Killer In Our Midst

Robert F. Mager

PublishAmerica

Baltimore

First printing

ISBN: 1-59129-809-1
PUBLISHED BY PUBLISHAMERICA BOOK PUBLISHERS
www.publishamerica.com
Baltimore

Printed in the United States of America

Welcome Fingers in the Soup

A work like this screams for expertise from an array of specialists, in this case generously provided (in the search for technical accuracy) by:

Bea Weaver, Captain, Miami-Dade Police Department; Detective Bob Ragsdale, Public Information Bureau, Phoenix Police Department; Detective Bob Brunansky, Homicide Unit (Cold Cases Squad), Phoenix Police Department; Robert Shutts, Chief Homicide trial lawyer, Maricopa County Attorney's Office; Lt. Ed Moore, Deputy Commander, Maricopa County Sheriff's Office; Detective Mike Hopper, Madison Street Jail; Lt. John M. Rankin, booking officer, Madison Street Jail; Elmer Withers, Carefree Town Marshall; Robert W. Bergstrom, Attorney and Counselor; Robert Metzgar, private investigator; Jim Ahern, crematory operator, Messinger Mortuary; Ken Barrios and Ron Salvatore, Matthews Cremation Group; Lori Schweighardt, Child Life Specialist, Phoenix Children's Hospital; Diane Dudley, Planned Parenthood; Judith Ingalls, M.D.; Nacho Estrada, master ventriloquist.

There's more. Manuscript reviews and moral support were willingly provided by David Cram, Libby Muelhaupt, Carol Adler, Connie Flynn, Eileen Mager, Di Bolger, Seth Leibler and Ann Parkman. Red-pencil slash 'n burn editorial assistance was offered by Eileen Mager and my insomniac mentor and writing coach, Rodney L. Cron.

Finally, it is customary for the author to accept all blame for errors and omissions. Oh, all right . . .

Robert F. Mager
Carefree, Arizona

CHAPTER ONE

Two hours past midnight, a grimacing man staggered across the well-manicured lawn toward the Bramwell Convalescent Center. Clutching his abdomen with both hands, he struggled ever more slowly toward the carefully disguised shelter for battered women only yards away. Two steps later, his weakening legs failed him. He stopped. Unable to drag himself further, he sank slowly to his knees. With a loud moan, he fell face down onto the well-manicured lawn. With a final, agonizing shriek . . . he died.

Security lights flashed on, abruptly lighting up the exterior grounds. Simultaneously, proximity alarms blared the residents into terrified wakefulness.

Startled, Tara Tindall dropped the pen she was using to sign out. "My God, George, what's happening?" But when she glanced up, the Center guard was gone.

Glancing through the front window, Tara saw him twenty paces beyond the entrance. Well out on the manicured lawn, he was pointing his gun at the head of the prone figure over which he knelt.

Since George seemed to have the situation in hand, Tara silenced the alarms and called the security company to cancel their response. For a moment she looked about the lobby, trying to decide how best to begin. She ended up scurrying along the corridor, hugging every one of the frightened women she could reach.

"It's all right," she soothed. "Don't worry, it's all right. You know nobody can protect us better than good old George Petacki."

With the residents somewhat calmer — at least for the moment — Tara rushed outside to the guard. "Oh, my God, George. Is he dead?"

George holstered his well-worn, nine-millimeter Glock. "You're the nurse. You tell me."

She stooped to check the neck for a pulse. Glancing at George she shook her head before turning over the body. "Just as I thought," she muttered, her questioning expression shifting to a grimace.

"What's just as you thought?"

"Nothing . . . I mean, I was just checking to see if I know who this is," she lied. She wasn't ready to reveal her growing suspicions. This is Willie Lamarka, Winona's husband. I recognize him from the scars."

"Sonuvabitch!" George drew his fit, six-foot-three-inch body to its full height, lips pinching. "This piece of garbage didn't deserve to be on the same planet with her. What the hell's a wife-beater like him doing dying on our lawn in the middle of the night?"

"Come on, George. You know our security is good and we do our best to keep our location secret. But you know how word gets around."

George grunted. "Any idea what killed him?"

She again bent down and examined the body's exposed skin for signs of a wound. She searched the clothing for bloodstains. Their absence moved her to sniff at the victim's mouth.

Standing, now only a few inches shorter than George, she brushed off her hands. "I can't be sure. But look here — " She pointed at the dead man's face. " — see the red skin? And the drool around the mouth? I'd say he's been poisoned."

"Holy smoke! Okay, I'll call it in." George barked into the microphone stitched to his lapel. He ended with, "Remember what we do here, Jim, so don't send any marked cars. And — for Chrissake — tell 'em not to respond Code Three. We don't need any more lights and noise than we've got."

To Tara, he added, "My son's on dispatch tonight, Tara. He says the guys'll do it right. By the way, Dr. Millston is gonna take the call, and I know his medical examiner's car isn't marked either."

Tara didn't answer. Absently chewing her lip while brushing back a tendril of dark hair hanging to one side of her oval, brown face, she considered her findings. *Now I'm convinced — somebody's threatening the shelter. The director? A staff member?* Though eager to add this third killing to her growing list, she turned instead to a more immediate responsibility. "I have to go tell the ladies what's going on, George. They're already upset and I don't want them to start any scary rumors."

"Okay. I'll wait here for the team."

She returned to the Center even more hurriedly than she left. Originally consisting of two large houses on adjacent lots, they had been combined into a single, ten-acre property to which several buildings had been added. Despite the chill of the air-conditioning, the atmosphere inside reeked of perspiring females, anxiety and cold fear.

Tara headed for the recreation room where the fretting women huddled. Before she could cross the lobby, women crowded around, bombarding her with questions.

"What happened?"

"Who is he?"

"Is he dead?"

"Ladies . . . ladies. It's going to be all right. Nobody can get in, and the police won't be coming with sirens and lights. But you must realize that with a dead body out there we had to call them. One at a time, please," she said, lifting her hands for silence. "Besides — " she attempted a smile, hoping to lighten the mood, " — a body on the lawn just doesn't fit our landscaping, does it?"

It didn't work; the clamor continued.

"Do you know who it is?"

"Is it somebody we know?"

"How did he die?"

Tara raised her hands again for silence. "I'll fill you in on the details as soon as I can."

She searched the fear-ridden faces for Winona, finally recognizing the bruised face of the gentle woman near the back of the room, one arm in a sling, the other comforting her two young daughters.

Speaking in a whisper, Tara said, "Winona, will you come to my clinic, please?" Smiling to reassure them, Tara led the two girls to a nearby sofa before leading Winona toward the small clinic in the far corner of the recreation room.

Behind them, their move triggered another ruckus of speculation.

"Please sit down," Tara invited, closing the door behind her.

Winona locked her jaws, eyes focused on Tara's, while settling into the vinyl chair. Wincing, she adjusted her broken right arm and pulled from her sling one of the small, dog-shaped hand puppets given abused children by a local entertainer. In a mindless kneading, she began crushing and worrying it as though squeezing comfort from the mangled object.

"Winona," Tara spoke softly, "the man on the lawn is your Willie."

Winona sucked in her breath. "Oh, my God!" When the news penetrated, she let out a long, slow breath. Her shoulders sagged, and tears made their way down her cheeks.

Tara handed her a tissue. "I'm truly sorry."

"Are you . . . sure . . . he's really . . . dead?"

"Yes, Winona, he's really dead."

"Thank God!" she whispered. Looking up with a fleeting, guilty expression, she added, "I suppose I should be sorry." She shook her head. "But I'm not. Every time he lost a fight, he took it out on us. Sometimes, he did it anyway. He used me and the kids like punching bags. I . . . I only wish I'd had the guts to kill him myself."

"It's over now, Winona. He's gone forever. You can start a new life without having to be afraid."

Winona grew a small smile. She lifted her head, a seed of self-assurance seeming to sprout. "Yes, I can, can't I?" Her expression brightened as she tissued away the last of her tears. Pushing herself to her feet with difficulty, she asked, "Can I go tell the others?"

"Of course." Tara opened the door. Immediately the waiting women crowded around.

"That was my husband who died out there on the lawn," Winona told them, good hand clasping her girls as if still protecting them from the corpse. "Prob'ly comin' to kill me for leavin' with the children." Her voice rose in volume with every word. "Now that sumbitch is dead . . . and I'm glad! *Glad.* You hear? I don't have to worry about being beat up by that mangy bastard no more . . . ever again!" She ended with her chin raised in defiance.

Satisfied that Winona was strong enough to carry on, Tara slipped back into the clinic and retrieved her secret record from its hiding place. She added the name, "Willie Lamarka," and the day/date "Monday, August 14," then stared at the results.

"My God!" she mumbled. "Three murders in three months. A murder every month. Each an abuser of our ladies. And the murderer's still at large." She felt her palms grow sweaty. "Whatever's going on here, I've got to get to the bottom of it. And in less than a month . . . before it happens again."

CHAPTER TWO

Late the following night, Tara paced to and fro in her clinic, waiting for the residents to go to sleep. Her watch suggested it should be soon.

She had already gathered her notebook, flashlight, and surgical gloves. She patted the key ring on her belt. Now ready for her "stealthy sleuthing," she checked her outfit. A black blouse, slacks and soft-soled shoes, seemed just right for what she had in mind. With her hair pinned tight against her head, she patted the key ring on her belt and declared herself ready. *I can get in real trouble doing this!*

Suddenly she gasped! *What am I thinking?* She examined herself in the mirror for a second time. *Good God! This outfit is a dead giveaway. If anyone sees me like this, my goose will be cooked, for sure.*

Tara took one last look at her burgling costume and rushed to exchange it for her regular nurse's uniform. There. Now she felt more confident.

She picked up her array of items, adjusted the key ring at her belt, and closed the door softly behind her. In the outer room, she paused to listen. Already after midnight, certainly no one was stirring after all the commotion the night before. But it never hurt to be cautious. She crept across the reception area, looking over her shoulder at every step, all the way to the director's office. Holding her breath, she tapped on the door panel.

No response. No sound. No light under the door.

Tara unlocked it, making as little noise as possible. To her ears, the click of the bolt sounded like a dropped anvil. Though she had her own key, there was no way she could explain doing this in the middle of the night. *If I'm caught in here, I can lose my job — and I can't afford that.* Then an even more frightening thought crossed her mind: *My God, if I'm caught in here, I can lose my life!*

Nonetheless, she entered, and crept to the locked records room at the far end of the office. She tried the same key. It worked! She slipped inside and released the breath she didn't know she was holding.

She flashed her light to locate the wall switch, and bathed the small room in a glare of fluorescent bulbs. A secure inside room — no windows — she now had no worries about using enough light.

9

Tiptoeing to the filing cabinets lining the inside walls, she pulled at a drawer. Locked. She tried another cabinet. Also locked.

Damn! Wouldn't you know it!

Turning off the light and shrouding her flashlight, she crept back into the outer office and went to the director's desk to tug on the center drawer. This one opened.

Careful not to touch anything, she swept her beam over the contents, looking for a cabinet key. There! It hung from a small nail tacked to the side of the drawer.

Noting that the back of the key faced the front of the drawer, she reached in . . . and, at the last instant, jerked back her hand. *Damn! I've got to be more careful.* Belatedly donning her surgical gloves, she lifted the key off the nail.

Back in the records room, Tara paused to calm her shallow breathing and trembling hands. *I'm not cut out for this!* Regaining reasonable control of her jitters, she used the key to open drawer after drawer, removing specific files. She spread them on the floor, read them, then made brief entries in her small notebook.

As she worked, she became even more confident she was on the right track. She also realized that from here on, she could no longer do this alone — she needed help.

She then collected the files and returned them to their drawers. Just as she relocked the last drawer, another equally strong suspicion settled about her head like an icy fog: *These findings could very well lead to a death sentence.*

Mine!

CHAPTER THREE

Detective Harry Shuman — "Harry, the Shoe" — to his colleagues — hunched over his keyboard in the headquarters' commons room. Letter by letter he pecked out a report due yesterday.

Startled by the rare interruption when Detective Charlie Drummel ambled in, he quit typing. "What's up, Charlie?"

"Just looking for a file. Hey, isn't it about time for your lunch?"

"So?"

"Can I watch?"

Harry's colleagues liked to watch him open his brown bag. He always arranged its contents into a neat row, studying it as though looking for clues before digging in. Sometimes, as a joke, he wrapped a piece of pie with a scoop of plastic ice cream on top. It made the reluctant dieters green with envy.

"Not funny. Now go detect something while I finish this paperwork." Harry poised his typing fingers.

Charlie picked up a manila folder and, waving it over his head, left as quickly as he'd come.

Harry resumed his staccato attack of his keyboard. Assigned to the Cold Cases Squad, he devoted his time to poking at unsolved homicides with his intellectual stick. Not a job for the impatient. Solving cases whose leads had long since been squeezed dry required intelligence and persistence. Shoe solved more than his share.

For the second time, he was interrupted. Sergeant "Dutch" Brunkel, huge, black and glowering came rushing in as if answering an emergency call. "Dammit, Shoe, are you still trying to solve that old Fiston case?"

Persistence was the only item on which he and his supervising sergeant disagreed. "Shoe," Brunkel complained, "give it a rest. We got hundreds of cases, and you can't spend all your time on just one."

"Come on, Sarge. You know I'm working on five cases right now, and I think I can *solve* this one." He shrugged. "With just a little more time."

Brunkel knew Harry was one of his best, but it made him feel good to do a little gratuitous prodding now and again. He pointed a finger in Harry's direction. "Put that Pellaway folder on my desk by sundown, or your ass will be tarred and feathered." Brunkel turned and rushed from the room as fast as he'd entered.

Harry shook his head and reached for his brown bag. *If the rest of the day is like this, I might as well build up my strength.*

The phone rang. He punched up the line. "Detective Shuman."

"Uh . . . hello." The female voice was firm, but hesitant.

Harry immediately visualized his caller as tall, dark, in her thirties and gorgeous. *What the hell*, he thought, *it doesn't hurt to fantasize.* "How may I help you?"

"They told me you handle unsolved cases."

"Yes, ma'am." *Promising*, he thought. *There's music in her voice.* "And your name is . . .?"

"Detective, I have some information I think will interest you." She took a deep breath. "But I'd like to talk with you face-to-face. Will that be all right?"

Anonymous phone calls weren't unusual, but no one had ever withheld a name until they knew him better. He should refuse to continue this conversation right now, but — what the hell — he liked her voice . . . intelligent and businesslike, with a certain sparkle. "Okay. What do you have in mind?"

"Would you be willing to meet me for coffee at that little tea shop on Adams Street? It's only a block and a half from your office."

"I've seen it, never been inside."

"That's why I chose it. It's not a cop hangout."

"You already checked it out?"

"Yes, and I'm . . . uh . . . kind of nervous about what I'm doing here. I'd like to meet you where we can talk undisturbed."

"Uh huh. Why do you want to talk to someone working cold cases?"

"Ah . . . if you'll let me, I might be able to help you solve a couple of your unsolved murders. Maybe some you don't even know about."

Harry sat straighter in his chair and pressed the receiver close to his ear. "Are you a private detective?"

"No, I'm a nurse. Would three o'clock, tomorrow afternoon, work for you?"

Harry didn't hesitate. "Sure. How will I recognize you?"

He heard a faint chuckle. "Well, I'm in my mid-thirties . . . and tall. I wear my dark hair up in a page boy. Because of my brown skin some people mistake me for Hispanic. Others think I'm more like a young Lena Horne." Her chuckle this time came out as a trill. "I'll be wearing a bright blue blouse over a white skirt, and red shoes. You'll recognize me . . . my friends say I'm gorgeous."

Unseen by Tara, Harry blushed. *Holy shit, she's a mind reader!* Aloud, he concluded with, "Okay, see you at three, tomorrow."

At ten minutes before three the following afternoon, Harry the Shoe, wearing light-colored slacks and a short-sleeved shirt, entered the Adams Street tea house. *Sure,* he thought, *thirties, tall, and gorgeous — my ass! With my luck she'll be fifty, fat, and frumpy.* He'd come deliberately early to case the restaurant before meeting his mysterious caller. It was a small establishment, no more than eight small tables and three booths. Flowered tablecloths, plastic flower centerpiece on each table, wicker chairs. *Somebody must have cleaned out a used-furniture store.* Yet, the unobtrusive ambience was relaxing. Someone had set the music volume so low he could hardly hear it. He liked that. That would make it easy to talk. It grated to have to strain during a conversation. What's more, the coffee smelled terrific, not like that swill at headquarters.

Harry scanned the room. Four tables were occupied by young couples dawdling over coffee or whatever. One was occupied by a dark-haired woman wearing a blue silk blouse tucked into a white skirt. Red shoes. Nice boobs too. She was in her thirties, tall, and definitely gorgeous. *I'll be damned!*

Her black hair, worn in a pageboy, bangs in front, curled inward at neck length. Her brown skin emphasized her beauty. Harry grinned. He couldn't help himself.

Tara watched Harry from behind her menu as he entered. From the first instant she knew the big galoot who looked so awkward in a tea room had to be the detective. While he scanned the patrons, she gave him a candid appraisal. About five-feet-eleven and forty-five years old, she guessed. Brownish hair just beginning to gray at the edges. Definitely nice shoulders! Less than two hundred pounds with a slight mid-riff paunch. *Probably doesn't work out as much as he should,* she thought.

She chuckled softly to herself as he sidled toward her. He wasn't "drop-dead handsome" — not by today's standards, anyway — but he did have an attractively rugged face with a good, strong jaw. Sort of a Humphrey Bogart type. *Oh, he'd do, all right . . . If I were looking. Which I'm not.*

When he approached her table, Tara rose and extended a hand.

Harry took it, nodded slightly on noticing the firmness of the grip. This was no withering female. There was substance here.

"I'm Detective Shuman," he said. "Call me Harry."

"I'm Tara, and thanks for coming. Mind if we move to that empty booth?" She pointed to a spot in the corner. "We're less likely to be overheard."

He smiled. "You always take command of a situation?"

"I'm a nurse. Goes with the territory."

A server swirled to their table in a flurry of short, ruffled skirts. They ordered coffee the same way — strong and without cream or sugar. Mostly they smiled and sized up each other until their cups arrived.

"Now then, Tara, how can I help you?"

"If this goes as planned, I'm going to help *you*." She held up a hand. "Please, I don't mean that to sound arrogant, but I have a hypothesis, and some information I think will interest an officer working on unsolved murders."

"I'm listening."

"I'll tell you this much about me before I begin. As I said, I'm a nurse. I work at a battered women's shelter here in Phoenix."

Harry, good at listening, absently scratched the scar on his forehead.

Tara stared at him for a long moment. "Look, Harry, as I said, I'm not a detective. So what I have to tell you may sound a little far-fetched. But if you laugh, I'll just walk out. I've thought long and hard about whether I should come forward at this time. I've even imagined hearing the raucous laughter when I told the police — "

"I understand," Harry interrupted. "If it'll make you feel a little easier, I've already decided you're not some kind of wacko who wants to tell me about the Martians she's seen."

"Thank you." Tara's shoulders relaxed as she continued, "I thought I should collect more information before saying anything, but the way things are going, I finally decided I have to take the chance."

Harry flicked a finger for her to go on.

"Our clients are women who've been beaten and raped by the scum of the earth. Mostly husbands or boyfriends. One girl was gang-raped. Several have brought their battered daughters with them. The mothers come to us after they can't stand the beatings, or after they can't stand to watch their kids beaten any longer. Or molested. Or raped. They're frightened. Their spirits are broken. When they finally get up the courage to leave, they bring nothing with them. Maybe a few keepsakes and medication." She shrugged. "These women are in bad shape." Tara stirred her coffee and gazed into the cup.

"I'm sure you know all that, but I feel I need to set the stage. These women have been given a raw deal; they're victims of the worst kinds of treatment possible, and they've no way of fighting back. They're mostly broke. They have little or nothing in the way of financial resources, and their self-confidence and self-respect have been pretty much destroyed. These are beaten women, in more ways than one." Her eyes glazed over. "In far more ways than one."

"May I ask how this ties into the information you said you might want to tell me?"

"Here's where it gets touchy. For me, at least. Recently I thought I noticed a pattern."

"What kind of pattern?" Harry, though anxious for Tara to get to the point, tried not to let it show.

"I noticed that several of the batterers, husbands and boyfriends, have gone missing. That's not unusual in itself. These guys are always skipping out on alimony and child support payments. Fortunately, your Missing Persons people find most of them."

Harry nodded. "The Missing Persons squad tries hard to locate these scumbags."

"But not all. One day, when I was looking for a client's file I was treating for . . ." Tara broke off and bit her lip. "That part's not important. Anyway, I opened the wrong file by mistake and it showed the resident's husband as deceased." She smiled playfully, "That means totally dead, you know."

Harry smiled in return. *I'm beginning to like this woman.* "I suspected you meant that. I'm a detective, you know."

"To tell the truth, after skimming through the file I was hoping he died the worst death possible — "

"Like being locked in a small room with three lawyers?"

"Well," she said, not changing expression, "maybe not *that* horrible. But close."

"And . . . "

"I'll bet you another cup of coffee he's on your list of cold cases."

"You're on."

"Ever heard of the case of Borland Buggles, nickname 'Tiny'?"

Startled, Harry's eyes widened. "Sure, he was a big mountain of a guy. Worked at a garage over on Nineteenth Avenue."

"He's on your list of unsolved cases, right?"

Harry shook his head slowly, looking directly into Tara's eyes. "No, he isn't. If I remember it right, he died of alcohol poisoning. *Wood* alcohol, I think. Not many people drink that stuff on purpose, but some do, if they can't afford anything else. So it was called an accidental death. Weren't any suspicious circumstances. The guy just sat on a barstool, probably spiked his beer with wood alcohol, then staggered out, fell down the concrete stairs onto his head. Died on the spot."

"Nothing suspicious?"

"I'd have to check the file, but I don't think so. The guy just drank the stuff and died. The whisky bottles were checked for prints, but all were accounted for."

"Was it a painful death?"

"Musta' been painful as hell . . . sorry." The light suddenly went on in Harry's eyes. "Wait a minute! Are you telling me he was the husband of one of your battered women?"

"Exactly."

"Holy shit!" Harry exclaimed, not bothering to apologize for the slip. "I don't remember that being in the report." Harry motioned the server for another round of coffee. "But, so what? His wife couldn't have done it."

"True. But somebody did. And Buggles was one of the most evil of the lot. Raped his eight-year-old daughter and made his wife watch."

"Okay, so he was a really rotten apple. But I still have to ask — so what?"

"So maybe somebody got away with murdering somebody in serious need of killing."

An alarm bell tinkled in Harry's inner ear. Murderers often justified their deeds by telling themselves their victims "needed" killing. "Yeah. If it *was* murder."

"It was murder."

"May I ask how you know that?"

"As you already know, they don't serve methanol — wood alcohol — in bars. Though it's not rare for *indigents* to die of methanol poisoning, of course. I know, I checked. But they don't do it in bars. And Buggles was far from indigent. He could afford to buy good booze."

Harry scratched his scar again and thought before responding. "I appreciate your reasoning, Tara, yet it could still be accidental."

Tara nodded. "Yes, but don't forget he was the husband of one of our residents and badly in need of killing."

"Lots of people are badly in need of killing, but they manage to live long and disgusting lives."

"Okay, then, here's another name on your list. Frankie Frangini."

Harry reached into a pocket, retrieved a breath mint, popped it into his mouth, and stared at her. "You gonna tell me his wife also lives at the shelter?"

"Girlfriend. Beaten to within an inch of her life before someone practically dragged her to us. If you could look at her wounds, you'd know." She sipped from her cup before continuing. "Frankie was a sadist."

"Yeah. Died like he lived, too. His body was found in an abandoned warehouse, beaten to death with a nail-studded two-by-four. Looked like a rage killing. The killer left a bunch of bloody fingerprints and footprints behind."

"The police ever make a connection between Buggles and Frangini?" Tara asked.

"No reason to. Buggles wasn't ruled a homicide, and they were completely . . . different . . . cases." Harry's voice slowed as he neared the end of his sentence. He stopped to glower at Tara. "Until *now*. I see: both were batterers and had a wife or girlfriend staying at your shelter." Harry fidgeted in his chair, his mind already orchestrating the opening moves of his investigation.

"I take it, then, you're interested in letting me help you with this?"

"More than a little, Tara. More than a little. Two of the worst batterers wind up dead — "

"Three."

Harry frowned. "Three?

"If you include the one who died on our front lawn the other night. Willie Lamarka. The latest. His wife and two daughters are residents at our shelter. I saw him a minute or two after he died. His pupils were dilated and his skin was red and still hot. I'm not into forensics, but it looked like poison to me."

"You're right about that. The autopsy showed belladonna. Not your usual choice of poisons. So, we've got three corpses, at least two killed by somebody who seems to be pretty good at it. If they actually are murders, that is. You bet I'm interested. You think somebody is going down the list of batterers and — "

"No," Tara interrupted. "From what I've been able to find out so far, only the most violent, sadistic, or destructive goons become victims. Especially those who prey on children."

"I'm not gonna ask you how you came to that interesting conclusion. Uh . . . got any *more* names?"

Tara sat without moving for a long time. "Harry, I don't want to be cagey, but I've got a lot more at stake here than you can possibly imagine. Before I tell you anything more, we've got to make a deal."

"What kind of a deal?"

"*I'll* provide you with information, and *you* keep me entirely out of your conversations with your buddies and your reports. I've got to stay completely out of this. I've got to! And you must promise to take no action until our next meeting."

"I — "

"Wait," she interrupted again. "Let me finish. The last thing I can afford is any sort of notoriety. More than my job may be at stake. So, if my information checks out, and you do your detecting thing, *you* get all the credit. The minute my name surfaces, we're through."

Harry thought about the proposition. Finally, he shook his head. "What you're asking is definitely against policy. This is police business, and we'll take it from here. You have no idea the risks you run investigating on your own . . . especially if what you're thinking is true."

"Harry, I have no choice. At the very least, I must find out if my suspicions are correct. So you'll either have to let me dig a little deeper, or you'll have to arrest me."

"That's pretty strong." Eyes boring into Tara's, he asked, "You going to want to be paid for this information?"

Tara's shoulders stiffened. A hard line formed across her forehead. For an extended moment she didn't speak. When she did, her words virtually tumbled out. In crisp, clipped tones, with a constantly rising inflection, she showed her pique. Citing page, chapter and verse of her background and perspective, she left no doubt about how she felt. She was still frowning when she finished. "Now you know how — and why — I feel as I do."

He gave a sheepish shrug, looking into her glowering expression. "Sorry, but I had to ask."

"Look! At this point I'm not even sure I'm right. I've still got some digging to do."

"Okay. In that case, we can consider you my CI — confidential informant. Nobody has to know you exist. Just tell me one thing."

She raised her eyebrows.

"Got any idea who's behind these killings?"

At first, Tara said nothing. Harry could see from her darting eyes she was considering and discarding possible replies to his question. "Harry, let me ask you a hypothetical question."

"Shoot."

"Suppose you weren't a cop, and you worked in an environment where everyone — *everyone* — who learned about these murders not only refused to help you — but cheered the murderer on?" She lifted a hand when she saw Harry was about to interrupt. "And suppose further, that when you finally collected enough information and made the connections, the evidence pointed squarely at your own *mother*."

Harry's eyes widened. "Whoa! That's just hypothetical, right?" A startling idea, he thought. *Maybe I should run a check on her mother.*

"Yes. Hypothetical. But it sort of summarizes the delicate situation I find myself in. It hints at why I'm being so cautious."

"Okay. I'm beginning to get the picture, and I'll go along with your deal. For now." Harry reached a hand across the small table and they shook on it. "I'll tell you flat out, though, I've been involved in strange situations before, but never anything like this."

"It gets better."

"How?"

"There are more murders."

"Jeezus! How many?"

Tara shook her head. "Not yet. I have more checking to do. With what I suspect, I have to be absolutely sure before I point a finger . . . even a hypothetical finger. You understand?"

"Yeah, I think I do. Sort of." It was clear to Harry that she suspected someone at the shelter. Someone well-liked. He said nothing, however, not wanting to scare her off.

Tara watched him finger his scar. "Pardon me for asking, but did you get that scar from a fencing match in old Heidelberg? I couldn't help notice it still seems to bother you."

Harry pulled his hand down. "Sorry. No, it was the result of over-exuberance on the football field during college. It only itches when I'm in an uncomfortable social situation."

"You're uncomfortable now?"

"I guess I must be. I seldom get to have meetings with gorgeous women."

Tara smiled and stood, signaling the meeting was over; Harry did the same.

"That's sweet. I can use that as a signaling device."

Harry cocked his head, frowning.

"You know. When I see you scratching it, I'll know to do something to make you more comfortable." That was accompanied by a friendly smile. "Can we meet here again next week? Same time?"

"It's a date."

"Remember, Harry. If my name surfaces — anywhere — I'm gone."

"Just be careful. If your suspicions are right, you could be putting yourself in danger."

"I've a feeling I already have."

CHAPTER FOUR

Head down, Harry ambled back toward his office. His usual street vigilance dulled by thoughts of the conversation just ended, he tried to organize his impressions of Tara and her revelations. His first thoughts were of Tara. *She's no nut, no crank caller, no spurned woman looking for revenge. She's a level-headed, professional woman who stumbled onto what she's convinced is an important discovery. She's no trained detective, but she is a trained observer. Heck, she even noticed me scratching my old football souvenir. In short, I've got to take her seriously.*

Harry stepped into a shaded doorway as he next thought about Tara's revelations. *She believes she's found a connection between some of my cold cases. All three victims she named were either husbands or boyfriends of women living at the domestic violence shelter at which she works as a nurse. That connection hasn't been made before. Probably because each man was killed by a different method, and one of them isn't even classified as a murder.*

There's more. Tara said only the worst of the worst will be on the murdered list. That meant the killer is selective. Why? Aren't wife-beaters, rapists, and child abusers equally qualified for retribution? What were the criteria by which the victims are selected? What's so special about . . .

Aha! Could the killer be a victim himself? No, not himself — herself. If the killer were really out to revenge the pain and torment inflicted by an abuser, it would have to be a woman. Well, to be technically correct, it would most likely be a woman; women are abused physically far more often than men.

Something else tweaked Harry's mind. *When describing her hypothetical scenario, Tara asked what he'd do if he made all the connections and decided the killer was his mother. His mother? That was a strange image, but it carried a strong implication. No, two strange images.*

First, Tara seems to suspect someone at the shelter. Second, her suspect is most likely a woman, probably someone in a position of authority. Her "mother" reference, and the fact that the shelter caters exclusively to women, appears to confirm that. Convinced his reasoning was sound, Harry stepped back into the hot sun and continued toward his office.

Something else about the conversation with Tara nagged at him. *What was it? Oh, yes. Her "hypothetical" description of a situation in which everybody who knew about the murders "pulled for" the killer. That suggests the residents might know some of the men were missing, and at least some of them had been murdered. Is that really true? Has she been spreading the word? No. I think she's looking ahead to when word does get around about the connections, and people begin choosing sides. Yeah, that's a better supposition. Besides, she did say there were more victims on her list.*

He slowed his pace even more. *Okay, how do I handle this? I've been given reason to believe some of our unsolved murders are connected, and that we have a serial killer running loose. A female serial killer. My informant says, if I'll play along with her, she'll give me information that will probably lead me to the killer. If I don't, she'll simply vanish and my information source will dry up. She made it clear she's in a delicate situation. She sure as hell won't give up anything more if I don't respect her conditions. Sure, I could take the squad in now and try clearing the cases without her help . . . but she's the one who made the connection, not us. She's on the inside, she has the sources, and she's sharp enough to carry on . . . with a little coaching from me.*

Nearing headquarters, Harry's thoughts turned to the investigation already underway. *What about Detectives Drummel and Skirms? They're already working the Lamarka case. Do I tell them what's what? No, not yet. They're not working a cold case . . . or a serial killer case. They're working a hot case. That's a helluva flimsy rationalization, but I'll go with it for now.*

That's it, then. I'll go along with her . . . for the moment, and treat her as a CI. She could be the key to solving more than just the three murders she's already mentioned. If that happens — zingo! — the big case I've always dreamed about.

CHAPTER FIVE

"Any word on the Lamarka autopsy?"

Detective Joan Skirms, standing five feet three in her bare feet, with flaming red hair and a tight-fitting aqua turtleneck, confronted Detective Charlie Drummel from behind her desk as soon as she entered the office.

Charlie nodded. "Yep. Just came in. The ME lists the cause of death as belladonna poisoning." He ran a barbell-callused hand through his thick brown mane. "No skinny on where he got it."

"Helluva way to die."

Drummel tapped the pages of the report. "The puzzling things are not only how the damned poison got into his system, but when — and where. The ME says he could'a ingested it anywhere from five to fifteen hours before he died."

"Hmm! That makes it sometime Sunday, before nine P.M."

"Sounds about right. But how many doses did he get? Was it all in one shot . . . or over a period of time. And how? Doc couldn't say. We're gonna have to run down the life he led. Maybe that'll tell us something."

"Anything else?"

"Not much. No strange fibers on his clothing; nothing unusual in his pants cuffs. Stomach contents suggest he 'bought it' some time after a hot dog lunch."

"Maybe the hot dog killed him." Skirms stood, stuffed her Beretta into a custom-crafted Galco holster at the small of her back, and stretched. The move enhanced the apparent size of her generous breasts.

Charlie Drummel waggled a pencil in their direction. "You got those registered as lethal weapons? Hmm. Mind if I check to see if they're loaded?" He moved as if to get up from his chair.

"Very funny. Bet you wish *you* had something worth registering. Okay, smartass, what else do we know about the vic?"

Drummel bent over an open folder on his desk. "Lamarka? DOB makes him thirty-three years old. Wife's name, Winona; age twenty-seven. Willie, a prizefighter, had a temper, probably why he's a drifter. Couldn't hold a job for long. I pulled his sheet — a couple of malicious mischiefs, three assaults, and a couple of simple robberies. Stole cigarettes from convenience stores. Nothing big. Except — ”

"Except?"

"Except he's got a restraining order against him to keep him away from his wife and daughters. Seems his hobby was beating hell out of them every chance he got. We had a team working up a case; said they were gonna arrest him tomorrow."

"Where did he live?"

Drummel riffled through the report. "Looks like a run-down trailer park in South Phoenix. Wanna check it out?"

"Sure. It's much too comfortable in here, don'cha think, what with the nice air conditioning and all? Might as well sweat off a few pounds."

"Jeez. I don't know if I'm gonna be able to put up with your cheerful outlook on life. C'mon, you drive, I'll navigate."

In an unmarked car, they drove south on Central, and hung a left on Baseline. From there, they threaded their way through side streets until they spotted the Happy Home trailer park.

"Happy Home?" Drummel snorted. "Looks more like Happy Junkyard."

Skirms parked close to the so-called office. What was left of a door stood open, so they went in.

A grizzled old timer sat behind a wooden desk that had seen better days. So had the old timer. With two teeth missing from his grin, and a beard that looked like a stranger to water, he couldn't have been a day older than two hundred. Booted feet on the desk, he was reading a racing form.

The two detectives showed their badges. "You got a resident name of Willie Lamarka?" Charlie asked.

The old timer put down his paper and scratched his beard. "Yeah. What about him?"

"He's dead."

The grizzled one dropped his feet to the floor and slammed a fist on the desktop. "That lyin' son of a bitch! He promised he'd pay me the back rent he owes by *yesterday*. I ain't seen hide nor hair of 'im. That sidewindin' son-of-a-bitch."

Ignoring the tirade, Skirms asked, "What else can you tell us about him?"

"Plenty! Always late with the rent. Never kept his plot clean — always full of trash and rusty car parts. Guy must'a been brought up in a junkyard. Beat hell out of his woman, too. Always pickin' a fight with somebody. Cops were here a couple times a week." He raised his eyebrows, obviously in search of gossip. "She dead, too?"

"No. She's okay."

The old guy ran a set of crooked fingers through the remains of his hair. "That's sumpin', anyhow."

"Did he have a car?"

"A beat-up old pickup. Red, mebbe ten, twelve years old."

"Got the license number? It would help."

"Think so." He shuffled in one of the desk drawers. "Here it is. Hell, if he's dead, you might as well keep the whole sheet." He handed the tattered page to Drummel.

Drummel wrote the number in his notebook, along with the make and model of the car, thanked the bearded one, and turned to Skirms. "Eighty-eight Chevy pickup. Matches the description of the truck we staked out last night. Let's go toss the trailer."

Approaching the aging trailer, both detectives squiggled their fingers into a pair of thin rubber gloves. Entering through the dented door, they paused a moment to drink in the scene, noses wrinkling from the stench.

"This shack can't be more'n twenty feet long. Not much of a home," Skirms observed. A leaky faucet pestered dirty dishes in the small aluminum sink. Empty beer bottles filled the small wastebasket. The place stank of mold and rotted food. Nirvana for the buzzing flies.

"Looks like the bed hasn't been made in weeks." Skirms peeked under the lone pillow before feeling under the thin mattress.

"What do you make of this?" Drummel called from the kitchen area. "Looks like our vic spent a lot of time clipping coupons."

"Does, doesn't it?" She riffled through a handful. "Looks mostly like those contests promising him he'd already won. Wait, look at these. He also clipped grocery coupons."

"Saving pennies while waiting for the big score."

After some twenty minutes of searching, they'd found nothing useful.

"Find any belladonna in the medicine cabinet?" Joan asked.

"Very funny. Nothing there but a bottle of aspirin and a rusty razor."

"Then how the hell did he get poisoned? There's nothing here, unless maybe somebody spiked his beer."

"Long shot. But we could take a couple empties back to the lab, just to be sure." Drummel scrounged a paper bag from his pocket and bagged two empty bottles still standing on the little sink counter. "I think we're done here. I'll call the crime scene guys to do some dusting. Might pick up some wild prints."

On the way to the office, Drummel summarized. "Okay, what've we got? A prizefighting drifter dies of belladonna poisoning on the lawn of a shelter for abused women."

"In the middle of the night — "

" — where his battered wife and two kids are hiding out. Was he trying to stalk her again? If so, why?"

"Maybe he thought she hired somebody to kill him, and wanted revenge. Why else would he try to get to her with his dying breath?" Skirms folded her arms across her ample chest, watching the traffic.

"Dunno. I keep coming back to how he got poisoned? And why? There was nothing at the scene. Nothing in the trailer. That leaves his truck — "

"And his place of employment." Skirms added, "And maybe a bar with a grudge-infested customer."

"Right. That would go to motive; once we know *that*, we can work on opportunity and method. Let's check out the truck and the job. So far, that's all we've got."

"Mmm, not quite," offered Skirms. "We also know that belladonna is not a commonly used poison. Probably because it takes so long to kill. But I think that tells us something about the murderer."

"That he's more careful and sophisticated than the average blunt-instrument killer?"

"Right! And that suggests premeditation."

Drummel tugged absently at an ear, his face wrinkled in thought. "The delayed action of the poison gave Lamarka plenty of time to die someplace else. Slick."

"There's something else. Poison is usually a woman's tool, but the perp can't be his wife. She hasn't left the shelter in more than a week. I checked."

Drummel nodded. "C'mon, let's get to work."

They drove to Willie Lamarka's last known place of employment, a rundown motel on Van Buren.

Skirms mused, "Y'know what's funny?"

"What?"

"Here's a guy who's got to know he was poisoned. He must've been in serious pain, and yet he tries like hell to get to the shelter. Why not a hospital, Charlie?"

"I still think maybe he thought his wife hired somebody to do him in, and wanted to beat hell out of her one last time."

"Maybe, and maybe he didn't start feeling the effects of the poison until he got to the shelter grounds. But how did he know where she was?"

"Y'got me," Charlie said, pointing to the motel they were approaching. "Here we are, I think."

She eased into a parking space outside the motel's reception area. Stretching their muscles when exiting the car, they entered and approached the desk to ask for the manager.

The young woman behind the desk, a girl appearing just about old enough to have completed high school, shot them an inquiring glance. Charlie showed his ID. She took a close look and, her tongue stud clicking against her teeth as she spoke, said, "I'm the manager on duty. How can I help you?"

When they told her why they were there, she turned and headed into a back room, presumably to check the records. Returning within seconds, she waved a saffron-colored, five by eight inch card.

"Here it is. Willard Lamarka was employed three weeks ago as a bus boy, and was fired one week after that."

"His problem?" Joan asked.

The young manager pursed her lips. "He couldn't hold his temper. Whenever something bothered him, he slammed the dishes around and dropped the aluminum trays, y' know? Always made sure he'd drop them right behind customers, too, like he was trying to scare them into a heart attack. He was a rude pain in — "

"Nice personality."

"So like what's he done?" the manager asked.

"He was murdered," Charlie said.

"Good! Nobody here will miss him. If you want help catching his killer, you've come to the wrong place."

"Wow!" Skirms said, "that's some attitude."

"Mebbe so, but he brought it on himself."

"Did he have a locker where he kept his personal things?" This from Joan.

"Just a hook on the wall, but it's been assigned to somebody else by now."

"Mind if we take a look where he worked?"

"I'll show you around."

After eyeballing the kitchen and dining room, they thanked the cooperative girl and headed for their car. "We're striking out," Charlie noted, as they drove toward headquarters. "We're no closer to the perp than we were three days ago."

"And from that manager's attitude, it looks like *that* state of affairs suits our good citizens just fine."

CHAPTER SIX

Thursday afternoon at three, Tara and Harry met in the same booth at the tea room. This time, Tara appeared in a more flowery, short-sleeved blouse, one she had made certain enhanced her skin tones. A flared green skirt, necklace of large, multicolored beads, and white shoes completed the outfit. She smoothed her skirt as she entered.

Harry also had dressed better than usual. Instead of his usual hot-weather attire, he wore a more formal, silver gray, button-down shirt, bottomed-off with gabardine, summer weight trousers. His thirty-eight caliber revolver rested in a holster under his belt.

"You're sure making things hard on me," Harry began, then blushed at the implication.

She grinned, eyebrows lifting. "Oh? How so?"

"You've given me information connecting two murders and a possible third, and I'm sworn to secrecy. That's definitely against policy, you know. I'm bending the rules here. A lot. We solve cases by sharing information and working as a team. I can get into a lot of trouble — "

"I realize that," Tara interrupted. "I really do. I know it's got to be tough to keep this to yourself. But it won't be for long. I promise."

Harry plopped his elbows on the table and leaned forward. "I'm bustin' a gut to know just how big this thing is. And who you suspect. And why. And on and on and on."

Brows furrowed, Tara twiddled the spoon in her coffee cup. Hesitantly, she leaned forward. "Harry, I've done some more research since last week, and I'm pretty sure these murders are the work of one person."

"How? The three weren't all poisoned, you know." He held his hands together in his lap to keep them from scratching his itchy scar.

"Lamarka was poisoned — "

"And 'Tiny' Buggles died of wood alcohol poisoning, probably because he was too drunk to know what he was drinking. Frankie Frangini was beaten to death. So we've got three bodies — but each died differently, and the only connection is that they all beat their wives and kids. How do you figure they were all killed by the same perp?"

29

"There's another connection. None of the three cases has been solved."

"I don't think that's much of a connection, if you'll pardon my saying so, even if true. And the Buggles case has been ruled an accidental death. As far as the Department is concerned, that one *has* been solved."

"So far as you know. I'll bet you a case of doughnuts it turns out he was murdered like the rest." Tara tapped a forefinger on his hand as she spoke. "But there's more. I went back and looked at the dates of the killings, and found what looks like a much stronger pattern."

"Which is . . . ?"

"All three were killed during daylight hours."

"Wait a minute. Lamarka died in the middle of the night."

"Yes, but you told me the ME said he might have been *poisoned* the day before."

Harry the Shoe leaned forward and touched her arm. "You've got a point. And what does that tell you?"

"It suggests the murderer has time on his hands during the day. If he's a working stiff, he works nights."

"That's a little flimsy, don't you think?"

"Maybe so," Tara conceded, "but there's still more." Tara removed a sheet of paper from her purse, unfolded it, and placed it in front of Harry. "Here's a list of the three murders — let me call the Buggles death a murder for now. It's in the order in which they were killed. Frangini first, then Buggles, and finally Lamarka."

Harry studied the short list.

Frankie Frangini	Monday, June 12
Borland "Tiny" Buggles	Monday, July 14
Willie Lamarka	Monday, August 14

He couldn't see where she was heading, but he nodded and said nothing.

"Now look at the dates on which they were killed. There's roughly thirty days apart. Notice anything else?"

Harry studied the marks on the paper she'd put in front of him. "I'll be damned." Harry ran his forefinger down the list as the realization came to him. "Just as you said. They all died on a Monday." He thought for a moment. "What's so special about Mondays?"

"I don't know yet, but this little chart suggests he'll kill again about three weeks from now."

"Whoa. Wait a minute. That's a pretty big leap from a sample of only three, don't you think?"

"I haven't told you about the other ones yet. Exactly six months before Frankie Frangini died, the body of a man named Broman Tarper was found in the desert — "

"I remember that case," Harry interrupted. "A small-time shyster. Shot in the back of the head from close range with a .22 caliber pistol. Two shots, execution style. I think the police report said it was a mob hit. Tarper did a little lawyering in his spare time, but his main business seemed to be loan sharking among the poor. The supposition was that somebody finally decided they'd had enough."

"He's the one. Was the killer ever found?"

"Police report said there were no leads. Murder weapon was never found. It's one of my cold cases. I don't think the police tried too hard."

"Uh-huh. Tarper had a wife living at the shelter at the time he died. She moved to Idaho the next day."

Harry sat up and looked directly at Tara. "No *shit*? Um, sorry."

"Yes. I happened to find the file in the . . ." her voice trailed off as she waved a hand in the air. "I found the file. It said he not only beat his wife, but kept her in a locked room and fed her only enough to keep her alive."

Harry's gaze shifted to the antique teapots hanging on the far wall, deep in thought. "That means there's a gap of five months during which our perp was inactive. Or laying low."

"Possibly, but don't forget there may be missing bad guys who've never been found. Maybe *they* were killed on a Monday . . . about a month apart."

"Can you get a list of the missing bad guys?"

"I can try. Not all the deceased husbands and boyfriends are recorded on shelter records. But I'll see what I can find . . . it may take a few days." Tara thought about the risk of being caught pawing through the Center's confidential files. She'd have to hold the number of midnight visits to a minimum. "But there *are* other shelters in our fair city — "

Harry slapped an open hand on the table, causing other customers to look up and turn in their direction. "Of *course*, there are! I'd forgotten about that. How *many* others?"

"If we're talking only about shelters for abused women, there are seven. All of them are smaller and considerably less well endowed than where I work. None of the others have a resident nurse, for example, but they do the same kind of work we do."

"I'll start right away matching their records to our cold cases list — "

Tara reached out a hand and squeezed Harry's fingers. "What about our agreement?" she asked, anxiety showing in her eyes.

"Sorry about that. You've given me information that could go a long way toward solving some of my cases. Not to run with it could be considered dereliction of duty, and I could probably put you in the slammer for obstructing justice." He said this last with a small smile.

Tara, also half-smiling, extended her joined wrists as if awaiting handcuffs. "Well, here I am."

Harry grasped her hands with a sick grin. Pressing them to the tabletop, he continued holding them, turning the impulsive gesture into a caress.

Slowly withdrawing from his grip, Tara changed the subject. "All right, Harry, see if this makes sense. You could run with the information you have, and maybe connect a few cases together. But with what you've got so far, I think if it gets out you'd only warn the killer to lie low." She paused a moment to let that thought sink in. "Have you made any progress with the Lamarka case?"

"Detectives Skirms and Drummel have been investigating it, but so far they've come up empty."

Tara nodded. "I'm no expert, but I don't think you've got enough evidence to make an arrest, even if you had a suspect. You said yourself we haven't actually proved this *is* the work of a serial killer. On the other hand, you could risk giving me just a few more days and probably catch a bad guy. An *active* serial killer who's still on the loose, and still killing. Which is more important?"

Harry's mind danced around the edge of his dream of "just one really big case." Shaking himself back to reality, he pretended exasperation and said, "You know, I'm getting a little tired of your impeccable logic, young lady. Maybe I'll arrest you anyhow."

Surprised, Tara asked, "On what charge?"

"Straight thinking in the first degree." Harry smiled, his eyes on the smooth brown skin of Tara's face, her perky nose and . . . *I'm beginning to feel too damned comfortable in her presence.* "You're right. We need to focus on catching the killer."

Tara reconsidered the person she thought responsible for the murders. Still resting her hands lightly in his, she said, "Harry, I'm really in a very precarious situation. I've got to find a way to make that go away before you take action. Give me just one more week to find a way out, and then you can move — whichever way it goes — *please?*"

Harry bit his lip to keep from asking for details . . . and her phone number." *Come on, Harry old boy, focus!* Whatever it was, it had to be related to her suspicions about the killer's identity. "Okay, one more week. But if there's something you want to tell me, or do, call me any time, day or night." He took a card from his card case, turned it over, and wrote his home phone number on the back. "I'm serious, Tara. You seem to be getting in pretty deep. If the killer suspects you're getting too close, well — "

"I know, I know — I can be the next victim."

CHAPTER SEVEN

Harry ignored the afternoon heat and hustled along the street with a new spring in his step. Reliving his meeting with Tara, he didn't even notice the rivers of sweat running down his chest into the waistband of his trousers. She'd given him the name of another murder victim on the cold case list. This was exciting news — useful in confirming the killer's pattern. He could check the date of death back at the office and see if the Monday/monthly pattern still held. If it did, they'd have less than three weeks to prevent the next killing. He really needed to start the Homicide Squad moving. But . . .

Something else made him feel good — spending more time with Tara. He was already looking forward to their meeting a week from now. He'd have to think about that. Why was he so attracted to her? True, she was comfortable to be with, but why?

He immediately answered his own question. She's attractive as hell, and she's intelligent. She's also a professional woman — not a detective, but someone he can talk to about subjects he wouldn't dare mention in more squeamish company. *That's it,* he thought. *She's not a detective or a police officer, but she feels like one.*

I wonder! He'd never been a star during all his years on the job — just a good, solid investigator who'd made it to the Cold Case squad on merit and managed to solve more than his case share. But he'd never solved a high-profile case. He'd never experienced the glory associated with a single "glamour" case in his entire career. Now there was a chance he could solve — or at least contribute to the solution of — a serial killer case. That'd make all the newspapers, and maybe he'd even be on television. Harry imagined standing on the steps of the courthouse — the Commissioner handing him a citation — surrounded by reporters while recounting the details of the capture. The image made him smile.

Better yet, maybe his superiors would stop calling him 'Turtleshoe' and teasing him about his meticulous perseverance with "hopeless" cases. Sure, he wasted a lot of time on cases the others just *knew* were unsolvable, but every once in awhile he hit pay dirt. He recalled the case of a sun-dried skeleton discovered to be that of a low-life petty thief. Nobody had expressed interest in finding out how its skull had gotten bashed — except Harry. He poked and prodded the fifteen-year-old case until he discovered a small scratch on the bone of the skeleton's ring finger. There being no claims on the bones by relatives, the remains of the skeleton were used for training purposes at the morgue.

On a hunch, he wondered whether the scratch might have materialized when the murderer violently removed a ring from the finger in question. Researching the files for living relatives still available for interview, he finally found a brother living in Casa Grande. A phone call netted an appointment with a brother proclaiming his willingness to answer any questions the police might have.

Harry showed up at the address on a Friday morning and was ushered into the presence of the dentist brother. As they exchanged greetings, Harry felt the ring on the extended hand. During Harry's questioning, the dentist confessed to the crime, relieved to be rid of the guilty knowledge he'd been harboring those many years.

"Hey, Shoe," Detective Skirms called. She and Drummel were leaving the headquarters building as Harry entered. "How's it goin'?"

"Fine," Harry replied, smiling. "Just fine." Then Harry remembered Drummel and Skirms were investigating the Lamarka killing. "Hey, how're you two doing with the Lamarka case?"

"Don't ask." Drummel waved a hand dismissively. "We've tracked it about as far as we can go, and we're still on square one. All we know is the guy died from belladonna poisoning. We don't know how it was administered — or when — or by whom. We don't even have a crime scene. Unless our neighborhood canvass turns up something, we're up the creek."

"That's about it," Skirms confirmed. She put her palms together in a pleading gesture. "Need another case, Shoe?"

"Thanks a lot. Have you talked with the residents over at the shelter?"

Drummel nodded. "Got a good description of Lamarka staggering and screaming on the lawn before his legs gave out and he dropped dead. Also interviewed his mother, who assured us he was a nice boy who didn't deserve to die. Ever hear that one before? But that's about it."

"Forensics?"

"Nothing useful. Enough to confirm the cause of death, but other than that, just stomach contents. Guy musta' taken the poison sometime after lunch the day before he died. No useful foreign fibers, no suspicious marks on the body. Nothing we can grab hold of. Hell, we can't even do much of a canvass!

The shelter is invisible from the street, what with all the trees and tall bushes, so there's practically nobody to talk to. I think Skirms is right — looks like we'll have an open case for you."

"Thanks a *lot*. Look, if you get a lead, let me know, fast. Okay?"

"Sure. Something special about this case, Harry?"

"No," Harry lied. "It just bothers me, that's all." What bothered Harry was his fear that by honoring Tara's demand to hold off another week he might become responsible for another homicide. *I'd never live that down.*

CHAPTER EIGHT

Sunday morning, Tara luxuriated in her tub as best she could, given it was a few inches too short for anyone but a midget. Idly, she wondered what sadist designed such a product. *It must be the same yahoo who designs all those forms with spaces too small to write in.*

The phone rang.

She reached out to dry her hand in the towel bunched beside the tub, and picked up her cell phone on a nearby stool.

"Hello, Tara?"

"Narena?"

Who else? Do you know another Narena Tanner who roomed with you in nursing school?"

"No, and I don't know any other placed named 'The Marvella Snitskin-Pruitt Children's Hospital, either."

"Hey! Don't knock it! That 'place' — as you call it — provides my livelihood . . . and anyone who donates twenty-million bucks to establish a hospital can call it anything he likes . . . so there!"

Tara grinned. "Okay, you win. What's up?

"Remember the volunteer entertainer I told you about — Jason Smalter? The ventriloquist?"

"Oh, yes. I remember him."

"It's Sunday, and he'll be at the hospital today around two. He's really a treat, and the kids just love him. You wanna come?"

"Guess so. You caught me in the tub, so it'll take a while. Where will I find you?"

"Meet me in the lobby at a little before two and we can go up to the pediatric floor together. I guarantee you'll laugh yourself silly."

"All right," Tara said. "Uh . . . how will I recognize you?"

"I'll wear a nurse's uniform, okay?" The "How-will-I-recognize-you?" line was a tradition. They'd howled with laughter on first hearing it in an excruciatingly bad movie years before, and found it too good to abandon.

"Right. And I'll wear blackface." They laughed harder than the tired joke warranted, said good-bye, and broke the connection.

Tara entered the hospital lobby a few minutes before two, having wasted ten minutes finding a place to park. The lobby was large, its walls painted with happy colors and dancing cartoon figures. The chairs actually looked comfortable enough to sit on. The complex pattern woven into the wall-to-wall carpeting was capable of titillating the curious for minutes. A manned reception desk stood guard over the end of the lobby leading to the elevators.

Curiously though, the lobby, fully occupied by those waiting for service, or by family members waiting for other family members, was almost completely devoid of conversation. Almost.

The otherwise peaceful scene was marred by one annoying exception — a squirming child on the lap of a visibly-embarrassed mother. The little girl, about two years old, wore a short, chocolate-stained dress over bulging diapers. Her screams, accompanied by kicking legs and flailing arms, seemed unabated, leading Tara to wonder how she breathed.

Narena waved as Tara entered. Tara strode forward to exchange hushed greetings. Narena's flaming red hair tended to hide her height — more accurately, her absence of height. At only five feet, one inch, her short stature motivated her always to stand and walk with head high and shoulders thrown back. Tara often wondered how she kept from falling over backward.

"What do you think of the opera so far?" Narena nodded toward the girl with the bottomless lungs.

"Sounds like somebody's pulling her fingernails off. One by one."

"I feel sorry for the mother."

Just then the street door opened to a pleasant-looking man. Medium height, balding, on the light side of overweight, approaching middle-age. His brown and white checkered jacket, bright green pants, wide yellow tie painted with a happy clown face, and porkpie hat, came with a large smile to complete the ensemble. He carried a black suitcase in one hand and a large plastic sunflower in the other.

Edging close enough to the screaming child to attract her attention, he pantomimed extreme discomfort. He dropped his suitcase noisily to the floor. He wrapped his hands around his head. He shriveled his body into a ball. He rocked back and forth as though in pain.

The screamer wasn't impressed.

He peeked at the screamer from between his fingers. Nothing changed. Holding the sunflower in his outstretched hand and pointing it toward the child, he waved his other hand over it while chanting, "Abracadabra, gobbledy gook." On the word "gook," the sunflower wilted, accompanied by the sound of a slide whistle. People in the room looked for the source of the whistle — none realized it came from the smiling lips of the ventriloquist in the bright green pants.

The screamer was still unimpressed.

Jason Smalter placed his suitcase four feet in front of the child and sat on it, facing the screamer. Holding the bottom of his tie steady between the outstretched fingers of his left hand, he placed his thumb into the hidden ring on the tie's back. By pulling the ring, he opened and closed the tie's painted clown's mouth, making it appear to cry.

The child screamed, and the clown tie cried along with her. Only more loudly! Jason continued to smile during the screaming duet, and the room full of waiting people laughed at the bizarre scene.

When the little girl realized she was the only human screamer in a sea of laughter, she looked intently at the crying clown. For a moment, she forgot to scream.

The clown tie seized the moment.

"Hey, aren't you supposed to be screaming?" the clown hollered, mouth opening and closing to the words.

The little girl stared at the painted clown, and closed down to a whimper.

"Well, that's a *little* better," the clown said, "but I'm sure you can do better than *that*."

Jason let go of the tie and, with a flourish of his right hand, pointed to his left hand, which by then was buried deep in the pocket of his brown checkered jacket. Suddenly there was violent movement in that pocket as a muffled voice cried out.

"Lemme out . . . lemme out!" the voice shouted. Jason jumped up in mock surprise and pulled his hand from his pocket. No longer an empty hand, it wore a ventriloquist's hand-puppet shaped like a cuddly dog with a porkpie hat. Just like Jason's. Its long ears flopped as the head nodded and turned, and the perky nose moved up and down as the mouth opened and closed. The dog's body consisted of a black-spotted white plush sleeve covering Jason's wrist. Jason brought the puppet close to his face and leaned backward to escape its verbal attack.

"Arf! Do you have *any* idea . . ." ranted the puppet, "do you have *any* idea how *disgusting* it is to have to hang around in that dark pocket? *Do* you?" Jason raised his eyebrows and appeared to cower.

"I hope you realize my food dish is empty," the puppet raved on, "and my pet elephant needs a bath."

During the dog puppet's spirited tirade, the screamer had completely forgotten to scream. She was now watching intently.

The dog bit Jason on the ear, and Jason yowled, "Owww! Cut that out!"

A small smile appeared on the lips of the totally entranced little girl.

"That's for making me miserable in that smelly pocket."

"I promise not to do it again," Jason said, sniffling.

The dog turned to the little girl. "I'll bet *you* wouldn't ever treat me like that, would you?"

The little girl shook her head.

"I'll bet if I lived in *your* house, you'd take *much* better care of me, wouldn't you?"

The ex-screamer nodded vigorously. The puppet dog then turned to Jason, and said, "*There.* You see? I've got a friend who would take much better care of me than you do. I think I'll go live with her instead."

Jason looked at the little girl. "Would you like Spot to live with you?"

The girl nodded again, vigorously this time, and squirmed off the lap of the relieved mother. As she reached for the puppet, it whipped its head around toward Jason in a dramatic gesture and said, "Good-bye forever, Mister Butterbrains. I'm off to a far, far better life than that stinky pocket."

With that, Jason removed the puppet from his hand and handed it to the little girl. "Spot is yours to keep now. If you take good care of him, he'll always make you happy."

When the little girl's fingers touched the puppet, the "audience" exploded in applause.

Jason stood and bowed low. Picking up his suitcase, he headed toward the hall where he'd noticed Narena and Tara were waiting.

They were grinning from ear to ear.

CHAPTER NINE

Greetings exchanged, Narena introduced Jason to Tara. "Jason Smalter is the most successful kid-charmer I've ever seen work," she said.

"Aw shucks," Jason said, shuffling a toe on the floor.

"That was a most amazing performance." Tara extended her hand to Jason. "Where did you ever learn to do that?"

"I took a correspondence course."

They stepped into an arriving elevator; Narena punched the "4" button.

"You're joking."

"No, it's true. Lots of ventriloquists started with the same course I took. I'd be glad to lend it to you, if you want."

"Maybe some day."

"*Anyone* can learn it. It's a skill, like anything else. I could teach you to do it in just a few days." Jason turned to Narena, and asked, "Got any special kids needing attention today?"

"Just one. The bed nearest the door. There's another new one, but she's still too traumatized to approach with a puppet. She's pretty banged up. Let's wait until next time."

Jason agreed, and the three stepped onto the carpeted floor of the pediatric pod.

The three stopped at the nursing station to make their presence known. Though a nurse with a tiny bear clinging to the stethoscope around her neck was busy preparing a tray of medications, six other staff members appeared to be doing nothing but trying to look busy.

"What are all these people doing here?" Tara whispered to Narena.

"Waiting for Jason," she whispered back. "Nobody misses him if they can sneak away from work."

When the milling group noticed Jason's arrival, they all smiled, and roared in unison.

A muffled roar responded from Jason's suitcase and everybody laughed.

"Hi, Jason, Narena," Teena Lanovin, the duty nurse, said, smiling broadly. Like everyone else, she found it impossible not to smile when Jason was around.

"Hi, Teena. Narena said you've got a special case for me to work with today."

"He's in the Skunk room. He could really use some of your magical treatment."

Each room had a name such as Dinosaur, Giraffe, or Kangaroo. The Skunk room was one of only three containing four beds; all the others had only two, or one.

"What's their favorite room?" Tara asked Teena.

"The Slime Room. Seems they all like whatever's grossest. In addition to the slimy stuff painted on the walls, the room has a big bucket of slimy worms the kids can squish their hands in. They love it."

The gaggle of unoccupied staff began moving toward the Skunk room.

Jason stopped outside the room, put down his battered suitcase, and reached in. Adjusting his hand inside, he lifted a lion puppet from the suitcase. The soft brown plush body reached all the way to Jason's elbow. The shaggy mane swished and the big brown eyes moved from side to side when the head turned.

"This is Gweedo the lion," Jason offered. The lion looked left and right, then smiled at Tara and said, "Bon giorno." After eyeing Tara from top to bottom, and back again, he said, "Mama mia. . . you look good enough to eat. Yum yum. Mangia! Mangia!" Gweedo's open mouth lunged at Tara's chest, who backed her breasts out of reach barely in time to avoid being devoured.

Jason, standing just to one side of the door to the Slime room, turned and pushed the lion around the corner.

Gweedo roared.

The two children inside who had already experienced the lion, roared back, then giggled.

Jason walked toward the new patient, as Gweedo called, "Wat'sa matta' you? You don' know how to say 'hello'? Mama mia!" The image of a cuddly lion with an Italian accent was too much for the spectators crowding the doorway. They laughed as though watching their favorite Marx Brothers movie.

"What'sa you name?" Gweedo asked the new boy.

"Christopher."

Gweedo roared, and tilted his head, waiting.

Finally, Christopher roared back. It sounded more like a squeak. Everybody applauded, Gweedo nodded vigorously, and Christopher was officially accepted into a very special group.

Jason moved back to address all three of the children. "Hokay," Gweedo said, looking at each in turn. "How about I tella you da story of da four big pigs?"

"NOOOO!" shouted the kids.

Tilting his head in puzzlement, Gweedo looked at Jason. "No?"

Jason shook his head. "No." Addressing the children, he asked, "What's the *right* name for the story?"

"The Three *Little* Pigs," they shouted as loudly as their conditions allowed.

"Oh, da t'ree *little* pigs, eh?" said Gweedo. Hokay. I tella you da story of da t'ree *little* pigs . . . and da big, bad alligator — "

"NOOOO!" shouted the kids, laughing and beating their hands against their beds. "The big, bad *wolf.*"

It went like that for the next half hour — Gweedo mangling the story at every possible turn, and the children shouting out the "right" version between giggles. During this magical time there was no way they could dwell on the traumas bringing them there. When at last the story was ended, Gweedo visited each bed to collect a hug from its occupant and to make a few personal parting remarks. Saving Christopher for last, he had Gweedo spend a few minutes cheering up the battered boy and making him a friend.

On leaving, the crowd escorted Jason to the next room on the day's schedule. There the routine was repeated, usually with a different story — Jill and the Greenstork, Pinocchio and Jiminy Cockroach, Snow Black and the 'leventy-leven Elves. Gweedo didn't discriminate — he fractured them all, much to the delight of everyone.

Concluding his performance in the last room on the schedule, Jason tried to return Gweedo to his suitcase. Gweedo resisted with all his energy. He thrashed and flailed, he shouted insults at Jason — mostly in Italian — and threatened dire consequences. Even after the lid finally was closed, his muffled voice was heard shouting to be let out.

In the elevator once again, Tara said to Jason, "I can't remember when I've had such a good time. I laughed until I cried, and I feel a lot better than I did before you arrived. I'm sure the kids do, too."

"Thank you," he said. "I really appreciate that. I enjoy the kids, and Gweedo does — "

At the mention of the name, a muffled voice seemed to come from the suitcase. "Hay, lady. You wanna come in'a my suitcase wit me? I gotta da big hot tub. We skinny-dip, hokay?"

Tara laughed and patted the suitcase. "Down, Gweedo, down."

Jason turned to Narena. "You should bring Tara to dinner some night. Maybe she'd like to meet Scrawk."

"Oh, my God, *yes*," Narena replied, touching Tara's arm. "That's something you've got to *see* to believe."

CHAPTER TEN

On Monday morning, Sergeant Glenn "Dutch" Brunkel, Homicide supervisor of the Cold Cases squad, waved Detectives Drummel and Skirms into his office. They shuffled in, as if expecting to be called on the carpet for their inability to solve the Lamarka murder. Brunkel nodded for them to sit.

"I've read your report on the Lamarka thing, but I'd like a summary from the horse's you-know-what."

The two detectives looked at Sergeant Brunkel as they collected their thoughts. "Big" was always the word that came to mind when they saw "Dutch" Brunkel. At six feet six inches, two hundred and thirty pounds, "big" was the only word that fit. He had been a go-getter as a street cop. After twelve years, he was promoted to sergeant and assigned to Homicide. Soon after, he was made supervisor. Nobody was surprised, and everyone thought it a good move. Brunkel, according to his detectives, was not only street smart, but shrewd. As long as they played straight with him, his detectives had his full support.

Finally Drummel got his act together. "Here it is in a nutshell, boss. This guy Willie Lamarka dies of belladonna poisoning on the lawn of the Bramwell Convalescent Shelter, aka battered women's refuge. He dies at two in the morning, presumably trying to get to his battered wife, currently in residence."

Skirms joined the conversation. "After completing the crime scene investigation, we checked out his residence, truck, and last known employer. We canvassed the neighborhood. Nothing. No drug trace in the truck, or in his trailer. Forensics had nothing to add other than Lamarka's fingerprints and stomach contents. He wasn't a junkie. So far, we don't know anything leading us to the perp."

"What *do* you know?"

"We know he wasn't a lovable character, and nobody except his mother is sorry he's dead. Matter of fact, the day manager at the honkytonk hotel he was fired from, said not to go *there* looking for help in finding the guy's killer."

"What else?"

"Not much. We know belladonna is rarely used for killing — takes too long to work for most perps."

"And," added Skirms, "it isn't that easy to get — not like cyanide, for example, or rat poison."

Brunkel nodded. "So what's next? You thinking about where the perp might have gotten the poison? About who has access to that unusual elixir?"

Charlie Drummel looked at Joan Skirms, nodding. "You know, he's pretty damn sharp."

"Ha. You think that's just because I'm black." Brunkel leaned forward, planted his elbows on his desk, and stabbed his forefinger in their direction for emphasis. "Well, that's probably true. I never told you this before, but when I was young . . . *I* was a white boy, too, just like you two palefaces."

Drummel and Skirms glanced at one another. With Brunkel, one could never be sure when he was pulling your leg.

"Yes, sir, I was lily white, just like you two homicide defectives. But when I got older, I got smarter . . . and the smarter I got, the darker I got. Finally, I got so damned smart I ended up a full-fledged black man, just like I am today." He paused and steepled his fingers, leaning back in his chair. "You two play your cards right and study hard, you might just wind up as black as I am."

Joan Skirms turned to Drummel, brows furrowed. "Y'know, he just might be telling the truth. I haven't noticed any makeup in his office, so maybe his skin color *isn't* painted on like we thought."

"I dunno," Drummel said. "Mebbe we ought to have forensics check it out. We didn't get our Dick Tracy badges just to take these cock-n-bull stories at face value."

Brunkel laughed. "Well, I guess you must be pretty good detectives, after all. But you've got to admit I had you going there for a minute." Then he drummed his fists on his desk. "All right, troops, time to get serious. What *are* your next moves in the Lamarka case?"

"We're investigating sources of belladonna, and we've got some more interviewing to do."

The three of them chewed on the case for another minute, then Drummel and Skirms stood as if to leave.

"Not so fast," Brunkel said, waving them back into their chairs. He reached for a piece of paper sealed in a transparent glassine envelope. He paused, then pushed the 9x12 inch envelope across the desk. "Now it's time to get really serious. What do you make of *this*? The governor sent it over this morning by personal messenger."

The detectives leaned forward to read the document. It was a one-page letter addressed to Governor Sylvia Feingold, written on the stationery of the law firm of Chilton, Gonzalez, and Tibbetts. CG&T was one of the high-powered law firms occupying an entire floor of a building near Twenty-Fourth Street and Camelback.

"H-o-l-y shit!" Drummel exclaimed. "Who'd be dumb enough to write something like *this*?"

"What do you make of it?" asked Brunkel.

"For one thing," Skirms said, "it was typed on the same typewriter Noah used when he schlepped around in his ark. Look at those letters — not one of them seems to be aligned with those on either side of it. And the impressions are uneven. I'll bet whoever typed it used only one finger."

"Yeah," Drummel added. "But it's the signature that gives it away as an obvious forgery. It's signed by none other than Wilfred Bilfington Tibbetts. I don't know how bright this guy is, but if he's a law partner in a big firm like C, G and T, he's got a whole army of typists who can do up his letters. And if he doesn't want anyone to know he's the author of the letter, why sign his name?"

"I like it so far," Brunkel said. "What do you make of the content?"

The letter read:

Dear Governor Shit-for-brains;
I don't know what makes you think yore so smart, but yore an asshole if you think you can get away with passing more taxes on us lawyers. And yore try at getting us ambulance chasers off the streets isn't gonna work neither. You just might have to be strung up or shot if you don't stand down.
Really pissed off. . .
Wilfred Bilfington Tibbetts

"The writer's obviously trying to disguise his intelligence," Skirms said. "Look here. He uses 'yore' instead of 'you're,' but then ends the message with the words 'stand down.' Idiots don't use that language. Also, note he uses 'isn't' instead of 'ain't,' which he would do if he were consistent. Looks to me like somebody wants to make trouble for Mister Tibbetts." Skirms lightly ran a finger over the outside of the transparent evidence envelope. "Anything on the letter itself?"

"It's already been dusted for prints — it's clean," Brunkel said. "I suspect you two can find out whether the stationery is genuine. Hell, you know the drill."

"*Us?*" Drummel exclaimed. "Mind if I ask why *Homicide* is involved in a crank letter?"

Sgt. Brunkel heaved his large frame out of his swivel chair and sat on the edge of his desk. "Three reasons. First reason, the Governor personally asked the Commissioner to look into it. And the Commissioner personally asked our very own Homicide Lieutenant Beatrice Stacy, who asked *me*, and I'm now asking *you*. Personally. Second reason, as you should know by now, shit runs downhill. Third reason, this crank letter contains a death threat." He held up his hands to forestall the objections he knew were about to be voiced. "I know, I know. Those aren't good enough reasons, but that's the way the poop stirs. Besides, you might consider this an entertaining little break from blood and gore. So let me see you smile. And I don't need to remind you to tread lightly while you're up in the rarefied air of the legal castles. We wouldn't want to disturb the sensibilities of God's chosen, would we?"

"You really serious about our taking on this Mickey Mouse case?"

"Tell you what — you do me this favor and I'll get Lieutenant Stacy to spring for a brand new coffee pot for the squad."

"Well, now . . . " Skirms spread her hands in resignation. "With an offer like that — "

"Just knock it off and get to work."

Heels clicked on the polished granite floor as the two detectives approached the elevator bank of Solini Towers on Camelback. When built in 1985, there was an outcry from the neighborhood over the proposed twenty-story building. As usual, money spoke louder than the will of the people, and cries of protest were ignored. Legal firms now leased most of the floors.

A squint at the polished brass directory by the elevators told the detectives what they wanted to know — the law firm of Chilton, Gonzalez and Tibbetts occupied the entire seventeenth floor. They punched for an elevator and rose into an environment reeking of money.

The door opened to reveal a thickly carpeted reception area decorated in tones of muted brown and mauve. A large curved cherry wood desk faced the elevators, driven by a reed-like woman barely out of her teens. Wearing a dark blue suit, she sported short black hair and a reluctant smile. "May I help you?" she asked.

The detectives flashed their badges and asked for Mr. Tibbetts.

The stern-faced one pressed a button on her console. "Mary, there are two detectives to see Mr. Tibbetts."

"He's with clients," the loudspeaker replied.

"I think you'd be wise to get him out of the meeting. Now!"

Two minutes later Mary arrived and gave the detectives a look that clearly shouted, "How *dare* you interrupt a man who sits on the right hand of God!" It was a pretty loud look for someone small enough to be blown away by a sneeze.

They showed their badges again, and Drummel said, "We need to talk with Mr. Tibbetts, as soon as possible."

"May I ask what this is about?"

"Just take us to Mr. Tibbetts." Mary, who considered herself a confidential associate — aka executive secretary — to Mr. Tibbetts, bristled and led them to her office. The detectives concluded from the physical layout that Mary worked for more than one of the legal eagles.

"If you'd tell me — "

"Look," Skirms said, leaning close. "If you don't bring Mister Tibbetts out of that meeting *now*, we're both gonna get down on the floor and throw a tantrum."

Seeing no other option, Mary got the message and buzzed for Tibbetts. "I'm sorry to bother you, Mister Tibbetts, but the director needs your signature." Their code for "Get your ass out here, now!"

Within seconds, the door to the office suite opened, and the lawyer appeared. The detectives flashed their badges yet again. "Is there somewhere we can talk?" Drummel asked.

"In my office." He turned and strode back in to the office from which he'd just emerged.

"What happened to the clients?" Drummel asked.

"They're in the conference room," pointing to the door on the other side of the office.

An unusual office, the detectives noted. Not a single piece of paper, or folder, or filing cabinet, was visible. Three pencils and a pen lay carefully placed beside the telephone. Except for the absence of a speck of dust, it would be easy to conclude the office was vacant. Instead, they concluded "anal-retentive." Control freak.

"Now then, what's this about?"

"Mind if we sit down?" Skirms asked.

"Please do." Tibbetts sat carefully in his leather lawyer's chair as though he didn't want creases to develop from the pressure of his butt. Five feet, six inches or so tall, a head of brown hair, he wore the lawyer uniform — dark suit, tie, buttoned jacket, neatly folded hankie in breast pocket.

"It's like this," Drummel began. "We're from Homicide — "

"Homicide!" Tibbetts exploded. "What has homicide got to do with *me*?"

"We were just about to tell you."

"Oh. Well, please do."

"First, we need to see a piece of paper with your signature on it. Any paper will do."

"What for?"

"Look, Mister Tibbetts, if we're going to get this over with some time today, it'd be better if you just went along." Drummel hoped his frowning stare would get the desired results.

It did. Tibbetts reached into a drawer, withdrew a small notepad, wrote his name, and handed it to Drummel.

Drummel motioned for Skirms to produce the threatening letter from the manila folder she carried. She handed it to Drummel, who made a quick comparison of the signatures. Noting the absence of obvious similarities, Drummel handed the glassine-enclosed letter to Tibbetts.

Tibbetts quickly read the short letter, and exploded. "What the fuck is *this*?" he bellowed. "You think *I* wrote this, is *that* it?"

"That's what we came to find out," Skirms said, voice even.

"This is bullshit! I've never *seen* this — this filthy thing before, and you should have known this wasn't my doing without having to ask. This — this is *bullshit*!" By now the lawyer was standing behind his desk waving his arms.

"It's an obvious forgery," admitted Drummel. "We saw that right off. Got any ideas about who might want to get you in trouble?"

"Absolutely not," the lawyer thundered. "I'm a respectable attorney, and I'm not about to engage in this sort of threat . . . and . . . and . . . il . . . illiterate language." Now he was sputtering.

"Any disgruntled co-workers? Disappointed clients?"

"Certainly not!"

"What about a colleague who wants to create a spot for himself over your mangled body?"

Tibbetts stopped then, and frowned. A moment later, he shook his head and said, "Nooo. Nobody. Certainly nobody at *this* firm."

Skirms said, "Any idea how the writer got a sheet of your stationery?"

"I suppose anyone could have taken it. We don't lock it up like we do checkbooks, you know."

"Does that 'anyone' include people outside the firm?"

"What are you getting at?"

"Could somebody — say a messenger, or somebody on the cleaning crew — take a sheet?"

"I . . . I suppose so. But they'd have to know where to look. We don't leave stationery just lying around," he repeated. "What kind of place do you think this is?"

"We're just trying to find out who did this." Changing the subject, Skirms said, "We'll talk to a few of the other employees. Maybe they'll know — "

"Now wait just a *minute*," exploded the lawyer for the third time. "You have no need to do that."

The detectives noted the fear creeping into the lawyer's eyes and glanced at one another.

"I'm going to call the governor!"

"She already knows. She's the one who put us on the case," Charlie Drummel said. "Don't forget, she's the person the letter-writer threatens."

Tibbetts' shoulders fell. "Yes . . . yes, of course." In a more cooperative tone, he added, "Look. Rumors fly at the speed of light in a place like this. If you start asking questions, somebody's bound to think I'm guilty of something. You know, 'Where there's smoke — '"

"We'll be the soul of discretion," Drummel said. "We'll start every interview by saying you had nothing to do with this, but that we have to find out who did."

The lawyer sat again, leaned forward. Planting his elbows on the desk, he cupped his head between his hands.

During the pause, Detective Skirms wrinkled her nose at the strong smell of furniture polish.

"Mister Tibbetts, have you ever been arrested?"

Tibbetts' head jerked up. "Have I *WHAT*? Why, how dare you — " Exploding seemed to be what he did best.

"Sorry. It's just routine. I have to ask."

Tibbetts blustered, "Well, of all the — I'm not answering any more questions without my lawyer present. This has gone far enough!"

Detectives Drummel and Skirms rose together. Skirms picked up the letter, returned it to her folder, and the two left the office.

Heading back to the lobby, Drummel said, "I'll bet a donut he's got a sheet."

"No contest. But I'll have mine glazed."

The following morning, Drummel and Skirms summarized their interview for Sergeant Brunkel. "Tibbetts got mad as hell when we asked if he'd ever been arrested, and the way he carried on got us thinking we'd better do a little checking."

"And?"

"Bingo. Three years ago he was arrested for beating on his wife and causing a disturbance in the process. It never came to trial because the wife refused to file charges."

"And the guy's a tight-ass," Skirms said. "There's nothing out of place in his office. Not a thing on his desk. Just a telephone, three carefully arranged pencils, and a pen, along with several coats of furniture polish. You can imagine what his wife must have to put up with living with a guy like that."

Brunkel grunted. He'd seen cases where assorted neatniks finally cracked because the rest of the world didn't share their obsession. "Tibbetts had nothing to do with the bogus letter to the governor?"

"Nothing at all," Skirms said. "We think whoever wrote the letter is hoping it will make us dig a little deeper."

Brunkel looked from Skirms to Drummel and back again. "What do you suspect?"

"Not sure," said Drummel. "But I got to thinking about the Lamarka case, and wondering whether there's any kind of a connection."

Brunkel, knowing when to sit and listen, said nothing, waiting for Drummel to sort out his thoughts.

"The Lamarka case is connected with the battered women shelter, and that started me thinking. Tibbetts was arrested for beating his wife. I was just wondering . . . "

CHAPTER ELEVEN

Tara reached for the ringing cordless phone next to the cereal box and punched it on. "Hello?"

"Tara? It's Harry. Can you talk?"

"Hello, Harry. Nice to hear from you."

"You, too. Look, Tara. Have you been watching the news?"

"No, why?"

"There's been another murder."

"Oh, my God! What happened?"

"A dead body — a naked dead body — was found this morning beside a deserted road in North Phoenix. The crime scene detectives think he was killed some time last night, then dumped from a car."

"Who was he?" Tara could hardly wait to hear the name of the deceased and compare it to her list.

"Man name of Leroy Luntz. Black, thirty-five, long record of child abuse, registered pedophile. He had a rolled-up snapshot of himself doing unspeakable things to a seriously bruised little girl. It'd been shoved up his anus . . . none too gently."

"But . . . but there wasn't supposed to be another murder for another two weeks. How could — "

"Tara," Harry interrupted, "*ours* isn't the only killer plying his gruesome trade out there, you know."

Tara's mind raced. The name was not on her list — not yet, anyway — but the dead man *did* fit her profile of a vicious abuser of women and children. "How did he die?"

"The barrel of a .22 caliber pistol, shoved into his ear . . . and left at the scene. No fingerprints, of course. Two shots. No exit wound, so the perp probably used hollow-point bullets."

"My God! Sounds like that man . . . Tarper, our first gunshot victim."

"Yeah. Not much blood that way, if any. There was something else." Harry paused, unsure how to proceed. Remembering she was a nurse, he said, "The penis had been shredded — "

"You can't be serious! Shredded how?"

53

"Because of the unusual condition of the penis, the ME did a preliminary as soon as the body got to the morgue. He found little specks of walnuts in the shredded foreskin. He thinks the shredding was done with some kind of hand-operated nut grinder."

"What a horrible way to lose your — "

"If you'd seen the rolled-up photo, you'd have probably wanted to give the grinder a crank or two yourself."

"I see what you mean," Tara said, thoughtfully. "He fits the pattern of our previous murders, though . . . doesn't he?"

"Don't think so. This one died from gunshot — "

"But that's the point. Each one was killed by a different method. That's his style, uh, what do you call it . . . his MO?"

Harry was silent as he studied the chart in his hand. "Almost. Lamarka and Buggles died from poisons, one from belladonna and one from methanol, and Buggles was ruled accidental."

"If it *was* accidental, it should be ruled '*stupid*ental.' I still think he goes on our victim list."

"And *both* Tarper and Luntz were shot, one in the back of the head and the other in the ear. But you're right that the killer uses different killing tools."

Tara smiled at the recognition of her sleuthing skill.

"Tara, the reason I called was this guy Luntz was not on your list, and didn't have anybody staying at your shelter. Right, so far?"

"Right."

"So that means whoever killed him *isn't* someone from the shelter. That is, it's not the person you suspect. You okay with that?"

Tara said nothing.

"I mean, it's pretty unlikely somebody from *your* shelter would go around killing bad guys buzzing around *other* shelters, don't you think?"

"I suppose so," Tara replied slowly, thinking hard about the implications of Harry's conclusion. She repeated the conclusion in her mind. If the killer was finding victims at *other* shelters, it would be very unlikely he would be someone employed at *her* shelter. Tara sighed as a great weight suddenly lifted from her shoulders.

"If you're right, it means the police should go full speed ahead and try to catch this guy before he strikes again." She paused before adding, "But somehow I hope they don't catch him too fast."

"I understand your feelings. Here's somebody sweeping the world clean of some really bad people. And you secretly want to cheer him on. I've felt that way more than once. But we *have* to stop him, Tara. What if he decides that for whatever reason, other kinds of people have to die? What if he decides the world needs to be rid of doctors accused of malpractice, or sleazy politicians, or lawyers who defend criminals? Or even incompetent manicurists?"

"Okay, Harry, I get the point. It's just that, well, think of the lives he's saving."

"It's a gray area, and something I'd like to discuss with you some cool fall evening over a suitable libation."

"I'd like that, too." She paused to give him time to make the next move. She was disappointed when he failed to suggest a time and place. *Maybe next time*, she hoped.

"Go ahead with your investigation, Harry, but my promise still holds. I'll continue to dig up information, but the minute my name surfaces, that'll be the last you'll hear from me."

"Why be so worried about your anonymity — now that your Director is off the hook?"

"What? How did you know — ?"

"C'mon, Tara. It's pretty obvious who you suspected. Why so cagey?"

She hesitated before saying, "What if the killer finds out I've been helping to catch him?"

CHAPTER TWELVE

"What's on your mind, Shoe?" Sergeant Brunkel gestured Harry to a chair.

Harry stared at his supervisor for a long moment before speaking. "I've got something I need to talk to you about. Mind if I close the door?"

"This looks serious." Brunkel waved at the door as Harry got up to close it.

"It is," Harry said, "and I'd appreciate your hearing me out before calling anyone else in. This could be a little sensitive."

Brunkel had learned to listen carefully to what Harry had to say, especially when he closed the door.

"It's possible," Harry began, "that we have a serial killer at work."

Brunkel's eyebrows raised. "Go on."

"It's like this. Three days after Willie Lamarka died on the lawn over at the Convalescent Center, I had an anonymous call from a woman. She wasn't a kook. She was simply trying to keep her identity secret until she'd had a chance to meet me and size me up. I met her that afternoon at a little sandwich shop — she'd already cased the place to make sure it wasn't a cop hangout. Turns out she works at the shelter, and wanted to tell me that Lamarka had a wife staying there."

"Why'd she call *you*?"

"She didn't. She called the switchboard, and Estonia handed her off to me — she'd asked for someone working on unsolved cases."

Brunkel gestured for Harry to continue.

"She told me that if I'd let her work with me, she might be able to help me solve some of the cold cases on our list — "

"What'd she mean by 'work with you'?"

"Just that she'd provide information as long as her name didn't surface anywhere during the investigation."

"Interesting. She suspects someone at the shelter, right?"

Harry nodded, grinning. "Yeah. I guess that's why you make the big bucks. Anyhow, I agreed, and told her that if I thought of her as a CI, I wouldn't have to tell anyone about her. She then told me she could tell me a couple of the names on our cold cases list, and proceeded to mention the name of

'Tiny' Buggles, and tossed out the name of Frankie Frangini."

"And the connection?"

"Each was either the husband or boyfriend of a battered woman living at the shelter."

"Interesting." Brunkel leaned back in his chair and steepled his fingers. "If I remember right, Frangini died from a beating and Lamarka from poison. And Buggles was ruled an accidental death. What makes her think we've got a serial killer running?"

"All three of them died about a month apart . . . all on a Monday."

"Hmm. A strong coincidence, but hardly enough to run with."

"She realizes that, and she's digging for more — "

"*She's* digging? I thought *we* were supposed to do that."

"She's on the inside and has access to the information. She's no dummy, Sarge. Well, we met the following week, and she came up with the name of Broman Tarper. Died almost exactly six months before Frangini, also on a Monday. Two twenty-two slugs to the back of the head — contact range."

"Whoa! Now you're giving me the willies. Coincidence is one thing — "

"The latest kill was two days ago — Leroy Luntz."

"Guy with the shredded penis?"

"That's the guy. Found naked on the side of the road. On Monday. Shot in the ear with a .22. Twice."

"Besides dying on a Monday, how does he connect? His wife lives at the shelter?"

"Not this one. That's what's helping convince my CI that the perp isn't someone from the shelter. Luntz used to beat both the wife and daughter. Both were hospitalized at least twice. But there's something better. The bullet fragments taken from Luntz match those taken from Tarper."

Brunkel leaned forward. "Now that *is* interesting. So let me see if I've got this straight. You've got four bodies so far — "

"Five, if we include Luntz."

"Okay, five. The middle three died near a month apart, on a Monday, the first died six months prior to those, on a Monday, and the latest died two weeks after Lamarka. Except that they all died on a Monday, the dates don't make a pattern."

"They will."

"Because your crystal ball says so?"

"Because my CI says she's sure she can fill in the empty months with bodies. She just needs a little time."

Brunkel frowned and began tapping a finger on his desk. "Now wait a minute. You come in here and tell me we've got a serial killer running, based on information from this unnamed woman. Next you tell me you're letting her run around investigating — on her *own*? Don't you think you're putting her in harm's way? And where the hell do you get off keeping this to yourself?"

"Until two days ago, she swore me to secrecy — "

"An *informant WHAT* ?" Brunkel scowled.

Harry thought he saw wisps of smoke curling from Brunkel's ears. "She's not an informant, Sarge. She doesn't have a clue who the perp is, so she's not informing on anybody. I told her I'd call her my CI so I didn't have to give up her name until she says it's okay."

"*Why*, if I may be so bold as to ask?"

"Because until we talked two days ago, just as you said, she suspected the killer was someone at the shelter and that she was in a delicate position. She doesn't want to lose her job."

"But — "

"I know, I know. I bent the rules a little, but she's a sizzling source of information. If she's right, we're gonna clear a basketful of cases, all at once. Besides, we don't have enough yet to even *begin* talking about this outside your office."

Brunkel leaned back in his chair. "You're right about *that*, anyhow. So what do you want from me?"

"I want you to make me the primary on the case, and let me work with this woman until I've something solid, one way or the other."

"If I let you do that without telling the people upstairs, they'll fry me in oil."

"Understood. But if you *do* fill them in now, the press and the brass will go berserk and scare the killer off. You *know* it'll leak. And if it turns out there is no serial killer, the brass will look — well . . . "

"I take your point." Brunkel stood. "Okay, Shoe, run with it. We'll keep it between the two of us for now, but this is definitely against procedure. So keep me informed. I mean it. I can't cover your ass unless I know everything you're doing."

Harry grinned, and shook the Sergeant's hand. "Thanks, Sarge. I'll make you proud."

"Just don't make yourself dead. Uh . . . you like this woman, don't you?"

"Yes." Grinning, he added, "She's black, sort of, but what the hell — "

"Get your ass out of my office!"

CHAPTER THIRTEEN

The following morning, the phone on the stool rang just as Tara opened the shower door. Still dripping wet, she grabbed it up. "Hello?"

"Tara, it's Harry."

"What's happening?"

"I just had a long talk with Sergeant Brunkel. I laid out the case in detail — without ever mentioning your name, of course, and he went along with it."

"What does that mean?"

"He's assigned me as primary investigator. Since we don't have enough evidence yet to prove we even have a you-know-what on the loose, he's letting me investigate quietly until we do."

"You mean in secret?"

"Yes. If the press ever gets wind of this, all hell will break loose. And if it turned out we're wrong, all hell will break even looser. So the three of us are the only ones in on it, for now."

Tara was excited. She'd already planned to make another midnight visit to the records room, and this news strengthened her resolve. "What are you going to do now?"

"I'll start by reviewing the files on the five victims — there may be connections we don't know about. Then I'm going to want to review the files at the shelter to — "

"I wouldn't advise that just yet," Tara interrupted, an edge in her voice. "Women's shelters are very touchy about people finding out where they're located, and go absolutely ballistic when someone wants to look at a record. Especially at *this* shelter — the director is a real Nazi when it comes to security, and protecting *her* women. She almost beat up on those two detectives who came out to interview some of the residents about Lamarka."

"Gotcha."

"I'm sure even George doesn't have access to records, and he's the Center security guard who lives there."

"Okay, then, tell me this. How come you've got access?"

"Who said I had access?"

"Come on, Tara. It's pretty obvious you're getting your information from somewhere. If they're so security-conscious, I doubt you're getting it from one of the residents or staff."

Tara was agitated at having been so obvious. "Uh, look, Harry. I don't want to say anything about this subject . . . certainly not over the phone."

"I understand."

"Give me a couple of days to see what I can find out, and then we'll meet and compare notes. You'll have reviewed the case files, and I . . . well, I'll see what I can find out. Okay?"

Harry was silent as he thought about the implications of Tara's plan. It was clear she must be getting her information from shelter records, but what kind of risk was she taking? Was she about to put herself in danger again?

"Tell me this, Tara. How much of a risk are you taking? Sergeant Brunkel said he'd kill me if I put you in harm's way."

"Not much. I'm very careful. Wait, I've just had an idea. We're going to meet again to compare notes, right?"

"Right."

"Okay, this Saturday a nurse friend of mine and I are going to have dinner at an Italian restaurant where one of the waiters is a character, a real hoot to watch. How about coming along for a drink and dinner and — "

"Sorry. Can't do it."

"Why not?"

"We don't socialize."

"I don't understand. Aren't you allowed to have friends, for God's sake?"

"Yes, we can have friends, but we don't socialize with CIs. The whole point of confidential informants is that they're confidential. It would be too much of a risk to be seen in public. So that's why I'm declining your invitation. But — and I shouldn't tell you this — I'll miss the pleasure of your company."

Well, I'll be darned! He really likes me. "And I'll miss yours."

"I'll call you in a day or two after I've reviewed the files. Until then, remember — there's a killer out there . . . and he may already be watching you. Be extra careful."

Late that night, Tara prepared to repeat her furtive entry into the records vault. Remembering the chill she felt when Harry said the killer "may already be watching you," she determined to be especially careful. Dressing in dark slacks and a long-sleeved turtleneck, she laced up her running shoes and checked her "tools" yet again — small flashlight, two pairs of surgical gloves, key ring, small note pad and pencil, five file folders. These contained records of patients she'd examined that day — she was expected to return them as soon as possible to the director's office. If challenged, she planned to use that as an excuse for being out and about. She had no idea how she'd explain the skulking garb.

She cracked open the door of her clinic and cautiously looked out to make sure no residents were in sight. Closing the door quietly behind her, she tip-toed across the commons room to the director's office. After a quick look around, she slipped her key into the lock. Once inside, she made sure the door was locked before making her way to the director's desk to retrieve the key to the records vault. Good. The middle drawer was unlocked. Before opening it, Tara paused to put on a pair of surgical gloves. Before moving from the spot, she looked around to make sure she hadn't accidentally dropped the other pair.

Inside the windowless vault, she turned on the light and held her eyes closed until they adjusted to the sudden change in illumination. She then went to work. Quickly removing files for the targeted months, she placed them on the floor. One by one, she scanned the files, made notes, and replaced each into its cabinet before continuing with another. An hour later she was finished, having been only partially successful in her search. Replacing the last file, she stood in the middle of the room, wondering where else she might look for the "missing" information.

Retracing her steps, she locked the vault, replaced the key in the desk drawer and cracked open the door. *Damn!* A resident was sitting at a writing desk. Tara hoped her letter would be a short one. Closing the door, she settled down to wait, her heart pounding. With a start, she remembered she hadn't removed her latex gloves. She did so, slipping them into her bra.

Ten minutes later, she peeked out again, relieved to see the resident had gone. Quickly, she slipped out and locked the door behind her. She whirled in panic when she heard the voice.

"Miss Tara?"

"Uh . . . oh . . . Mrs. Tanaka. I thought you'd gone to bed."

"Almost. I just went off to the ladies room for a minute. I'm almost done with this letter." She looked closely at Tara. "Is something wrong? You look a little pale."

"No. I'm fine. Well, maybe I overworked a little today. I was just on my way home and, uh, had to return some files before I left."

"I see." Her raised eyebrows said she didn't believe a word of what she had just been told.

Tara said good night and returned to the safety of her clinic without further incident. Closing the door, she quickly headed for a chair and sat down. Her heart was still pounding from the close call, and she needed time to regain her composure.

When at last her hands stopped shaking, she tore off her skulking clothes and fumbled into her street clothing. Stuffing her notes into her purse, she turned out the lights and headed for home. That night, her troubled sleep was punctuated by dreams of shadowy monsters chasing her naked body up an endless flight of stairs.

CHAPTER FOURTEEN

Captain Darryl Portono, Homicide Chief, peeled an orange with his bone-handled pocketknife. Carefully placing the peelings on a tissue, he slowly sectioned the fruit, studying each before putting it into his mouth. Portono was balding, and usually soft-spoken. He seemed to linger over each thought while his brain cells convened a meeting to select the words he would say next. Impulsive was not a word anyone would use to describe him. Competent, insightful, but not impulsive. This careful selection of words made Portono seem wiser than he was, but the pauses led subordinates to conclude he must be president of the Slow Talkers of America. That impression, however, was not mentioned in his presence.

"Dutch," he said to Sergeant Brunkel, after demolishing the carefully-peeled orange, "I've just talked with the Commissioner. He's had another query from the Governor's office about that threatening letter from that lawyer . . . Tibbetts? Where do we stand?"

"Tibbetts, right." Brunkel leaned forward and rested his elbows on his knees. "He didn't have anything to do with sending the letter. As I wrote in my report, the letter was a forgery. We don't have a lead on who might have sent it yet, but our investigation did lead to some interesting information."

"As I recall, you said this Tibbetts fellow became rather irate when asked if he'd ever been arrested." Brunkel kept his patience in check while Portono paused yet again. "I suppose you looked into that?"

"Yes, sir, we did. He'd been arrested for beating his wife. She didn't press charges, so there was no arrest. But something else came up."

The captain bunched his eyebrows, urging Brunkel to continue.

"Drummel and Skirms asked around — very discreetly I might add — and verified their hunch that Tibbetts is one tightly wound guy. Short tempered, easily offended, meticulous. Also, he's one angry man."

"How do we know that?"

"Joan Skirms just 'happened' to bump into Tibbetts' wife at the supermarket. She was sporting a black eye that looked pretty raw. When they got to talking, she admitted to Skirms that her husband thought the eggs she served that morning were too cold. She also confided that she'd leave him in a minute, except that all the assets are in Tibbetts' name. She's obviously putting up with a lot to keep from becoming destitute. She's being held in bondage by the assets. Skirms said something else was bothering the lady, too, but she seemed afraid to say anything more."

"So what is he so angry about?"

"Just about everything. One of his colleagues told Charlie Drummel he'd been passed over — again — for a prestigious award he's been lusting after from the American Bar Association. That's the small thing. He's also being sued over a car accident he apparently caused. Also, it seems he sold some worthless swampland to some elderly people in Florida. That was a mistake. They're suing him, too.

"Sounds as though Tibbetts is skirting on the edge. Anything else we should know about?"

"It's only a rumor, Captain, but we've also heard he knocked up a sweet, young thing, then beat her to within an inch of her life when she refused to get an abortion. If that turns out to be true — "

"If it does," Portono added, "we'll step in and clip an inch or two off his wayward cock." He waved for Brunkel to go.

The last statement was so completely out of character for the normally soft-spoken captain, Brunkel left the office with his mouth agape.

CHAPTER FIFTEEN

When Harry answered his phone, without preliminaries Tara said, "We've got to talk. I've got something you should know as soon as possible. Can we meet today?"

Harry thumbed through his daily planner and eyed the pile of folders on his desktop. The desire to see Tara won out. "Today would be fine. Same place, same time?"

"Would it be okay if we met someplace more private? I'd like to be able to speak freely."

"Got anything in mind?"

"I'd suggest a bench in front of the opera house, but it's 110 degrees outside. How about the lobby of the Hyatt? We can find a quiet corner, and that's just a short walk for you."

"Sounds good. What time?"

"If we meet at eleven, we should be done with our business in time for lunch. Are you allowed to buy your snitches lunch?"

"Only if they're beautiful wenches and I'm trying to pry information out of them. You qualify on both counts. You're on. We meet at eleven."

A few minutes before the hour, Tara gave her car to a valet and strode into the hotel lobby. She found Harry sitting in a corner furnished with two overstuffed chairs book-ending a small table. Exchanging greetings, she noted that Harry seemed pleased she wasn't any more eager to end the handshake than he. When the handshake could no longer be considered anything other than overt hand-holding, they both laughed.

"Thought I'd never say this about a cop, but it's nice to see you again, Harry."

"Nice to see you, too — and I never thought I'd say that about anyone, even an attractive woman bent on poking her nose into police business."

"This is *my* business, too, and you know it, so don't give me that crap."

"You win. So what did you want to tell me?"

"I checked some more records. I was looking to see if I could find the missing bodies."

"The missing bodies for the empty five months between the Broman Tarper and Frankie Frangini killings, I presume?"

Tara nodded. "I'm sorry to say I didn't find any . . . and I was so *sure* they'd be there." Her bowed head emphasized the disappointment in her voice.

"Don't beat yourself up. There's nothing that says there have to be bodies for each of those months." He reached forward to put his hand on hers. "Maybe the killer took a vacation, or got locked up for drunk driving. Any number of things could have put him on hold. Hey, maybe he ran out of victims."

"Not a chance, but I'm still convinced I'm right."

Harry smiled. "*I* think you're right, too." Before Tara could continue with her report, Harry interrupted. "Let me tell you what *I* found in the case records."

Tara perked up at Harry's optimistic tone.

Harry leaned closer. "I went back over the cold case files and didn't find anything new. But remember that though cold cases are *unsolved* cases, they are still open. They don't give us *closed* cases to work on."

"So?"

"So cases ruled as suicides or accidental deaths are considered closed."

Tara immediately understood the implication. "That's right!" Now she could hardly wait for Harry to continue. "So what did you find?" she asked, putting her hand on his, squeezing gently.

"On April 10 last — a Monday — the body of a thirty-seven year old man was found in a flophouse on Washington Street about two miles from here."

"How did he die?"

"Shot himself in the head with a Saturday night special."

"Are they sure it was suicide?

"Yes, they're sure. Though there was no note, there was powder residue on his shooting hand. No forensics to suggest it wasn't suicide."

"Darn!"

"What is unusual — to us — is the deceased had been arrested several times for child abuse. The abuse was bad enough for Child Protective Services to remove his little girl from the family and put her in a foster home."

"What was his name, Harry?"

"Ramin Zander. Ring any bells?"

Tara shook her head slowly. "No, but maybe his wife never got to a shelter."

"That's possible. The day after Zander shot himself, she disappeared. She hasn't been heard from since."

Tara thought for a moment. "Harry, how did he shoot himself in the head?"

"I don't understand — "

"I mean, *where* did he shoot himself in the head?"

"He put the barrel in his ear and pulled the trigger . . . wait a minute, I see where you're going. That naked body with the shredded penis, Leroy Luntz. *He* was shot in the ear."

"Harry, I think we should think about this suicide the same way we think about Buggles. Buggles is a suspicious accidental death, and this is a suspicious suicide. What did the autopsy say?"

"There wasn't one. It seemed cut and dry, and the ME already had a backlog. What's more, Zander died long before we put out a watch for suicides and accidentals. What are you thinking?"

"I saw a cop show on TV last night. The killer gave his victim some kind of drug to pacify him, then put the gun in the victim's hand and helped him blow his brains out. That got powder residue on the victim's hand. That, along with a note, was enough to convince police it was suicide."

Harry smiled. "Sounds like a typical TV scenario."

"What's wrong with it? Do suicides *usually* put the gun barrel into their ear?"

"No, they don't. But in this case, there wasn't any physical or forensic evidence to suggest anything but suicide."

"Maybe another look would prove differently."

"Maybe. Okay, you may be right about Zander, and Buggles. Both expressed violence toward women, and both died on a Monday. That's a whole lot of coincidence to swallow. But I've another one, Tara."

"You do?"

"Accidental death. Man in a seventh floor apartment was washing his windows and fell out.

"When?"

"February fourteen, Valentine's Day. A Monday."

"What else do you know about him?" Tara asked.

"Not much. Seemed pretty clear it was an accident. The water bucket and squeegee both fell with him. No evidence of foul play. He died of a broken neck, along with a bunch of other things."

Tara stared off into space. "I see."

"But I confess this one looks a little hinky. Week or two before the guy died, his wife and daughter left town — no forwarding address. Nobody seemed much concerned at the time, but in retrospect . . . "

"I understand. What was the name?

67

"Darryl Dunbar. Known as 'Dummy' Dunbar — not too bright, I understand. The primary investigator, Charlie Drummel, checked with the neighbors; they seemed to think falling out a window was about his speed."

"So where are we? You've dug up two victims who died on a Monday. Both fit unfilled dates, and both had daughters. You know for sure that one of the daughters was mistreated enough to be taken from the home. But . . ."

Harry waited for Tara's thought to form.

" . . . but neither name is familiar. Neither of the mothers was at the shelter. Not ours, anyway. Oh, that's right, one moved away and the other disappeared. So their *not* having been at the shelter doesn't weaken my kill-a-month hypothesis."

Harry said, "They may have been ruled accidental, and a suicide, but there's just too much coincidence when they die on the unfilled Mondays. We've got to keep digging, Tara. And quickly. There's too much at stake if we're right about this. If this is the work of a serial killer, we've got to catch him before he strikes again."

"I can't argue with that. Now then, *I've* got something to report. I didn't find any more names of dead husbands, but I did find the names of two good candidates."

"Candidates?"

"Likely victims. They're not dead yet, but I'll bet it won't be long. Not if our killer stays true to form. One is a guy named Runny Pilanski . . ."

"I'll bet his friends call him 'The Nose'."

" . . .Well, his wife, Esther, was brought to the shelter a week ago by a friend. The poor woman was so beat up she could hardly walk."

"What made her decide to make the break?"

"He wanted her to have sex with some of his friends — and she refused."

"Imagine that."

"Yeah, and that's why he beat her so badly. She still can't feed herself — both arms are in casts."

"Who's the other candidate?"

"This one's even worse, if that's possible. Three days ago a mother and daughter signed in. The daughter's ten, and apparently the husband has been raping her regularly for the past couple of years. The wife didn't want to believe her daughter's story for a long time — she was in full denial. But when she caught him in the act, that was the last straw. Instead of being guilty about it, he pleaded with her to come join them in the fun."

"Nice people you hang out with."

"Ha! Look who's talking. The husband works for an upholstery company on Seventh Street." She handed Harry two 3x5 cards, one with information on Runny Pilanski — the other, on a José Gonzalez. "This guy's wife's name is Estrella, and the daughter is Conchita. It's all there on the cards. My source said the police are putting a case together so they can arrest the creep."

Harry studied the cards. "I think you're right — these are good candidates. I'll touch base with the rape squad, and we'll keep an eye peeled."

"Okay, so we've proven we have a serial killer at work, right?"

Harry tapped the cards on the table. "We have, and we haven't. What we've got are seven bodies — that's a fact. Also it's a fact that four of them were murdered; Tarper, Frangini, Lamarka, and Luntz. Buggles was ruled accidental, but is a possible homicide. The other two, Dunbar and Zander were ruled accidental death and suicide. They're also possibles, according to your theory."

"But they all died on a *Monday*. About a month apart."

"Almost. Luntz died two weeks after Lamarka was killed, so he breaks the pattern . . . but he's the only break in it so far."

Tara threw up her hands in exasperation. "Jeezus, Harry, how much do you *need*?"

"Look. I agree with you, we've got a serial killer at work. But let's look at it objectively. We don't have a witness, not for *any* of the kills, and we don't have a suspect. We don't even have a clear pattern in the way he kills — sometimes it's poison, sometimes it's gunshots, and one was beaten to death. That one, by the way, doesn't fit the pattern at all. So when I lay this out for my boss, the first thing he's going to ask me is why we think this is the work of a single killer."

"You can point to the pattern of monthly Mondays, for one thing. Then, you can describe the victims and ask him if he doesn't see a similarity . . ."

Harry applauded. "You oughta join the prosecutor's office. But we still only have a loose case. The crime scenes — and we don't even know where all the crime scenes were — were remarkably lacking in forensic and physical evidence. So until we have a suspect, we're still skating on thin ice."

"You're forgetting one important thing," Tara said.

"What's that?"

"You said the bullet fragments that killed Luntz matched the ones that killed Broman Tarper."

"You're right. Now *that's* a piece of information hard to ignore. It's still circumstantial, but that can't be coincidence. If there was only one killing, that would be one thing. But the minute word gets out that the police department thinks there's a serial killer loose in our fair city, it will start a firestorm of public reaction . . . fanned by the media, of course."

"Tell you what. Give me a few more days to nose around — yes, yes, I'll be careful. Don't forget, if our schedule is right, another murder is due a week from Monday."

CHAPTER SIXTEEN

Tara drove into the parking lot, stopped in front of Bellissimo's and got out. She handed her key to one of the red-shirted valets waiting to serve.

"Wow," she said, looking at the entrance to the restaurant.

"This your first time at Bellissimo's?" the valet asked.

"Yes, it is, and I'm already impressed."

"This is a pretty special place. I'm sure you'll enjoy yourself."

Tara ran her eyes around the entrance to the Italian restaurant. The huge round door was shaped like one end of a large wine cask. Split down the middle, the two halves were opened by pulling on solid brass bungs.

Once inside, Tara was immediately surrounded by music and merriment — and cool air. While making her presence known to the red-shirted hostess, she heard the sound of a polished tenor voice, accompanied by a skillfully-played accordion. Though she wasn't an opera buff, the aria sounded familiar. As the hostess checked the reservation chart, Tara's eyes lingered on the red — and white — checkered tablecloths. On the center of each sat an old pot-bellied Chianti bottle, the lit candle in its snout offering cheerful illumination. The red napkins, folded into an inviting spire, accented the decor. *How do they do that?* she asked herself.

Tara followed the hostess to a booth overlooking the restaurant, where Narena was already dipping bread into a small bowl of olive oil and garlic cloves. After exchanging the usual "kiss-in-the-air" greetings, Tara slid into the booth beside her friend.

"What do you think so far?" Narena asked.

"Fabulous. Why haven't I heard of this place before?"

"Maybe because it's an opera buff hangout."

Tara laughed. "Who would have guessed?"

"Well, we're within three blocks of Symphony Hall and the Herberger Theater, so the place jumps with the theater crowd."

"I don't care who comes here. I love it already."

"Here comes our waiter."

Just then Jason Smalter arrived, also dressed in the restaurant's costume — a red silk shirt with long puffed sleeves, and tight black pants. A red silk bandanna around the head completed the waiters' ensemble — except for one thing. In addition to the clothing, Jason "wore" a colorful six-inch-tall parrot puppet on his left shoulder. Attached by a leather harness under his shirt, the puppet was animated by a small remote-control keypad secured to Jason's left palm by a flesh-colored stretch-band. The four buttons operated small solenoids mounted inside the puppet. By pressing combinations of the four buttons, Jason could make the parrot's head turn left or right, or the beak open and close. The fourth button raised its bushy eyebrows.

"Good evening, ladies," Jason said with a smile. Nodding at Narena, he added, "It's nice to see you again. May I bring you something from the bar?"

"Scrawk!" shrieked the bird. "You late! What'sa matter you? You no got a clock?"

"Calm down," Jason said to the bird. "These ladies are good friends, so be nice to them." To Tara, he said, "Sorry about that. This is Scrawk, and he doesn't always mind his manners."

Narena and Tara laughed.

"Ha!" the bird hollered. "You talk-a manners?" Turning his head toward Tara, the bird continued in his high-pitched scratchy voice, "You watch-a dis guy he don' spill calamari sauce on your pretty dress."

"That's enough," said Jason, pretending embarrassment. The women gave him their drink orders and he headed for the bar, the bird scolding him until they were out of sight.

"You've got to admit," Narena said. "Just the *idea* of an Italian parrot puppet is enough to make you laugh. It's even funnier than an Italian lion. But when he *really* gets going, he'll nag Jason until everybody falls on the floor laughing."

"He really is a very good ventriloquist. I can't even see his lips move when he's standing right in front of me." Tara opened her menu. "Okay, what do you recommend?"

As they pondered the menu, Jason returned with their cocktails.

"Don' drink too much, now," Scrawk admonished. "You get-a drunk, somebody take advantage an' squeeze-a you boobies."

Jason pretended outrage. "Now you just *behave* yourself, Scrawk, or you'll get tossed out on your ear."

"Hooo-eee. Look-a da fat boy talkin' big."

Jason served the drinks amidst laughter from the surrounding tables as well as from Tara and Narena. Both women ordered an antipasto salad and a plate of calamari from the appetizer menu.

"The appetizer plate is big enough to feed a small army," Narena advised. Just then a mezzo-soprano voice from the other end of the restaurant burst forth with a rendition of *The Habañera*, an aria from the opera *Carmen*. Much to Tara's surprise, half a dozen diners joined in — with obviously trained voices. Tara couldn't help but hum along.

When Jason returned with the salad, Scrawk turned to the diners at the next table and shouted, "Hey, look-a da Mister Bumblefingers serve-a da salad." Jason tried to ignore the outburst, and again feigned embarrassment.

"Hey, Scrawk," called a diner from an adjacent booth. "How about a song?"

Scrawk immediately responded with a screechy rendition of *O Sole Mio*, much to the raucous delight of the diners. Just then an ear-piercing shriek shattered Scrawk's solo, followed by the sound of dishes breaking as they hit the floor. In a flash, Jason whipped off his apron and rolled it into a loose ball. Ever alert, he'd noticed the shriek was forced from a woman who had tripped and fell two tables away.

Before Tara or Narena located the source of the disturbance, Jason was on his knees beside the woman slipping his rolled apron under her head.

"Are you hurt?" he asked, his voice soft.

"I . . . I don't think so. Wh . . . what happened?"

"I believe you slipped and grabbed a tablecloth to try to break your fall." Jason carefully brushed the linguini from the dazed woman's torso.

"I think I'm okay. Help me up, please."

By this time the woman was surrounded by staff, picking up the broken pieces and swabbing the floor. Jason helped her to her feet.

"You have a nice trip, lady?" Scrawk joked.

"Stop that," Jason scolded. "Remember your manners."

"Thank you," the lady said to Jason. "You've been very helpful."

A man who seemed to be her husband moved to Jason's side and said, "Thank you for your thoughtfulness . . . and your lightning speed," extending his hand as he spoke. When Jason grasped it, a tightly folded fifty-dollar bill changed hands.

While the remainder of the evening was filled with good food and laughter, Scrawk occasionally accepted invitations to join diners at other tables in song. The banter continued with the patrons at nearby tables or booths. This table-hopping was a good thing, as it turned out — it gave patrons time to pause in their giggling long enough to eat their dinners.

All during the evening, Jason's serving ability was ridiculed by Scrawk.

"Hey, what'sa matta you? You don' know da butter plate goes on da left?"

Later. "How many times I gotta tell-a you, don' put-a your t'umb in-a da soup?" And to the patrons: "Hey, lady! You eat-a dat pasta an' you get too fat to play da squeezebox!" The customers took the banter in good spirits. They also left larger tips, whether or not they'd been served by Jason himself.

The serving staff loved Jason and his Italian parrot — the tips, after all, were shared by all. The patrons seemed to love Jason's being humiliated by the bird, and Jason's "hang-dog" look of embarrassment. The management loved Jason because he filled the restaurant with customers every Thursday, Friday, and Saturday evening.

After their dessert, Tara said, "I can't tell you how grateful I am you brought me here. This has been simply wonderful, and I couldn't eat another bite. Uhh . . ." Tara wanted badly to confide her suspicions about the serial killer. She wanted to tell Narena everything that had been going on; talking about it might help her clarify her thoughts and maybe give her a new insight or two. Her promise to Harry to keep the project secret for now, however, made her hesitate.

"Uhh . . . what?"

"Nothing. I just got to daydreaming, that's all."

"Don't give me that crap," Narena retorted. "I know you better than that. So give."

"All right. There is something I want to talk to you about, but I can't. Not yet. But soon, I hope. Please don't be angry, but I promised."

"Don't let it keep too long. Call me any time you want to talk, okay?"

"Yes, I will."

They paid for the dinner and walked to the entrance together. While waiting for their cars to be brought to the door, Narena said, "When are you going to come over to the hospital again? Jason is there on Tuesday and Saturday afternoons, you know."

"I'll have to look at my schedule and call you. But I'm looking forward to it. Maybe I'll be able to talk by then."

CHAPTER SEVENTEEN

All the way home, Tara hummed, still enchanted by the magic of the evening. Later, as she lay in bed, her mind returned to her immediate problem. Solidly convinced her hypothesis regarding the monthly Monday kills was right, she was still unable to fill in three of the "empty" dates with victims. *Who knows how many he killed before our first known murder of last December 13?* It was frustrating to have unfilled dates — it was even more frustrating not to have a suspect. Worse, the killer could be anybody. Sleepless, she decided to get up and lay out her plan for the week.

Step one, she proposed to bring her "murder chart" up to date. She had to see where they stood. Next, she planned to contact the other shelters and try discreetly to find out whether they had a dead husband or boyfriend on any of the "empty" dates. Third, she penciled in the library — a look through their newspaper files. Surely, something of value would turn up.

"This is so darn frustrating," she mumbled. She'd discovered the work of a serial killer — she was sure of it — and yet couldn't think of a likely suspect. The shelter director was ruled out, which was a relief, but she couldn't think of anyone else who . . . "Wait a minute! What about George Petacki, the security guard? Oh, no, he *couldn't* . . . he's a retired *cop*, for God's sake! On the other hand, he'd do *anything* to protect 'his' women."

Tara couldn't stop trying to fit George into the image of the killer. He had the opportunity, and the means. But why? What could be his motive? "And besides, he's such a nice man, so severely devoted to shelter residents."

Retrieving more paper, she began writing out her plan for the next few days. She started by updating her chart, then underlined the dates for which there wasn't a body. Yet.

Date		Victim	Method
12/13,	Mon	Broman Tarper	(gunshot to head)
1/10,	Mon	?	
2/14,	Mon	Darryl Dunbar	Accidental? (fell out window)
3/13,	Mon	?	
4/10,	Mon	Ramin Zander	Suicide? (gunshot to ear)
5/8,	Mon	?	
6/12,	Mon	Frankie Frangini	Beaten to death
7/10,	Mon	Tiny Buggles	Poisoned (wood alcohol)
8/14,	Mon	Willard Lamarka	Poisoned (belladonna)
8/21,	Mon	Leroy Luntz	(Gunshot to head)

The following day, a refreshed Tara reviewed her updated chart and called for appointments with people she knew at other shelters. She was successful in all but two instances. There simply were no convenient times when she could be welcomed. She was invited to call back later. Copying the three dates remaining in question onto separate cards — it wouldn't do to hint at her real motive for the visit — she listed the addresses, names, and phone numbers for her scheduled visits. Her quest for the missing bodies had begun.

Before leaving the house, she rehearsed several versions of a tactful approach. "I wonder if your records show any of the husbands or boyfriends of your residents died on any of these three dates." But what would she say if they asked *why* she wanted to know, which they surely would?

Finally hitting on an idea, she concocted a cock 'n bull story. "We're conducting a study having to do with recently deceased batterers." It was lame, but should be good enough to satisfy curiosity.

Sandwiching visits between her regular duties, she completed all but one of her appointments during the next three days. Wednesday afternoon found her completely discouraged. With only one more visit to make the following day, she'd learned nothing of value. The women she talked to were cooperative enough, but produced no evidence of relatives who had died on or near the dates Tara provided. Like other shelters, they knew of husbands who had skipped out to avoid various obligations, but none of the missing had yet been stamped "deceased." That didn't prove none had died, but it was disappointing. *Harry's right . . . detective work can be a royal bore.*

Having found nothing promising at the other shelters, she called the public library and quickly verified they indeed had back issues of newspapers on microfiche. She planned to scan through the papers on and around the three empty dates.

"If you'll come with me," the librarian said, "I'll set you up at an idle microfiche station. Tell me again what dates you're interested in?"

Tara told her, and they wended their way to the back of the main room. Once the correct fiche had been inserted, she began her search. This wasn't the first time she'd searched on fiche, and she remembered that on each and every previous occasion she'd gotten sidetracked by articles totally irrelevant to her purpose.

Finally, she approached the first date and slowed her search. She read the issues starting from three days before a target date, to three days after, looking for articles about accidental deaths, suicides, and murders. She then read the obituary page, just in case.

Tara looked up two hours later and massaged her eyes — for her, fiche-reading always led to eye-strain. She closed her eyes for a few minutes while squeezing the back of her neck.

Suddenly her head jerked up and she slapped a palm against her forehead. "What is the *matter* with me?" she exclaimed, loudly enough to attract the attention of those nearby. Putting a finger to her lips to signal her intent to be quiet, she thought, *I could have stayed at home and simply searched the Internet.*

Sheepishly, she returned the fiches to the librarian, thanked her, and went home. Embarrassed with her lapse of memory, she booted her computer and searched the Internet for the same information she'd hunted at the library. Again, she'd found nothing of value — other than a history review of the last six months. *Amazing*, she thought, *how many things happen in such a short span of time.* What she did, she chastised herself, was to waste a lot of time.

Reluctant to report on her lack of progress to Harry, she still called him. She finally admitted to herself that her attraction to Harry was growing, and she was now actively seeking opportunities where they could be together. She hoped he felt the same way.

"Detective Shuman."

"Hi. It's Tara."

Instantly, the voice softened. "I'm glad to hear your voice."

"You are?" Tara's mood soared, and she forgot all about the non-news she was about to report.

"Yes, but it's not enough — I want to *see* you, too."

"Mmm, that can be arranged." In a low sultry voice, she said, "Your place or mine?"

"Brazen hussy. Look here, madame, we have things to discuss, and I agree that a private venue would be best. Would it be too forward of me to suggest meeting at *my* apartment? Say, five o'clock today?"

"I don't know . . . "

"How about if I promise not to make imprudent advances?"

"It's not that. I was just thinking about my work schedule for today. I promised I'd have a chat with one of the residents. But I can change that. How late do you think we'll be?"

"Well," Harry said, pretending to ponder a very weighty situation, "if all goes as planned, I think we should be finished by midnight. With a little luck, maybe later. It's that . . . the sharing of . . . ah . . . information may take longer than we think. I'll plan to fix a little something for us to eat — in case of emergency, that is."

Tara smiled her pleasure into the phone. "I suppose I should be coy and — "

"Come, now. You know as well as I that nurses can't be coy. It's not in their genes. Five p.m. Okay?"

"Okay, but I thought you didn't socialize."

"This won't be socializing. It will go under the heading of pumping a snitch."

Tara chuckled into the phone. "Whatever it is, I'm for it."

Harry gave her the address and directions for locating his apartment complex. "But you have to promise you won't give away my secrets to any of these insensitive detectives around here, should you ever run into them. I already get enough ragging as it is."

Tara had no idea what he was talking about, but decided this was not the time to ask. The warmth flowing through her body left no room for mundane details. When they broke the connection, she immediately began preparing herself for the "sharing of information" and for "pumping of the snitch." It was barely three o'clock.

A few minutes after five that afternoon Tara turned into the tree-lined street off Camelback Road, located the address, and parked. After one last primp in the rear-view mirror, she located the ground-floor apartment number, whistling as she jabbed a finger toward the bell button. With her finger still in mid-air, the door opened.

Ushering her in, Harry exclaimed, "Wow! A vision of loveliness, if I ever saw one."

Tara bowed, causing the scoop-necked red blouse to reveal the black bra cupping her ample bosom. "Thank you, kind sir. You're looking pretty spiffy yourself." She pointed to his open-necked blue shirt, tan slacks, and sandals.

Harry couldn't take his eyes off the smooth brown skin nestled in the bra. Had that move been deliberate? He hoped so. "Please come in, said the spider."

Tara entered and, placing her hands lightly on his shoulders, offered a peck on his cheek.

"What did I do to deserve that?"

"Nice men who compliment women on their looks often earn rewards for their efforts."

"In that case, I'll spend the evening saying nice things about your red blouse, your white skirt, and definitely about your red shoes. And there really is something about the way your hair curls inward at the neck that I like. There — how's that?"

"You're racking up points. Ka-ching! Ka-ching!"

"Let's work in the living room, such as it is. It'll be more comfortable than the kitchen table."

They walked into the apartment, and Tara saw her image of a typical man's lair. Though there were no socks strewn about, or clothing casually thrown over chairs, there were also no signs of a woman's touch. The furniture seemed to have been selected for comfort rather than style — none matched — and the books littering the coffee table were definitely masculine. Several issues of *Soldier of Fortune*, one of *Guns & Ammo*, and an issue or two of *The American Rifleman*. Most prominent, however, was a thick blue book titled *Practical Homicide Investigation*.

Pointing to it, Tara asked, "Is that your bed-time reading?"

Harry chuckled. "Hardly. Nine-hundred page books are too heavy to hold on my belly when I'm trying to doze off. But for a textbook, it's pretty darned interesting. Wanna see some pictures of dead bodies?"

"No, thank you. But I wouldn't turn down the offer of a drink."

"Sorry, I'm forgetting my manners, such as they are. Homicide detectives aren't exactly known for their social graces, you know." Harry headed for the kitchen, where he retrieved some ice from the small fridge.

"I think you do very well in that department."

"What department?" Harry called from the kitchen.

"The social graces department. I feel very comfortable in your presence, you know. Probably more comfortable than I should. Is that part of your technique for ferreting information from unsuspecting informants?"

"No. It's because I like you . . . but you didn't hear it from me. What can I fix for you?"

"Scotch and ice would be nice, if you have it."

"Done." Harry brought her the requested scotch, and poured a bottle of Beck's beer for himself.

"Cheers," Tara offered. They clinked glasses.

"That's better," Harry said. They placed their drinks on the coffee table. "And now, to work. You first."

"I'm afraid I struck out this week, Harry. I visited five shelters and none of them found any record of deceased boyfriends or husbands on or near the three empty dates. This morning, I went to the library and looked up old newspapers on and around the dates in question. There's a lot of interesting stuff, but I couldn't find any stories about murders that fit. I even went back to look for suicides. My score, so far for the week, has been a big fat zero." Tara sighed. When she saw Harry grinning, she asked, "What? What'd I say?"

Harry leaned forward and took Tara by the arm. "Nothing at all. Don't be too hard on yourself because you didn't find anything. If you want to be a detective, you learn to live with a lot more disappointment than that. What I'm smiling about is that I *did* find something."

Tara brightened. "You did? What?"

"Remember Darryl Dunbar, the guy who fell out his window while washing it? The accidental death?"

"Of course."

"Well — you're gonna love this — I talked Sergeant Brunkel into convincing Captain Portono to reopen the investigation of Dunbar — and of Ramin Zander, the suicide. A team of detectives went over the case files, this time looking for indications of murder." Harry paused.

"Well? Come on."

"That was just a dramatic pause. The detectives reviewed the interviews with Dunbar's neighbors, and then took a closer look at the crime scene photos."

"And?"

"There wasn't anything new. There was no autopsy, you may remember. But when the detectives again looked at the photos of the body's exterior — taken when the body was on the slab at the morgue — they noticed a round bruise in the pubic hairs above the penis."

"Jeezus, Harry, the guy fell seven floors. You'd expect — "

"Not *there*. You expect to find broken bones, of course, and bruises on those parts of the body that hit the ground — like elbows and heads. And knees. You *don't* expect bruises on parts of the body not likely to hit the ground directly, like the pubic area."

Tara leaned forward expectantly.

"I talked to the detectives and asked them to guess how that bruise could have been made if Dunbar was a murder rather than an accident." Again, he paused.

"Will you stop with the dramatic pauses, Harry, and tell me what they *said*? I can't stand this suspense."

"Okay. Their best guess is that — if he were murdered — remember the murderer didn't leave any forensic evidence behind, he was probably pushed out the window with a hard shove by the end of a broom handle. They didn't find a broom in the apartment, so if that was the way it happened, the murderer took it with him."

"Did any of the neighbors see a stranger with a broom?"

"Sharp. No. The detectives asked about that specific point, but no one saw a stranger coming, or going."

Tara got up to pace. "Will the case now be called a murder instead of an accidental death?"

"Unlikely, but it sure strengthens your hypothesis. It's a lot more plausible now that he was murdered since the bruise has been noticed. It would make a prosecuting attorney's job a little easier."

"What about the other case . . ."

"Ramin Zander? Even better. Zander was labeled a suicide because it appeared he shot himself in the head, his fingerprints were all over the gun, and because there was no evidence of a struggle. There wasn't a note, but that's not rare in suicide cases." Harry stopped to take another sip of beer.

"Harry Shuman, you've got to be the most exasperating story teller I know. Tell me what happened already."

"Okay. The detectives looked at the Zander case the same way — they assumed it was a murder masquerading as a suicide. When they looked at the bullet fragments removed from Zander's head, the detectives remembered that Leroy Luntz was shot in the ear. So they had forensics try to match up the bullets." Harry paused, and smiled.

Beyond exasperation, Tara shouted, "Harry if you don't stop that, I'm gonna come over there and strangle you! Did they match — like Luntz's and Tarper's?"

"Yes, they matched . . . sort of."

"What the hell do you mean by *that*?"

"A low-velocity, twenty-two caliber hollow-point bullet will shatter when it hits a skull. So what we're talking about is the matching of one set of bullet fragments with another set of bullet fragments. Forensics is certain, but a good defense attorney could put some doubt in a jury's mind."

"I see. Even so, this is great news. Instead of having four certain murders, and one possible — Buggles — we now have six certain murders and one possible. Doesn't that mean something to you?"

"Oh, yes. I think we've got enough evidence now to support a serial killer theory, and I've already laid it out for Brunkel and Capt. Portono."

"You have? When?"

"This morning. A meeting is scheduled for Friday morning — that's tomorrow — so I can lay it out for the entire task force, and get them started on the investigation."

"Where will they start?"

"Probably by reviewing the victims' case files to see what we've got. Then they'll profile the killer and start interviewing. Remember, we're sure there's a killer on the loose, but we don't even have a whiff of a suspect . . . but we haven't been looking. That's where we'll start."

Harry stood and, taking Tara's hands, lifted her to her feet. "You've done a great job, Tara, and I can't tell you how glad I am your first phone call was bucked in my direction." He moved close to her. "Now it's my turn to offer a reward." Harry took her face in his hands and kissed her lightly on the forehead.

"That was very nice, Harry," she whispered, voice abruptly husky, "but for pungling up seven bodies, a kiss on the forehead can only be considered a small down payment. Very small." She pulled his head to hers and, with lips parted, kissed him on the mouth. Wrapping her arms around his neck and pulling him closer, her tongue danced with his until she felt a definite swelling in the region of his groin. It made her proud, and warm all over. She didn't want to let go.

When finally she allowed him to pull away far enough to speak, he mumbled, "It's been so long, I'm not sure I remember how this game is played, but I'm definitely a willing participant. I assume that kiss was in payment for one of the *other* bodies?"

Tara gently nipped his ear. "It'll soon come back to you — all you need is practice. Fortunately, we have five more bodies for which you can express your appreciation." Hungrily, she kissed him again, lightly scraping her fingernails across the flesh of his neck until his bulge grew to its maximum.

Five languorous kisses later, Tara nibbled on his chin. "Would it be possible to continue this discussion in a more comfortable position? There are still at least two more bodies to thank me for . . . you know, the two that aren't quite dead yet." She took his hand and led him toward what she had noted was the bedroom.

"You must promise not to tell a soul about what you are about to see here. I already get enough razzing." He led her the rest of the way into the room and turned on the light.

Tara scanned the room to discover what required a vow of silence. She soon saw the small desk beside the dresser. It was covered with stamp-collector's gear — magnifying glasses of various sizes, tweezers, small glassine envelopes, stamp books, and more. "Harry, you're a philatelist!"

"Naw. I'm just a run-of-the-mill stamp collector, but if you ever breathe that outside this room, I'll be doomed. Please promise you'll not mention it."

"I promise — but there's a price for my silence."

He spent the next two hours paying the price. Fortunately, he had a small supply of condoms in his Hope Drawer. It was a labor of love.

Much later, Tara raised herself on one elbow and drew circles around Harry's nipples. "Y'know, for a guy who doesn't socialize, you're very good at making a girl feel warm and fuzzy all over. You don't seem to have forgotten a thing."

Harry frowned, pretending confusion. "I'm flattered you're pleased, but there were one or two places there where I still felt a bit rusty. Do you suppose we could practice a little more?" Without waiting for a reply, he rolled on top of her, mumbling something about learning being enhanced by repetition.

Later, he flopped down at her side and said, "I meant to tell you earlier — before I was so completely distracted — but you smell terrific. What's the fragrance?"

"Jasmine. Like it?"

"Mmm, fabulous. It tastes as good as it smells." Harry mumbled this as he slowly ran the tip of his tongue around her nipple. Still later — after more practice — he tapped her chin with a forefinger. "You hungry? We never did seem to get to the dinner part of the evening."

"Yes, now that you mention it."

"I'll fix a little something. Then I'm going to have to ask for a timeout."

"Timeout?"

"I need about an hour to prepare for tomorrow morning's briefing. I've never had a big case like this, and I want all my ducks in a row." After a slow scan of her body, he leered. "Then the practice can resume. Okay?"

CHAPTER EIGHTEEN

"All right, all right," Brunkel called to the detectives waiting for the briefing to begin. "Find a seat so we can get started."

The briefing room was filled to overflowing. Detectives from the Homicide and Rape Squads occupied every one of the sixteen chairs. Even the medical examiner was present. The banter slowly waned, but low-volume murmuring continued. Brunkel's hulk stood motionless until all conversation stopped, then he began.

"First, somebody close the door. Next — and pay close attention to this — this is a *confidential* briefing. I will *personally* disembowel anybody who leaks what you're about to hear. Got that?"

"Jeezus, Sarge, you sound serious," a voice called out.

"You better believe I'm serious. Now then, are there any members of the press in the room? Look around and make sure. We can't afford to have the press inflaming the city before it's absolutely necessary. Anybody who leaks to their press pals will be out on his ass before he can fart. Got it?"

"We got a double murder, Sarge?" a voice asked.

"Some politician get whacked?" called another.

"No," Brunkel replied. "What we've got is a serial killer running loose in our city."

There was an eruption of response, most of them, "Holy shit!" or its intellectual equivalent. When the hubbub died down, Brunkel continued, "The existence of this killer was discovered by none other than our own Harry the Shoe. I've put him in charge of the investigation."

"Why Turtleshoe? It takes him all day just to brush his teeth." Laughter erupted, but died quickly when Brunkel glowered.

"Why? Because Shoe is the one who sniffed out the existence of this killer while the rest of you were sitting there with your fingers up your asses, that's why. And because he has a source who's been helping him dig up the victims, so to speak."

"How many?"

"Seven so far, and if the killer's pattern holds, another is due next Monday." There was another chorus of "Holy shits," along with whistles. "How do you know there's gonna be another killing on Monday?" asked Charlie Drummel.

"Look," Brunkel said sternly. "Just listen to what Harry's got to say. He'll lay out the whole story, then answer all your questions. After that, he'll make the assignments. With my blessing."

Harry stood behind the battered wooden lectern vacated by Brunkel and placed a stack of paper on the table beside him. "It began a little less than three weeks ago when I got a phone call from a woman who'd been bucked over to my desk. At the time, she had a suspect in mind and was very nervous about losing her job."

"Who is she? What's her name?" someone asked.

"I'm getting information only as long as I keep the name of this person to myself. The minute the name surfaces, the source will disappear. So I'm classifying the source as a CI for now. So, let's get to it."

Harry handed out his sheet listing the victims and the dates they died, after which he related the rest of the story. He started with the Lamarka killing, then explained what Drummel and Skirms had learned during their investigation. He nodded at Dr. Millston, the ME.

Millston stood. "Lamarka was killed by belladonna poisoning. That's a rather unusual poison to use for murder, since the victim could fly from here to New York before feeling its effects. But that means he was killed by remote control — we don't know where he ingested the poison, but we do know he died somewhere other than the scene of the crime. Ingenious. There wasn't any other useful forensic evidence, except that Lamarka died at least several hours after eating a junk meal."

"Thanks, Doc," Harry said, and continued to explain what he knew about each of the killings. He ended with, "That's it. Any questions?"

Nearly everyone shot up a hand and began speaking at the same time. Harry pointed to Detective Drummel.

"What do we know about the perp?"

"We know he prefers to kill on a Monday and, with one exception, his kills come about a month apart. That suggests his Mondays are free . . . he's not an eight to five wage slave . . ."

"Like some people we know," someone offered.

"We also know he's very selective in his choice of victims. This isn't just some nutcase killing everybody in sight, nor is he killing to satisfy sexual perversions. There's never any evidence of semen or sexual molestation. And he never takes anything from his victims — except in the case of Leroy

Luntz, who was dumped naked on the side of the road. The perp took his clothing. He confines his kills to guys who physically beat or rape either wives or girlfriends, or their children. But he's even selective within that group. Instead of killing anybody who harms women or children, he seems to kill only the worst offenders — those who've been most vicious or damaging — like child rape."

"Got any suspects?"

"Let me come back to that. I'd like to finish reviewing what we know about the perp. As you see by the sheet I handed out, he seems to kill about once each month on a Monday. You'll notice there are three open dates — January tenth, March thirteenth, and May eighth. We're convinced that he killed on those dates as well — we just haven't located the bodies yet."

"Why don't you assume he was in the pokey at that time, or at the track?"

"Good question. Here's why. Darryl Dunbar was originally marked down as an accidental death, and Ramin Zander was labeled a suicide. As a result of your own re-investigations, we now know they were carefully disguised murders. The bullet fragments from Zander's gun match the fragments we took from Leroy Luntz and Broman Tarper. Since we've finally filled in *those* two monthly Mondays with murders, we're assuming you'll be able to fill in the empty dates, too.

"Now on to the suspects. The first victim we were aware of was Willie Lamarka, the August fourteen kill on your chart. He died on the lawn of the Bramwell Convalescent Center — a shelter for battered women." Harry reminded himself to be careful with his next words so as not to reveal Tara's existence or identity. "His wife was a resident at the shelter at the time, and we assumed Lamarka was trying to reach her when he died."

"Good riddance," mumbled a voice, followed by several "Amens."

Harry continued. "Several of the victims had wives, girlfriends, or children staying at the shelter as well, so we thought at first the perp might be someone working there. *Everybody* there has a motive, after all — they'd all like to see these creeps taken out. But, for now, we'll rule out the women who are hiding out there — they may have motive, but most are too banged up to handle the job."

"Who's there beside the residents?" asked Detective Joan Skirms.

"Well, there's George Petacki. He's the security guard and lives in a little cottage right on the premises. He's a retired cop — his son works Dispatch downstairs. There's Tara Tindall. She's a nurse who *doesn't* live on the premises, but who gets to choose her working hours. Sometimes she works days, sometimes nights, sometimes a little of each. Then there's the Director, Dr. Marla Benarez. She *really* hates the creeps that mangle her residents. We could see her for the killings, if she had the opportunity. She's not a likely candidate, but we should check her out anyhow. Aside from a small cleaning staff, occasional social worker visits, and the usual delivery guys, that's about it."

"In other words, no suspects." This from a rape squad detective, Anita Solarez.

Harry nodded. "That's about it. But I'll tell you what's different about this case — half the population of the Valley has a motive!"

Brunkel perked up at that assertion. "How do you figure that?"

"Look at it this way. Who might want to harm somebody who mangled their daughters? The parents of the victims for one. Who else? The grandparents of the victims. Who else? The siblings of the victims. If I were the father, or the brother, of a woman torn up by the perp, *I'd* sure have a motive to kill. Wouldn't you?"

Nods followed the question.

"Then," Harry continued, "there are all the people who work with the victims — health care workers of all kinds. And we think most of the women of the Valley would like to get their hands on the creeps who deliberately destroy the lives of women and children — "

"You got that right," Skirms interrupted. "When we investigated the Lamarka case, we talked to a hotel manager where Lamarka worked. She told us not to come looking for help from anybody there to find the creep's killer. I kinda suspect a lot of other people are gonna feel the same way once this shit hits the media."

"And that," Sgt. Brunkel said forcefully, "is exactly why we have to keep this case quiet until we're ready to make an arrest. We don't want our good citizens obstructing our investigation because they're rooting for the killer."

Harry answered several more questions, after which he handed out the assignments he and Brunkel had agreed upon. "We need to concentrate on two things. First, we need to take a fresh look at the Buggles case. If it was a homicide, we want to know it. We've also got to go into the shelter files to see if we missed any bodies that might fit the three empty dates you've got on your sheet. Second, we need to find us a suspect . . . and fast. The bright side is that even though we've got a few million people with motive, we can cut the suspect pool way down just by eliminating those who work on Mondays."

"Have family members been interviewed for motive?" Solarez asked.

"Not yet. That's one of the things on your action list. You know the drill . . . talk to family members, co-workers, landlords, neighbors. Oh, and try to find out where the victim was going when he was killed. We gotta move fast on this one and close him down before he strikes again. And before this leaks to the press . . . and the copycat killers."

Sgt. Brunkel heaved his large frame out of his chair and towered over the group. "By the way. I want to ask everyone to move this investigation along, even though you didn't know you were dealing with a serial killer until now. And one last thing. When this case finally leaks there's gonna be a firestorm of demand for us to *do something*. If that happens before we're ready to announce an arrest — which we're not even close to — we're all gonna look like a bunch of Keystone Cop assholes. If that ain't your cup of tea, you'd damned well better keep this case under your hats and your noses to the grindstone. And remember this jolly item — if Harry's hypothesis is right, there's another killing due in three days. Dismissed."

CHAPTER NINETEEN

Earlier that week, a humming man clicked a light, stepped down the wooden stairs to his basement workbench, and began preparing for his next act of kindness. Placing the books under his arm onto the workbench, he spread them out where he could more easily make the difficult choice. These college textbooks were old friends, after all, but now one would now have to be sacrificed for radical surgery. Should it be the chemistry text? No, no, much too valuable. The mathematics text? Not for a moment. The Merck Manual? No. It was well-thumbed and, though a few years old, still useful. The sociology text? Yes, that's the one! It was just the right thickness for the purpose — hard-bound, with an old-book look about it. It would have to be the one sacrificed on the altar of "mankind improvement."

First, he measured to make sure the length of the book would accommodate the entire hypodermic syringe, plus an inch or two for the dowel. Next, he drew a penciled rectangle on the second leaf of the book, outlining a space large enough to accommodate the syringe. Selecting a sharp Exacto knife, he carefully cut along the line, scooping out the excised pages. When the pocket was deep enough, he lined it with enough cotton batting to hold the hypodermic firmly in place.

Moving to the wall of bookcases at one end of the basement — they served his special purposes better than typical basement shelving — he tripped a well-concealed latch and pushed open a section serving as the hidden door to his secret pharmacy. Stepping inside the small room, he turned on the light and reached into a drawer for a small box. Back at his workbench, he opened the box and withdrew one of the five-inch hypodermic needles he'd ordered from a veterinary supply house a year earlier.

Attaching the needle to the syringe, he pushed the needle through the pages at the top of the book and settled the syringe into place in the cotton nest. Satisfied with the fit, he clamped the closed book into his bench vice and drilled a hole into the center of the pages along the bottom of the book. Selecting a one-half inch wooden dowel rod from his stock bin, he pushed one end into the hole until it touched the plunger of the water-filled syringe. With a pencil, he marked the dowel at a point four inches beyond the edge of the book. After cutting off the excess and smoothing the edges with sandpaper, he re-inserted the dowel into the hole. Taping one end to the plunger, he was ready for a trial run.

He continued to hum as he worked, placing two sheets of blank paper on top of the closed book, and then placing the other three books on top of the paper. There! The paper would hide the protruding needle, and the stack of books would hold the paper in place, at the same time helping him look like a university student. It would also help distract his victim's attention from the needle-prick.

To test his work, he tacked a pillow to one of the bookshelves at chest height. That done, he bumped his book stack against the pillow, injecting it with water by pushing against the dowel with his belly. It was awkward, but it worked well enough to convince him that daily practice would prepare him for action by week's end.

The remainder of the week he planned to spend making sure he and his victim would converge in the same place at the same time.

The following Monday morning, the humming man filled the hypodermic with the poison he'd selected for its reaction time. He had to dilute it so it would act quickly, but still slowly enough to allow him time to leave the scene. Then he completed preparation of his lethal stack of textbooks.

While driving the twenty minutes to the site he'd selected, he reviewed the results of his practice runs, hoping to avoid the frustration he experienced on the days his victim either didn't show up or the traffic light had conspired against him. *If the light isn't red when I need it to be red, I'll either have to put myself in danger by waiting, or cancel the run and waste another day.*

Having planned his escape route, he parked a block away from the busy intersection targeted for his mission. Carrying his stack of books in both hands, he walked slowly toward the victim's place of employment, careful not to jab a stranger by accident — it would be unfortunate to harm someone he considered undeserving of such treatment.

As unobtrusively as possible, the humming — and now smiling — man stood near the entrance to the Kotapai Cleaners and Dyers Establishment . . . and waited.

Inside the cleaners, "Runny" Pilanski worked over a hot steamy press. Sweat poured off him, soaking his soiled white t-shirt and staining the waistband of his shorts. Though the building was air-conditioned, the heat of the press, added to the muscular exertion required to operate it, was stifling.

Pilanski finally noted the time — lunch break. Finishing the trousers in the press, he placed them on a hanger, rinsed his face and hands in the cracked porcelain sink in the corner, and told the manager, "Goin' t'lunch."

Stepping outside the door, he breathed deeply to rid himself of the cleaning chemicals' stench. He never noticed the man leaning against the building next door holding a stack of books.

Pilanski turned left to walk the three blocks to his favorite sandwich shop. As he often said to his friends, "I don' give no shit fer the food there — I jes' like to look at them chicky-chick co-eds bounce their boobies and swish their asses." He strolled along at a pace allowing him to ogle every one of the young female college students he passed. At this time of day, there were many.

The humming man followed close on his target's heels. His heart rate increased and his breath grew more shallow with each step. Beads of sweat formed on his forehead. He feared his clammy hands might let the books slip from his grasp. He looked straight ahead, keeping his eyes on his target. He was terrified of these "contact kills" where he had to be close to his victim — he much preferred the belladonna ploy when circumstances permitted.

As they approached the busy intersection, he was relieved to note that the traffic light had turned red, causing pedestrians to bunch at the curb, primed to surge forward when the green signal appeared. To prevent the needle from puncturing passersby, he inched his way to a spot just behind the left shoulder of his intended victim. Surrounded by chattering students, he waited.

When the light turned green, the gibbering lemmings surged forward. The humming man quickly jabbed the needle into the flesh of one Runyon "Runny" Pilanski, pushing the plunger forward with his stomach while ramming the stack of books into his victim's back. A second later, he dropped to his knees and allowed the books to fall to the ground. His head was already bent over, eyes looking at the ground, when Pilanski turned to say, "Hey, watch where yer goin'."

The crowd pushed Pilanski along — apparently not noticing the man on his knees fumbling with his books.

The humming man, hands trembling from the danger he'd just survived, remained on his knees pretending to collect his books. While doing so, his sweaty hands removed the needle from the hypodermic and placed it quickly inside the hollowed book, careful not to touch the tip. *It wouldn't do*, he thought, *to accidentally jab an innocent bystander offering to help*. His sleight-of-hand completed, he stood and, with his book stack held in both hands, turned left and strolled the single block to his car.

Pilanski, just a short stroll from the sandwich shop, already visualized the female flesh about to inflame his sexual fantasies. Then, halfway along the block, he began to feel strange. First his eyelids didn't work right. Soon, his face became numb. By the time he reached the next corner, he couldn't lift his head from his chest and was having trouble catching a breath. Standing on the curb waiting for the light to turn green, he clutched at his chest — his lungs were no longer able to take in air. Desperately gasping, he staggered. When he lost consciousness, he fell headlong into the street.

Traveling at twenty-five miles an hour, the SUV driver barely slowed as she ran over the prostrate body and drove on.

CHAPTER TWENTY

An hour later, Harry the Shoe and Sgt. Brunkel were discussing the investigation's progress when Brunkel's phone rang.

"Corporal Petacki, sir. Dispatch. Sorry to interrupt, but you wanted to know about any accidental deaths as soon as we heard. There's been a hit and run."

"When?" Brunkel barked.

"About an hour ago. Tempe police put out an APB. Guy named Pilanski tripped and fell into the street — SUV ran over him. He's dead. According to witnesses, the driver never even slowed down."

"Who'd you send to the crime scene?"

"Drummel and Skirms. They're there now."

"Good. Tell them we'll be treating this as a possible homicide until we know different."

"Yes, sir." Brunkel put down the phone.

"And the *name* of that victim," Harry said, standing and dramatically lifting a finger into the air, "is Runny Pilanski. Right?"

"Son-of-a-bitch!" Brunkel growled. "How the hell could you know *that?*"

"Superior powers of deduction. Plus, I'm a detective. I detect things."

"Cut the crap, Harry. How'd you know?"

"My source gave me two likely candidates for the next kill. Pilanski was one of them."

Brunkel stared off into space for a long minute. "Well, we *were* expecting a kill today. To tell you the truth, I was hoping your CI was wrong." He looked at Harry. "Harry, we've got to stop this guy, and fast. Sure as *hell* we've gotta stop him before he does it again."

"No argument there."

"Besides riding herd on the team, what's your next move?"

Harry reached into his pocket and handed Brunkel a folded sheet of paper. "Here's a copy of the updated case summary. We now have seven homicides, not counting this one. I've asterisked the names of those with a relative hiding out at the Bramwell shelter."

The sergeant looked at the chart Tara had provided. He tapped a finger on the paper.

"What do you make of the Frangini killing? Frankly, it bothers me."

"Yeah," Harry said, "it bothers me, too. Doesn't fit the pattern. Compared to the other killings, it's just too violent. Our serial perp doesn't kill in a rage. Everything is too neat at the crime scenes, at least the ones we know about. His use of poison suggests he'd rather kill by remote control than make physical contact with his victims."

"Are you thinking we've got *two* killers at work?"

"Could be. The MOs are completely different. Our serial killer is neat, organized, and goes to great pains to leave nothing behind. The Frangini killer, on the other hand, kills in a rage, is disorganized, and leaves the crime scene with bloody footprints and fingerprints, while also leaving the murder weapon behind."

Brunkel tossed the pencil he'd been waggling onto the desk. "I agree. You think we should take his name off the list and try to make somebody else for it?"

"Not yet. The kill *did* happen on one of the Mondays, so until we know something different, I'd just as soon leave things as they are. If we hold back our suspicions about a second killer for now, maybe we can use that when we get a suspect."

"Good point. Keep reminding the team that the first one breathes the words 'serial killer' will feel the wrath of Brunkel. Now go find this guy."

Harry arrived at a chaotic crime scene in a huff. The covered body still lay in the street where it had been mangled by the SUV. Yellow "Crime Scene" tape demarcated an area so large it choked traffic to a trickle. The entire right lane of traffic had been blocked, as had the sidewalk, reaching one hundred feet up the block. Alerted that this might be a serial killing, the detectives were taking no chances on having evidence destroyed.

A traffic officer waved his arms in the middle of the intersection trying to keep the traffic moving, but the impediments posed by the yellow tape, police cars, media trucks, and pedestrians proved too much — the result was chaos for the police, circus time for the gawkers, and hell for the motorists.

The pedestrians clogging the street and sidewalk provided one advantage, however — the detectives caught some witnesses among them before they got away.

"Where were you when the SUV ran over the man?" Detective Drummel asked one of them.

Pointing, the young woman said, "I was standing right on the corner waiting for the light to turn so I could cross. This guy next to me seemed to stumble, and then he just fell into the street — right in front of a big blue SUV. Driver ran over him and — just kept on going."

"Did you notice him before you got to the corner?"

"Uh . . . no."

"So you don't know what direction he came from?"

"Sorry. I just didn't notice him. He was holding his chest when he fell, if that means anything."

"One more question. Was the driver of the SUV male or female?"

"I dunno. I was watching the poor guy get run over."

Other witnesses recounted similar stories. Only one young woman felt pretty sure she had noticed him a few yards before reaching the corner.

"He seemed to be stumbling a little, or staggering. I thought he was drunk." She pointed. "We were coming from that direction."

"Thanks. That's helpful." Detectives gathered names and addresses, and took spectators' photos.

When he reached a breathing space, Drummel waved Harry over and briefed him on the situation. "Looks like a hit-and-run. The SUV driver never had a chance to slow down — the vic fell right in front of her — witness said she thought it was a female driver talking on her cell phone. Whoever it was sure as hell is gonna get nailed — and nailed hard — for leaving the scene."

"That all we know?"

"Well, one witness said he thought the vic's face looked kinda' blue when he fell, but that could'a been a shadow or something."

"What did the ME say was the cause of death?"

"Seems pretty obvious it was the SUV, but the ME doesn't wanna commit himself until after the autopsy — knowing we're treating it as a homicide."

"Any physical evidence?"

"Not a shred. Wait, I take that back. The driver's license in his wallet said his name is Runyon Pilanski — home address about a mile from here. There was thirty-seven dollars and change. Nothing else in the pockets except a small beat-up pocket knife and a comb. The guy was hardly what we would call a middle-class citizen."

"Thanks, Charlie. Stay with it. This is the right day and date. If it turns out to be homicide . . . well, you know what we're up against. Just stay with it."

"By the way, the ME said he's pretty backed up and it may be a couple of days before he gets to the autopsy. But hell, I guess dead guys can wait a couple of days."

"Yeah, but *we* can't!"

CHAPTER TWENTY-ONE

"Narena, I've *got* to talk to you. As soon as possible." Tara's crushing grip on her phone matched the urgency in her voice. "Something's happened and I must talk to someone."

"I've been wondering how long you were going to keep it bottled up. How about coming over to the hospital for lunch? We can talk outside under the misters. Then we can go up and watch Jason perform for the kids — it's Tuesday, you know."

"All right. Can we talk in private?"

"Sure. If the tables are full we can grab a bench or sit on the lawn."

"Okay. I'll show up around eleven."

At a table in the courtyard, they arranged their meager lunch of fruit salad and cola. The mister above their heads cooled the 109 degree air enough to allow them to think about something other than the heat.

"So tell me all about it," Narena urged.

"To begin with, I was just called in for a meeting with the Director. You remember Dr. Marla Benarez?"

"Never met the woman."

"Well, she's a strong director, but fair. She's really militant about protecting the residents — she was a victim of domestic violence herself. She also goes out of her way to protect her staff. That's why the meeting was so hard for her."

"Okay, so she's superwoman."

"She told me the shelter was having serious financial difficulties — donations are down substantially — and that she might have to give up the nursing slot. Narena, I may soon be out of a *job*!"

"I thought you told me the shelter was well-endowed."

"It is. But most operating expenses are supported by donations."

"Uh-huh. How long do you have?"

"Don't know." Tara mulled her situation while drawing lines on a paper napkin with her fingernail. "She said it wouldn't be before the end of the month, but that's only a couple weeks off."

"Sorry to hear it. How do you feel about it?" Despite her no-nonsense demeanor, Narena was a good listener.

"I really haven't had time to think much about that. It's something of a shock because I wasn't expecting it. I should have, I suppose — after all, other shelters don't have the luxury of a full-time nurse. But it'll mean I'll have to drop the other thing and start looking for a job. Narena, this is a disaster."

"What other thing?"

"Before I tell you, I have to say that this is the most confidential thing I've ever told you. It may sound melodramatic, but lives really are at stake. I know you'll keep the secret, but it's so sensitive I just had to warn you."

Narena leaned forward. "Now you've really got my attention. And my word. So tell me, already."

"There's a serial killer loose in the Valley, and I'm helping the police to find him."

"You're what? Wow!"

"Yes, 'wow!'"

"How come you're helping the police?"

"I was the one who discovered the killer exists." Tara launched into a truncated recital of her discovery through their latest finding and her coming up blank. "If I could only find the bodies that belong in those three empty dates — but I've searched the records and come up blank."

"There are other shelters, you know."

"Yes, and I've asked them to check their records for those dates. *They've* come up blank, too. It's driving me crazy. I just *know* the killer murdered somebody on those dates."

"Wait a minute," Narena said, suddenly alert. "You said the killer only picks on guys who've beaten or raped women or children. Well, not all victims end up in a shelter, you know. Some of them end up in a hospital — "

"Of course!" Tara shouted as she banged a fist on the table. "How could I be so blind? Of course, they do! My God, it's been right in front of me all along. I've been so focused on the shelters, I'd forgotten that abuse victims also end up in hospitals — "

"And in morgues . . . and in foster homes. And I think most of the child abuse cases are taken directly to one of the trauma centers downtown."

"Right." Suddenly Tara understood what she needed to do next. "Narena, I've got to start checking hospital records and — "

"Hold on," Narena interrupted. "You think hospitals are just gonna let you paw through their confidential patient records?"

Tara's shoulders sagged. "You're right, of course." She stared into the distance as her mind searched for a way around the problem. "Uh, maybe you could check the records for the three empty dates?"

"*Me*? I don't see how — "

"Please, Narena. You've got to help me." The pleading in Tara's voice was as plaintive as her grip on Narena's wrist was strong."

"Mmm . . . well . . . maybe I could find a way to sneak a peek. But what would I look for? We don't get murder victims — the police morgue does."

"Darn!"

"What we get is the victims of the murdered abusers."

"That's it!" Tara said. "That's it! That must be how the killer finds his victims. He has to get his information somehow. He could just as easily find abuse victims in hospitals as in shelters, couldn't he? Narena, you've got to help me check the records." In her growing excitement, Tara chewed the end off her cola straw.

"Whoa, there, my impetuous one. Suppose I do look at the records — which I can't promise — but if I do, what do I look for?"

"Look to see whether there were . . ." Tara's voice trailed off, having spotted the flaw in her reasoning. "I see what you mean. Let's say the killer finds a battered woman — or child — patient registered here on one of the three dates. He couldn't kill the batterer on the same date . . . it would take time to prepare, wouldn't it?"

"Of course. So I'd have to look for dates *prior* to the date he killed someone. But I'd have to know who he killed before I can check whether his victim was a patient. I'd need a name to check against."

The two women sat deep in thought. At long last, Narena spoke. "I think you have to give this some more thought. Don't forget, he could learn about abuse victims in other ways as well."

"What other ways?"

"Well, suppose he reads the newspaper and runs across an article about some woman who was beat up by her husband. He can check it out to see if the guy is a candidate for killing. There are probably other ways, too, that he can find his victims. In bars, for instance. Then, maybe, he has a way of getting information from Child Protective Services."

Dejected, Tara said, "I guess you're right. Damn! I was so sure I had it all worked out."

Narena reached a hand out to squeeze Tara's arm. "You're on to something big here, though. What you've told me so far is one helluva story."

Tara nodded. "You can see how the loss of my job will interfere with my finding the killer — "

"Hey, wait a minute," Narena interrupted. "What about the police? Isn't that what they're supposed to be doing?"

"Yes, of course. But if it weren't for me, the police wouldn't even know there *is* a serial killer on the loose."

"Okay, girl. So a big point for you." Her finger drew a "1" in the air. "But I still don't see why you have to stick your neck out — and probably put yourself in danger — to catch the guy."

"Not to catch the guy, just to find out who he is. I'll let the police do the catching."

Narena tilted her head. "How generous of you." She stared at Tara for a long moment. "Come on, tell me the real reason you want to play amateur sleuth."

Tara lifted her eyebrows in mock wonderment. "You always were a mind reader." She looked at the back of her hands, then turned them over to study her palms. "All right. Here it is. For one thing, if I can find out who the killer is, I might be able to keep my job."

"How do you figure that?"

"Well, if I can get a little credit for discovering the name of the killer, it might give me some positive publicity, and the board might lean over backward to keep me on."

"Uh-huh."

"You've got to admit, I'm in the perfect position to do it. I'm on the inside, so to speak, and have access to information the police might find difficult to get, and I can move freely around the shelter."

Narena looked at Tara for a long moment. "That's not the real reason, is it?"

"My God, you're perceptive!" She took a long sip of her cola, reluctant to divulge her deepest secret. "Okay, there's more. This is something else I've never told anyone. Look, Narena, I really enjoyed working at the hospital, until the arrogance of the medical staff toward the nurses got to me. Now I've got a job I love at the shelter. I get a lot of respect — "

"But?"

"But I'm making a lot less than I did at the hospital, and I'd really like to enjoy at least a few of the luxuries of life. I hate to say this, but though I feel I'm providing a useful service, I'm in a dead-end job and . . . and I've kinda lost my enthusiasm for working only with victims. For a change, I'd like to be able to do something about preventing people from becoming victims. I think there'd be a lot of satisfaction in keeping some creep from destroying a child." Tara paused, then shrugged her shoulders as she decided to confess her secret. "Okay, here it is — for a long time now I've dreamed of a life in law enforcement."

"You? A cop?" Narena shook her head in surprise. "I'd never have guessed."

"Don't you see? I'd be working among people dedicated to keeping bad things from happening, instead of among people who spend their lives trying to put broken lives back together."

Narena tilted her head. "Uh-huh . . .?"

Tara looked down at her laced fingers. "Uh, okay. My dad was a cop. Sometimes he'd tell us about some of the things he did. I really admired him, especially when he told us about crimes he kept from happening. I was impressed, even though it might only be a shoplifting he prevented. But the thing I admired most was that he got along with my friends — bonded with them as though we were just one big happy gang of kids. Then — "

"Then?"

"He was killed during a burglary. Narena, I still miss him a lot — he promised to help me get into Police Academy."

"So you see yourself out on the street — in blue?"

"No, not a street cop, of course. I know it sounds crazy, but I think I could really make a contribution; maybe the rape squad . . . or something in forensics . . . or juvenile missing persons. I've got a good background for it, I think."

"And you believe your finding this killer will give you a leg up on a cop career?"

"That's about it."

"Tara, I admire you a whole lot . . . but I can't help feel you're walking a dangerous path. Think about it. You don't know anything about the law enforcement world — except what you learned from your dad, and if there *is* a killer in the Valley, he gets one whiff of what you're up to . . . well . . ."

"I promise to stay way in the background."

"Yeah, sure, as if you could." Narena looked at her watch. "Oh, my God, we've got to hurry to catch Jason at work."

Tara and Narena met Jason in the lobby just as he entered, and exchanged greetings. "Hi, Miss Tara, Narena. Good to see you again."

"Lemme out! Lemme out!" shouted the muffled voice of Gweedo the lion.

Jason whacked the suitcase to quiet the lion puppet, as the two women chuckled. "Sorry about that," Jason said. "When he sniffs beautiful women, he gets a little hard to handle. Uh, no screaming kids today?"

There being none in need of soothing, they headed directly for the elevator.

"What have we got on today's agenda?" Jason asked Narena.

"The battered child from last week who was too medicated to talk to is a lot better today. I think a little dose of Gweedo might be just what she needs."

"Okay, I'll see what we can do."

When they approached the four-bed room, Jason had Gweedo poke his head around the door and roar. There was an answering roar from the kids in the beds, accompanied by giggles.

After some jolly bantering, during which Gweedo greeted each by name, Jason said, "Today I'm going to tell you the story of Grumpy Stilted-skin."

"NOOOO," roared the kids. "Rumplestiltskin!"

Jason then told the story, mangling the fairy tale at every twist and turn, with Gweedo and the kids shouting out corrections as loudly as they could. When the story ended, Jason and Gweedo stopped again, as they did every visit, at each of the beds for a private conversation and a hug. He'd saved the little battered girl for last.

"Hi," said Gweedo, gently. "My name's Gweedo. You have very pretty eyes."

The girl said nothing.

Jason wanted Gweedo to say something nice about the little girl's hair, but it was totally concealed by bandages. "That's a very nice doll. Is she your friend?"

A small nod.

"Can you tell me her name? I'd like to meet her."

In a weak voice, "Suzie."

"Hi, Suzie. My name's Gweedo. Nice to meet you. What's your friend's name?"

"Anna," said the little girl, pretending to speak through her doll.

"Oooh, that's a pretty name. My sister's name was Anna. You seem to be wearing a lot of bandages. Did you fall out of an airplane?"

Small smile. "No, silly. My mommy hits me when I'm bad."

"I can't believe a pretty girl like you could ever be bad. What bad thing did you do, rob a bank?"

Another small smile. "No, silly. I didn't drink all my milk, and I'm not supposed to waste anything." Though he tried hard to prevent it, Jason's eyes brimmed and a single tear slid down his cheek.

Jason worked down his mental checklist of points to cover in gaining the confidence of the child, first making sure the child understood that Gweedo wasn't real. Gweedo then leaned closer and the two of them spoke softly for several minutes. The tiny microphone hidden in Gweedo's furry mane transmitted the conversation to Jason's earpiece. Finally, Anna smiled and put her arms around Gweedo, squeezing the lion in a bear hug.

Once Jason completed his visits to the other rooms, he nodded at Narena, signaling that he wanted to talk with her in private.

Narena turned to Tara. "Tara, Jason and I need to talk for a few minutes."

"Of course." She reached out to shake Jason's hand. "Thank you for letting me watch a master at work. You are truly wonderful with those kids. And I'm still in awe at how quickly you managed to help that woman who slipped at the restaurant the other night."

CHAPTER TWENTY-TWO

Driving toward home, Tara gnawed on her conversation with Narena.

Of course the killer might find victims at hospitals. But how? It was one thing to check the center's records for files where husbands or boyfriends were stamped "deceased." That provided a link between the name of a domestic violence victim and the name and date of the death of the killer's potential victim.

But did hospital records have a similar policy? Did *they* mark husbands and boyfriends "deceased" on their records when they learned of their demise? Unlikely, but she'd have to find out. If they didn't, how could she tie the names of the battered women, or kids, to their killer's victims?

She couldn't. What to do? Staring at the road without seeing it, she asked herself what she did during her skulking missions at the shelter. *Well, look for records that tied a deceased abuser to an abused relative. But that won't work with hospital records. I'd first have to find a body, confirm it was that of an abuser, then look at hospital records to discover if an abused victim had been a patient two to three weeks prior to the date the abuser died.* She guessed it would probably take that long for the killer to set up a kill.

Tara smiled, pleased with her reasoning. So far, so good. Next step: Where to find a list of dead abusers? She considered several possibilities, then slapped her forehead as the answer flashed onto her mental screen.

Harry the Shoe! He's got a whole list of unsolved cases. That would give her names and their dates of death. She could start there. Accidental deaths and suicides wouldn't be on the list, of course, but those cases could be ferreted out and re-opened later, if needed.

Once she had the list, Narena could begin to search, and Tara could return to the Internet to hunt for domestic violence stories dating up to three weeks before the kill dates.

There's a fly in the ointment, Tara thought. She'd have to ask Harry for the list, and he'd want to know why she was asking. Hmm. That's it. She'd just tell him she wanted to check the list so she could decide whether an idea she'd come up with was any good. Pretty lame, but it was true, and it might fly.

She dialed Harry's number where he sat alone, as usual, in the "commons room."

"Hello, Harry."

"Hi. What's up?"

"Two things. First, can you fax me a list of the names on your unsolved list, along with the dates of the deaths? Please?"

"I smell the stench of an amateur sleuth meddling in police business."

"You wound me."

"Cut the soft soap. What do you want it for?"

"I believe that information is public. If it is, I need the list to test out an idea I have. I want to see if it's any good."

"Excuse me while I roll up my pants. It's getting a little deep in here. What are you up to, Tara? And do you realize the list of unsolveds is several hundred names long?"

"Ouch." That revelation made Tara wince. And think. "Uh, I don't need the entire list, Harry. Just the names and dates of death of abusers." Tara warmed to the subject. "Seems to me your unsolved cases have all been investigated, and abuser information would be in the files. Right?"

"Sometimes. That kind of thing doesn't always come up, especially if the vic was never arrested for abuse."

"Even so, it would help if you could get me the names of the ones that *are* shown as abusers in the files."

"Uh-huh, and why do you want such a list?"

Tara didn't want to lie to Harry. She was working hard to gain his trust. On the other hand . . . "Harry, I don't want to have to lie to you, so let me just say I have an idea that may or may not have merit, and I'd like to check it out before telling you and making a fool of myself."

"Okay." Harry adopted a stern voice. "But I've told you before, this is a dangerous game. Even more dangerous because of the kind of person we're dealing with, which I'd rather not talk about over the phone." After a pause, "All right, I'll get a clerk to sort the list for dead male abusers — I assume you're only interested in males — and fax it to you. But you be damned careful what you do with it. I know you, and on top of that I'm becoming very fond of you. If you get yourself killed, I'll never speak to you again!"

"Thanks, Harry." That was said with as much warmth as she could stuff into a telephone. "Now for the second item on the agenda."

"Uh-oh."

"Harry, I really want you to come to dinner with me Saturday evening..."

"But I already told you we don't socialize with our CIs."

"That's a load of crap, and you know it. Besides, we aren't exactly *strangers*, in case you've forgotten."

"Oh, that's right, isn't it?" Harry lied, chuckling to cover his embarrassment. "But that incident seems so l-o-n-g ago I'd almost forgotten. Uhh . . . I can't be sure, but my memory might improve with a refresher course."

"You send me that list and I'll give you more refresher than you can handle. Now say 'yes,' and be quick about it."

"Okay, where are you dragging me off to?"

"Bellissimo's. It's a special Italian restaurant."

"I've heard of it. But I'm still uneasy about this."

"I expect to have new information for you by then. Something is afoot, and I see no reason you can't enjoy yourself while getting briefed by your *very* confidential informant."

"All right. You've convinced me."

"Good. I'll pick you up Saturday at six p.m. Jacket, no tie."

"Wait a minute. *You're* picking *me* up?"

"Just be ready. You're gonna have the time of your life."

"Narena, I'm ready to fax you the list."

"How many names in all?"

"Only seven within the date ranges we talked about. You know what to do?"

"Yes, compare the files for the names on your list, with relatives who were patients somewhere between two and four weeks before the guy got killed. Right?"

"Right."

"This may take awhile. I don't have all that much time, and I'm going to have to be kind of cagey about it."

"I understand. Please do the best you can. My entire future may rest in your hands."

The humming man re-read the note he'd scribbled. Scrawled in pencil, it named names — Estrella Gonzalez, seven-year-old daughter of Conchita, father named José, home address, and his place of employment. It also described the extent of Conchita's and Estrella's injuries, along with the date of hospital admission. The man shook his head despondently. Will there never be an end to the violence? His eyes misted at the thought.

Committing the information to memory, he burned the wrinkled paper and began preparations for his next act of kindness. First, he'd locate José and verify that he met his criteria for someone who should "go away." Then he would follow José long enough to permit selecting just the right method. Only when he felt adequately prepared would he make his move. It wasn't exactly how he'd intended to spend his life, but it was what he *had* to do. He could still hear his mother screaming before she died; maybe . . . if he did just one more . . . the screams would go away.

The following morning, Sergeant Brunkel waved Detective Harry Shuman into his office. "Thanks for popping in, Harry. Any progress?"

"The task force has gone over the cases and summarized the physical and forensic evidence. They're on the streets now, interviewing victims' families and so on."

"Run it down for me."

Harry opened his notebook. "Okay, I'll take 'em in chronological order. Broman Tarper was shot — two .22s at close range in the back of the head — execution style. We've got bullet fragments, and they match those taken from Leroy Luntz. But no gun, and no useful forensics, other than the fragments and the powder burns."

"Keep going."

"Frankie Frangini was beaten to death with a spiked two-by-four. Lots of blood on the scene. We've got bloody footprints around the body, and bloody fingerprints on the weapon — pretty well smudged — a bloody two-by-four with nails sticking out one end. This one still bothers me, Sarge. It's the only case involving a rage attack on the vic, and the only case where the perp was careless enough to leave prints. Something else. If he's the serial perp he's got to suspect we're looking for him — full bore. But that doesn't drive him into hiding — he still goes on killing."

"You're still thinking the Frangini thing doesn't belong on the list?"

"That's what I'm thinking. But we still leave it there for now — just in case."

"If the rage killer isn't our serial perp, that opens up one of the Mondays. Go on." Brunkel leaned back in his chair, steepled his fingers, and closed his eyes.

"Borland Buggles is the guy who killed himself by pouring wood alcohol in his beer. Or so we'd assumed. We haven't been able to prove this one was murder — all we've got is that he died on the right Monday to fit the pattern."

"Didn't anybody else die on that Monday?"

"Sure, but we checked them out and they've either been cleared or pending."

"Okay. Go on." He made a stirring motion.

"Next, Willie Lamarka was poisoned. We know the poison, and approximately when it was administered. And we've got stomach contents. But we don't know where it happened, or how. We only know where he died.

"Leroy Luntz followed. He was shot in the ear by the same gun as Tarper. Again, we've got the bullet fragments, powder burns, and that's all. His door was locked from the inside, but this isn't one of those locked room mysteries."

"Why not?"

"Because if the killer got into the vic's room on some pretext, it would be no trouble to lock the door behind himself on the way out."

Brunkel nodded agreement, adding a "hurry up" gesture.

"Darryl Dunbar got pushed out a window — originally ruled accidental, now considered a possible homicide. All we've got is an unexplained bruise around his pubic hairs — we think he was shoved out the window with the end of a broom handle. We've re-interviewed his neighbors, and they didn't see any strangers going in or out.

"Ramin Zander — I'm giving you this one out of sequence — was where we got lucky, sort of. He was the suicide — though we had no note or gun — gunshot to the ear. On re-opening the case, we've re-classified it as a homicide. Originally, we thought vagrants stole the weapon, but bullet fragments match those we took from Tarper and Luntz. We've run the serial number through NCIC, but no hit. We checked with the manufacturer and learned the gun was made in 1923, long before anybody ever thought of creating a National Crime Information Center. Even so, we got the name of the dealer it was sold to. When we tried contacting the dealer, it turned out he's been long gone — also deceased. As in totally dead. That's where the trail ends. No one knows how many hands that gun has been through during the last seventy odd years.

"Or how many kills are hanging on it."

"The most recent is Runny Pilanski. Died on Monday. Killed by a hit 'n run SUV driver talking on a cell phone. Looked like an accident at first, but the medical examiner says he was stabbed in the lower back by a needle laced with curare. So it's a confirmed homicide. Somebody injected him with curare. When it hit him shortly thereafter, he fell into the street and got run over."

"Isn't curare a little unusual in this day and age?"

"Yes and no. It's still used as a muscle relaxant before surgery, so it's available to anesthetists. I suppose every hospital with a surgery unit would have some on hand. But it isn't easy to get. Drugs like that are locked up pretty tight."

"Yeah, but you and I know there are ways. So where do we stand?"

"Well, the rape squad is going through the records of the other shelters, looking to interview relatives of the vics. So far, no new names have surfaced. But they're not done yet. Only the Bramwell shelter houses, or has housed, relatives of our vics. That makes us want to take a closer look at the Bramwell staff to find out how our killer is getting his information. We're checking alibis for all the shelter staff, especially the director."

"So you think someone at the shelter might be the killer?"

"Could be. To put it bluntly, Sarge, we don't have much in the way of evidence. We have enough to prove we've got a serial killer, but even that's circumstantial. We don't yet have anything that points us in the killer's direction."

"What about your nurse CI?"

"You've known all along, haven't you?"

Brunkel raised his eyebrows in an attempt to look innocent. "As you've said, that's why I get the big bucks."

"To tell you the truth, I think she's a little closer to finding a suspect than we are, but I don't have a solid reason for saying that. Just a hunch. I keep warning her not to put herself in harm's way, but there's nothing we can do short of locking her up."

"So?"

"So the task force is meeting in an hour to sketch out a profile. We think we know quite a bit about the guy, and we're gonna try to come up with a reasonably good description. That might point us in a direction to run. If not, I'll try to convince you to get us a profiler. Or somebody with a crystal ball."

"Good idea, Harry. Keep me informed."

"All right, all right, settle down, gang. We've a lot of ground to cover." Harry waved his arms to subdue the hubbub. It didn't work. There was, after all, case-related information to exchange, as well as departmental gossip to spread, all interspersed with jovial banter. Harry stood immobile at the lectern until the room quieted.

"Okay. I just briefed Sergeant Brunkel on the evidence we have for each of the kills. So he's up to date on that. And I told him we'd be profiling the perp on the basis of that evidence. He's anxious to know what we come up with."

"So are *we*," a voice offered from the back of the conference room.

"So let's do it." Harry rolled a fresh whiteboard into view, and handed the marker to Joan Skirms. "Would you please do the honors, Joan? My writing is just about unreadable."

"Just like a man," Skirms chided. "Always ask a woman to do the scut work."

"Boos" erupted from all corners, followed by a blizzard of crumpled paper aimed in Skirms' direction.

"Come on, guys," Harry pleaded, "we have to get serious. There aren't many days before the next kill is due. If the press gets wind of a serial killer before then, we'll all be in deep shit." Gradually the horseplay ended, and the profiling began.

"First, you've all reviewed the case files of the victims, so let's just call out what we think that tells us about the perp. Later, we'll organize it into something more coherent. Ready?" Hands immediately waved in the air.

The spirited session continued until all offerings were posted. When there were no more entries, the team just stared at the board, trying to make sense of what they'd produced.

"Holy shit!" Detective Charlie Drummel said. "Look at that! What we've got is a serial killer with a conscience who's *not* sexually motivated — "

"Yeah," piped another detective, "and one who's intelligent enough to be very neat and very, *very* careful."

As the discussion continued, two more items were offered before the group ran dry. Harry thanked them, and said, "Charlie, Joan and I will organize what we've got, and send you a copy. Feel free to write all over it with ideas, and get it back to me as soon as you can. I'll say it again: We know a lot about this guy, but we don't have a whiff of a suspect. And time is getting short."

"Wait a minute, Harry. We forgot something." This from one of the detective teams.

"What?"

"This guy has access to exotic poisons. That oughta' point us in the direction of somebody well-connected enough to get at those poisons without arousing suspicions. I suggest we start looking at hospital personnel . . . and maybe even pharmacists . . . as likely suspects."

"Sounds good," Harry replied. "Run with it."

Joan Skirms' hand flew up.

"Go," Harry prodded.

Skirms spoke slowly, carefully forming her sentences as her thoughts coalesced. "Harry, would it be possible to get medical records of the abusers' victims?"

"What are you thinking?"

"To learn more about the perp's killing pattern, it might help to know about the type and extent of the damage being done by his vics."

"Go on."

"Well, say we learn that the perp only kills guys who have done a particular kind of damage to wife or kids . . . or girlfriends. That might give us some input for the psychological profile."

"Good thinking. Check with the shelters and hospitals and see if you can't get them to part with at least a little medical dope."

Harry the Shoe, Skirms, and Drummel spent the next hour organizing the input from the task force. "Jeezus," Drummel said, "I had no idea we knew so much about this guy."

Harry wasn't as optimistic. "If we know so damn much, how come we don't have a suspect? Let's get copies of this profile to all the team members . And remember to mark it CONFIDENTIAL." Harry took one last look at what they'd drafted.

Profile

Kills only on Mondays; therefore, he's probably not employed on Mondays. Kills approximately once each month.

He's selective: all known victims are violent male abusers: never kills women or children.

He's not a sexual killer; there's no rape, sexual mutilation (one exception), dismemberment, or cannibalism.

He never robs his victims. He has resources; he's not broke.

He employs different MO's to kill:

3 poisonings (belladonna, curare, wood alcohol)

3 gunshots to head with .22

1 shoved out the window

1 beaten to death

He's known well enough by gunshot victims to get close.

He's a non-violent killer (exception: the beating kill)
He doesn't kill in a rage (exception: Frangini)
He's careful, leaves little evidence behind, suggesting he's a man of some intelligence.
He knows something about firearms.

Implications: He's older, rather than younger (probably 40-45), intelligent, fairly well educated, has a wide variety of skills and contacts, as well as access and knowledge of drugs. Plus, he has a conscience. He's not looking to avenge a wrong done to himself; instead, he's looking to punish those who hurt women and children.

Harry stared at the profile, willing it to tell him the name of the killer. Why did the killer leave the gun at the scene of the staged suicide? He must know he'd left a clue behind. He must know we'd match the bullet fragments from all three gunshot killings. Did he think his suicide staging was good enough that we wouldn't think to tie it to the other murders? *Does he want to be caught?*

What was it Tara said? He only kills the worst of the abusers. That matches our conclusion that he's a selective killer — that he doesn't target just any abuser. So how does he find his victim candidates? Could he be getting his information on the street? From loose conversation in bars? Does he have access to a shelter's files? Is he getting his information from someone else? An accomplice, perhaps? Someone who feels as the killer does about abusers? If he does, then somebody out there knows the identity of the killer. Harry tapped a pencil on the profile.

Too many options . . . not enough time.

CHAPTER TWENTY-THREE

"You're not gonna believe this, Captain," Detective Drummel said, opening a case file as he sat in Captain Portono's office, along with Sergeant Brunkel.

"What am I not gonna believe?" Portono asked.

"The Tibbetts thing has taken a nasty turn."

"Close the door."

Drummel did, and continued. "Remember we heard a rumor he'd knocked up an underage girl and then beat her when she refused to get an abortion?"

"Yeah."

"Skirms got nosy and started interviewing abortion doctors. Hit pay dirt on the second try. The girl had had an abortion. When she told the doc why she was asking, he knew exactly which case she was talking about. Name of the girl is," he glanced at the file, "Tammy. Tammy Tibbetts —

"*Tibbetts*? Son-of-a-bitch!"

"Twelve years old."

"Son-of-a-double-bitch!"

"The doc did the abortion — first trimester — it wasn't illegal. When he was done, Tammy handed him a check for five thousand dollars. The check was drawn on Tibbetts' law firm, and was noted 'For consultation.'"

"That does it," Portono said. "He's now crossed way over the line, and is in deep shit. Once this comes out, he'll probably be bounced from the firm. And it *will* come out." Pause. "Statutory rape and incest — Christ!"

"He oughta be disbarred. The doc said she showed up for the abortion with a black eye."

"Take somebody big over to talk to him — give the bastard a scare and see what he has to say for himself. Better yet, do that then bring him here to be interviewed."

"I'll take Larry Cummings," Drummell offered. "He's big enough to scare anybody. You don't want us to talk to the girl first?"

"No. Leave her alone for now — she's been through enough already. And I hope I don't need to tell you to tread carefully. That law firm wields a lot of clout."

Drummel perched on the edge of Larry Cummings' desk. "How'd you like a chance to do your bad guy act?"

"What'cha got cookin'?" Cummings was not only big, but fierce. Football shoulders, shaved head, bushy mustache, gold earring. Nobody messed with Larry Cummings . . . especially when he gave them "The Look." How were they to know he was a pussycat?

"We need to talk to a fancy lawyer. Just found out he knocked up his twelve-year-old daughter and beat on her to convince her she wanted an abortion. Wanna come?"

Cummings heaved his six-foot-three-inch frame out of his chair. "Wouldn't miss it."

Showing their badges to the receptionist at the law firm of Chilton, Gonzalez, and Tibbetts, Drummel and Cummings padded their way down the hall to Tibbetts' office. The icy look their badges evoked from Mary, Tibbetts' stone-faced secretary, mimicked the response they'd received on their first visit.

"We need to talk to Mr. Tibbetts, and don't waste our time."

Into the intercom, the secretary repeated the get-out-here-*now* code phrase, "Mr. Tibbetts, the director needs your signature."

Less than a minute later, Tibbetts opened the door to his office. When he saw Detective Drummel, his face darkened with a scowl. "*Now* what do you want?"

"Do you want to talk here, or someplace more private?" Drummel asked.

Tibbetts reluctantly led them into his office and closed the door.

"We need to ask you a few questions about your daughter."

Tibbetts froze, his face draining to white. His eyes darted from one detective to the other, his knuckles losing color as his hands balled into tight fists. "What about my daughter?" he asked, almost in a whisper. "Have you been talking to my daughter?"

"Not yet," Drummel said, "and we're hoping we won't have to. But we need to talk to you about the circumstances of her abortion, and we'd rather do that downtown."

"Why can't we talk here?"

"It will be better if we talk downtown. It shouldn't take long."

"Do we have to do it *now*?" Tibbetts' face caved in until he wore the expression of a beaten man. His shoulders sagged and he looked as though his head was suddenly too heavy to hold up as he stared sullenly at the floor.

"I'm afraid so. We need to do it now."

Tibbetts sighed and the air seeped from his lungs. Slowly his fingers caressed the highly-polished desk. "All right. I'll just get my jacket." Stepping into what looked like a small half-bath with toilet and sink, he closed the door.

As soon as Drummel heard the lock click, he realized he'd made a terrible mistake. "Gun!" he shouted to Cummings. "Break it down!"

Cummings instantly threw himself at the door. When his shoulder was just inches from the door, an explosion rocked the air. Cummings bashed through just as Tibbetts fell to the floor. Blood and brain tissue erupted from his head, splattering wall, mirror, toilet, and floor.

The secretary screamed in the outer office.

"Sweet Jeezus," Cummings said. "He killed himself. He just walked in here and shot himself."

"Don't touch anything," Drummel said, unnecessarily. He was already on his cell phone calling for a crime scene unit. Reaching into his pocket for Tibbetts' business card, he gave the address to the dispatcher. "Tell Sergeant Brunkel and Lieutenant Portono that Tibbetts just shot himself."

The door to the office opened and several people crowded in the opening. "Stay back," ordered Drummel, waving his badge in their faces. "There's been an accident and no one will be allowed in until an investigation has been completed. So just calm down, everyone. The police are on the way."

That announcement started tongues wagging anew, and a host of questions were thrown in their direction.

"What was the explosion?"

"What happened?"

"Did Tibbetts kill himself?"

"Did you shoot him?"

"No, we didn't shoot him, but I can't tell you anything until the investigators have completed their work," Drummel responded. "Until then, please keep everyone away from this area."

"He's due at a directors' meeting in ten minutes. Will he be able to make it on time?" someone asked.

"No, he won't be there at all. You'll have to carry on without him. Look, I promise all your questions will be answered as soon as the investigators do their thing. Now please go back to work."

Go back to work! he wanted to shout, but knew that would be like asking a bunch of horny teenagers to hide their eyes while strolling through a glass-walled whorehouse.

"What did you actually say to him?" Brunkel asked. After the crime scene unit arrived and Drummel had briefed them on the events leading to the suicide, he and Cummings had returned to headquarters and headed directly to Brunkel's office.

"I told him we needed to ask him some questions about the circumstances surrounding his daughter's abortion. He turned all kinds of white and shriveled like a sun-dried prune. When I next told him we'd like to discuss it downtown, he said he'd just get his jacket and stepped into his little washroom."

"You let him out of your sight?"

"He wasn't under arrest at the time — but dammit, it was still a mistake on my part. I knew what was going to happen the instant I heard the lock click. Larry was inches from bashing in the door — he was actually in mid-air — when we heard the gunshot. Less than a second later, Larry crashed the door open and we saw Tibbetts falling to the floor. The gun was still in his hand, and blood and brains were all over the place. Larry pulled the door closed, and I called the Crime Scene squad."

"Seems odd, doesn't it?" Brunkel mused. Here's a guy you just asked to come in for a few questions and he blows his brains out. Hardly seems reason for such extreme measures."

"I dunno," Drummel said. "He was arrested for beating on his wife, he's got two active lawsuits pending, and he just got caught boffing his twelve-year-old daughter. Got her pregnant and made her get an abortion. Incest, statutory rape, fraud, mail fraud, and who knows what else."

"Okay, you made your point."

"Besides, this guy was really wound up tight. I think he might have exploded for a lot less."

Brunkel nodded. "Write it up."

The two detectives got up to leave. "Charlie, stay a minute," Brunkel said, nodding for Cummings to leave. With Charlie back in his chair, he said, "If I remember right, this whole thing started when somebody sent that flaky threatening letter to the governor."

"Yeah. It was pretty clear somebody wanted us to take a closer look at Tibbetts — somebody who wanted to get him in trouble."

"Any progress in finding the miscreant?"

"I'll check, but I don't think so. We've been pretty busy with the serial killer case."

"I realize that. But I've been thinking." Brunkel leaned back and steepled his fingers. Finger-steepling seemed to make his brain work better. "I was just wondering whether there might not be a connection."

"Between the serial killer case and Tibbetts?"

Brunkel nodded. "Try this on. As we know, the killer only kills guys who damage women and children. Right?"

"That's what it looks like."

"That means he operates by some sort of standard. He doesn't just kill at random. Well, just suppose . . . just suppose that while he's trolling for victims, he finds some who aren't bad enough to kill — by his standards — but who are bad enough to deserve *some* kind of justice. Again, by his standards. So instead of killing them, he makes trouble for them, like he did for Tibbetts."

"Jeezus, Sarge, that's one helluva theory. Want me to see if maybe there are some *other* Tibbetts-type cases in the bushes?"

Brunkel nodded. "But get somebody else to do it. You've got enough on your plate working Shoe's task force. Have 'em start by looking for hinky-looking harassment cases. But fill Harry in first. Hell, you know the drill."

CHAPTER TWENTY-FOUR

"Tara, I think I've got one!" Narena said.

"Got what?"

"A name. Get something to write with."

"Got it right here. Shoot."

"Okay. I was looking through the records and ran across the name Zander. When I checked your list, sure enough, there it was. Marcella Zander, daughter of Ramin Zander, was admitted on March 23 — about three weeks before Zander was killed. She had two broken arms and a badly disfigured face. Three days later she was sent to the trauma center."

"Good work, Narena. You deserve a medal."

"Wait. There's more. I talked to the nurse assigned to the case, and she said the little girl was brought in by neighbors. When they tried to notify the mother, they couldn't find her. She'd just disappeared. They finally found the father in a bar, drunk as a skunk. Said he had no idea where his wife was."

"You're terrific. I'm just about to leave to pick up Harry — we're having dinner at Bellissimo's tonight, and I'll tell him the good news. His people can take it from here."

"Got a couple more minutes? There's more."

"What've you got?"

"Well . . . I'm not sure about this one, but here goes. I found an abuse case where a seven-year-old boy was admitted on March 1st, about two weeks before one of your empty dates — March 13. Could that be one of the victims you're looking for?"

"What was the name?"

"The little boy's name was Elijah Baruna — mother Kalima, father Abdul. I don't know if the father is still alive or not, but maybe the police can check it out. Think so?"

"You bet. I'll tell Harry about that one, too. You're an absolute dream, Narena. This proves that the killer doesn't find his victims only at the Bramwell shelter. And that suggests the staff there are in the clear."

"I suppose. But how does the killer get his information about the residents?

119

Wouldn't he have to have someone on the inside?"

"Not necessarily. There are lots of places he could get it. Overheard conversations. Newspapers. Besides, if he's got some sort of accomplice at Bramwell, he must also have one at your hospital, too."

"Uh-huh. Maybe. Actually, too many maybes. Heck, anybody with access to information could be the killer, you know. Hey, even our own Jason — maybe he sends his puppets out to do the dirty work." Narena laughed at her own joke.

Tara put her phone down with a shaking hand, Narena's words ringing in her ears as goose bumps tightened her skin. "No," she whispered, thoughtfully, "it *couldn't* be."

Harry's front door opened as Tara stepped out of her Honda. He pulled the door shut behind him and called, "Never let it be said that Harry Shuman was ever late for a date. Especially with a beautiful woman."

"You only keep the ugly ones waiting, is that it?"

Harry delivered a light kiss to her cheek and swatted her on the behind at the same time. "That's for the sassy greeting."

"Oww. I didn't know you were into S&M."

Harry swatted her again. "Mmm! I'm not, but I might be persuaded. That's a very attractive bottom you have there, young lady, and I'm sure it could use more attention than it's been getting." He made circles on her backside with the palm of his hand.

"Get in the car, you horny toad. I've some hot news."

Driving toward Bellissimo's, Tara repeated her conversation with Narena. "I've got the names and dates written down — it's in my purse. Your guys can take it from here, right?"

"Right. That's good work, Tara. I won't ask how you got that information. I just hope you didn't put yourself at risk."

"Thanks for not asking. I didn't." She didn't mention Narena's casual joke about the killer's possible identity. "Will it help?"

"Yeah. The hospital info will tie the Zander thing more tightly to the killer — I'll get a team looking for the mother. That Baruna case is also a good lead." Harry put a hand on Tara's knee. "Don't be disappointed if we don't find a corpse to match the name, though. It's not unusual for corpses to disappear forever."

At the restaurant, Tara handed her car keys to a waiting valet. Stepping out of the car, they were immediately surrounded by the roasting Arizona air.

KILLER IN OUR MIDST

"Jeezus, it's hot," Harry said. "It must be 105 degrees, even at this time of the evening. Hope their air conditioner is working."

"You didn't have to wear a tie, you know. Loosen up a little — take it off."

"You're just trying to get me naked so you can ravish my poor defenseless body."

"Later, Harry, later." They luxuriated in a welcome wall of cool air on opening the door to the restaurant. Inside, they made their presence known and the maitre d' ushered them to their table.

Harry studied the details of the environment and drank in the ambiance. "You were right. It's a neat place. I especially like the red 'n white checkered tablecloths and the candles in the wine bottles. Nice touches."

At that moment an obese man two tables away stood and began singing the *Toreador* aria from *Carmen*. The accordion player sitting on a small riser at one end of the room immediately picked up his instrument and provided robust and skillful accompaniment.

"What the hell?" Harry said, surprised.

Tara laughed. "Oh, didn't I tell you? Some of the patrons are professional singers — or voice teachers — and this happens periodically throughout the evening."

"Actually, it's kinda' charming. Oh-oh, here comes that waiter you told me about."

"Good evening, Miss Tara." Jason, with Scrawk sitting on his shoulder, bowed low before Tara.

"Nice to see you again," Tara replied. Turning to Harry, she said, "This is my friend Harry Shuman. *Detective* Harry Shuman."

Immediately the puppet on Jason's shoulder erupted in a frenzy of activity. "Scrawk," he screeched. Turning his head toward Jason, he hollered, "He did it! He's a da guilty one."

"Did what?" Harry asked, grinning.

"Mama mia! Puts 'is finger in da minestrone. I gotta da eyes to see, and I *see*! Take 'im away! String 'im up!"

By now the patrons at several nearby tables were listening to the exchange with great amusement.

Jason feigned embarrassment. "Don't mind Scrawk, sir, he's always showing off to get attention."

Scrawk screamed, "Basta!"

Harry stared at Jason and the puppet, trying hard to figure out how it was operated. Because the puppet was so animated, it was hard to keep his eyes on Jason's lips to see if they were moving. He needn't have bothered — they weren't.

"He's a good ventriloquist, isn't he?" Tara said.

"Uh-huh." Harry turned to Jason. "And a parrot puppet with an Italian accent is a helluva clever idea. How do you operate it?"

"By remote control — a little keypad in my left hand." Jason held his left palm open where the diners could see it.

Harry raised his brows. "Did you make the mechanism yourself?"

The waiter said, "Yes. I'm a natural born tinkerer."

"You must be a pretty skilled mechanic."

Jason beamed. "Thank you, sir. Would you like to order a cocktail before dinner?"

They ordered, and Jason turned to leave, with Scrawk venting feigned irritation at every step of the way.

Tara and Harry laughed and giggled their way through dinner, watching Scrawk harass Jason over his serving skills at every opportunity.

"Hey, what'sa matter you? How many time I gotta tell you — da butter plate goes on da *left*!"

"Eh, goofball. Why you no bring more wine?"

"Hey, fat boy. You no see dey need bread? What'sa matta you?"

Along with similar barbs, these filled the evening with smiles. The music added even more spirit and delight. When they'd finished their espressos, Tara paid the bill, over Harry's objections.

"Hey, you're treating me like a kept man."

"Not a bad idea. Just shut up and enjoy it. You'll get your turn soon enough." Tara tipped generously, and they got up to leave.

Jason thanked them for coming. Shaking his head, Scrawk hollered, "Wot? You no arrest dis bum? You be sorry. You be sorry. You let him poison everybody wit his finger in da minestrone."

Harry smiled and waggled a finger at Scrawk. "You behave yourself or I'll arrest *you* for causing a disturbance." The banter continued as Jason accompanied them to the door.

While they ambled toward Tara's car, Harry said, "That was a great evening and I'm glad you talked me into it. When I don't throw something together for myself, I usually go to some cop hangout, eat crap food, and talk shop. It gets pretty boring. This was one helluva treat."

Tara smiled at the compliment all the way to his apartment.

When she drove into Harry's driveway, Harry said, "Y'know, I'm not sure how to handle this."

"Handle what?"

"Usually, *I* take the lady home, and then try to get into her pants."

"Not to worry. It's the same thing, except in reverse. Or, you can pretend you brought *me* home and do your usual thing."

Harry led her into his house and closed the door. "Would you like a drink before I unleash the animal in me?"

Tara laughed. "No, thank you. I've already had enough to weaken my defenses."

"In that case . . ." Harry took her hand and led her toward the bedroom, but stopped just short of the door. Taking her in his arms, he kissed her tenderly. "You know, you'd better be careful. I could get used to this kind of life — especially this part."

Once in the bedroom Harry tried to remove Tara's blouse.

"Oh, no, you don't. It's not your turn."

"What's that supposed to mean?"

"Never mind." Tara looked slowly around the bedroom for a suitable implement. Finding none, she asked, "Got a shaving brush?"

"Sure. What for?"

"Just get it."

He did, and handed it to Tara. "That all?"

"Not in the least. Now I want you to take off that tie, and everything else not nailed on, and then I want you to lie on the bed — face up."

"What about you? Don't *you* get to take something off?"

"In good time, sir, in good time. Just do as you're told."

Harry wasn't sure what Tara had in mind, but he complied with her command. By the time he'd removed his shorts, he was fully aroused.

Tara approached him, brandishing the shaving brush. "It's a hard decision," she said, frowning. "I can't decide whether to start at the bottom . . . hmm . . . or at the top." With a Cheshire smile, she decided to start at the top. "Just lie still."

Sitting on the edge of the bed and leaning toward Harry, she exposed the full curve of her breasts as her scoop-necked blouse folded away from her chest. She lightly brushed Harry's forehead, his chin, his chest, and continued slowly working her way downward. By the time she got to his pubic hairs, its centerpiece screamed for release.

"Hurry," he moaned.

Still Tara took her time, and went on making Harry crazy . . . at length. For an hour not one reference to the crimes entered her mind, or his.

Much later, while driving home, Tara mused about her growing fondness for Harry. *He really is sweet. Once you get behind the public image of the hard-nosed homicide detective, he's sensitive, gentle and yes . . . even talkative at times. So much for the "we don't socialize" myth.*

Picking up her cell phone she realized it was after midnight, too late to call Narena. Her mind returned to Narena's off-hand remark about Jason. *An absurd idea.* Yet she couldn't tear it out of her mind.

"Okay," she asked herself, putting it into words, "What if it were Jason? Could it be? Yes . . . he has access to hospital information. But what about shelter data? He has no contact with any shelter . . . or does he?" She pondered, driving ever more slowly. Finally she pushed harder on the accelerator. "Stop it! This is silly!"

Still the doubt persisted, nibbling at her brain like a mouse gnawing on cheese. *I have to do something to get this out of my system. It's an injustice to Jason even to suspect such a thoroughly kind human being of such heinous crimes. But what can I do?*

While turning into her driveway, the idea came to her. *I need to learn more about him — that's what!* She mentally massaged several possible approaches, then settled on a plan. *Tomorrow I'll go watch him perform at Narena's hospital. It can't hurt to ask him some questions designed to show interest in his work.* Her mind chilled. *But what if I'm wrong about Jason's innocence? Won't I be sticking my neck out?*

She brushed the threat aside, parking her car. *I have to know.*

CHAPTER TWENTY-FIVE

That same evening, Jason Smalter had removed the parrot puppet from his shoulder and carefully placed it and the control pad into its home-made, custom-fitted case. Dressing in street clothes, he punched out and headed for home. This time, however, the drive was not filled with pleasant thoughts of laughing customers complimenting him for his entertainment. Tonight he was uneasy. He recalled the hard — and surprised — look he'd received from Tara when Scrawk jokingly hollered, "He did it!" before accusing him of putting his finger in the minestrone. Her look shouted, as loudly as any words, that she suspected him of something. *Could* she suspect him? Did she *know*? Impossible! Tonight, he decided, his imagination was decidedly paranoid. He'd discuss the situation with his good friend and confidante, Scootch.

He drove to the detached garage behind the house. They didn't build garages that way much any more, but Jason found his offered special advantages. Activating the remote opener for the door, he drove in and parked. Tired from an especially busy shift, he shuffled slowly toward the house, musing about the garage he'd just exited.

It, along with the house — and the old mortuary next door — were built shortly after World War II ended. Then, the neighborhood had been at the edge of town, though located only a few blocks west of Central Avenue.

He stopped before entering the house, considering the two buildings sitting side-by-side or . . . he laughed, remembering . . . "cheek by jowl" as his Dad used to say. Moving from Sicily to Phoenix, his Uncle Salvatore had purchased the property and built the mortuary, as well as the house next door, as an investment. This was his dream come true. Though a mortician all his life, the scarcity of Sicilian real estate never allowed the luxury of living quarters apart from the cramped mortuary. Jason scowled at the irony. In Sicily, Salvatore was awash in Mafia money earned for the "special services" he provided with his crematory. Yet he never seemed to have any time to enjoy the luxuries he could well afford.

Salvatore had willed the property to Jason's father, baptized Luigi Bellisto Scintilliano. He inherited it on Salvatore's death in 1980. Finally sickened by the cold-bloodedness of Mafia violence, the jealousy, the revenge killings, the maimings, and the grieving widows, Luigi brought his son Benito to the United States and settled in New York City. Trying to distance himself from everything Mafia, he changed their name to Smalter, simply because he could find no Smalters in the phone book. He became Lawrence Smalter, and his son, Jason Smalter.

After a year, during which he'd discovered New York to be little different from Sicily insofar as organized crime was concerned, he again moved them . . . this time to Phoenix. There, he took over operation of his inherited funeral home — but with less and less enthusiasm. Just as before, the local Mafia occasionally deposited an "extra" body in his garage. Always at night, of course, and always accompanied by lots of cash.

Jason, though tired and glad to be home, still had work to do. Pulling on his glue-stained "shop shorts," he opened a bottle of beer and stepped down to his basement workshop. Basements, he thought, were another amenity seldom seen in the desert. Of course, back when this house was built by a mob-connected contractor, it contained every special feature his uncle demanded. The basement was one of them, including the secret crematory beneath the "public" one on the main floor of the mortuary next door. Unfortunately, his uncle could operate the secret basement crematory only when the one above was operating. Simultaneous operations blended the smoke from both into the same chimney. Because the legitimate upstairs crematory was used less and less frequently, delivery of "extra" bodies had to decline. Such deliveries gradually dwindled to nothing.

Jason clicked on the incandescent lights over his large workbench. The familiar sights and smells warmed him. Wood, plastic, and acrylic body parts littered the bench. Others huddled in bins marked "Legs," "Arms" and "Misc." The smell of glue comforted his nostrils, and the sight of colorful fabrics stirred his soul. He hummed in contentment.

"I was wondering when you'd finally get home," Scootch, his understanding companion, scolded. With gray hair and trench coat, the old man with the bulbous nose and raspy voice sat against the wall on an old Remington ammunition box. This perch above the workbench allowed him a commanding view of the entire room. That he was a puppet didn't bother Jason an iota — he was used to conversing with puppets as though they were alive. The first rule of ventriloquism was, after all, "If *you* don't think of them as alive, nobody else will."

"It was a very busy evening, Scootch. Very busy."

"Good tips, I hope?"

"Very good indeed. I haven't counted it yet, but it should be close to two hundred fifty dollars."

"If ya made such a good haul, how come you're schlepping around with a long face?"

"Bad news. We may have to do another one." Jason shook his head. "Bad, bad business."

"Well, don't just stand there hanging your head, tell me about it." Jason always found "discussion" with Scootch a useful way to think through problems.

"I got the information a day or two ago. I told you about it. Estrella Gonzalez, seven-year-old daughter of Conchita and José. I'm going to try to talk to Estrella tomorrow at the hospital. If it's as bad as I think, I may have to make José go away."

"Well," cackled the old man, "it won't be the first time you did a good deed."

"No, but it's not the kind of deed I'd prefer doing."

"Don't give me that bullshit, Jason, you know more people would die if you didn't send those vermin away."

"I still don't have to like it. Actually, I hate doing it . . . but I still hear the screams." Jason was silent while he thought about poor little Conchita Gonzalez. "There's something I want to talk to you about."

"You know I'm a good listener."

"Except when you're full of sass." Jason paused, organizing his thoughts. "I had two customers tonight who disturbed me. One was that Tara woman I've told you about."

"The one works at the women's shelter?"

"Yes — glad you remembered. She brought a companion tonight. A detective."

"Oh-oh."

"'Oh-oh' is right. When she introduced him, Scrawk hollered for him to lock me up."

"For what, pray tell?"

"Same old schtick — putting my finger in the minestrone. It was all done as a big joke, of course . . . but it made Tara look at me real funny."

"Funny peculiar . . . or funny 'ha-ha'?"

"She stared at me. Her eyes got big and round, and her eyebrows lifted a little. I immediately thought, 'She's on to us.' I don't know how she could know, but my gut got all squirrelly."

"You gonna put her on the list?"

"No . . . not yet, anyway. You know how I feel about doing women. It's not what I do. Especially after seeing my mother . . . I'll need to find out for sure. She's such a nice lady — really seems to enjoy my work. I'd hate to have to . . . well, I don't even want to think about it."

"Yeah, I know how you feel. But it wouldn't be the first time, would it?"

"No, unfortunately. But it was only once — I cried while I did it — and that woman did worse things to her children than . . . what do *you* think I should do?"

Scootch's lips didn't move when he "spoke," but that didn't matter. Jason was used to creating both sides of a conversation. "Remember, Jason — Don't put out a fire that doesn't exist."

Jason looked up, surprised at the comment. "You surprise me again, old friend. But I take your point. If she shows up at the hospital again, I'll try to sound her out."

"Be careful," Scootch warned. "This could be dangerous. You can't afford to be caught. Not now. There's still so much to do. Remember your upcoming presentation."

On entering the hospital the following afternoon, a chill went through Jason's body when he saw both Narena and Tara waiting for him in the lobby. He didn't expect to see Tara again so soon. Slipping easily into his persona as the jolly entertainer, he smiled broadly and looked around the lobby for a screaming child to mollify or another good deed to perform. *No one?* He shrugged and strode toward the two women. He greeted them with a wave of his porkpie hat, adding a deep bow.

"To what do I owe the pleasure of your company on this sunny afternoon?" he asked Tara.

"Narena thought we night catch Gweedo in action before heading out to a dinner and movie."

"A splendid idea. Absolutely splendid. I am always eager to fulfill the wishes of a beautiful lady." In the elevator, Jason asked Narena, "What's on the agenda today?"

"The usual, except that we're a little light on patients this weekend. We do have one little girl, Conchita Gonzalez, who came in a few days ago. Pretty banged up — rape victim. Somebody from the rape squad tried talking to her. Somebody from Social Services also tried, but she won't talk to anybody. Looks like she's still in shock. The police said they're going to match the DNA from the semen found on her to that of her father." She looked away. "And his three brothers. They're working up enough evidence to arrest them all."

"May I try?"

"As a matter of fact, they're hoping you will, even though it's against hospital policy to allow volunteers to do anything therapeutic."

"I promise not to do anything therapeutic. I'll just try making contact. Listening can work wonders."

"I was hoping you would."

Working his way from room to room toward the one where the molested girl lay in pain, Jason spread smiles and laughter in every direction. After a few hilarious minutes telling a fractured fairy tale to the two other children in the room, he and Gweedo moved to Conchita's bedside. Jason noted she was awake, but unresponsive. She hadn't moved during his deliberately short performance.

"Hi," Gweedo said gently. Turning to Jason, Gweedo said, "This is a very pretty young lady. I love her pretty hair. I'll bet her eyes sparkle when she's happy." It was important to begin by allowing the little girl to establish a comfort level with the puppet.

To Conchita, Gweedo said, "Hi. My name is Gweedo. Would you like a little doll to play with?"

When Conchita nodded slightly, Jason handed the girl a small colorfully dressed doll. She cuddled it in her arms.

Speaking to the doll, Gweedo said, "Well, you're a pretty little doll. Can you tell me your name, please?"

There was a pause while Conchita decided on a name. Speaking through the doll, she said, "Maria." Barely audible.

"That's a pretty name." Focusing on the doll, Gweedo asked, "Can you tell me the name of your new friend?"

Speaking again through her new doll friend, "Conchita."

Gradually, as Gweedo earned Conchita's trust, she began to respond. Before long, she moved to put an arm around Gweedo, and Gweedo leaned toward her to make the task easier. Then they talked. Gweedo listened, offering words of encouragement from time to time. A few minutes later, tears began streaming down Jason's cheeks as Conchita poured out her hurts to the sympathetic lion puppet.

At long last, Gweedo gave Conchita a tender peck on her cheek, told her he would return in two days, and told Jason it was time to say good-bye. As they turned to leave, Jason tried unsuccessfully to hide his tear-swollen eyes.

Jason motioned Narena into an unoccupied room along with Tara. He said, "Can Miss Tara hear this, too? I think she deserves to know." He didn't really think that, but it would give him another opportunity to observe Tara's reactions.

Narena looked from one to the other. "Any information you get from the children is held in the strictest confidence, you know that." She sighed. "But then, I've known Tara for a hundred years and she's always been the soul of discretion." She nodded for Tara to join them.

"The picture isn't a pretty one," Jason began. "The father is a hot-headed man with a short temper who shouts and beats his wife when she refuses to go to bed with the men he brings home. When she gives in, they do it right in front of Conchita, and that frightens her a great deal. She said when that happens she tries to hide her head and take her mind to far away places.

"Apparently one of the men took a fancy to Conchita and tried to buy her services from her father. There was a screaming match, the father hit the mother, and then tried to rape the little girl. She said he 'messed all over her,' but I gather he didn't manage penetration. But he hurt her pretty badly. She's scared to death another man will come and make her do what she called 'dirty things.'"

"Oh, my God," Tara said, shaking her head. "How is it possible for *anyone* . . ."

"If I were you," Jason said to Narena, "I'd try to keep all males out of her room. At least for a few days."

As they headed toward the lobby, Tara put a hand on Jason's arm and said, "Thank you for including me in that conversation. It reminded me again of just how evil people can be. When I saw the tears in your eyes, my own eyes misted, too. You must hurt a great deal when listening to those kids tell their stories."

Jason looked down at his shoes. "I never get used to hearing about the evil things done to these poor children."

"You know, you're truly an incredible asset to the community. I'd really like to know more about how you do what you do."

"You would?" Jason's head snapped up as tiny alarm bells sounded.

"I've been interested in ventriloquism ever since, as a kid, I saw an act at a variety show. The ventriloquist had a dummy dressed in a king costume. The dummy pretended to have taken a correspondence course to learn how

130

to become a king. The skit was a hoot. I've never forgotten it."

"I'd be glad to talk to you about it anytime," Jason offered, his mind racing to find a safe course of action.

"How about tomorrow?" Tara asked. She was well aware that tomorrow was Monday.

"Oh, I'm sorry. Tomorrow's Monday — Gweedo and I have been asked to perform at a political luncheon downtown. It's a fund-raiser for the governor, I think. Frankly, I'd rather spend the time with you." Jason furrowed his brows and thought for a moment. "How about a week from Thursday? I'm going to be pretty busy until then."

"All right. A week from Thursday it is."

"If you'd like to come to my workshop I can show you how I make the figures — the puppets. We call them anything but dummies, you know. I'm sure my other little friends would be delighted to meet you." Jason smiled. "But you'll have to promise not to call them 'dummies.' If you do, they'll find ways to get even."

With barely a perceptible pause, Tara agreed. They exchanged phone numbers, and Jason offered his address.

After exchanging parting comments, Jason picked up his suitcase and left.

"That," Narena said, "was a strange thing to do. Are you really planning to visit his workshop?"

"Yes. Why not?" What she didn't say was, *Narena, I've got to know!*

CHAPTER TWENTY-SIX

The following day, Jason began his preparations by staking out the home of José Gonzalez. He had to know how many people lived in the house, and when people entered and left. Having learned that Gonzalez resided in a working-class neighborhood, Jason chose to drive his old Ford pickup for his surveillance. Parking down the street from the house with the junk-strewn yard, Jason placed his notebook on the seat beside him and settled in, to observe. It was boring work — he wondered how detectives stood the dreary hours sitting in a car just watching. To fill the time, he imagined a series of scenarios he might use to relieve Conchita and her daughter Estrella of their awesome burden. As he pondered, he nibbled at the cold hamburger he'd bought on the way to his stakeout location. Absently, he wished he'd remembered to add mustard.

By Wednesday, he was convinced José now lived alone — both wife and daughter were in the hospital, and there were no casual visitors. Now, when Gonzalez left his house, Jason followed. But not too closely. He followed him to work in the morning at a small foundry in South Phoenix, and to his favorite bar when he left work in the afternoon.

He followed into the bar, trying to sit close enough to overhear conversation. This was easy — Gonzalez had a loud voice.

Jason followed him when he picked up a woman and took her home for a romp, then followed him when he returned her to the bar from which she had been harvested.

By Thursday, Jason knew enough about José's predictable ways to formulate his plan. He returned to his basement workshop.

"I think I'm ready, Scootch. This one definitely lives alone, and his brothers don't come around if the wife isn't there for them to savage."

"I know what you're thinking," Scootch said in his cackly voice. "You're gonna use the belladonna ploy."

"That's what I'm thinking."

"But how do you know this guy will send it in? Is he a coupon collector?"

"I haven't been able to find that out. But I think I've got something even better. Wanna hear it?"

"Do I have a choice?"

"This guy talks and acts like a sex maniac. I think if he's offered a free collection of really hot girlie photos, he'll bite. Especially if there's a tinge of S&M in the offer."

"Ya think he can read?"

"I've checked that out, too. He gets the newspaper every day and never fails to take it with him when he leaves for work. It's not proof, but it's close. What do you think?"

"Y' can't win if y' don't play. Go for it!"

Jason sat at his Macintosh G4 and loaded his PowerPoint software. Using fonts often used in mail solicitations, he composed a scorching advertising piece. The headline screamed that José Gonzalez had ALREADY WON a book of the hottest, sexiest, completely explicit photos of the most exotic women — and girls — from around the world ever collected. Pictures taken in every position were promised. Jason even downloaded a photo from a pornographic website, positioning it in the center of the page.

There was no obligation, nothing to buy, no money to send in. All Gonzalez had to do was fill in his name, address, and age on the reverse of the ad, place it in the "Verification Envelope" provided, and seal it. He was to place the sealed "Verification Envelope" into the larger, pre-addressed and pre-stamped mailing envelope, seal it, and drop it into a mailbox. That was all. What's more, if he mailed the envelope within twenty-four hours of receipt, José would also receive a pair of velvet-covered handcuffs. Absolutely free!

Jason put an official-looking border around the page, added an official-looking heading, and printed it. When satisfied with the ad, he burned the disk, knowing experts were able to resurrect erased data. He dumped the ashes and pulverized them with his heel.

Next, he tripped a latch and pushed open the hidden door to his "pharmacy." Removing his supply of belladonna from the little cooler, he mixed it with a special ingredient to soften the taste of the poison. Now, he was ready to prepare his bait.

Donning a pair of surgical gloves, he folded the advertisement and placed it inside the large envelope that would contain both the "Verification Envelope" and the return-mail envelope. Next, he carefully applied a swipe of the poison to the flaps of each of the two envelopes — he needed two envelope flaps to be sure of a lethal dose. After letting the flaps dry, he placed both envelopes into the mailing envelope.

The final step was to dampen a small sponge with distilled water, moisten the flap of the mailing envelope, and seal it. He was now ready to strike. After replacing his paraphernalia and washing the surface of the workbench with alcohol, he drove to the main post office. Still wearing his surgical gloves, he mailed the bait.

Tara watched with interest from her Honda parked across the street.

José Gonzalez, pleased with himself, couldn't remember ever winning anything in his entire life. Now he had, and he looked forward to receiving his prize — a book of sex-drenched photos and, because he'd been quick to return the Verification Envelope, a pair of velvet-covered handcuffs. Hot damn! Those would come in handy — his ticket to a very satisfying weekend.

Saturday evening he put on a fresh T-shirt and shorts and drove his rusted VW a few blocks to Tico's, his favorite watering hole. He ordered a beer at the well-scarred bar, sipping as his eyes scanned the dimly-lit room. At the other end of the bar he noticed a woman he'd seen several times before — no prize, but not a dog, either. When she looked in his direction, he raised his bottle and smiled. He took her returned smile as an invitation. Picking up his money and bottle, he settled on the bar stool adjoining hers.

"Hi," he ventured.

"Hello, yourself."

"I've seen you here before. I'm José."

"Maria." She wore a midnight-blue low-cut blouse, and a yellow skirt much too short for the weight and thirty-some years she carried. They conversed in Spanish for a few moments, then switched back to English. "I've seen you, too. How come you always alone?"

"My wife, she don' like bars. Buy you a beer?"

"I only drink Kahlua here."

José ordered her one.

"At home I make my own special drink. It's stronger than Kahlua, but not as strong as tequila or scotch."

"Sounds good. How about makin' one for me?"

Maria looked him up and down, obviously sizing him up — wondering if it was safe to take him home, apparently remembering she'd seen him here several times. As he'd never gotten out of line during those occasions, she agreed. "Okay. I live down the block. We can walk." It was already a little after midnight, but she could sleep in until time for Mass.

José paid for the drinks, and they walked the half-block to her apartment building. It wasn't much to look at — badly cracked sidewalk, graffiti-stained walls, bulging screens in the windows. They climbed the outside stairs to the second floor.

"This is pretty nice," he said, grinning. "You got nice furniture."

"I'll go make my special drink. You gonna like it." She went to the kitchen area, rattled bottles and glasses, and chipped ice cubes from a tray." Returning with two glasses containing a dirty-brown liquid, she handed him one. Lifting hers, she said, "Viva!" and downed the four-ounce glass in one gulp.

José followed suit. "Jeez, that's good. What you got in it?"

Maria beamed. "My special mix. I make another?" She reached for his glass, but he suddenly grabbed his stomach with both hands, doubled over, and moaned.

"Aargh. What you put in that drink?" he said through gritted teeth.

He felt his face getting hot and his vision blurring. His mouth was dry, and his heart beat so loudly he could hear it thumping. His pulse beat more rapidly. Suddenly he began to sweat. The mild discomfort he'd felt in his belly since dinnertime had gone far beyond a simple stomach ache.

"You poison me, you puta!" he shouted, trying to squeeze the pain from his stomach. The aches only increased.

"I no poison you! I drank same as you. You *saw* me!"

Suddenly José lashed out and punched her in the gut. When she doubled over from the sudden pain, he punched her hard on the side of the head. She fell to the floor, yelping like a beaten dog.

"You bitch. You poison me!" he repeated. "I kill you!" He cursed her in Spanish.

By now his skin had turned bright red and he began to stagger, trying to keep his balance. Ten minutes later he clutched his stomach and bent over in a grinding convulsion. He wet his pants. Sinking to his knees, he writhed in pain. With a strangled moan, he fell to the floor, twitching. Three minutes later, after a final muffled screech, he died.

Maria, crying hard through her pain, watched in disbelief as José twitched on the carpet, drool leaking from his mouth. She watched until he was still. Then, using the furniture as a crutch, she dragged herself up and looked again at the corpse in her apartment. "My God," she said, "What am I gonna do?"

She dialed 911.

CHAPTER TWENTY-SEVEN

Striding into Brunkel's office, Harry found Charlie Drummel deep in discussion with the sergeant.

"Why the urgent meeting so early on a Monday morning?" Harry butted in. "What's up?"

"Poor Harry," Brunkel replied. "You only get called in for an early meeting, but Charlie here had to drag his sorry ass out to another middle-of-the-night crime scene."

"What happened?"

"Fill him in, Charlie," Brunkel said.

Drummel outlined his visit to the Maria Coreza apartment. "The officer on the scene had already interviewed Maria when I got there. She was still pretty upset, and still hurting from the blows she took from the guy. She'd met him — his ID shows him as a José Gonzalez — at the bar on the corner. Pico's. They decided to have a drink at her place. She fixed the drinks and after downing just one, he doubled over in pain. He decided she'd poisoned him and beat her up. A little while later, he died. She called 911."

"When did he die?" Harry asked.

"About two a.m. Why?"

Harry ignored the question. "What was the cause of death?"

"The ME on the scene said it looked like a poisoning, but he won't know for sure until the autopsy. What are you thinking?"

"In a minute. Did this Maria person do it?"

Drummel shook his head. "Doesn't look like it. The drink glasses were still on the sink — we bagged 'em — and she apparently drank from the same batch. The lab's got the glasses and the pitcher. No, I don't see her as the perp."

"Okay," Harry said, "here's what I'm wondering. I'm wondering whether this isn't another victim of our serial killer. He dies early Sunday morning — an *almost* Monday — poisoned by persons unknown. There's no evidence the poisoning occurred at the scene of death. So the vic got the poison somewhere else, just like in the Willie Lamarka case."

Brunkel leaned his bulk forward in his swivel chair, and riffled through a case file on his desk. "Wait a minute," he said. "The last kill . . . Pilanski, right? That was only two Mondays ago. If this *is* the work of the serial killer, he's changed his monthly timetable. Why?"

"Maybe he feels we're closing in and tried to get one last kill in before we catch him," Drummel offered.

"In your dreams," Brunkel said.

"What if he found a victim he thought couldn't wait another two weeks?" Harry mused.

"That's a possibility. Nothing says he *has* to stick to the one-a-month formula."

"Besides," Drummel added, "he's deviated from that pattern before."

"Right," Harry confirmed. "He may not even know he's killing on a schedule."

"Okay." Brunkel heaved his bulk from his chair and towered over his visitors. "We'll wait to see what the autopsy shows and take it from there. But if this guy's planning to kill more often, we'd better close him down before this leaks to the press and the citizens go berserk. Harry, set up a meeting of the task force — as many as can make it — for ten this morning."

Harry tried to start the meeting promptly at ten. It didn't happen. At five minutes after the hour, Sergeant Brunkel leaped to his feet and took center stage. In his most threatening voice, he said, "Button it. We need to get on with this."

The hubbub quieted to silence as Brunkel glowered, in turn, at Anita Solarez, rape squad; Harry the Shoe, task force leader; the Homicide Reaction Team, detectives Charlie Drummel, Joan Skirms, "Dinky" Dirnbaum, and Helen Pau. The others were hitting the streets, interviewing.

"Listen up! Our perp is getting more active, and we gotta close him down. Now! Harry, take over."

Harry stood and pointed to the large whiteboard summarizing the information they'd collected to date. "We think we've found another one. It happened some time ago, but it fits the pattern. Anita will fill us in on the Baruna case in a minute.

"For now, here's where we are: we've interviewed almost all the personnel at the shelters. Haven't found anything that points us to a suspect. We also know the perp trolls for victims at hospitals." He looked up. "By the way, break in any time you get an idea.

"Our killer also may be finding victims in other places, but so far, we don't have any evidence of that." He nodded toward the rape squad representative, "Anita?"

Anita Solarez stood. "Harry told me his CI recently turned up a suspicious abuse case at the Snitskin-Pruitt Children's hospital. Elijah Baruna, a seven-year-old boy, was admitted March 1 of this year. It was clearly an abuse case — a bad one. About two weeks later, the father, Abdul, disappeared. Hasn't been heard from since."

"What's significant about that?" Skirms asked.

Solarez jabbed at the victim schedule on the whiteboard. "March 13 is one of the empty Mondays on our chart. Get it? Badly abused boy is checked into a hospital; two weeks later his father vanishes."

"We believe he's one of our killer's earlier victims, Joan. The timing's right," Harry emphasized.

Solarez picked up the recitation. "Missing Persons is looking for the father. So far, no trace . . ."

The door to the conference room burst open and Anita froze in mid-sentence. All heads turned as a uniformed lieutenant rushed in waving a note pad.

"Sorry to interrupt, but I just received a call from Kay Delaney, crime reporter at the Republic. She has a tip from a 'reliable source' that we're investigating a serial killer. She wants confirmation."

"Shit! Someone's leaked." Brunkel slammed his palms on the desk. "What'd you tell her?"

"The usual. Told her I'd get back to her. But she said to hurry. She's on a two-hour deadline."

"If I find out who leaked," Brunkel growled, "I'll pull his guts out through his nose." He waved a thumb over his shoulder at the intruder. "Now lissen up. Lieutenant Steven *Carver* here is the Public Information Officer in this department. *Not* any one of you, and he is the only — repeat O-N-L-Y — one who will talk to the press about this case. Refer all inquiries to him, no matter *how* short the deadline, no matter how they whine and plead."

"What do you want me to tell her?" Carver asked.

"Why tell her anything?" Drummel wondered aloud.

"If we don't, she'll make it up!" Brunkel stormed. "You don't think she'll ignore a hot tip like a serial killer just because the police clam up on her, do you? Now go back to work while we talk to Captain Portono, and decide how to handle this fink. Better yet, go out and nail that bastard!"

Wednesday morning was different in Phoenix. Overnight, the desert temperature dropped all the way to eighty-five degrees. The residents called it a "cool" morning.

Little else changed. The backup-beeper cacophony provided by the construction trucks still started shortly after the 4:30 dawn. Newspapers thumped onto lawns and porches of sleeping homes. Another sunny day was on the rise. It would be another glorious day in the desert — until unsuspecting readers opened their morning newspapers.

There, on the front page, a headline screamed:

SERIAL KILLER LOOSE IN VALLEY
Police silent about details

By Kate Delaney, Crime Reporter
Police are quietly investigating a serial killer believed to be roaming the Valley. They refuse to release details lest it hamper their investigation.

Lieutenant Steven Carver, Public Information Officer, Phoenix Police, confirmed only that the murder of José Gonzalez, three days ago, may be the serial killer's latest victim. The killer, however, is believed responsible for the deaths of at least nine victims in the past nine months.

All murders took place in or near Metropolitan Phoenix. Police refuse to give any specifics about the killings, or reveal any evidence linking the assaults to a suspect. "We can't afford to jeopardize our investigation," Lt. Carver said.

According to a profile prepared by a task force headed by Detective Harry Shuman, the killer most likely is living in or near the downtown area. He is active mainly during the day, and is polite and "normal" in appearance. He will be perceived by others as quiet, patient, and considerate. He seems to be selective in the choice of victims, targeting only men committing violence toward women and children . . .

Tara gasped as she read the remainder of the article, then reread it. "Oh, my God!" she blurted. "It's *him!*"

She dialed Narena, hoping she hadn't already left for work. "Narena? Have you seen the morning paper?"

"Slow down, girl. No, I haven't. What's got you so riled up?"

"It's him!"

"Who's him?"

"Jason. *He's* the serial killer! It's in the morning paper — front page. It's got to be him!"

"Is he mentioned by name?"

"No, of course not. They don't know who it is yet, just that there is a serial killer on the loose. Oh, my God."

"Take a deep breath," Narena soothed. "So what makes you so sure it's him?

"The article describes him to a 'T'."

"Come on, Tara. There must be thousands of men who fit the description, whatever it is."

"Yes, but they named José Gonzalez as the latest victim. He's the father of the — "

"Yes, I remember," Narena interrupted. "That's different. Wait a minute. Isn't today the day you were supposed to visit Jason's workshop?"

"Tomorrow."

"Well, if you're so sure it's him, you're really not going, are you?"

Tara hesitated. "I suppose I shouldn't." She glanced again at the article as her mind whirled. "But I was looking forward to seeing the workshop . . . and I promised. Besides, he's always been kind and polite to us, hasn't he?"

"But if he's a killer — "

"He's always been kind and gentle with the children, too, and he's provided a lot of useful information — "

"Stop it, Tara. You're trying to talk yourself into something far too dangerous. Let the police deal with it."

"We can't just sic the police on him because I *think* he's the one. Think what it would do to his reputation if he's innocent. I have to give him the benefit of the doubt." The speech solidified her conviction to keep her date.

"Aren't you afraid of what he might do to you?"

"Of course I'm afraid, but I've got to know."

"And if it *is* him? What'll you do then?"

"I . . . I don't know. But I'm certain he wouldn't hurt *me*. He knows us, Narena, and besides, I don't fit his criteria for picking victims. You know as well as I he only kills men who've battered and raped wives and children."

"Uh-huh. Tara, don't do it. Call your detective friend and let him deal with this."

"I just *told* you. I can't do that until I'm absolutely certain. I can't destroy him just because I *suspect* him. I've *got* to keep the appointment." She didn't mention again the vision still dancing in her head — the vision in which newspapers heralded her as the fearless woman who identified the serial killer and, as a result, got to keep her job at the shelter. Or, better yet, managed to land a job in law enforcement. How proud her father would be.

"I think you're being foolish, Tara. *Please!* Call the police!"

"The minute I'm sure, that's exactly what I'll do. I don't want to *catch* him, Narena, I just want to know who he is. I'll call you the minute I leave his workshop. I promise. It'll be okay."

"What if *I* call the police?"

"I'd never speak to you again. I mean it. If I don't call within two hours, *then* call. Promise?"

Narena hesitated. "All right. I promise. But if you're wrong, you may be *dead* wrong."

"Wait a minute."

"What?"

"I just remembered something. When I took an abnormal psychology course in college we had to go on a couple of field trips to a mental hospital. I remember having a marvelous conversation with a man who sounded very well versed in lots of subjects."

"So?"

"So later I found out he was one of the inmates."

"You're kidding. Why was he locked up?"

"Well, he was perfectly normal in every way, except that he was obsessed with the idea that he'd written thirty-two national anthems. It wasn't true, but nothing could shake him from that belief."

"I don't see what — "

"Don't you see? Jason is normal in every way, except that he can't stand guys who commit violence against women and children. That's why he won't hurt me."

Grudgingly, Narena conceded, "You may have a point. But I still think you'll be putting yourself in danger. Please, I ask you once more — don't go, Tara. I don't want to lose my best friend. If you're wrong, you may be *dead* wrong."

CHAPTER TWENTY-EIGHT

"It's Open Line Wednesday," the talk show host began, opening a telephone connection to the first caller of the program. "Larry, you're on the air."

"Uh, I just wanna say I think that serial killer guy is doing the right thing. If he's only getting rid of guys who beat up on women and kids, more power to 'im."

"Thanks for the call, Larry. Darla, you're on the air."

"I agree with the previous caller. The entire justice system is about protecting the *criminals*. It forgets all about the victims. I think it's about time we do something more than just wring our hands and weep for the child killers."

"Thank you. Theodore, you're on the air."

"I can't believe these callers are cheering for the killer. Don't they realize he could start killing *other* kinds of people as well?"

"What kind of people, Theodore?"

"Well, he could start killing burglars, or anybody who didn't agree with his political philosophy, for example. If he isn't caught, what's to stop him from killing at random?"

"You have a point there, but the police said he seems to be selective in his choice of victims."

"For now, maybe. Still, even if he doesn't branch out, killing is wrong and he's got to be stopped."

By late morning the airwaves sizzled with talk shows discussing the serial killer in their midst. Callers chose sides, as if rooting for favorite football teams. By mid-afternoon, informal polls revealed an almost even split among those advocating the killer should continue his "good work," and those finding his lawless "crusade" abhorrent. Many cited the Bible as evidence to bolster both "for" and "against" positions. "Thou salt not kill," the law-abiding quoted. "An eye for an eye," rebutted the avengers.

The story hit the six o'clock news, causing TV station switchboards and web sites to light up with demands for more information. Police phone lines clogged with the onslaught. Finally, the police public information officer had to record a brief announcement to be played for those wanting more details.

Detective Harry Shuman stood uncertainly before a seated gathering of the brass. He had no idea what this was all about, but decided that any meeting in the office of Major Bea Stacy, Chief of Detectives, was serious. The added presence of Sergeant Brunkel and Captain Portono, Homicide Chief, confirmed that notion.

Harry stared around the wall of concerned faces until Capt. Portono spoke. "Tell us what's new with the serial killer case."

"After that," Bea Stacy added, stabbing her pen at Harry, "tell us what you're doing to close him down."

"What's new is we've learned the perp selects victims not only from one of the women's shelters, but also from at least one of the hospitals, and probably trolls other places as well. We also believe — and we're holding this information back — we've got *two* killers working, not one."

Stacy frowned. "What brought you to that conclusion?"

"The MO of one of the killings isn't even close to that of the others. The serial killer is organized: the maverick is disorganized — he killed in a rage and left evidence behind; the serial killer is cool, calm . . . and smart. Also new: the serial killer now seems to be killing every two weeks instead of just once a month."

"Anything else?"

Harry looked at Sgt. Brunkel. "One thing, but I haven't even discussed it with Sergeant Brunkel yet. Okay if I keep it to myself until I do? It's very sensitive."

The Chief of Detectives stood and banged a hand on the table. "What the hell could be more sensitive than a serial killer running around making us all look like a bunch of one-legged ass-kickers?" she stormed. "We've got to *move* on this, Harry, and if you know something, spit it out. Now!"

"I appreciate the urgency of the situation," Harry countered. "What I have, though, relates only to the rage killer."

"I don't care *what* it relates to. If it has anything to do with this string of murders, I want it on the table. And I want it *now*. I'm sure everyone in this room can keep it to themselves." Her eyes scanned the nodding heads.

"All right. We've been re-interviewing the staff at the shelters — especially the one where Willie Lamarka died — trying to find out how the perp gets info on his potential victims." Harry paused to take a breath. "There's a security guard there who's very protective of the resident women and gets mad as hell when he thinks about the scumbags who've damaged his charges."

"You make *him* for the killer?" Stacy asked, a deep frown marring her otherwise attractive face.

"Possibly. But we're still investigating."

"What's so sensitive about *that*?"

"He's an ex-cop. His son is 'on the Job.'"

Bodies stiffened and lungs emptied in unison. Quietly, Stacy said, "I see." She turned in her swivel chair to look out the window. "How confident are you that he's involved?"

"Fifty-fifty. As I said, we're still investigating. There's another suspect."

The chief of detectives swivelled back to face Harry. "Who?"

"The director of the shelter is also extremely possessive about her residents, and really gets her dander up when some mere male tries to enter the kingdom. I can visualize — easily — her mauling some bad guy in a rage."

"Or maybe just feeding information to the killer?"

"That too! If we find such a source, we'll sweat him — or her — for the killer's identity."

Stacy nodded, and turned to Capt. Portono. "Darryl, can we try to smoke him out by giving out more information to the press? Maybe on the type of victims he kills?"

"I'll talk with the PIO. I think he'll go along. At minimum, it should make some of the violent batterers think twice about chasing their women to a shelter . . . or putting them in a hospital." Portono produced a remote smile. "Actually, I rather like the thought of making those vermin sweat a little."

"Let me know what you decide." She turned back to Harry. "Any other plans for shutting this guy down that you haven't mentioned?"

"We're checking timelines at the pediatric hospitals — tracking forward two-three weeks from the date of admission to see if we can connect a male victim to the admission. Also, we're interviewing relatives of the battered victims — brothers, fathers, grandfathers. If the killer is one of them, we'll smoke him out, and I've got a team re-visiting what few crime scenes we have, just in case we missed something. If anybody can think of something we're not doing, I'd like to know about it."

"I have a question," Brunkel said. Heads turned in his direction. "Is everyone here familiar with the Tibbetts case?" Recognition nods all around. "Briefly — this is just a theory — the killer may have two levels of punishment. Violent batterers who damage their women beyond the ability to recover deserve the ultimate sanction. Lesser batterers, however, seem to deserve lesser treatment. Like our 'friend,' lawyer Tibbetts. We don't know for sure Tibbetts is the work of the serial killer, but on the assumption he is, Harry has someone looking for similar cases. Harry?"

"We've found two possibles. First one happened more than a year ago. Guy's car engine melted down. Seems someone poured sulfuric acid all over the engine compartment. Odd, don't you think?"

"What happened to the guy?"

"Nothing to the guy, but it totaled his Mercedes. The interesting thing is he'd twice been arrested for beating on his wife."

"And the other one?" Brunkel asked.

"Even stranger. This one goes back about two years. The guy was a prominent minister in town. Hired to conduct a funeral service for the deceased wife of a wealthy sports figure. Two hundred people showed up, but when they opened the casket for the viewing, the body was missing. The investigation revealed the minister was diddling some of the choirboys."

"What happened to the body?" Brunkel asked.

"They finally found it stuffed into a casket in another viewing room."

"What I'm thinking is . . . " Brunkel said slowly, "is that if you interviewed some of the people close to those cases, you might learn something more about the killer's profile."

"I'll get somebody on it this afternoon," Harry agreed.

Stacy rose. "Close him down, Harry, close him down — *fast!*"

CHAPTER TWENTY-NINE

After a nervous lunch, Tara prepared for her appointment with Jason Smalter. Aware of the danger she might be facing, she dressed accordingly. White sleeveless blouse tucked into a pleated blue skirt, dark blue rubber-soled shoes. Not exactly her favorite outfit, she told herself, but one allowing maximum movement if she needed it. In her bedroom, she reached into the back of a dresser drawer for her new .25 caliber, Beretta semi-automatic pistol. Not much of a gun for stopping power, she thought, but maybe good enough to get her out of a jam. Having completed the fourteen-hour gun-handling course, she now had a license allowing her to carry it concealed. *I just wish I had more time to practice using it.*

She worked the slide to ram a cartridge into the chamber, and set the safety. She added another cartridge to the clip, slid the loaded pistol into the special gun compartment of her white purse, and slung its strap over her shoulder. Unable to think of anything she'd forgotten, she headed for the meeting with Jason Smalter.

Also at home, Jason paced the floor, as uneasy as Tara, only a few miles away.

"You know you're asking for trouble . . . you know," Scootch warned.

"You're repeating yourself, old friend, and yes, I do know . . . but it can't be helped. I think she suspects, and I've got to know." Jason continued to fill a hypodermic from a small vial as he talked to, and for, himself. Easing a protective cover on the needle, he placed the hypodermic in the pocket of an old lab coat he used as a shop apron.

"What do you think you're gonna do with that thing?"

"Don't know. Nothing, I hope."

In truth, he didn't know *what* he was planning to do. But he was sure he didn't want to be arrested — not now! He considered commitments he'd made — and be forced to default on — if he were arrested. The battered children he had yet to relieve of their pain. The award he and Gweedo were scheduled to receive from the hospital for his work with the children. The lecture he and Gweedo had planned to present at the ventriloquists' convention in San Francisco. The homeless kids they had yet to perform for at the governor's Halloween party. The lecture he was invited to present at the prestigious Psychotherapist Council.

"You're walking a dangerous path here, and I don't want any part of it," Scootch said. "What'll you do if you find out she knows? Tell me *that*."

"I'll — I'll use the hypo to make her drowsy. That'll give me time to think about what to do."

"I don't believe it. Killing women is not your style. It's what you're fighting against . . . or have you forgotten?"

"I know, I know. But if I have to protect myself, I'll just have to do it. It's not the first time I've sent a woman away, you know."

"Yeah, you keep telling me that. But for what *that* poor excuse for a mother did to her kids — and their dog — you should'a sent that bitch away a lot sooner than you did. Even so, it took you three months to get over it, didn't it? You cried every night. Like I said, it's not what you do."

"Yes, yes, I know, but — "

"No buts. Don't forget, *this* woman is kind and gentle. And she likes you."

Jason looked at Scootch for a long time. "You know I don't want to — it's wrong to send people away — but if they catch me, they'll execute me for sure. Worse, they might just put me in jail for a long time. I don't think I can stand that." Jason squeezed his hands together. "I've got important things to *do* before I let that happen."

The doorbell rang, and Jason bounded up the basement stairs. "Don't go 'way," he shouted over his shoulder. "And keep your mouth shut."

Tara smiled when Jason opened the door — his pale green T-shirt sported the slogan, "Help a Dummy, Hire a Ventriloquist."

"Hi, Miss Tara. Please come in."

"Thank you. Love your T-shirt." Tara's glance noted the spotless living room, the tasteful over-stuffed furniture, and the clown puppet sitting on the edge of the piano. "This looks like a very comfortable home. Do you do your own decorating?"

"Thanks." Jason chuckled. "Yes, I like plain but comfortable furnishings. Let's go down to the workshop — it's cooler there." He guided Tara toward the basement door. "Please watch your step. The journey down can be a little treacherous."

Once in the basement, Tara breathed deeply, wondering if there was a deeper meaning to Jason's comment. "It *is* cooler here, and it smells so . . . so workshoppy. Is that glue I smell?"

"Among other things. Glue, leather, styrofoam, wood, acrylic. You name it, you're probably smelling it."

"Who's that sitting on the bench?" she asked, pointing to the figure.

"That's Scootch. That old guy is supposed to be my friendly side-kick, but he's turning into a nagging old man." By now Jason had slipped his hand around the puppet's controls.

Scootch turned to Jason. "Is that so? As if you didn't *need* a keeper."

"Cut that out. Say something nice to Miss Tara."

Turning to Tara, the puppet said, "You look like much too nice a person to be hanging out in a dump like this. Run while you still can."

Tara laughed. "He's positively charming," she said, stroking the white hair. "I'm glad to meet you, Mister Scootch."

Scootch bowed to Tara, then turned toward Jason. "There. Didn't I tell you she'd be even prettier than you said she was?"

"Scootch is an impossible flirt, Miss Tara. Just ignore him. Let me show you around the workshop," Placing the puppet on the workbench, he explained the making of the head molds and construction of the various body parts.

"Fascinating. How do you control the mouth and eyes?"

Jason placed a clean towel on the bench. He put Scootch there, on his stomach, and removed Scootch's wig. He then opened the flap in the back of the head, exposing the mechanism.

"Gweedo, the lion you've seen at the hospital, is a soft puppet; I put my hand into his head to open and close the mouth. Scootch, on the other hand, is a 'hard puppet.' His head is made of plastic — some are made from wood." He showed Tara how each of the controls on the headstick inside the puppet's body linked up to the eyes, lips, and mouth. With Jason's hand wrapped around the headstick in the puppet's back, Scootch continued to interrupt the explanations, allowing Tara to see the controls in action.

"Now I understand how you can make your — figures — move so realistically." Tara decided now was the time to probe gently toward the purpose of her visit. "I've been especially impressed with how Gweedo can get so close to those poor battered children."

That simple statement sent alarms ringing in Jason's head. *She knows!* But he had to be sure. "Thank you. Gweedo will be pleased when I tell him he's got a fan."

"Does he really get the children talking about how they got hurt?"

"Yes, he does. It's not uncommon for ventriloquists to be called on for that kind of service. Kids will tell things to puppets and dolls they would never tell an adult. Therapists use dolls and puppets all the time."

"How does that make *you* feel?" Tara wasn't sure what to say to determine Jason's guilt or innocence.

"I enjoy making the kids laugh, of course, but when we talk to the kids who've been . . . well, it makes me very sad. Sometimes I tear up when I hear those innocent kids telling all the bad things that have been done to them. You saw it yourself. They're just so helpless." He looked down at his hands.

Heart pounding, Tara decided it was time to take the plunge. Even if Jason were the killer, she was intellectually convinced this gentle, sensitive man would never harm her. In her heart, however, she wasn't so sure.

"When Gweedo talked with little Estrella Gonzalez, did she tell him how she got hurt?" There! She'd said it. She looked at Jason as innocently as she knew how. But the look in his eyes told her he knew she knew! *Oh, God, what have I done?*

Jason stared at Tara, his face expressing sadness. *Yes! She knows!* Jason wanted nothing more than to run and hide — anything to keep from thinking about what he knew he had to do.

"Yes," he said slowly, "Gweedo talked with Estrella. She told him about all the things that had been done to her — the things I told Nurse Narena about. You were there. I wept." He paused, his eyes locked to Tara's. Sliding his hand into his lab coat pocket, he gently wrapped his fingers around the loaded syringe. He still didn't know what he would do after he used it.

Narena looked at her watch for the thousandth time. Tara must have been with Jason for almost an hour by now! *What should I do?* If she called the police and Jason was innocent, it would be beyond embarrassing. Worse, it would probably damage Jason's reputation. She knew very well that the falsely-accused never completely shake off the cloud of suspicion. On the other hand, if she *didn't* call, and Tara *was* in danger, she would never forgive herself for not acting.

No contest! A reputation against a best friend's life! She punched in Jason's *number*. The line was busy. She called two more times with the same result. Wondering if perhaps the phone hadn't been deliberately left off the hook, she looked at her watch yet again and reluctantly decided to wait a few minutes before trying again.

"I can appreciate how you must feel when Gweedo listens to the children tell their stories," Tara said in a gentle voice. "It isn't easy to listen to those stories of fear, of helplessness in the face of violence, especially from children. I know, because I hear them at the shelter all the time. I never get used to the tears, the despair, the massive injuries, or the stories of anger and rage that go along with the beatings. It makes me want to strangle the creeps who cause such suffering." While speaking, her gaze darted around the room. *He knows I suspect him. I've got to distract him until I can find a way to get out.* "By the way, you never told me how *you* can hear what the children are saying when they're talking softly to Gweedo."

Jason reached for Gweedo's suitcase and put it on the workbench. *I really, truly don't want to make this nice woman go away*, he thought. *But what choice do I have? If I don't, they'll lock me in jail.*

He opened the case and placed Gweedo on the bench. "Look closely at the front of his collar," he said, pointing with his left hand as he slipped his right hand into the lab coat pocket. "There's a microphone there connected to a tiny transmitter inside the body, with a short antenna sewn to the inside of the collar. Go ahead and feel it."

Intrigued in spite of herself, Tara leaned over the puppet and felt for the antenna wire inside the collar. As she did so, Jason edged behind her and, with a quick motion, jabbed the hypodermic needle into the fleshy part of her buttock and pressed the plunger.

Tara shrieked, more from surprise than pain. An instant later, when the reality of what had happened exploded inside her brain, fear began to make her skin tingle. "My God, Jason, what have you *done?*"

"I think the charade is over, don't you?"

"What do you mean?"

Jason sighed. "It won't work, Tara. Your eyes and your questions tell me you know what I do. I'm really sorry."

"I . . . I don't know what you're talking about."

"I'm really very sorry, but it's over."

"Have — have you poisoned me?" She fought the panic welling up inside her.

"Heavens, no, it's nothing like that. It's just a muscle relaxant that will make you a little drowsy."

"You — you're not going to kill me, are you?" Tara backed away from the bench, eyes wide, palms held outward as if pushing away an unseen enemy.

Jason looked puzzled. "Kill you? Certainly not. I don't want to hurt you,

Tara. You must know that. But I have to do something — you can see that, can't you? If I let you go, you'll tell the police and then I won't be able to make anyone else stop hurting the children. Don't you agree the world is better off after these vermin have been sent away?"

"Yes, yes I do, but . . . but I wouldn't tell anyone about you. I promise." Tara felt her muscles loosening, her body going limp. She backed against a supporting beam to steady herself, to keep her from sliding to the floor. Every fiber in her body screamed for her to sleep — every neuron of her *mind* screamed for her to stay awake.

Narena looked at her watch; ten minutes had passed since the last time she looked, but only five since she last received another busy signal from Jason's number. *Why hasn't Tara called? Twenty more minutes and I call the police.* She tried to concentrate on her work, but her thoughts kept snapping back to Tara, and the danger she might be in.

Jason looked at the clock on the wall above the workbench. *Less than forty minutes and the cremation service begins next door. I must have her in place by then.* "You must be feeling a little sleepy by now. Wouldn't you like to lie down?" Putting an arm around her to keep her from stumbling, he gently led her to the gurney kept in readiness along the wall.

She tried to resist, but her muscles refused the message. "No . . . please. I won't tell anyone. Please let me go, Jason. You know I would never do anything to hurt you." Her words were slurred and she spoke barely above a whisper. "Wh . . . what . . . have . . . you . . . done . . . to . . . me?"

Jason picked her up and placed her on the gurney. Stroking her hair with an unexpected gentleness, he bent nearer and whispered into her ear. "There, there. It's going to be all right." Reaching for the Velcro straps, he added, "This is just to keep you from falling off." He fastened the straps across her chest, then he secured her ankles and wrists. "We only have a short way to go." Inside his mind, the rising crescendo of his dead mother's screams made him wince. "Go away! Leave me alone!"

"Go away? Where?" She shook her bound wrists. "How? Where are you taking me? Please, Jason. I promise I won't tell. I'll give you anything you want . . . any . . . thing. I . . . I . . . " Though fear shot a jolt of adrenaline into her blood stream, it was getting harder and harder to stay awake. *I'm so sleepy . . . so very sleepy . . . but I have to stay awake. I've got to! It's my only hope.*

"That's it," Narena mumbled, extracting her hand from the patient's one she was holding. To the patient, she said, "You'll have to excuse me for a few minutes. I've an urgent phone call to make." Deciding to call from her own cell phone rather than from the phone at the nursing station, she sprinted from the room and down the hall to the locker room where she kept her purse. Grabbing it quickly, she fumbled for her cell phone. In desperation, she turned to the table behind her and hurriedly dumped its contents on the surface, causing several items to spill onto the floor — including her cell. "Damn." Hoping it still worked after the fall, she picked it up and punched in 911.

Jason rolled the gurney away from the wall. Activating a hidden latch, he grunted as he pushed a section of the cinderblock wall inward on its ancient, hidden track. A dark tunnel was revealed as he swung the heavy door to the right. Musty air seeped into the basement, moving slightly to equalize the temperatures in the two spaces. Jason turned an old porcelain light switch, bathing the brick-lined, arched passageway in dim amber light. Returning to the gurney, he began to push Tara into the tunnel. "It's not far, Tara. Just next door."

The sight of the tunnel pushed Tara near total panic. She fought against the rising claustrophobia. "But *why*, Jason? Why are you doing this?"

"I must, Tara. I must continue my work. It's little enough, but I must do what I can."

"What are you talking about?" Tara was now mumbling. *He must be mad*, she thought, but had to distract him any way she could. "What are you talking about?" she repeated, her voice just a whisper.

"About what I do to those men who beat women and rape children, of course." He stopped rolling the gurney and moved to where Tara could see him as he spoke. "When I make one of those evil men disappear, I save lives, don't you see?" *And the screaming goes away for a while, too.* Jason shook his head wistfully. "But there are so many of them, you know. They're everywhere. Beating, maiming, raping. They've got to be stopped."

"Yes, they do. I agree with you. But that's what the police and the courts are supposed to be doing," she argued. "Isn't it?"

"Of course it is. But you see how impotent they are. As soon as the police arrest one jackal, the courts put him right back on the street. And the victims continue to pile up . . . and suffer. Nobody cares about the victims. I'm just doing what a lot of people would like to do themselves. Doing what they know in their hearts is right."

He looked at his watch and continued pushing the gurney through the cobweb-infested tunnel. He had less than twenty minutes left to synchronize activation of his secret crematory with the one in the mortuary above it.

Tara screamed. Jason heard it more as a squeak.

"Sorry about the cobwebs. This passageway hasn't been used for some time. Mortuaries just don't do many cremations now that the neighborhoods have built up around them."

"What are you talking about?" Her mind skittered . . . if she could only sleep . . . "What cremations?"

"They're mostly done at the cemeteries now, to keep people from complaining about the odors."

Then Tara understood, and screamed again — but only inside her head.

Jason heard only another prolonged squeak.

"Hello, *hello*? Detective Shuman? The operator said you're in charge of finding the killer." Narena's words tumbled out as fast as she could form them. "You've got to do something, fast. Tara's in danger."

"Please slow down a little, Miss. I can't understand you."

Words spilled from Narena. "My name is Narena Tanner, a friend of Tara Tindall. She knows who the killer is and has gone to meet him at his workshop. Please! If he suspects Tara knows, I'm afraid he'll kill her."

"Who'll kill her?"

"Jason Smalter. The ventriloquist entertainer who comes to our hospital twice a week. Tara's convinced he's the killer."

"I know Jason Smalter. Do you have his address?"

"Yes. Right here." Narena fumbled through her purse for the wallet for the slip of paper with phone number and address. Momentarily panicking, she remembered that items had fallen to the floor when she dumped her purse on the table. On hands and knees, she patted the floor until she found the wallet leaning against a wall. Breathing rapidly, she read the address and number into the phone. "Do you know where that is? Tara said it was next door to an old mortuary."

"Yeah, it's only a few blocks from here. I'll leave right now!" Harry slipped his pistol from desk drawer to belt holster and ran for the door.

CHAPTER THIRTY

"Please don't kill me," Tara pleaded, voice feeling a little less slurred. And a little stronger. *Maybe the drug is wearing off.*

She twisted her wrists against their restraints. *Yes!* She was regaining her strength — just a little, but she was sure of the improvement. Her mouth didn't seem quite as dry as when they'd entered the tunnel. She could breathe a little easier.

"It's not what I want to do."

"But why, Jason. You know I won't tell anyone."

"I've already told you. I *have* to do it . . . I still hear my mother screaming whenever I hear about bad men hurting women and children."

"But . . . but Jason, you don't kill women. You only kill the bad men who hurt women."

Tara's argument sent Jason's mind into turmoil. *She's right. I don't kill women. And yet, if I let this woman go now, she'll expose me. My work would end . . . but the screaming wouldn't. Can I trust her not to tell?* Shaking his head sadly, he decided no, he would have to make her go away.

They reached the end of the tunnel, and Tara felt as if she had been wheeled into a dark cavern. Jason stopped the gurney and reached to the wall for the light switch.

Tara heard the switch click, and, through a lifting fog, saw a room bathed in soft incandescent light. Twisting her head left and right to see where she was, she noted the room was bare but for a single item — a large brick oven with a black iron door on one end . . . just at the height of the gurney.

Oh . . . my . . . God! He's going to cremate me! Tara screamed — this time it sounded like a high-pitched gargle. *Think, Tara, you've got to focus your mind and think. It's your only chance.*

"There's no need to be alarmed. I'll make sure you won't feel a thing."

Tara scrambled for things to say that might make Jason change his mind. She grasped at straws. Anything to make him stop — or slow down. "Jason, there's something you've got to tell me before . . . you know . . ." She couldn't bring herself to say it.

"What?"

"You're such a kind and sensitive person, and you do so much good with your entertaining and with the kids. How can you do so much good, and then kill people?"

"I *am* doing good by making bad people disappear. I don't think there's anything strange about that, Tara."

"But you're *killing* people."

"Not really . . . I'm *saving* lives. Most people don't want to think about it, but we're in a war against evil. You know the kind of people I make go away. Nobody knows how many more would be hurt if somebody didn't do something." Jason positioned the gurney in line with the black iron door at the end of the furnace.

"I . . . I understand that, Jason," she said, her mind reeling, "I really do. After all, I work with the *victims* of the bad people you make go away. But how can you be such a compassionate man, then turn around and kill people?"

Jason stopped, frowning in puzzlement. "But I don't kill people. I just make the bad men go away."

At that moment Tara finally understood Jason's reasoning. *He really, truly believes he doesn't kill people. In his mind, he just "sends them away" — makes them disappear.* "I think I understand. But why do you have to 'send them away'?"

"Oh," he said, finally understanding her question. "I was born in Sicily." He said it as though the comment explained everything.

"I don't understand."

"My father — God rest his soul — and his three brothers were all involved with Mafia activities. When I was a little boy, I used to sit with the family around the kitchen table and hear all the talk. They'd talk about making people 'go away' as though it was no different than . . . well, than suing someone. You know, if someone does you a wrong, you sue. In the Mafia neighborhoods, if someone does you a wrong, you hurt them. Or made them disappear."

He sounds as if he wants to tell me about his past. If only I can keep him talking long enough . . .

"Oh, I *saw* a lot of the violence. I wasn't supposed to, I guess, but there was so much of it I couldn't help it. My uncles sometimes took me with them when they were going to do something — I was just a child, you see, so they got me to carry the pistol or lupo — "

"Lupo?"

"Sawed-off shotgun. That's why I was there to see it when the violence

155

happened. I suppose I got used to it without even knowing it."

"Did they ever make *you* do something bad?"

"No." Jason snorted. "I think they thought that if I only watched, and didn't actually do anything to anybody, I wouldn't grow up to be like them — they really didn't want that."

Jason swung wide the black iron door to the crematory. The hinge moved with a high-pitched squeak, crying out for a few drops of oil.

Tara looked at the darkness of the oven. "I'm really sorry to hear that, Jason." She tried to put as much compassion into her voice as her strengthening condition allowed. *What else can I ask him? What can I say to make him change his mind? Think, Tara, think!* "How did you get to this country?" *Oh, God, that's lame.*

"It was my father, bless his soul." Lame or not, Jason seemed eager to talk about his family. "When my mother was murdered — shotgun blast — by accident, I was standing only a few feet away. She screamed and I cried. Her blood was everywhere. That was the turning point for my father — he finally couldn't stand it anymore, you see. And . . . "

"And . . . ?" *I've got to keep him talking.*

"And I *still* hear her screaming inside my head.

Tears filled Jason's eyes and cheeks as his voice choked at the memory. "After that, Father wasn't ever the same. They weren't supposed to attack each others' families, you see. He'd gotten so fed up with all the casual violence . . . and the revenge killings . . . and the widows . . . that one day he just packed and moved us to New York."

"Jason, was your mother the only family member they killed?"

"Oh, God," Jason wailed. "I can't talk about it. Please, I can't talk about it."

"But you've got to talk about it, Jason. You're about to send me away, and I think I have a right to know *why*. Who else did they kill — send away?"

Tears streamed down Jason's cheeks. In a whisper, he said, "My little sister."

"How did it happen?"

"She was only four. Just a little girl . . . a beautiful, innocent, little girl." Jason pulled a handkerchief from his pocket and wiped the tears from his eyes, only to have them well up again.

"How did it happen?" she repeated. *I've got to keep him talking.*

"She was *there*. She was hiding behind my mother, holding on to her skirt." Jason paused, the pain of the memory showing in his eyes and tensed muscles of his face. "When the shotgun blast killed my mother, some of the pellets must have gone between her legs and into my sweet little sister."

"Oh, God! I'm sorry, Jason. I really am." Tara noticed her voice was still regaining strength. She also noticed her claustrophobia was receding. She was still near panic, but able to focus a bit better. *Narena, call the police!*

"It wasn't until they moved my dead mother that they found my sister lying underneath her. Dead. Nobody knew she'd been hurt until then. Nobody even knew she was *there*." Jason wiped his eyes again. "How could they *do* such a terrible thing?"

Please, Narena, call the police. "How did you decide to settle in Arizona?"

Jason thought for a moment. "Oh, that. We settled in New York." Tara thought Jason seemed to relax a little at the change in subject.

"But we lived there only a year before my father saw things weren't much different in New York than in the Old Country. When Uncle Salvatore died, my father inherited this property here in Phoenix — a small mortuary with the little house next door. So he packed us up and moved us. He operated the funeral parlor for a few years until he died. When I inherited it from him, I sold the mortuary and stayed in this house next door. The funeral director who bought it is pretty old now and doesn't take on much business."

Jason looked at his hands. "I wasn't interested in becoming a funeral director — oh, did I tell you I almost went to medical school?"

"No, you didn't. Why didn't you?"

"My father was too poor to send me. My uncles offered to pay my way, but I decided to study pharmacy instead."

"You never told me that."

"It's true. I worked in a pharmacy for a while — they were happy days. I got to talk to the customers — I made many friends there. But there were so many old people in pain — they couldn't get pain medication from their doctors, you see — I began selling them what they needed, just to make them more comfortable. They finally found out what I was doing, and took away my license." Jason shook his head. "I guess they'd rather see people in pain."

"So now you just work at the restaurant?"

"Yes. I have a trust fund, too — my uncles' doing — and I perform with my puppets." Jason was reminded to look at his watch. "Oh my, I've been talking so much I almost lost track of time."

He pushed the gurney up against the open oven door and tightened the restraints binding Tara to the thin plywood sheet on which she was lying.

"Please don't, Jason." Panic rising once again, she began to whimper at the fate awaiting her inside the dark oven. Once more she began straining against the restraints, but was unable to free herself.

"Don't worry, Tara," Jason said sadly, "You know I wouldn't hurt you. I'll give you something to make you sleep." Reaching into his shirt pocket, he withdrew a small syringe filled with a yellow liquid. Holding it in front of Tara's face, he smiled and said, "See? You won't feel a thing."

"Wait, Jason. Listen to me. *Please!*"

"This is not what I want to do. I'm sorry, but time has run out." He began to push her from the gurney to the rollers mounted on the bed of the oven.

"*Please*, Jason! If you let me go, I promise not to tell what happened here today. I swear it."

He slid her feet in first, then her thighs.

"Jason," Tara pleaded in desperation. "Don't you *see*? If you do this thing, it will be just like the time they killed your mother — "

"What? What did you say?" Jason stopped and moved to stand by her side. "What did you say?"

"Don't you see, Jason? If you kill me, it will be just like somebody's killing your mother — all over again." Now that she had regained his attention, her words came faster and faster. "I'm not a mother . . . yet . . . but I hope to be someday. I want to have children, too . . . a beautiful little girl, like your little sister."

"I don't . . . "

Tara saw her pleading was having an effect. "Oh, please, Jason!" she begged, "I want to be able to cuddle my own children, just like your mother did with you and your sister. I want to be able to watch them grow up, just like your mother watched you grow up. Just like she nurtured you, I want to comfort *my* children. If you do this thing to me it will be just as if she were being killed all over again . . . and — as if you were doing it, this time . . . and the screams you hear will be even louder. Besides, you'll be violating your own rules about who you send away. And you'll be just like *them*. Oh God, don't you *see* that?"

Jason hesitated while Tara's eyes were still able to see the concrete ceiling of the dimly-lit room. "Be like who?"

"Until now, you've just been killing — sending *bad* people away."

"That's the *only* kind I make disappear," he said, gesturing with the syringe.

"But don't you *see*?" she pleaded, as loudly as she could manage. "If you kill *me*, you'll be just like *them*! You'll be no better than the evil men you send away!"

Stunned, Jason threw up his hands as if to ward off the horrible thought. The sedative-fill syringe slipped from his grasp and shattered onto the floor.

CHAPTER THIRTY-ONE

Sirens screaming, Harry and the backup team screeched to a stop in front of Jason's house. Hearing the radio call, a TV team was right behind them, already pulling equipment from their van.

Detectives Drummel and Skirms drew their weapons and ran toward the back of the house in response to Harry's motioning.

Harry bounded across the sidewalk. At the front door, he punched the doorbell again and again. When there was no response, he banged on the door with his gun. Still no response.

"Police," he shouted. "Come out with your hands in the air and you won't be hurt. Do it now!" No response. Reaching for his cell phone, he fumbled for the notebook on which he'd written the number Narena had given him. He quickly punched in the number. One ring . . . two rings . . . three rings. No answer. "Open up," he shouted again. "Police."

Hearing the commotion, Drummel returned to the front of the house and stood near Harry as they aimed their guns toward the door.

"To hell with it," Harry said in complete frustration. Backing away from the door, he got set for a running start.

"Wait," Drummel said. "We don't have a search warrant. We don't even know for sure this guy really *is* the killer. You sure you wanna break it in with cameras rolling?"

"No choice. He could be killing her right now. I've *got* to! Back me up." What he didn't say was that he was taking the risk because the thought of something happening to Tara put a knot in his gut. "We can't take any chances." He ran at the door and bashed his shoulder into the old wood, splintering the jamb. He crashed into the house.

His gun leading the way, he quickly spotted the open basement door and ran toward it shouting, "Tara . . . Jason?" Leaping down the last three stairs, he landed in a crouch, ready to shoot. Taking in the scene at a glance, he saw Jason with his back turned, fiddling with the straps of an empty gurney standing against a wall. Tara was nowhere in sight.

"Stop what you're doing and put your hands in the air," he shouted, pulse racing, adrenaline pumping at full throttle. "Now!"

Jason complied instantly.

"What have you done with Tara?"

"Why, nothing at all. She's gone upstairs to the bathroom."

Harry ordered Jason to turn around and put his hands on the bench. Again, Jason complied. Harry patted him down and handcuffed his hands behind his back. "Jason Smalter, you're under arrest for the murder of — of Frankie Frangini." Frangini's was the first name that came to Harry's mind. *Hell with it. We can sort it out later.*

As Harry read the Miranda rights, Jason's mouth dropped open, his head tilting in puzzlement. "Who? I've never heard of anyone named Frangini."

"All clear," Harry shouted toward Drummel, who crouched in a shooting posture halfway down the stairs. "Go up and keep the press out of the house. And find Tara. We'll be up in a minute."

Drummel disappeared to carry out his task.

Leading Jason by the arm, Harry said, "We're going upstairs now. Tara had better be all right."

As they reached the top of the stairs, Tara staggered into view, her face ashen, hair mussed, front of her blouse wet. "What's going on?" she asked of Drummel. "I . . . I was freshening up and heard a lot of shouting."

"Are you all right?"

"Yes . . . yes, I'm fine. Why wouldn't I be?" She stood straighter to bolster the illusion she was unharmed. *Physically, I'm fine . . . but I'm a nervous wreck.*

Harry reached the top of the stairs, overhearing her last comment. "Because Narena called 911 and said you were in danger."

"Oh, I can explain — "

"It'll have to wait 'til we get to headquarters. Let's go." Harry started their trio moving toward the stairs. "There's a TV crew with a camera running outside, and neither of you is to answer any of their questions."

Tara hung back. "Wait. You were supposed to keep me in the background."

"Yeah. And you were supposed to *stay* in the background!" Harry said, the irritation in his voice not lost on her. "That was before we knew we had a serial killer on our hands, and while you still suspected someone at the shelter. It's too late for that now. Once they know the story, I suspect the press will turn you into a big heroine."

"Oh, God, Harry, they *mustn't*. They *can't*. The cops will swarm all over the shelter and the creeps will find us and try to get at their women. Can't you *do* something?"

"I'll do my best. Just don't say anything until we've had a chance to talk downtown. Then you can tell your story."

With Tara leading the way, Jason and Harry followed her up the stairs and out onto the porch. Unexpectedly, applause erupted from the mourners gathered on the porch of the mortuary next door. The screaming sirens had disrupted the cremation service and everyone had trickled outside in time to witness the drama.

The TV camera crew hadn't missed a moment — Harry bursting in through the front door, the trio emerging from the house, and the applauding mourners. No sooner had they reached street level than a reporter pushed a microphone into Harry's face. "Is this the serial killer?"

"We're just taking this man in for questioning."

"Is he under arrest?"

"No."

"Why is he in handcuffs then?"

"Just a precaution."

"How many did he kill?"

"I'm sure the public information officer will have a statement later in the day."

The microphone was next pushed into Tara's face. "What's your name, honey? Did he hurt you? Did he hold you hostage?"

Tara bristled. "No. I'm fine. Now go away and leave us alone. This isn't a circus, you know. Go away."

"Charlie," Harry said, "take this man downtown. I'll bring, uh, the lady, as soon as I brief the responding officers." He saw no reason to mention her name in public.

"Am I under arrest?" Her furrowed brow signaled her confusion about the rapid unfolding of unfamiliar events.

"No, of course not. Right now you're a material witness, and we need to ask you some questions about what happened here. All we know is what your friend told us, and it isn't much."

"*Nothing* happened here," Tara lied. "We were talking, that's all. He showed me his workshop and his puppets. Period."

Harry sneered. "Yeah, right! From the way you look right now I'd say a helluva lot happened. We'll talk about it later."

"I don't think I'll have anything useful to say."

"Yeah? Well, that's what we need to find out."

CHAPTER THIRTY-TWO

"We interrupt this program to bring you this special news bulletin. Less than an hour ago, the police arrested a suspect believed to be the serial killer..."

In a voice dripping with self-importance, the announcer described Harry crashing through the door to Jason's house, followed by a description of him bringing Jason to the porch in handcuffs. The report ended with some film of the curious mourners applauding on the porch next door.

"The suspect was apprehended in a daring capture by Detective Harry Shuman . . ."

"My God, Harry," Tara said, "that's the third time we've heard the same story in the last fifteen minutes. How many times are they going to repeat it?"

"They'll milk it for all they can. Catching a serial killer is big news."

After Jason had been questioned at police headquarters, he was taken to the Madison Street Jail down the street to be booked, fingerprinted, photographed, and locked up. It wasn't until days later that the media frenzy began to die down.

Tara waited in the squad room, while Harry obtained a search warrant allowing police to take a blood sample from Jason. He then laboriously attacked the inevitable paperwork.

During the paperwork marathon, other detectives took Tara to an interrogation room and questioned her about her visit to Jason's workshop. Stubborn to the end, she refused to tell investigators anything about the tunnel and what happened in the crematory room. *I promised not to tell in exchange for my life, and I will keep my promises.* She was, however, expansive about Jason's workshop and its inhabitants. When the frustrated detectives gave up, Harry offered to drive her to the car she had left parked at Jason's house.

During the drive, Harry struggled to keep his anger in check. *What the hell's the matter with you, woman?* He kept his eyes focused on the road.

"You're famous, you know," Tara said, pretending nothing had changed between them.

Harry grunted. "I don't want to spoil the moment, Tara, but you and I know I'm not the hero of this piece." The edge to his voice showed his anger. "It's no good, Tara. Why didn't you tell the investigators what happened in the basement?"

"I had nothing to tell them."

"Bull! They know you're lying, you know."

"I don't care. I told them all I could. I want *you* to be the hero, Harry. We agreed on that, and — "

"And if you told them what happened, they'd *know* I'm not a hero. Is that it?"

"That's not it and you know it. You burst into that house all alone, and you went down to the basement, knowing Jason could be holding me hostage, standing there waiting to shoot you. You thought I was in danger of my life. It took a lot of courage to do what you did, Harry. And *that's* what I told them . . . because every word of it is *true*." Tara turned to face him, hoping to charm him out of his anger.

"I appreciate the vote of confidence, but what did happen down there?"

Tara hesitated, lowering her head. "I've told them everything I can."

"That means you know more than you're telling. Were you asked if Jason admitted to the murders?"

Tara squeezed her lips together.

"I hope you realize you'll be called as a hostile witness at the trial. Maybe even arrested before then for interfering with an investigation."

"I told them everything I can," she repeated.

"How about telling *me*?"

"I can't."

"Why not?"

"I just can't . . . not yet." Tara was torn. She didn't want to lie to the police, and especially not to Harry whose intimacy she cherished. But she had promised Jason she wouldn't tell if he let her live, and she couldn't bear thinking of herself as a woman without honor. Desperate to change the subject, she said, "But there's something *you* can do for me."

"Oh, and what might that be?"

"You can follow me home and rub some of my sore muscles. It's been a very tense day and the feel of your strong fingers would be very relaxing." She wanted very much to find something that would dissolve his anger.

"Sorry, Tara, but this just isn't the time. I've got a lot of paperwork to do right now."

Jason Smalter sat in his small, barren cell, cold and alone. In the confusion of the arrest he'd neglected to ask for his sweater — just sitting in this air-conditioned cell made him shiver. He longed to be outside in the heat of the evening. His newly issued prison garb — pink underwear and overalls of black-and-white horizontal stripes — wasn't enough to keep him warm.

But it had been a harrowing, and surprising, afternoon; he welcomed the solitude. Still bewildered about the rapid stream of events leading to his present predicament, he let his mind drift back to its beginning. There was no question about it — it was, he thought, one of those situations of "he knew she knew," and "she knew he knew she knew." Finally, he could continue the charade no longer; he had to take action. It was the hardest thing he'd ever had to do. At the last moment, she said something making a bright light explode inside his head. He'd needed time to work through the effects of that emotional skyrocket. It had made him light-headed, as though a great weight had been removed from his chest. Whatever had happened — he wished he could remember what it was — made him realize that the vivid image of his blood-spattered mother crying out for revenge was at long last beginning to fade. Somehow, he no longer felt he had to "send people away."

The next thing he remembered, was their locking him in a small interrogation room. Except for the little wooden table and the two uncomfortable chairs, it was completely bare. Oh, there was a telephone on the table, but he didn't think it was there for his personal use. He sat for what seemed like hours — they'd taken his watch and other possessions, so he couldn't be sure. He *was* sure he was being observed, however, so he tried to remain calm, and moved as little as possible.

At long last, two detectives entered. Both wore short-sleeved shirts open at the collar. One carried a small tape recorder. They introduced themselves, but he didn't remember their names.

After reading him his rights again, he asked timidly,

"Is it really true that I have the right to remain silent?"

The detectives glanced at one another. "Yes, it is."

"Then I don't believe I have anything to say."

The black detective didn't seem upset by that announcement. "We just want to ask you a few questions to clarify some of the details of your arrest. Do you know why you've been arrested?"

"I believe the policeman who arrested me said something about murdering a man, but I don't remember the name he mentioned. I was very upset."

"Frankie Frangini."

"That was it. But I've never heard that name before. Was he a bad man?"

The detectives had looked hard at him, then at one another, before continuing.

"Am I going to need a lawyer?"

At that very moment the most amazing thing happened. The door opened and a stunning, red-headed woman strode into the little room. She was tall and fair, and in addition to her perfectly-coiffed hair, she was dressed like he imagined the president of a very large corporation would dress.

"Excuse me, gentlemen," she said. "I am Mr. Smalter's attorney in this matter. This interview is over."

Jason couldn't believe it. The interview over? Why, they hadn't even gotten out the rubber hoses yet.

"Hello, Countess," said the black detective.

To Jason, his long face said it all — the presence of the Countess was bad news. "What the hell are *you* doing here?" the detective continued. "This ain't some class action case where you can suck up another million or two in fees."

"And I'm glad to see you, too, detective. As I said, I'm representing Mr. Smalter in this matter." The iron in her voice was unmistakable. "This interview is over."

After some verbal skirmishing, the detectives had left the room and he was alone with the . . . the Countess?

She turned to him and said, "My name is Caliana Tunesco — call me Cally — and I want to represent you in this case."

"I'm — I'm overwhelmed," Jason managed to reply, "and flattered, but I'm sure I couldn't possibly afford your services." Jason could tell by her demeanor and expensive suit she was no nickel-and-dime attorney.

"Don't worry about that. I'm offering to take the case *pro bono* — free of charge."

Jason was stunned. After all the bad things that had happened, this was more good news than he was prepared to handle. "I — I don't know what to say."

"I'll tell you what to say. This room is being monitored by a video camera and a microphone, so your job is to say nothing at all. Absolutely nothing. From now on, you talk only to *me*. Understand?"

"But — "

She interrupted by jabbing a finger in his direction. "*Not* another word."

They'd come to take him to the jail then. Handcuffing him again, they led him to a police car and drove three blocks to the jailhouse — Madison Street Jail he thought they called it. Inside, they took off the handcuffs and made him turn out his pockets and give them his shoes and socks. Standing in his bare feet on the same concrete floor on which drug addicts, drunks, and the diseased, stood they had him lean against the steel plate mounted on a wall so they could search him. This done, he had to enter a tiny room and walk through a magnetometer naked to show he wasn't carrying contraband. It was totally humiliating.

I've never felt so ashamed in my life.

Worse, the pervasive smell of sweat, urine and vomit made him gag.

That's when they let him get dressed, photographed by a camera mounted near the ceiling, and then fingerprinted in another room down the hall. To get there he had to pass several cells in which people staggered around drunk, fell to their knees and threw up, or just passed out on the floor. Jason thought surely this must be the worst possible thing that could happen to him.

He was wrong.

Finally, in handcuffs and shackles, they took him to the sixth floor. There, they put him into a maximum security cell — alone.

Later that evening, his attorney — he liked the sound of that — met him in a visitation room. She tried to comfort him and told him she'd meet him at the arraignment, probably the following morning.

"Until then," she'd warned, "don't talk to anybody. It's your right." She smiled then, and seemed to soften a bit. "I'm very good at what I do, Mr. Smalter, and I'll do my very best for you." She stopped when she turned to leave, and turned back. "Is there anything you need?"

"My friend Scootch. He's one of my puppets, the white-haired fellow sitting on my workbench. I could use his company. I'm sure it will be very lonely here."

"I'll see what I can do."

Jason had never even been inside a jail before. He worried what would happen next. Holding his head in his hands, he thought he understood why so many prisoners vomited during the booking ordeal. He shook his head in wonderment at his lack of knowledge about how the justice system worked. And then another thought occurred to him. *Why, that attorney didn't even ask if I was guilty.*

CHAPTER THIRTY-THREE

Sergeant Brunkel closed the door to his office, carefully arranged himself in his chair, and stared hard-eyed at Harry the Shoe. "I don't get it, Harry," he said, shaking his head. "What the hell ever possessed you to pull a bonehead stunt like that?"

"Like what?"

"Knock it off. You know damn well what I'm talking about. Bashing in a door with gun drawn, no search warrant — no vest — the TV camera's rolling? What made you think we had enough evidence against this Smelter guy to arrest him — or any evidence at all? Have you become suicidal all of a sudden? Come on, explain it to me. If you can."

"I had probable cause, Sarge — exigent circumstances. I had reason to believe the lady was in mortal danger." Harry explained the call from Narena. "I didn't know it, but the latest murder convinced my CI this Jason Smalter was the killer. She started trailing him around to find out for sure. She says she didn't want to accuse anyone without really good reason. I assumed when she told Narena — her nurse friend — that Smalter was the killer, she knew what she was talking about."

"Uh-huh. So how did she end up in his basement?"

"She began to suspect him while visiting the pediatric hospital and realized he could be getting information about his victims from the battered kids. So she showed interest in his work as a ventriloquist. That led to an invitation to visit his workshop — "

"Yeah. 'Come up and I'll show you my etchings,' said the spider. Go on."

"She called her friend Narena. Told her Jason was the killer and that she was heading for the appointment to make sure. Narena was alarmed, but Tara was convinced Smalter wouldn't hurt her — she didn't fit his criteria for victim selection. Narena wanted to call the police right then and there, but Tara pleaded to be given two hours at Smalter's workshop. Narena had ants in her pants the whole time, but as promised . . . she waited. She finally called 911 and was bucked to me."

"And you picked up your lance, climbed onto your white charger, and thundered away to save the lady in distress."

"Something like that. Only she wasn't in distress. I don't know what happened down there, but by the time I stormed the castle walls, Jason was alone in the basement fiddling with the straps of a gurney."

"Where was your CI?"

"In the bathroom freshening up. I dunno, Sarge. Something happened down there — she was pretty shaken up when she came out of the bathroom — but she won't talk to me about it. She won't even tell me *why* she won't tell me."

"Why are you so sure something happened?"

"The change. She goes in scared, certain Smalter is the killer — Narena said as much. Some two hours later they're acting like nothing happened. She looks mussed up, her face is white as a sheet and her blouse is wet. It doesn't add up. Something *happened*."

"Look, Harry, no matter what happened down there, the press is making you out to be a hero for catching a serial killer, and the brass upstairs isn't going to discourage them. They figure we can use a little good press about now. They're busting their buttons for a chance to tell the press how they caught a serial killer."

"So why don't I feel like a hero?"

"Harry, I know how you're feeling, but I'm telling you to go along with it. It'll be good for all of us." Brunkel chuckled. "Something else. It ought to scare hell out of the woman-bashers — now the copy-cats will be after the creeps this Smalter guy hasn't killed yet."

Harry nodded his acquiescence.

"So what's your plan?"

"First thing is to tie Smalter to the crimes. We're getting a search warrant so we can toss his house and match his shoes to the bloody footprints we got from the Frangini crime scene."

Brunkel made a note on his desk pad. "What else?"

"We're taking a closer look at the physical evidence we've collected on the other cases. But I gotta tell you, I'm not sure there's much there that'll connect him to the kills. If Smalter's the perp, he doesn't leave much behind. We've got to find more evidence."

"What about the Tibbetts case?"

Harry frowned. "You lost me."

"Maybe Smalter is the guy wrote the letter that went to the governor . . ."

Harry nodded vigorously and poked a finger toward Brunkel. "Right. The *signature*. If Smalter signed that letter, we've got him, although I'm not sure for what, other than doing another good deed by calling attention to the Tibbetts pervert."

"The ADA can sort that out. You seem to be on the right track, as usual. Go to it."

Harry began to rise, then froze half-crouched and stared off into space.

"When you go glassy-eyed like that I know you've got a bug up your ass. What is it?"

"I just had a wild idea. It'll sound crazy, but here it is. Tara told me about Scootch — that's the name of the sidekick he told Tara he talks to while he works — the alter ego he discusses his troubles with. Tara told me ventriloquists talk to their dummies all the time. Part of their practice routine. She said this Scootch dummy was sitting on the workbench while Smalter showed her how things worked. This morning I learned that Smalter had the Countess ask to have this Scootch brought to his cell. Said he could use the company."

Brunkel knew enough to keep quiet when Harry was working through a thought.

"I was thinking maybe we ought to interview the dummy."

"What makes you think that would help?" Brunkel managed to say with a straight face.

"This Scootch dummy has got to know what happened in that basement. He's a witness."

Brunkel frowned and remained silent. Seeing Harry's face droop, he said quickly, "No, no, I like it. It's a crazy idea, and we just might get laughed out of the Department, but if he's as close to this dummy as you say, it just might work. But we'd have to be very careful how we set it up. I can just see the headline if the press gets wind of it. 'Hero detective interrogates dummy'."

"And the subhead will read, 'Dummy demands lawyer.'"

Brunkel added, "Yeah, and the political cartoon will show you beating on it with a rubber hose."

They laughed longer than the joke warranted. It'd been a long day and the release of tension felt good.

"Ahh," Brunkel said when he finally realized the state of affairs. "We'll think on this again tomorrow, but . . . right now . . . I'm taking you, the department hero, out for a celebration. On me."

CHAPTER THIRTY-FOUR

Cally Tunesco knocked on the door of the room off the visitor's area where Jason already waited. When the jailer unlocked it, she entered and motioned to the guard. "Can you give us a few minutes?"

The jailer left and locked the door behind her.

"I'm afraid I struck out on the dummy. To be honest, they laughed when I asked about bringing it in. Sorry."

"That's all right. Thanks for trying."

"How are you holding up, Jason? Did you manage to sleep any, last night?"

"A little. What's going to happen to me now?"

"This afternoon we'll go downstairs to the court for the arraignment. Once the case is called, it'll take only a minute or two for the charge to be read accusing you of the murder of Frankie Frangini. We'll plead not guilty, of course. I'll try to get the judge to set bail, but this is a murder case."

Jason smiled.

"You find that funny?"

Jason looked up and shook his head slowly. "I didn't have anything to do with that murder. I never even heard of anyone named Frangini until the detective who arrested me mentioned it."

Tunesco's eyebrows raised. "You *didn't*? Well! Well! Won't they be surprised when they discover the bloody footprints don't match anything in your closets." She looked hard into Jason's eyes. "They won't, will they?"

"No, they won't. I tell you I had nothing to do with that murder. I swear it."

She made a note in a red leather notebook with a gold ball-point pen. "Try not to worry."

"They're going to execute me, aren't they?"

"Not if I have anything to say about it," she smiled with confidence. "And I intend to have a *lot* to say."

The arraignment went as Cally had predicted, except bail was denied. Cally tried to convince the judge Jason wasn't a flight risk, but the prosecutor argued that, "This is a capital murder case and Jason should be remanded without bail. There are nine murders here, not just one."

In the end, the prosecutor had her way, and Jason was led back to his cell.

The arrest of Jason Smalter still led the stories on the ten o'clock news. By then the arrest itself was old hat, though the footage showing Harry bursting single-handedly through the door, then appearing with the suspect, was repeated many times. What was new was the description of Jason Smalter himself. Reporters seemed surprised to learn that Jason was a well-known volunteer entertainer at the Marvella Snitskin-Pruitt Children's Hospital, revered by all who knew him. And that he had amused all who saw him at work. The newspapers took delight in contrasting his life of community service with his alleged life of crime.

"How can such a mild-mannered man do the terrible things of which he stands accused?" they asked. That didn't stop them from spinning bizarre theories, however, to explain the apparent contradiction.

Another reporter had discovered Jason's employment at Bellissimo's. Interviews with Jason's satisfied customers followed:

"I can't believe he did it. Jason's a scream . . . and that parrot on his shoulder is even funnier."

"Jason? I'm certain they've arrested the wrong man. We won't make a reservation there unless they guarantee Jason will be our server."

"He's an incredibly talented entertainer, as well as a fine waiter. If you've never heard a parrot with an Italian accent, be sure to book one of his tables for dinner. You'll have a ball."

Yet another reporter spent the afternoon interviewing neighbors and victims of the men Jason had allegedly murdered.

"If he *is* the killer, I thank my God for a man like Jason. He saved my life and the life of my baby."

"He's been our neighbor for seven years. Always smiling and pleasant. Never forgets our children at Christmas. I will pray for him."

"Death penalty? For what? Doing what the police should've been doing all along? Some justice system — ha!"

"If somebody hadn't killed *my* vicious husband, I'd be dead by now."

A nurse from the pediatric ward of the Children's Hospital summarized, "Jason sheds real tears when he hears the stories battered children tell his cuddly lion. It rips your heart out to watch. No way a man like that can be a murderer."

During the next twenty-four hours, network reporters and TV crews poured into Phoenix. Filling up hotel rooms, they got into each other's way trying to interview everyone even remotely connected with the big story of the serial killer arrest.

Colima Sanchez, Jason's housekeeper, claimed, "I clean his house two times each month. I know all the corners and closets. I never find nothing look like a killer's tools."

An interview with the police Public Information Officer must have brought chills to the city's violent predators. "Though it's early in the investigation, our evidence clearly shows the killings to be the work of one person," he said. "We also know that if Mister Smalter is the serial killer, he targets only men who have been violent toward women or children."

The PIO went on to describe some of the killer's victims, concluding by saying, ". . . and if I were a wife-beater I'd be shaking in my boots worrying that I'd be next."

"But why should they worry . . . now that Smalter's behind bars?" a reporter asked.

"Because a high-profile case like this almost always brings out the copycats. I'm afraid our police force may be in for a busy month."

"Serial killers are always sadists who attack their victims sexually, isn't that right?" another eager reporter asked.

"No, it isn't. Though serial killers usually rape or in some other way violate their victims sexually, that's not the case here. There is no evidence at all of sexual misconduct in the cases under investigation."

By the following noon, the talk shows were again churning the airwaves with the story. Heated debates took up all sides of the issue.

"Jason is guilty of the most heinous crimes imaginable."

"He didn't do it. Jason was doing the work of God. Judge not lest ye be judged."

Some rebutted with, "He was doing the work of the Devil."

A fourth viewpoint attacked the police. "What husbands do to their women is no business of the law. Jason was saving lives, and besides, the cops should be taking the drunk drivers off the streets instead of hounding poor Jason."

"Jason is nothing but a vigilante," a final argument warned. "Men like him must be stopped. What's to keep anybody else from doing the same thing?"

Every talk show host continued the informal polling. The results showed that up to seventy percent of their listeners favored clemency for Jason. Then a new voice was heard, "Hello, Claudia, you're on the air."

"Yes. I want to tell everyone that I'm the chairwoman of *Women for Jason*, and that there will be a rally in front of the court house at nine tomorrow morning. Every woman who's ever suffered the brutality of a Neanderthal husband or boyfriend should be there."

"Okay, you got your message on the air. May I ask the purpose of this *Women for Jason* movement?"

"We want the authorities to know we women are sick and tired of being swept under the rug. We're victims, too, you know. Over and over again. Jason's doing what the police and courts can't — or won't — do, and we're taking up a collection for his defense."

"Wow! That certainly should send a message. Thanks for the call."

"We've got a problem, Sarge," Harry said, idly flipping pages in his notebook.

"You're gonna tell me the bloody footprints at the Frangini crime scene don't match any of Smalter's shoes. Right?"

"How the hell did you know that?"

Brunkel waved a hand toward the telephone. "I just talked to the ME. They're not even close. Smalter wears a size ten, and the bloody footprints are at least a twelve. That means, Shoe, that unless we come up with evidence tying this suspect to a crime within the next few hours, we'll have to cut him loose. The Countess pleaded her client 'not guilty' at the arraignment this morning when Smalter was charged with the Frangini thing."

"Can't we find some excuse for keeping him a little longer?"

"Not with the Countess on file as his defense attorney. She'd scream all the way to the Supreme Court. No, sir, you've got to get your gang to work and burn shoe-leather. Take a team out to Smalter's house and give it another going over. *Now!* Go back and take shoe sizes at the shelters — hospitals, too. If Smalter isn't the perp, somebody else is, and he's still out there. Get everybody you can find to work on it. You know what'll happen when the press finds out we had to let him go?"

"Nothing good, that's for sure." Harry struggled to his feet and headed for the door, only to turn back. "At least we know we were right about a second killer. I'm on my way." *So much for the hero celebration. But it was nice while it lasted.*

CHAPTER THIRTY-FIVE

Detective Harry the Shoe and his team of investigators scoured Jason's house for a second time in as many days. It was a fruitless search. "They found not one scrap of useful evidence in the house or basement workshop, just a lot of puppets and parts." The lab boys summarized in detail. "We inspected every nook and cranny, every drawer and every closet's contents, even dismantled wall sockets and light fixtures. Nothing! Either the guy's as clean as a new penny or he knows all the tricks."

"C'mon, guys," Drummel reminded unnecessarily, "unless we can tie the perp to these killings, the DA'll have to cut him loose. He could run, and there won't be anything we can do about it."

"Hey, isn't Skirms reviewing the case files again?"

"I just checked with her a few minutes ago. She hasn't found anything we can use. With the exception of Frangini, it still looks as though the other kills were done by the same perp, but we can't make Smalter for any of them. Dammit, we're missing something."

"Tara, I've got to talk to you. It's urgent."

"I can't leave the shelter for another four hours, Harry. Can we do it over the phone?"

"These phones leak like sieves. All right if I run out to the shelter? I could meet you out back for a few minutes. This is urgent."

"I suppose. I'll meet you on the back lawn in fifteen minutes. There's a little bench there."

Harry headed out the door before the phone stopped vibrating in its cradle. Within minutes he had driven into the driveway leading to the delivery entrance of the shelter and parked.

Tara waved as he closed his car door. "We can sit here for a few minutes," she said, pointing to a concrete bench. "Now, what's so urgent?"

"Tara, Jason was arraigned yesterday for the murder of Frankie Frangini. We thought it was a slam-dunk, but when his lawyer pleaded him 'not guilty', we began feeling a little uneasy. An hour later we discovered the evidence doesn't point to Jason at all. *Nothing* matches."

"I don't understand what you're telling me."

"Tara, unless we can find evidence that ties him to at least *one* of the murders, he's going to be released any minute now."

Tara didn't know how to feel about that unexpected development. She was glad he was arrested for the murders — she knew he was guilty. Even so, her spirits soared at the thought of Jason going free. She understood why he did what he did. Besides, she liked him. A kind and gentle man, he enjoyed being kind and helpful to others. But no matter how evil his victims, she didn't condone his actions . . . justice was a job for the courts. She shook her head, confused at her ambivalence.

"Tara, you've *got* to tell me what happened in the basement."

Tara's eyes widened. She hadn't expected that to be the purpose of Harry's urgent visit. Her body stiffening, she looked away.

"All we have is Narena's statement that you told her Jason is the murderer, along with her 911 call announcing you were in danger. You've got to help us."

"What happens if you have to let him go?"

"*Jeezus*, Tara," Harry exploded. "We arrested the man because you made us believe you were in danger. How can you just sit there now and not tell us what you know?"

"I promised."

"You *promised*?" Harry shot to his feet, then paced in fury. "You made a promise to a man you believe to be a serial killer?" Harry couldn't believe what he was hearing. "Promised *what*, for God's sake?"

Tara's body sagged. "I promised I wouldn't tell what happened in the basement if he wouldn't hurt me . . ."

Harry stopped pacing and stood facing her, slamming a fist into his palm. "I knew it! Something *did* happen down there. He threatened you, didn't he? Tell me, Tara. Did he try to kill you?"

Tara's head drooped, her right hand nervously rubbing the knuckles of her left. "I . . . I can't."

He stopped in front of her, planting his feet and jamming his fists onto his hips. "Look, Tara. This isn't a game. When I report this conversation to my superiors they may have you arrested for obstruction of justice. It's as simple and as serious as that."

Tara looked up to see Harry facing her, hands on hips. His look said he meant every word. But she'd made a promise to Jason in return for her life. She couldn't go back on her word. Her mind raced. How could she give him what he needs without breaking her promise?

Desperation forced a small thought into her brain and nourished itself into a tiny reed of hope. "Harry, I can't tell you what happened . . . but I'll tell you something that might help you."

"Hurry, Tara, the clock is running."

"There's a secret tunnel in the basement — "

"What? Where does it go? What's it for? How do we find it?" Harry reached for the phone in his pocket.

Tara told him, and Jason punched Drummel's number into his cell phone. "Charlie?" Where are you now?"

"We just buttoned up out here at the Smalter house. We're about to — "

"Stop. You've got to go back. There's a secret tunnel in the basement."

"What? No way. We thumped every wall — "

"Never mind that. Here's how to find it. Stand with your back against the workbench. The tunnel is behind the wall you'll be facing."

"No way! There's nothing there but a concrete block wall."

Harry told him how to find the hidden latch. "You'll have to push pretty hard — the door is part of the cinderblock wall itself, so it's heavy — that's why you didn't hear anything hollow when you thumped. It swings on a track arcing to the right. Got it?"

"Sonuvabitch! Hold the phone — I'm heading down the stairs." Drummel stood with his back to the workbench to get his bearings, then strode across the room and reached high above him to feel for the latch. Hearing a faint click, he pushed, then pushed harder as part of the wall began to move inward. "You're right. The wall moves inward." He breathed the musty air moving into the warmer room. "Phew, the air's pretty stale. You say there's a light switch?"

"Yeah. It's an old ceramic one you have to twist."

"Got it." Drummel entered the tunnel with gun drawn. "Where does this go?" he asked when he'd bathed the musty tunnel in pale amber light.

Harry heard only a crackling — the phone signal was now blocked by the brick wall and several feet of earth above it. He returned the phone to his pocket and sat beside Tara. Wiping her tears with his handkerchief, he said gently, "Thanks, Tara."

"What will happen to me now?"

"Depends on what we find. If we find evidence that'll tie him to the murders, nothing. If we don't, we'll have to ask you some more questions. You're our only *living* witness." He stressed "living."

"But I didn't see any murders . . ."

"That doesn't matter. You were part of something that could give us some vital information. Tara, we haven't had any luck in nailing this killer. We've got lots of circumstantial evidence, but nothing pointing to Jason as the doer. Dammit, I put a lot on the line by trusting your intuition; now you're trying to pretend the whole thing was just a lark — "

"That's unfair."

"That's a pretty shabby thing to do to a guy who busted his ass to save your very lovable neck. Almost lost my job." He rose facing her and poked a finger at her nose. "As much as I wish it were otherwise, you're likely to play a key role at the trial of Jason Smalter."

CHAPTER THIRTY-SIX

Cally strode toward Jason's cell, followed by a jailer.

"Pack your bags, Jason," she called. "You're getting out of here."

Jason, curled into a ball in one corner of the old bunk, opened his eyes. "Huh?"

"You're free to go. They don't have a case against you and the judge had to grant us the habeus."

The jailer signaled for the door to be opened. When he heard the click, he slid it open. Jason looked around to make sure he had all his possessions — which were none — and stepped into the corridor, shoulders sagging with relief. "I guess I still don't understand what's happening."

"I'll explain as soon as we get you out of here."

The out-processing took more than an hour. To Cally, it seemed as though every clerk worked in slow motion. There were stacks of forms to be completed and signed, Jason's few pocket possessions to be released, before the two of them walked out of the jail into the heat of the fall, desert day. Cally led him to her car in the parking lot and drove out as quickly as she could.

"We've got to get you someplace where they won't find you without some effort."

"Why?" Jason asked. "I thought I was free."

"For now. They're pretty pissed about having to let you go, and they're going to bust a gut to find a reason to arrest you again. Home is the last place you want to go right now."

"But I didn't kill that Frangini person."

"It won't matter. There are eight other murders they want to hang on you." Cally wanted desperately to ask Jason if he was the serial killer. If he admitted the crimes, she wasn't ethically bound to report it — only crimes he confessed he *intended* to commit. In the end, she decided it would be better not to know. "First, though, we've got to stop at the police station and get your suitcase out of the property room. Shouldn't take long."

"Can I ask you a question?"

Cally stopped with her hand on the door and turned to face Jason. "Of course, but let's do it on the run."

"Why are you doing this for me?"

Cally paused only a moment before she replied, her voice hard as granite, "Because I know what its like to be locked up for something I didn't do."

"Harry? Can you hear me, Harry?" Drummel stood in the dimly-lit secret room under the old crematory. When he realized why his phone wasn't working, he raced back through the tunnel, up the basement stairs and out to the porch. Punching in the number again, he finally heard Harry's voice. "Harry? You won't believe this."

"Wait one." Harry pulled to the curb and stopped his car. "Go."

"The tunnel extends into a room under the mortuary next door, and there's a crematory in that room."

"So? It's a mortuary."

"Yeah, but get this — there's no way in or out of the room except through the tunnel. No doors, no stairs, no windows. Nothing. No way can it be part of the mortuary upstairs."

Mind racing, Harry said nothing.

"Harry? You there?"

"Yeah, I'm here. Hold on a minute." A few seconds later his voice boomed into the phone. "Jeezus! That's it! The crematory. That's how the perp gets rid of some of his bodies. He just cremates 'em in his own private furnace."

"Holy shit!"

"I'll bet that's what happened to the bodies for the missing dates. Charlie, get back down there and close that door before any of the evidence is disturbed. Plaster crime scene tape all over the place and get the lab boys in there as fast as you can."

"Okay, but I didn't see anything in that room other than the furnace."

"Doesn't matter. There's bound to be some leftovers in the oven."

"Leftovers?"

"Never mind. Just do it. Talk to you later." Harry disconnected, and immediately punched in Sergeant Brunkel's number. Drumming his fist on the steering wheel while waiting for the connection, he cursed the maddeningly slow circuits. Finally, he heard Sergeant Brunkel's voice. "Sarge? Shoe. Is Smalter still in custody?"

"No. They had to let him go. His lawyer was about to tear down the place."

"How long ago?"

"About twenty, thirty minutes."

"Damn!" Harry filled Brunkel in on what Drummel had just told him.

"That's interesting, but until the crime scene gang is finished, we won't know if we have anything to go with. Stay with 'em, Harry, and keep me informed."

Word of Jason's release raced like wildfire through the jail, the court house, and into the media. Within minutes, the news was flashed across the airwaves.

"Alleged serial killer released for lack of evidence," was the theme, embellished by rehashes of the murders of child rapists and women batterers. Radio talk show hosts made it a point to repeat over and over that the "alleged" serial killer was again on the loose and that anyone contemplating mayhem against women and children had better think again. Only one such host suggested that if Jason were indeed "not guilty," the killer should be described as "still on the loose."

"Junaya, you're on the air."

"Well, you don' know he the killa'. He ain't had no trahl yet. Ah think you jest tryin' to stir up the public so you kin git more folks to listen to your honky station."

"Thank you, Junaya. Mike, you're on the air."

"What kind of a police force do we have if they catch the guy and then can't hold on to him?"

"Mike, I understand your frustration, man. But the guy ain't had a fair trial yet and — "

"Yeah? How fair is it to let him go so he can go out and kill some more innocent husbands?"

"Aha. Mike, could you be one of the husbands he'd be gunning for, by any chance . . .?" No answer. "I guess Mike hung up. Carlana, you're on the air."

"You remember that woman you had on from the *Women for Jason* movement?"

"Yes, of course. What about her?"

"Could you give me her name or address or something so I can send a check?"

"You want to send financial support for a killer?"

"No. Not for a killer. I want to help make sure he gets a fair trial so *both* sides of the story can come out — whatever they are."

"All right, stay on the line and one of the staff will give it to you off-line." The following three callers made similar requests.

Sprinkled throughout the calls were those from desperate women hoping to get their full names and addresses on the air so Jason would please kill their rotten husbands or stalking boyfriends.

Similar callers deluged every talk show chewing on the release of Jason Smalter, on his chances of a fair trial in the midst of the widespread publicity, on his probable whereabouts, or on the date of his next murder. Few paid attention to the issue of his guilt or innocence.

The police switchboard lit up, routing all calls to Detective Steve Carver, Public Information Officer. He repeatedly released as much information as he could without endangering the ongoing investigation. He was a busy man. By the end of the day, his telephone ear burned.

It was an even busier weekend.

Television news teams camped in the street, using the police headquarters building as a backdrop while continually interrupting their regularly scheduled programming with yet another "breaking news bulletin."

"Shoe? I need to talk to you as soon as your little feet can carry your ass down here."

"Be there in five." Harry finished typing the sentence he was writing into the report of the "tunnel caper," and scampered for Brunkel's office.

"Sit," Brunkel said, pointing at a chair. "We got the handwriting report on the Tibbetts signature. They compared it with Smalter's signature, and they're pretty sure he wrote it."

"Pretty sure? What's that mean?"

"It means Smalter was trying to imitate Tibbett's signature, and was therefore copying the Tibbetts style as closely as he could. There are enough points of comparison, though, to give the DA a good case that Smalter was the forger."

Harry sat back in the chair and propped his left ankle on his right knee. "Okay, so say Smalter wrote the letter and forged the signature. Where does that get us?"

"It is my distinct impression that *you* are the detective. So detect."

Harry made a face. "I just hate it when you do that. Okay, mister high and mighty, here's what I think. Smalter writes the letter and signs Tibbetts' name, knowing we'll see through the forgery in a minute. So will the jury. They'll know he was trying to call attention to Tibbetts and, since no fraud was

182

involved — he didn't forge a check or anything else — I don't see a crime was committed worth chewing on. All it does is let us charge Tibbetts with threatening the governor, and that won't be worth two cents." Harry rose and began to pace. "However — " Harry said, swirling toward Brunkel and jabbing the air with a finger.

"Aha. I believe I detect the smell of a detecting detective."

"It does give us something to talk to Mr. Smalter about next time we meet up with him."

"To wit?"

"How does he get his information? How does he find out who's in serious need of killing? He doesn't seem to want to talk about his kills, but maybe we can get him to brag about the ways he's screwing over the lives of his lesser victims."

"Lesser victims. I like that. What does the ADA say?"

"I talked to 'Buns' Markova about it yesterday. She agrees there's nothing there worth wasting time on. Not when we've got nine murders to prosecute."

"You keep that up and one of these days you'll call her 'Buns' to her face."

"Already did. I apologized, and she confided she was kinda proud of having earned *some* kind of nickname. I guess she was feeling a little invisible among all the big people."

"You're lucky. One of our young lawyers made the mistake of calling her 'Tits' Markova."

"Yeah? What happened?"

"She belted him one. Couldn't see out of his left eye for three days. Anyhow, we'll keep the Tibbetts thing in our back pockets — you never know when it'll be just the card we need."

CHAPTER THIRTY-SEVEN

Dr. Fred Millston, Medical Examiner, placed a bulging briefcase on the small conference table in the office of Captain Darryl Portono, Chief of Homicide. Millston had called Portono at his home the evening before to make the appointment — he hoped Portono's home phone would allow a private conversation. "Police departments have more ears than sense," he was fond of saying. "The matter I want to discuss is disturbingly sensitive."

"Sorry I bothered you at home, Chief, but something touchy has come up. Frankly, I'm not sure what to do with it."

Portono got up, told his secretary he would be unavailable until further notice, and closed the door. "Is there anyone else we should have at this meeting?"

"I'd rather let you make that decision, if you don't mind."

"All right." He motioned for Millston to proceed.

Millston let out a long breath, leaned his forearms on the table and laced his fingers tightly together before speaking. "This is going to be difficult. Bear with me if I don't tell it well." He reached into a pocket and unfolded a somewhat wrinkled piece of paper he found there. "This has to do with the murder of Frankie Frangini. I believe you're familiar with that case?"

"Yes, of course." No offense was taken at the implication the chief might not recall the "fly-in-the-ointment" case.

"When the ADA had to release Jason Smalter for lack of evidence, Homicide sent the teams back out to do a more thorough investigation of ground they'd already covered. One of the teams was assigned to investigate the staff at the Bramwell Convalescent Center — battered women's shelter — to see if they could find a suspect matching the considerable physical evidence we collected at the Frangini crime scene. But of course you know all that." Millston paused before continuing.

"I take it you hit pay dirt?"

Millston nodded. "Good news and bad news — very bad. The director of the Center, Dr. Marla Benarez, is known to be totally militant and aggressively protective of her residents, so Detective Shuman asked that she be checked out very carefully. She was. Her feet were obviously smaller than the size twelve shoe-prints found at the scene, but it's no trick to wear larger shoes to mislead pursuers. When she was asked for a DNA sample, however, she hit the ceiling and threatened all sorts of dire actions. You know — how dare anyone suspect her of anything but the loftiest of motives, and so on. Team said she sounded like somebody trying to hide something."

Portono nodded, but heard that line as many times from the guilty as from the innocent.

"While Dr. Benarez was being interviewed, another team talked to George Petacki, the security guard. He's a retired cop, as you probably know, but the teams were ordered to be thorough and check out *all* the staff. To make a long story shorter, Petacki was quite willing to talk to the detectives — Drummel and Dirnbaum — and suggested they go with him to his home, a cottage on the property, where he had something to show them.

"This seemed a little unusual, but they went along with it and walked with Petacki to his house. They accompanied Petacki to his bedroom, where he proceeded to dig a sealed cardboard file box from the back of a closet. It was labeled, 'Hand deliver to the Medical Examiner — Confidential.' He asked the detectives to hand the box to me personally. In private."

Portono shook his head sadly. "I don't like the smell of what I'm guessing happened next."

Running a nicotine-stained hand through his hair, Millston nodded. "When Petacki told the detectives the box contained everything they needed, they thought he was talking about evidence against Dr. Benarez, the director. So they did as they were asked."

"That was a mistake. But go on."

"As soon as I was alone, I opened the box. It contained a pair of bloody shoes — size twelve, a blood-spattered shirt, and a large brown envelope containing three file folders." Millston reached into his briefcase and placed three file folders on the table in front of the captain. "These contain photographs of the most depraved acts anyone could possibly commit against the women who, in better days, were Frangini's wife and two daughters." He wiped a knuckle over the dampness in his eye and shook his head. "Darryl, I spend my days and nights looking at the victims of the most grotesque variety of perverted acts, but they pale by comparison."

Portono sat perfectly still, allowing Millston to finish his narration.

"I've got to tell you, Darryl, if I had seen these pictures while Frangini was still alive, I might have gladly killed him myself. But I wouldn't have been as merciful as Petacki apparently was. I'd have made sure the demented sonuvabitch would have taken *days* to die." Millston leaned back in the chair and sighed. "Nobody knows about the contents of this box but you and me. As I said, I didn't know what to do with it — I guess I thought you'd want to be filled in before it was entered into the evidence book."

"Thanks, Fred. I appreciate your thoughtfulness." Portono ran his fingertips along the edges of the folders. "Why in the world would a retired cop — I assume he had a clean record?"

"Squeaky. I've been thinking about that myself. Darryl, this man spends his working days around victims of some of the worst cowards of all — wife beaters, rapists. When he was on the job he used to have the authority to *do* something about those scumbags. Now, he's expected simply to grin and bear it."

"I see your point. Probably he just couldn't take it one day or something, and went out and beat one of them to death."

"Uh-huh. I hate to say it, but I'll bet it felt good, too. Can anything be done?" Millston asked.

"About Petacki's situation?"

Millston nodded.

"I don't know. We can't suppress the evidence — sooner or later you'll have to put it on the record. The detectives who handed it to you know the box exists and will be curious about its contents." Millston banged his open palms on the table and stood. "Oh, my god! You don't suppose Petacki has gone and done something foolish, do you?"

"You mean like eat his gun? I've wondered about that."

"Why didn't you say something?"

Portono looked directly into Millston's eyes. "Fred, I was thinking if he *did* pull the plug . . ."

"I see where you're going. That *would* solve the problem, wouldn't it? Jeez, I really feel sorry for his son."

"We really ought to find out what's happening there."

"If he did pull the plug, we'd know about it by now, wouldn't we?"

"Probably. Tell you what. Give me an hour to think about this. But unless I can come up with something better, I'll take it directly to the commissioner and ask his advice. No matter how this goes, he needs a 'heads up' before this hits the press. Then I'll ask you to fill Brunkel and Shoe in on what's going down."

"Shoe?" Millston asked.

"He's heading the investigation. He needs to know. I'll get back to you as soon as I know something."

"What'll I do with the evidence?"

"It should be safe in my desk for an hour or so." Millston got up to leave. "Fred, what have you found out about the stuff my guys bagged at the funeral home?"

"My lab rats are working it now. I'll call you as soon as it's processed."

CHAPTER THIRTY-EIGHT

Tara dragged herself through her Monday shift. It was the hardest workday of her life. Everything reminded her how angry Harry was with her. Since their Saturday confrontation, he hadn't contacted her, and everything she looked at seemed to tell her their relationship was melting into nothingness. Worse yet, she didn't know what to do about it.

Totally frustrated, she threw on her jogging outfit, fled out the door, and ran down the street as hard as she could manage. Later, winded, hungry and exhausted, she dropped onto a park bench to watch an old man feed the pigeons crowding around him. For some reason, it angered her that neither the old man or the pigeons seemed to have a care in the world. Holding her head between her hands, she began to sob.

"Excuse me." The old man had come near to sit quietly beside her on the bench. "Excuse me, but I was saddened to see you . . . surely it can't be as bad as all that." His voice was soft and soothing. "Please . . .I mean no offense."

"It's all right," she said. "None taken."

"You know," he continued, "I've sat on this very bench when I've felt overwhelmed by events, and somehow just sitting here always seems to help."

Tara looked up into the wrinkled face then, warmed by the smile crinkling the skin around the old man's eyes. "Thank you," she managed to mumble.

"Tell me. Can you remember something that happened to you as a little girl that made you think the world was coming to an end?"

Tara was puzzled by the change of subject, but searched her memory in spite of herself. "Yes. I think I was seven. I didn't get the pony I was sure Santa was going to bring me."

"Did your world come to an end then?"

"It did for that day. I'd already told all my friends I was getting a white pony and would give them all a ride. I was totally wrecked when I thought about having to tell them the pony never came."

"What happened when you told them?"

Tara paused as she recalled the moments. "Nothing much, as I remember. They'd pretty much forgotten all about it."

"So . . . would you say the disaster just sort of dissolved into thin air? Without any help from you?"

"Okay, now I know what you're doing." Without willing it to happen, Tara smiled.

He reached out and put her hand on his.

"Thank you," she continued. "Now you tell me something. Are you an angel or something sent to cheer me up?"

The old man handed her a small bag of peanuts and said, "Why don't we just sit here a bit and feed these insatiable pigeons?"

While they sat together, tossing food to the cooing birds, Tara breathed more deeply, her racing mind slowing to a lazy trot. Gradually, she began thinking about her situation without the distortion of a roiling haze of emotion. It was as though she saw the entire world through dispassionate eyes . . . as long as she stayed within the soothing aura of this strange and wonderful man.

All right, she thought. So, she knew Jason was the serial killer — he as much as told her so. And she was relieved he'd been arrested for his crimes. Yet, she was even more relieved when they let him go. Maybe she didn't understand the legal part of it, but she was glad he was now free. He was much too valuable to be locked up in a cell with — with what? Criminals?

For a moment she sat, stunned. *I don't think of Jason as a criminal. I can't! Instead, the events in the basement made me want to put my arms around him like a protective mother.*

Then there was Harry to consider. Tara really felt bad about how she'd treated Harry. She knew he was angry with her for withholding information, but how would she have felt about herself if she'd broken a solemn promise to Jason? It's not as though she'd made the promise to a wanton killer — it was made to a man weeping over what he was about to do. Harry wouldn't see it that way, though. He'd think she was just being stubborn.

Wasn't there something she could do to make him understand? She really didn't want their friendship to end this way. With her fondness for Harry growing, did she dare think "relationship?"

Tara was startled when she felt the sharp talons of a landing pigeon dig into her knee. Looking up, she and the old man giggled.

"He likes you," he said.

"Sure," she said. "I'll bet he likes anybody who looks like a food dispenser. I'm curious, do you come here often?" After a pause, they both laughed again at the cliché she had just uttered.

"Every day," he replied. Pointing, he said, "I live just over there. I teach — try to teach — violin to the neighborhood urchins. Feeding pigeons calms my nerves after a day of listening to screeching attempts to saw their instruments in half."

"Well, sir, you've certainly calmed my nerves, and for that I thank you." She grinned, "If we should meet again, I promise *not* to bring a violin."

The man took Tara's closed hand in his. "I don't read stars," he said, "or even palms." Opening her hand, he added, "But I do read pigeon food." Then, gazing intently at the peanuts in her hand, he pronounced in a most sonorous voice, "I see your problems will soon be solved in your favor, your wishes will be granted, and you and he will live happily ever after."

Live happily ever after? Did he mean Harry? Whatever made the man say a thing like that! Was he a mind reader?

Tara trotted homeward where a cool shower beckoned. Images of the soothing water rolling down her body made her quicken her pace to a leisurely jog. When she dropped her keys and wallet on the kitchen table she went immediately to check for phone messages. There was only one, from a caller whose name she didn't recognize. Was this another pesky telemarketer? Unlikely. They didn't expect callbacks. She tapped in the number.

"Cally Tunesco speaking."

"This is Tara Tindall returning your call."

"Oh, thank you so much, Ms. Tindall. I represented Jason Smalter during his recent encounter with the police, and I need to ask a favor."

What could she possibly want? "How can I help you?"

"This may seem a bit odd, but I'd like you to call my number from a public telephone."

"May I ask why?"

Short pause. "Ah, it would be better if you don't. Your phone line may be tapped."

"*What?*" Tara looked at her handset as though expecting to see an electronic bug attached to its skin.

"Please don't be alarmed. I don't know for sure that it is — this may be an unnecessary precaution. But will you humor me and make the call?"

"Yes, of course." It had been a while since Tara had used a public phone and she wasn't sure where she could find one.

As though reading her mind, Cally said, "You'll probably find one at your nearest service station."

"Oh, thank you. I'll call you in about half an hour. I just got back from a jog and need to rinse off."

"That'll be fine."

Now what is this all about? Tara stripped and stepped into her shower.

Twenty minutes later she drove into her local service station, found an unused phone and dropped in the correct change. Her call was answered on the first ring.

"Ms. Tindall? Thanks for calling back. There's someone here who wants to talk to you."

Before she could reply, a male voice came on the line and said, "Miss Tara, it's Jason."

"*Jason*? My God, how *are* you?"

"Just fine. I've been worried about you."

"Me? That's very kind of you, but why would you be worried about me?"

"Well, you know . . . what with all the unpleasantness and all. I've been worrying whether the police have been harassing you — "

"No," Tara interrupted, "they haven't. And I haven't broken my promise to you, either."

"Thank you." Tara thought she heard a sigh of relief. "I'm really sorry about what . . . well, you know."

"Jason, where are you?"

"I can't say right now. But I'm fine, and I have almost everything I need."

"Are you hiding? The police aren't looking for you, are they?"

"No. Not right now, anyhow. But if they knew where I am, I'm sure they'd have me followed. They're trying to put me in jail again, you know. I just don't want to make it too easy for them. Jail is the worst place in the world. Miss Tara . . . I'm really sorry . . . about everything. You know I wouldn't hurt you for the world."

Tara didn't know what to say to that. "Thank you. You said you had *almost* everything you need?"

"Yes, I'm really lonely without Scootch — Gweedo helps, but Scootch is the companion I can talk to about serious things. I've made a little sock puppet, but it's not the same without my old friend."

"I understand. If you like, I'd be glad to ask Detective Shuman if you can have — "

"No, no, please don't do that. They'd find out where I am. I'll be fine for the time being — until all this is over."

Tara and Jason exchanged innocent pleasantries for a minute more. "Jason, it's been really good talking to you. I'm glad to know you're all right. May I talk with Ms. Tunesco again?"

"This is Cally."

"Is there something I can do for Jason? He sounds so lonely."

"No, but thank you for asking. I'll see he keeps in touch with you. He's very fond of you, you know."

Tara hung up the phone slowly, thinking about Cally's last remark. *Jason's fond of me? Well, I'll be damned.*

CHAPTER THIRTY-NINE

"I'll be damned if I do, and damned if I don't." Assistant District Attorney Titiana Markova paced the office of District Attorney Barney Malloy sitting quietly behind his mahogany desk. He'd learned to keep quiet while Markova was on a tear.

"It would be one thing if this damned serial killer was a rage killer, or a sexual predator, or a rotten bastard. But no, he's got to be a mild-mannered friggin' hero in the eyes of Jane and Joe Public." She waved her arms for emphasis as she ranted. "If I tear him apart in the courtroom, the media will tear *me* apart." She jabbed a finger in his direction. "And you, too, in the media. Have you seen the latest polls?"

District Attorney Malloy, a forty-three-year-old ex-football jock, leaned back in his leather swivel chair. "I believe they show the public is rooting for the killer. The great unwashed are thinking unkind thoughts about the criminal justice system."

"Jesus H. Christ, Malloy, they think we're actually *hounding* this Smalter guy." She shook her head and spread her arms wide. "I just don't get it. We're trying to uphold the law and protect them from guys like Smalter . . . and all of a sudden *we're* the bad guys. He's even got a high-priced lawyer, for God's sake."

"Yeah. Like we're jealous because this Smalter guy is doing what they think *we* should be doing." He sneered, "Like they have any idea what a justice system is all about — or even give a damn."

"We've got to get some solid evidence on this guy. Once we do, I'll nail him to the effing flagpole." Her rage finally vented, she plunked herself into a chair opposite Malloy. "Heard anything from the lab rats about the crematory analysis?"

"Nothing yet. Wait, I did get a call from Millston this morning. Said they'd have something by tomorrow."

"What's taking them so long? You'd think they were being asked to provide a definitive analysis of the Turin fucking Shroud."

"You any idea how much stuff they vacuumed from the bed of that crematory? A lot. ME said it looked as though the thing hadn't been cleaned in years. It might even have fragments left over from the dinosaur era."

Markova snorted. "So what do we do now?"

Titiana Markova, standing only five foot three, was easily mistaken for a wimpish woman, in spite of the jet-black hair stacked high on her head. This faulty impression immediately crashed and burned when her courtroom adversaries realized they were dealing with a tigress. A penniless immigrant from Russia, when a child she was taken in by another immigrant who promptly mistreated her. She never forgot. When she told him to shove it, he threatened to turn her in to the New York KGB. Her response was to push him down the stairs. After making sure he wasn't dead, she took his money, and made for Chicago.

A sympathetic priest gave her a job keeping the church in pristine condition. By luck, noticing his "cleaning lady" had a brilliant mind, the priest pulled strings. Twisting the arm of one of his wealthy benefactors, Titiana found herself enrolled in University of Chicago Law School.

A creditable student, she was not brilliant . . . until her encounter with mock court. That day, acting as a prosecuting attorney, Titiana burst into life, then soared. Ever since, her entrance into a courtroom transformed her into another person — a virtuoso prosecutor. It was her domain — her arena — her life. *They* were the lions, *she* was the gladiator. She even imagined herself her as a leather-clad gladiator with whip in one hand and snare in the other.

"What do we do now?" Malloy repeated. "Just this. Sit tight until we get enough evidence to lock up the perp. I've a feeling the ME is going to shower us with good news very soon. Then we'll unleash our secret weapon — 'Buns' Markova, who — Ta-da! — will proceed to make heroes of us all!"

Detectives Shuman and Skirms tromped up the stairs and across the porch of the Hermosa Funeral Home on Kaliche Street. While pushing on the bell button, Harry said, "Thanks for coming along, Joan. I want to get a feel for the scene out here. I still think something went down we don't know about, and I'd appreciate your letting me take the lead. Look around, if you can, and see what you can find."

"Anything in particular?"

"Mainly, we want to know how much this guy knows about what goes on next door at the Smalter residence."

The door opened. An elderly man in an equally elderly black suit and white hair said, "Good afternoon, madame, sir. May I help you?"

Harry flashed his badge. "I'm Detective Shuman, and this is Detective

Skirms. May we come in? We have a few questions."

The man stood firm in the doorway. "I am Juan Hermosa, the funeral director here. Have I done something wrong?"

"Nothing like that, sir. We'd just like to ask you a few questions about the house next door."

Hermosa moved out of the way and beckoned them in. "Please come this way." Leading them to a parlor whose furniture had seen better days, he invited them to sit. "Now then, how may I be of service?"

"How long have you owned this establishment?"

"I believe it must be a little over twenty years. It is fully paid for, so this cannot be about my being behind in my mortgage payments."

Harry smiled. "Look, we're here about that thing that happened next door last week. It has nothing to do with you. We're just filling in some background."

"Was that man really the serial killer? He hasn't been back since you arrested him, you know."

"Yes, we know." Harry loosened his tie. "I believe you have a crematory here in this building."

"Yes, that is true." Hermosa frowned, wondering what interest the police could possibly have with his crematory.

"May we see it, please?"

Hermosa led them into a somewhat larger parlor. Several rows of chairs faced the front of the room. Built into the wall was a mahogany door with no handle. An altar stood next to the door, draped with a white silk banner. Hermosa stood behind the altar and revealed a small control board. "I take it you would like to look inside the furnace?"

"Yes, please."

Hermosa flicked a switch. Without a sound, the mahogany door opened. Another click and subdued lights came on, illuminating the face of the oven. "When we cremate, we place the wooden casket of the deceased on this set of rollers. The casket is then slowly fed into the oven. It is only after the door is closed that the gas fire is lit."

Hermosa reached under the altar and retrieved a flashlight. Handing it to Harry, he said, "Would you like to inspect the inside?"

The two detectives looked into the oven. Unlike the oven hiding beneath it, it was clean.

Harry was satisfied there were no illegal immigrants hiding there. *Now where the hell did that silly thought come from?* Handing the flashlight back to the funeral director, the two at last got to the point of their visit.

"Mr. Hermosa, how often do you use the crematory?"

Hermosa shook his head. "Not very often any more. I'm getting too old to take on much work, and besides, the neighborhood is getting so crowded there are always a few complaints when I do use it. It's an old one, you see... installed around 1956, I understand. There have been many improvements since."

"Can you tell us how often the interior is cleaned?"

"After every use. The law requires it."

"We're particularly interested in three dates. Would you be so kind as to check whether you had cremations on January 10, March 13, or on May 8?"

"Certainly, but I confess I am curious to know why you are asking." Hermosa went to a desk and rummaged for a record book. Finding it, he leafed through the pages for the requested dates. "Would you tell me the dates, again, please. My memory isn't what it used to be."

Harry repeated the dates. "No, nothing on January tenth . . . wait a minute, here it is. April tenth. Poor Mrs. Feldstein was cremated on that date, may she rest in peace. And May 8? That was a Monday. We don't often . . . wait. It says here that on May eighth we cremated a Mister Samuel Salerno. I remember that now. At age ninety-five he was roller-skating with his great-grandson, fell down and broke his neck. Died instantly, bless his soul. We did a nice job — "

"Thank you, Mister Hermosa. Just one or two more questions. Has your crematory always worked properly? Have you ever noticed anything unusual about its operation?"

"I don't understand what you are asking."

"I'm sorry. I don't know how to be more specific than that."

Hermosa thought for a moment. "No, we've never had a problem with it. Oh, once in a while the rollers stick, but only when we forget to do the proper maintenance."

Harry decided against telling Hermosa about the crematory in his basement. "Last question. Have you ever noticed any strange activity next door?"

"There used to be some cars driving in and out late at night, but that was many years ago."

They thanked Hermosa for his help and headed back to their offices. "Well," Skirms said as she drove, "he seems like a decent man. I'd be surprised if he had any sort of hand in anything shady."

"Yeah, me too. Let's get back and look up those dates. I've a hunch we've just hit the jackpot."

CHAPTER FORTY

Sergeant Brunkel stepped into Captain Portono's office to find Chief of Detectives Stacy and Detective Harry the Shoe already seated. Portono waved at Brunkel to close the door before joining the others at the small conference table.

"This is about the Petacki matter," Portono began. "I believe you've all been filled in." Nods from around the table. "Good. Here's how it is. I've talked to the commissioner. After he thought about it awhile, and probably conferred with one or two others, here's what he decided. First, there's no way the evidence can be suppressed or swept under the rug. It's too strong and just too incriminating. Besides, we don't work that way. However, before we book Petacki for homicide, we'll ask him to come in and tell us his side of the story. There may be mitigating circumstances we don't know about and, of course, we'd like to give him the benefit of the doubt. Agreed so far?"

Again nods from around the table. "Second point. We want to keep this quiet until we decide how we'll handle it. Still agreed?" More nods. "All right, then. Third point. We want to keep this low key. Therefore, since Petacki handed the box of evidence to your man Drummel," he motioned toward Brunkel, "Dutch here will ask Drummel to visit Petacki — wearing civvies — and ask him to come by for a chat. He won't be under arrest. The commissioner feels that since he voluntarily handed over the evidence — for whatever reasons — he's unlikely to bolt." He looked around the table. "Anyone not okay with that scenario?"

Heads shook.

"All right, then. The confidential interview will take place in this room. Shoe, this is your case and, unless you say otherwise, you'll conduct the interview. We'll chime in with questions. Bea, do you think that arrangement will be too intimidating?"

"No, I don't think so. After all, Petacki knows what he did and didn't do, and his giving up the evidence as he did suggests he's anxious to tell his story."

"It's settled, then. Remember, this stays with the people in this room.

With the exception of Detective Drummel, of course. Harry, you'll swear him to secrecy. Right?"

"Yes, sir."

Harry raced back to his office. He was concerned about the Petacki case, but he was much more excited about what he'd find when he looked up the dates he'd discussed with Juan Hermosa at the funeral home. Grabbing his phone, he called Missing Persons. "Gabby, this is Shoe. Need you to look up some dates."

Gabby Forello, two hundred pounds and growing, memorized every name on his "missing" list, often allowing him to produce useful information without having to access records. "What d'ya need?"

"Missing person reports for these two dates — on or about March thirteen, and May eight, last year. Looking for missing males, probably between the ages of twenty and forty. Got anything that fits that profile?"

"Sure," replied Gabby, laconically. "March fourteen, a man named Abdul Baruna was reported missing. Hasn't been seen or heard from since."

"Bingo!" Harry banged a closed fist on the desk. "What about the May eight date? Anything near that?"

"Yup. Guy named Andy Harper, nicknamed 'Cowboy', was reported missing on May six. Close enough for you?"

"Bingo again. You're an effin genius, you know that? Will you marry me?"

"Not on the kind of dowry you can afford to pungle up. I'll wait 'til you make your millions."

"Any other candidates for those two dates?"

"Nothing within two weeks either side, except for the usual runaways."

"Thanks, Gabby, you've made my day. I owe you a dinner."

Harry broke the connection and fingered his rolodex for Narena's number at the hospital. Though he announced himself as Detective Shuman, he was nonetheless bounced from one office to another. Finally, someone confessed that Narena wasn't on the premises, and wouldn't be until tomorrow. "Damn!" Harry hated it when he was frustrated while following a hot lead. Well, he'd just have to wait until tomorrow.

A thought popped into his brain, and he slapped his forehead. "Tara!" he said to the dead phone.

"Look, lady," Harry said to the snooty woman answering the phone at Tara's shelter, "I just told you who I am. I am Detective Shuman — *Homicide*

Detective Shuman — and I need to talk with Tara Tindall. *Now*." He listened to the bluster for a moment, then interrupted. "Look, whoever you are, I'm trying to be polite here, but I can assure you that if I have to come over there with a squad of police officers, they will arrive with flashing lights and sirens, and you may just be arrested for obstruction." He paused to listen for a moment. "That's better. Now either go find her or send somebody else. But do it now."

Harry waited less than twenty seconds before Tara came on the line. "What in God's name did you do to that poor woman, Harry? She's terrified."

"Good. I merely threatened to bring a busload of police down there if she didn't get you to the phone."

"What's happening?"

"I'm unable to contact Narena; they said she won't be in until tomorrow. Rather than fight them over the phone for her home phone number, I thought I'd ask you. Come to think of it, I often think of you."

She hesitated. *He's thought of me?* A wave of relief swept over her. *Does that mean he isn't angry with me anymore?*

Finally, she said, "Narena took the day off today, but I think you can reach her at her apartment."

Harry wrote the number in his notebook.

"May I ask what's so urgent?"

"Things are heating up, Tara. I can't talk over the phone . . . you understand. How about if I call you as soon as things settle down?"

"Fine, but does it have to do with the project we've been working on?"

"Look! I know your curiosity is eating you up. I'll fill you in when I can."

Harry punched in Narena's number and waited through nine rings before the phone was picked up. "Narena? This is Harry Shuman. Remember me? You called me the other day to give me an urgent message from Tara."

"Of course, I remember you. Has something happened to Tara?"

"No. She's fine. I just need a little information. As quickly as I can get it."

"I'll do what I can."

"When you were looking for missing or deceased husbands, remember telling us about an Abdul Baruna? His wife and kid had been admitted to your hospital around last March thirteen."

"Yes, I remember . . . but I don't recall the details."

"Can you look up that info again without getting yourself in trouble, or will I need to support you with a search warrant?"

"No, I guess I can do that. You want the dates his family were patients here?"

"That, and as much as you can find out about Abdul. Especially about Abdul. Physical description, name of his doctor, that sort of thing."

"I don't know. If he wasn't a patient here . . ."

"That's okay. Just find out what you can, okay?"

"All right."

"There's another one, too. You didn't give us the name of an Andy Harper, so maybe none of his family members were booked into your hospital."

"Booked?"

"Sorry, 'admitted.' He was reported missing around May eight last year. Could you check the records up to three weeks back from that date?"

"The name doesn't sound familiar, but I'll look. How fast do you need it?"

"Yesterday. Narena, this is hot, so I need it as soon as I can get it. If you get anything, call me at my office number, any time, day or night." He gave her the number. "And thanks!"

Harry broke the connection and alerted Dispatch to forward calls from Narena Tanner as soon as they came in. Then he went home to a restless evening. He thought of calling Tara and offering to take her out for a drink, but thought better of it when he realized he wasn't up for the possible consequences.

Now I know I'm getting old. When was the last time I turned down a possible roll in the hay? Besides, his anger over Tara's reluctance to "come clean" still lingered.

The following morning, Harry bounded up the last flight of stairs when he heard a phone ringing on the third floor. There were lots of phones on the third floor, but Harry willed this call to be for him. It was. He made a mad dash for his desk and all but leaped the last four feet with his hand outstretched. Breathless, he managed to say, "Detective . . . Shuman."

"Harry? Doctor Millston. I've got the analysis you've been panting after."

"Hot damn!"

"No — not damn — analysis. Can you come over — ?"

"Don't move a muscle. I'll be right there." Harry bounded back down the same stairs, out the door of the headquarters building, across the street, jogging the full distance across the block-wide parking lot separating headquarters from the morgue. By the time he arrived, he was totally winded. "Jeezus," he grunted, holding on to the door while catching his breath, "I really need to get back in some kind of shape."

Finally able to breathe without panting, he went directly to the lab where the techies worked on the crematory gleanings. He found the ME staring at the stainless steel surface of a table holding an assortment of charred items. "Pay dirt," Millston said, waving a hand over what looked like the debris from a fireplace.

"That looks like the scuzz I clean out of my fireplace."

"Exactly. What we have here are the cremains from the Smalter crematory, and a fine collection it is. Why, we can practically read the history of the past fifty years or so from this . . . scuzz."

"What the hell is that big shiny thing?"

"That, my good man, is a titanium hip replacement, which puts you well on the road toward discovering the identity of the deceased."

"Jeez, I thought everything got burned up during a cremation."

"Far from it . . . far from it. At the risk of telling you things you already know — for which I apologize in advance — allow me to make a few brief remarks about the wonders of cremation."

"Will there be a quiz?"

"No, but you may cream your pants when you discover the evidence we have here for you. To begin with, a cremation is a fire, which you know. You also know that bodies are cremated fully clothed, usually in a wooden box. What you may not know is that cremated bodies are often buried with a variety of other items — bibles, books, mementos, framed photos, and more. You also know from your experience with the fires you've investigated that fires don't burn evenly. What you may not have had reason to notice is that this is also true of cremation fires. They don't burn evenly, either."

Harry listened intently. He was eager for Millston to get to the point, but an interruption would only delay that moment. He waited.

"When crematory chambers are cleaned out, all sorts of things are left behind — more than you might imagine — and we have some of them here." He spread his hands over the table. "Observe the cremains." He picked up the strangely-shaped object.

"This," Millston said with a flourish, "is, as I said, a titanium hip-replacement. It wasn't harmed during the cremation."

"How come?"

"Because, considering its age, the furnace it came from probably operates at a temperature of between twelve to fifteen hundred degrees Fahrenheit. Titanium melts at a temperature of three *thousand* degrees."

"Hot damn. All we need to do is find the doctor who installed it and we'll have the identity of its owner."

Millston's mouth formed into his Cheshire Cat smile. "Ohhh, I don't think you'll have to go to all *that* trouble, young man." He pointed to an object on the table.

"Okay, so you've got a cigarette case."

"Faulty deduction. It may look like a cigarette case to your unschooled eye. It's made of steel — the fake gold finish has melted off. But this item was not made in the USA, and I think you'll find the interior much more interesting than cigarettes."

Harry picked up the item and snapped it open — rather, he tried to snap it open. Millston handed him what looked like a tiny chisel. "You can pry it open with this."

Harry did. "Jesus H. Christ," he exclaimed. "It's an address book. How come it didn't get burned up?"

"When the fire got hot enough for the body to begin burning — it wasn't in a box when that happened — the case fell out of the disintegrating pocket. It's weight must have caused it to fall through the rollers and settle to the bottom of the chamber, where it was protected from the hottest part of the fire. Even if it hadn't, it still wouldn't have been destroyed."

Millston motioned Harry to follow him to a display case on the far side of the room. "This is my . . . uh . . . scuzz collection. Every one of these items survived a cremation."

Harry studied the items through the glass-enclosed cabinet.

"See that book there? That was a family bible. Still is. It didn't get burned. Oh, the outer pages have been singed and scorched some, but the interior of the bible is perfectly readable. Like new. That's because the pages are so tightly compacted against one another it's hard for them to get enough oxygen to burn."

Harry scanned the other items on display — a variety of hip replacements and other prosthetic devices, glass eyes, staples, belt buckles, dentures, and a generous collection of bone fragments.

"I believe you'll find the name of a doctor or two in that address book you are holding. I suspect a persistent detective like yourself will find that little book your magic key into the life of the deceased. And I will be willing to let you have it for a mere lavish dinner — no liver, please — at a respectable restaurant."

"Done. You're a wizard, Doc. Thanks. And thanks for the lesson — I hope it doesn't have to come in handy any time soon." He turned to leave.

"Wait a moment. Don't you want to know about the other poor blokes beamed to the great beyond in Smalter's fiery transporter?"

Harry turned and shook his head. "Jeez, Doc, you mean there were more?"

"Yes, indeed. This Smalter chap wasn't a very good housekeeper, it seems. The cremains of two other bodies were collected from the chamber, along with a generous helping of Smalter fingerprints on the crematory door."

Shoe's attention was now firmly riveted on Millston. "Go on."

"Mr. Titanium-hip here was the most recent victim — "

"How recent?"

"I'm afraid we don't do carbon-dating on such young items, my dear detective, but my lackeys say he was cremated within the year."

"What about the other two?"

"Can't tell. They've been cremated at least twice or thrice, remember, so their remains have been pretty well warmed-over. From the size of his bones, however, we know one was a big man — two-fifty or so. The least recent was an average-sized gonzo with no recognizable features. Certainly nothing as convenient as a titanium hip, with initials, or a denture. But my gnomes are certain their cremains can't have been reposing in the chamber for longer than a year. Without any DNA to tie these to, that's the best we can do."

"Hot damn! That's more than I hoped for. Thanks again, Doc. Great work. We've got him now for sure. Lemme know when you want the dinner."

Harry was elated with the news. Baruna had savaged his family into the hospital two weeks before he was reported missing. Now he knew where Baruna got missing *to*. That information, along with Smalter's fingerprints on the oven door should be all they need for a conviction.

Striding briskly, approximately two feet off the ground, Harry clutched the steel-enclosed address book and hustled to his office. Totally oblivious of the sweat trickling down his breastbone, he sniffed — at last — at the possible realization of his secret dream hanging in the 104 degree air.

Courthouse steps, here I come.

CHAPTER FORTY-ONE

Harry strode jubilantly into Sergeant Brunkel's office wearing a wide grin. "We've got him, Sarge."

"Got who?"

"Jason Smelter. The serial killer."

"Oh, him."

"What the hell's wrong with you? You look as though your dog died."

"Yeah," Brunkel grumped. "Just about." Brunkel continued to stare off into the distance. "It's the Frangini thing. They're interviewing George Petacki first thing in the morning. I believe you were asked to do the interviewing."

"You got a problem with that?"

"No. I'm just sitting here stewing. I'm really hoping he'll have something to say that'll make it go away. But I don't see how it's possible."

The bad press and embarrassment resulting from the arrest for murder of one of their own would be as welcome as a mother-in-law at a seduction. If it couldn't be avoided, every effort would be made to put the arrest in the best light possible.

"I knew George when he was on the job. Good man. Far as I know, there are no blemishes on his record. None. What the hell could have gotten into him?"

Harry let Brunkel reminisce about his friendship with Petacki without interrupting. Finally, Brunkel looked directly at Harry and asked, "So what brings you here all smiley and cheerful?"

"I'm sorry about the Petacki thing, Sarge. I really am. I know how you must be feeling. I'll handle it as gently as I can."

"Thanks."

"I came about the serial killer case. We've got the goods on our man."

"We had him once before, remember?"

"This is different. I just came from the ME's office." Harry described the evidence he'd been shown, and then pulled the address book from his pocket. "With the names in this book I should have the identity of Mr. Titanium before — "

"Mister who?"

"That's how the ME refers to the most recently deceased. He left a titanium hip joint behind when he made an ash of himself." He smiled at his feeble play on words. "We'll know his real name before the end of the day. That, with Smalter's fingerprints on the oven door, should be more than enough for a conviction."

"Whoa there. Just hold on a minute. Before we run off with only half a cock, I suggest we run this by Markova. We don't want egg on our faces twice in the same week. Let's find out what she says about the evidence."

"Okay, I'll call her right away. And I promise not to say anything about the bird's nest she wears on her head."

That got a small smile from Brunkel. "A wise decision. One that may allow you to live another day." Brunkel shook his head to clear the cobwebs. "While you're checking with the ADA, get someone to verify the name of the vic as soon as you can, so we'll have something firm to put on the arrest warrant."

Harry headed for the door, then turned. "Uh . . . for what it's worth, Sarge, I'm betting Petacki had a damned good reason for not reporting the incident."

Detective Charlie Drummel found the clinic in an aging strip mall on Cave Creek Road, and parked. There were plenty of parking spaces available. On entering, his quick scan showed him a waiting room with three well-worn over-stuffed chairs surrounding a small table covered by a dog-eared collection of women's magazines.

Could there be a law against stocking something of interest to men? Drummel ruminated over the sexist waiting room while eyeing the elderly receptionist day-dreaming behind a sliding glass door. *I guess it just wouldn't do to let your customers get too close to the providers of service.* He shrugged as he remembered that police worked behind barricades of metal detectors, too, plus locked doors, steel bars and bullet-proof glass. *Oh well.*

He clicked his badge on the glass. "Anybody home?" he called.

Madame Droopy-Eyes slowly pulled open the glass window. "If you're a patient, sign the book."

Drummel waggled his badge closer to her nose. "Police business. I'm here to see Doctor Strether. As soon as possible."

"He's in with a patient. You can wait over there."

"He may be in with a patient, but if you don't go in and tell him I'm here, I may have to arrest you for obstruction of justice."

The Old One peered more closely at the badge, and then at Drummel.

Seeing he was serious, she roused her considerable bulk from her chair — Drummel could almost hear the fat jiggle as it flowed. Shuffling back to a door, she opened it without knocking and went in.

She wouldn't do that if he were with a patient, thought Drummel. *She probably interrupted his nap*. In less than a minute, the door opened again and the doctor shuffled out to the reception area. "I'm Doctor Struther."

"Detective Drummel," Charlie offered, showing his badge. "I apologize for the interruption, but I'm here on police business and I need some information, as quickly as I can get it. Time is of the essence."

Doctor Strether, a small, completely bald man with an alert face and hooked nose, said, "How can I help?"

"You had a patient with a titanium hip replacement about a year ago."

"Had?"

"He's dead. I need to know his name, and anything else you can tell me about him."

Strether hesitated.

"I know — doctor-patient confidentiality — I respect that. But the man we're discussing was murdered and we're trying to find his killer."

"Well, now, that's different. His name is — was — Abdul Baruna."

"Did you do the hip replacement?"

"Heavens, no. I referred him to a specialist." Strether fumbled with a small file box. "Doctor Yuan — good man. Want his phone number?"

"Please." Drummel wrote down the information. "Can you tell me anything more about Mister Baruna?"

"Humph. I might call him a lot of things, but 'mister' isn't one of them. He was a foul-mouthed, insensitive slob — reason I knew right off who you were talking about. I treated his wife and daughter several times for 'falling down stairs.' That's what they always say when they're beaten up by their husbands. I hope you find his killer and give him a medal for his good deed."

Drummel called on Doctor Yuan thirty minutes later. He verified that he had actually performed the hip replacement on one Abdul Baruna.

"You say he was murdered? How, if I may ask?"

"Cremated."

"You mean doused with gasoline or something and set on fire?"

"No, doc. He was cremated. In a crematory."

"Mmm. Too bad. I like my version better."

By now Drummel was getting the message that Baruna wasn't going to get many votes in the Mister Congeniality contest. Drummel returned to his desk and reported his findings to Shoe.

"Good work, Charlie. I'm on my way to talk to the ADA. If she says we've got enough for a conviction, we'll issue an arrest warrant on this Smalter guy. Any idea where we can find him?"

"C'mon, Harry. He's probably in China by now."

"I know that." Facetiously, he added, "I just thought you might have noticed which way he went when he left the house here."

"Matter of fact, I did. He left in the car of his fancy lawyer."

"No shit? You're a genius, Charlie. Thanks."

CHAPTER FORTY-TWO

The commissioner's conference room contained several people, *not* including the commissioner. George Petacki had entered looking sharp in the uniform issued by the shelter, carrying a very old and scuffed leather briefcase held closed by two frayed straps. He approached the conference table and stood stiffly at attention.

"Relax, George," Captain Portono encouraged. "Have a seat."

"Thank you, sir."

"Do you know everyone here?" Not waiting for a reply, Portono introduced those present. "Lieutenant Stacy, Chief of Detectives; Dr. Millston, Medical Examiner; ADA Markova, Sergeant Brunkel, Supervisor of the Cold Cases squad, and Detective Harry Shuman, also Cold Cases squad. Harry's here because he's leading the investigation into the incident which brings us to this meeting."

Petacki nodded in the direction of each as he or she was introduced.

"This is an informal meeting, George. You aren't under arrest, and you willingly accepted our invitation to discuss the matter of Frankie Frangini. Is that correct?"

"Yes, sir."

"I think this will go better if you'd drop the sirs and ma'ams. Okay?"

"Yes, sir . . . yes."

"Because Harry's in charge of the investigation, I'd like him to briefly review the events that brought us to this meeting."

"As you all know, we've been investigating a series of nine murders — so far — all of which we believe are the work of one killer. Except one. Eight of the murders were committed by an organized killer who carefully left as little evidence behind as he could manage. The ninth, we believe, was a rage killing, performed by someone who left a great deal of evidence behind." Harry looked around the room to see if there were any comments. There being none, he continued.

"During our re-investigation of possible suspects, our detectives called on you, George, at your workplace. Without prompting, you invited the detectives to your home. Again without prompting, you went into the closet and handed a sealed box to the detectives, on which was written something like, 'To be hand-delivered to the medical examiner." Harry studied George's intense expression. "Am I correct so far?"

Petacki tugged at the bottom of his jacket. "Perfectly correct."

"Would you tell us, then, what you found when you examined the contents of the box, Dr. Millston?"

Millston opened a folder and reported the contents in detail. Millston closed the folder, ending with, "There were also some pictures. That's it in a nutshell."

Harry nodded toward Portono to signify he'd concluded his summary.

Captain Portono fiddled with a pencil before continuing. "George, since you voluntarily offered evidence clearly tying you to this, ah, event, we'd like you to tell us why you chose the course of action you did. Before you begin, would you like some coffee? Something stronger?"

"Thank you. Water would be fine."

After a short break during which various liquids were served, George began his story.

"As you know, I work as the security guard at the Bramwell Convalescent Center. Actually, it's a shelter for battered women. A few of them bring their children when they've finally had more than they can take. These women and children are victims of some of the most vicious scum of the earth. Their victims come to the shelter with broken bones, torn faces, broken heads, and more. It always tears me up when I see what's been done to them.

"But there's been nothing I can do about it. When I was on the job, there were at least a few things I could do, but now I have no authority to take any kind of action. That's been eating at me for a long time. Still does."

"How did you meet Frankie Frangini?" Stacy asked.

"In a bar. I was having a beer with a couple of ex-cops, telling war stories. Pretty soon we began hearing loud guffawing from a booth opposite the bar where we were sitting. There were three assholes — excuse me — three pitiful excuses for human beings, drinking beer and laughing about all the things they did to their women. It sounded like a pissing contest to see who was the worst sonuvabitch on the planet." George was so engrossed in his story he ignored his slips in verbal etiquette. It wouldn't have mattered; this group had heard it all many times.

"I tuned into the conversation — hard to avoid it — and heard one of them call another 'Frankie.' Something clicked, and I remembered one of the battered women at our shelter had a husband named Frankie — heard the staff talking about it when his wife showed up. So I sat at the bar wracking my brain for a last name. It drove me nuts that I couldn't think of it. It musta' been half an hour later when it clicked. I overheard the word 'frangipani' from another conversation, and the name suddenly came to me."

"What did you do then?" Portono prompted.

"I hollered, 'Hey, Frangini' at him, and he looked up and said, 'Yeah? You talkin' to me?' I guess I said something like, 'Hell, no. I don't talk to assholes like you.' You've got to understand that here I was, looking at one of the scumbags who put one of the disfigured women in my shelter, and there wasn't anything I could do about it." Several nods and understanding glances rippled around the table.

"Well, this Frangini guy got up and walked over to me — I think he was trying to show off in front of his buddies. 'You got some kind of beef with me, old man?' he says. 'Naw,' I said, 'Your kind ain't worth a spoonful of shit.' His buddies laughed at that and Frangini got pretty hot under the collar. He was spoiling for a fight, but I guess he figured his buddies would laugh him out of town if he took on a gray-haired old man. He glowered a bit, then went back to his booth."

"Was that the end of it?" Harry put in.

"No. As I was driving home I noticed I was being followed by a beat up cream-colored Chevy. I kinda' suspected it was Frankie, and I didn't know what to do. I wasn't about to lead him to my house, and if I led him to a police station he might just take off."

"You were still pretty angry at this time?" This from Stacy.

"Yes, I was, ma'am. I drove around a while to make sure it was a tail, and then finally had an idea. I drove to an old warehouse district where I know the night watchman. I guess I thought if I could find him we could scare Frangini off."

Petacki was obviously coming to the climax of his story. Everyone in the room leaned forward, not wanting to miss a word.

"I drove up to the warehouse where I thought I'd find my buddy. Didn't see him, so I stopped and got out of the car. Before I got to the warehouse door, Frangini banged into the back of my car, jumped out, and started after me with a knife."

Harry broke into the narrative. "You still got the bruises on your car?"

"Yeah. There's a dent in the rear fender and some paint scratches. You can check it out."

Harry gestured for Petacki to continue.

"Anyhow, this guy comes screaming at me waving that damned knife and I'm scared shitless — I haven't been in a street brawl for a lot of years — and I didn't have my gun." Petacki paused, rubbing his hands together as he re-created the scene in his mind. Grimacing, he continued.

"There was no way I could avoid the attack. He jabbed at me and I jumped back from the thrust. That made him laugh . . . and overconfident, I guess. Mostly, it made me madder. I lunged at him, hoping to get him in a bear hug and get the knife away from him. When I reached for him, he cut me in the arm. I tripped him and he went down. That gave me time to pick up a two-by-four I'd seen lying on the ground — "

"The one with the nails in it?" Harry asked.

"Must be. I didn't notice the nails at the time."

"Go on."

"Frangini was back on his feet by this time. He still had the knife, so I just started swinging away with the two-by-four. I guess I hit him a couple of times. He staggered some, but wouldn't let go of the knife. Finally, I got in a lucky blow to the head and he went down and stopped moving. I checked for a pulse — there wasn't any. I guess I was a little disoriented and didn't know what to do, so I just drove away."

"You just drove off?" Brunkel's turn.

"By that time my head was filled with thoughts about my son, about how it would look when I got arrested for murdering some scumbag. He's on the job, you know."

Heads shook in sympathy.

"He was getting married in a few days and I couldn't bear the thought of ruining his wedding. I knew it was the wrong thing to do, but I wasn't thinking straight. So, yeah, I just drove off! I knew you'd catch up to me eventually, and it wasn't as though I was fleeing or anything like that."

"You said you just drove off," the ME said. "What happened to the knife?"

Petacki reached down to his battered briefcase and extracted a plastic bag. "It's in this bag. I didn't even know I'd picked it up until I got home and found it on the floor of my car. His fingerprints should be on it — that's my blood on the blade." He pushed the plastic bag toward the center of the table.

Beatrice Stacy, Chief of Detectives, joined the questioning. "I believe you said you were disoriented and just drove off, thinking about your son. Yet you had enough presence of mind to pick up the knife."

"Like I said, I wasn't thinking clearly at that time. I didn't even realize I'd picked it up until I got home."

"So your fingerprints will be on the knife as well?"

"I don't know. I suppose so." Petacki stood, removed the jacket of his uniform, and rolled up his left sleeve. Pointing to the scar on his biceps, he said, "This is where the bastard cut me. It's not deep, but it bled some."

"Have you talked to your son about the incident?" This from Brunkel.

"I took him fishing last weekend and told him all about it. He was pretty bummed out — more worried about me than anything — but once he heard the whole story and that I had turned over the evidence, he was pretty supportive."

"Do you remember ever seeing this night watchman friend you told us about?"

"No, I don't. I wish he'd seen the whole thing go down, though."

"Maybe he did," Brunkel responded. "If you'll give us his name and address, I'll check it out."

Petacki turned toward Caption Portono. "What will happen to me now? Am I under arrest?"

Portono looked around the table, thinking. "First, we need to check out your story and confer with the commissioner. By the way, he chose not to be here today so you could feel more relaxed about telling your story. You owe him one for that."

"Please convey my appreciation for his thoughtfulness."

"I'll ask the ME to examine the knife, and Sgt. Brunkel will have his investigators check out the night watchman, your bar friends, and the bartender. And your car. Unless there are objections from around the table, we won't arrest you before we know the results. If your story of self-defense holds up, then there is no crime and we won't have to arrest you at all."

He looked at Markova, who poked a thumb into the air signaling her agreement. To lighten the mood, Portono added, "Of course, we may have to fine you a round of beers for carrying an unlicensed two-by-four."

Petacki's head snapped up at the unexpected laughter. "I'm really sorry I let the job down," Petacki said, breathing a little easier at the change in mood. Shaking his head, he added, "I just couldn't bring myself to ruin my son's wedding and — "

"George," Brunkel interrupted, "I'm sure there isn't a street-experienced cop anywhere who hasn't wanted to do exactly what you did. More than once."

CHAPTER FORTY-THREE

Harry left the Petacki interview with a long face, trudging slowly toward the DA's office. Petacki's self-defense story was totally believable, but his failure to report the incident wouldn't do his career much good. *Bummer. I wonder how his son really feels about it. Hope they're still okay with one another.*

Entering the elevator that would take him to the ADA's office, he gave up trying to predict how it would play out.

"Ah, there you are, Detective." ADA Titiana Markova closed a folder and stood, reaching out her hand. "I understand you have new evidence pertaining to the serial killer case." Her tailored gray suit, unadorned by jewelry, made her look like the fierce litigator she was.

"I do. And a new victim, too." Harry outlined the new case against Jason. He described the secret crematory, the cremation of Abdul Baruna, the significance of the cremains, and the circumstances of Smalter's arrest in his basement.

The ADA listened attentively during the recitation, jotting a word or two on a lined, yellow legal-sized pad.

Harry pointed. "I thought you'd be taking notes on your laptop there. I thought it was welded to your . . . hand." He had been about to say "bellybutton," barely catching himself in time.

"The laptop is indispensable in the courtroom. But the pad is still a useful tool." Changing the subject, she said, "Now let's see if I've got this straight. You've discovered this secret tunnel and crematory that doesn't connect in any way to the funeral home above it. Right?"

"Right."

"And you've discovered that the cremains you found in the oven belong to one Abdul Baruna. You're absolutely sure about that?"

"Yes. The doctor who installed the titanium hip joint confirms it. He always initials his joints."

"The next question has to do with how we tie the deceased to Smalter. You say his fingerprints are all over the oven door?"

"That's right. That's confirmed."

"And you say that Smalter is the only one with access to the tunnel and oven?"

"Nobody even knew it existed until Tara Tindall — the one in the basement with him when he was arrested — told us about it."

"And you say Baruna put his family in the hospital about two weeks before he was cremated, and this is the same hospital where Smalter's dummy talked with his daughter?"

"No doubt about it."

"And this Tara person confirms that Smalter tried to kill her?"

Harry frowned. "Not exactly."

Titiana looked up from her notepad. "Just what does 'not exactly' mean?"

"She won't say what happened in the basement. She apparently made some sort of promise to Smalter — probably to save her life — and she refuses to tell us about it."

"She likes him?"

"Hell, Titiana, half this town is in *love* with him. According to the press and talk shows, he's a hero — he knocks off the bad guys while the cops sit on their hands."

"Yes, I'm well aware of the polls. Tell me, *are* you just sitting on your hands?" Markova quickly raised her palms to forestall Harry's objection. "Question is, do we have a case? Let me sum it up from the defense point of view." She stood and adopted the manner of a trial lawyer.

"First, we have the cremains of a positively identified body. Second, the cremains were found in a crematory to which only the suspect had access. Third, Baruna disappeared two weeks after his family showed up at the hospital. Right so far?"

"Right."

"And from that we are to conclude that Jason Smalter cremated Baruna because he fit Smalter's criteria?"

"Right again."

"Wrong, boy-o."

"What the hell do you mean, wrong? It's airtight."

"Is it, now?" Markova began pacing her office, pretending to be the attorney for the defense. "Ladies and gentlemen of the jury," she began in a strong voice, pointing to the coat rack in the corner. "The prosecution alleges that my client was responsible for the untimely death of Mister Baruna. Let's look at the flimsy evidence."

Harry winced.

"We concede that Mister Baruna is deceased, and that his remains were found in this," Markova made a deprecatory gesture, "this secret crematory. What has *not* been established is that Mister Baruna died as a result of the *cremation*. He could have died from a heart attack. He could have committed suicide. In other words, he could have been dead for hours, or days, or even months, before his remains were placed in that oven. There is absolutely no evidence to show otherwise."

"Yeah . . . but you've got to admit, at least that's desecrating a corpse."

Titiana ignored Harry's objection. "That being the case, what does it matter if my client's fingerprints were found on the oven door? It's irrelevant. As for the defendant learning via the hospital that Mister Baruna 'needed killing,' according to the prosecution, that's simply absurd."

Harry's face grew longer.

"There is no shortage of people who had access to the same information. The nurses, the doctors, all the way down the list to the janitor — anyone who entered that hospital room."

"You're telling me we don't have a case?"

"No. I'm telling you what the defense will do with your case."

"Then I don't know what the hell you're telling me." Harry's frustration was by now visibly leaking out of his pores.

"I'm telling you you've got a case, but it isn't likely to be a slam-dunk. Cally Tunesco is only a corporate lawyer, but she's a brilliant one — no dummy, that woman. With the case you've got, she'll be able to sow enough doubt in the jury's minds to get an acquittal. Especially if, as you say, half the population would like him freed to get back to doing his so-called 'good deeds.' And that's *all* she has to do — sow doubt."

"So where does that leave us? We were just about to issue an arrest warrant."

"It's like this. I can come on strong with the evidence you've described, and I can make the jury believe Smalter is the killer of Baruna . . . until the defense has its turn. Then the jury will begin to have doubts. And a reasonable doubt is all it takes."

"So?"

"So two things. First, you have no witnesses to the deed — you don't even know whether the oven was the crime scene — so it would help if you could put Smalter and Baruna in the same room together. Where did Smalter meet Baruna? How did he lure him into the basement — if that's where he killed him? Is there evidence to show he stalked Baruna before killing him?

Harry, my boy, there's got to be more. Go find it!"

"You said *two* things."

"Three, actually. Second, this Tara person you say has clammed up. Get her to tell you what happened between her and Smalter. If she won't, charge her with obstruction. Better yet, after you've arrested Smalter — again — and she still refuses to talk, I'll issue a material witness order. If that doesn't encourage her to talk, we can arrest her.

"Third, you've told me this is a serial killer and that there are other murders. Do you intend charging Smalter with those as well?"

Harry fidgeted in his chair. "We'd really like to, but I'm not sure the evidence is even as strong as what we have against Baruna."

"Reason I bring it up is this. If you could charge him with other killings, I could then make an issue of the pattern — the monthly Monday pattern — and weave a tighter rope of circumstantial evidence. If you don't charge him with other murders, the defense won't even let me mention the 'monthly Mondays' pattern. I suggest you get your gang back to work."

"You saying we shouldn't arrest Smalter?"

"Is he a flight risk?"

"Don't think so. But he hasn't been back to his house since he was released. We don't know where he is. But then, we haven't been looking."

"It's your call, but if you have to let him go a *second* time, the public will be absolutely convinced Smalter is doing a better job on the bad guys than the cops. That, or you're relentlessly hounding an innocent man."

Harry returned to his office wrapped in a cloud of gloom. Head down, hands in pockets, he shuffled along with "Why me?" thoughts nibbling at his synapses. *Shit! What the hell more does the woman want? A smoking oven?*

CHAPTER FORTY-FOUR

"Tara, can we meet?" Harry didn't want to make this call. He wanted to see Tara again — his yearning for her grew more every time they parted. He didn't want to have to tell her the bad news.

"Yes, of course. You have news?"

"I can bring you up to date on what's been happening, if you'd like. I have to leave for about an hour, but, barring emergencies, I'll be in the office the rest of the day. We could meet here after lunch."

Tara didn't miss the formal tone. *After lunch? At headquarters?* "You're still angry with me, aren't you?" She wondered what she might do to make that go away. There must be something that would dissolve his anger toward her.

"Under the circumstances, I think I'm controlling myself pretty well. It's a little hard to warm up to someone who's impeding my investigation."

"Harry, you know damned well why I can't tell you what happened. When the time is right, you'll be the first to know. Now how about knocking off this frosty attitude. Can't we still be friends, at least?"

Harry softened a little. "Tara, we're friends. I think I'm just miffed because our friendship doesn't seem to be as strong as your commitment to a serial killer — especially now that time is of the essence."

Wow! He really is angry. Can I find a way to defuse that anger? "Harry, you're right . . . and I'm sorry."

"Okay. I just called to bring you up to date, tell you your testimony will be more crucial than I thought, and warn you the ADA is planning to arrest you unless you're more forthcoming. Just thought you'd want to know."

Tara was stunned. She realized intellectually there would be a consequence for her silence, but had no idea that keeping her promise to Jason would be *this* severe. Arrested? For what? Keeping a promise? It didn't make sense. Shaken, Tara asked, "When are they planning to — to arrest me?" It was hard even saying the word out loud.

"Probably not until after we collar Jason, and the ADA begins pulling her case together. Maybe a week — maybe two. If I can, I'll let you know when it's imminent. Until then, you may want to think some more about what you want to do." Sadly, he added, "Good-bye, Tara."

Oh, my God! Tara looked at the dead phone, dazed by the abruptness of Harry's termination. *He just said 'good-bye' and hung up. There wasn't any warmth in his voice at all. Yet he did sound a little sad when he hung up. He must be bitterly frustrated. He wants so much to catch the killer, and he's convinced I'm standing in his way. Maybe I am, but why can't he understand my side of it?* She'd made a promise in exchange for her life — that should mean something to him. After all, she couldn't just renege because Harry and his troops couldn't find enough evidence.

Harry gently returned the phone to its cradle. *Damn!* That didn't go the way he wanted — at all. He'd have welcomed another opportunity to be with her, pissed as he was that she was putting herself in danger of being arrested just to keep a promise to a killer. *Jeez*, Harry had thought she was a lot more sensible than that. Tapping a pencil on the desk, he thought about her predicament a few moments longer, then turned his mind to his own troubles.

"Sarge, got a minute?"

Brunkel waved Harry into his office and motioned him to a chair. When he completed the note he was making, he leaned back and gave Harry his full attention. "Why the gloom, Shoe?" It was Brunkel's turn to ask about a perceived funk. "Your furrowed brow and drag-ass demeanor tells me there's trouble in River City."

"I talked with Markova about the Baruna thing. She says we've got a good case, but only until the defense gets its turn. Thinks the defense will be able to throw enough doubt on the jury to make a conviction questionable. Dammit, Sarge! I haven't been this frustrated over a case in years."

"What does your recalcitrant CI have to say?"

"She's not budging. I told her the ADA was thinking of getting a material witness order so she can be arrested, but she still wouldn't budge. I got really gigged off at her and hung up. Not what I had in mind."

"Harry, take a deep breath."

"Markova said she'd like to make an issue of the monthly Monday pattern — thinks it will help her case. But to do that she's got to charge Jason with some of the other kills." Harry threw up his hands in a gesture of resignation.

"And?"

"And the evidence on those kills is still too thin. We know the pattern and the evidence tie the kills together, but we don't have much that ties them to Smalter. She even told me how the defense can weasel Smalter out of the

Baruna kill, for God's sake."

Brunkel listened with steepled fingers, saying nothing. When Harry finished pacing and waving his arms, Brunkel leaned forward, put his elbows on his desk, and said, "May I make a suggestion?"

"Why else would I be standing at the feet of the master?"

"Let's hold off on the warrant until we find out whether we can put the arm on Smalter whenever we want him. See if you can find out where's he's holed up, and whether he's planning to take off. Meanwhile, get the team back out to dig up some more evidence. Third, go over the evidence you already have and see if we can make a case against Smalter with any of the other victims."

As Harry got up to leave, Brunkel added, "You started this, Harry. Now find something that'll finish it in style."

Harry sat at his desk, case files neatly arranged in front of him. His plan was to summarize the available evidence for each of the cases and stack the files of those for which he thought the ADA could make a case. He reviewed his data and combined as much as he could on one chart, including the method by which the victims died. Since they now knew George Petacki killed him, the Frankie Frangini murder no longer belonged in the serial murder count. He deleted it.

He added a dot before the victims known to have had family members at a battered women's shelter, and a plus sign before those family members at a hospital. Then he wrote three Xs for confirmed murders. The chart was getting pretty bulky and complicated, but — for him — it did the trick.

He stared at the results. Two Mondays were still unaccounted for. Since no one really knew when the killing began, he left only those Mondays open. And, there was no reason the killer had to kill once a month . . . probably just more convenient that way, like the Sunday killing of Gonzalez. Or was there a reason they hadn't determined yet? Nonetheless, the pattern was striking. It would be a damned shame if Markova wasn't able to get his chart into evidence.

He finally left the Buggles name unmarked. No evidence, yet, whether that was a murder, suicide or just plain stupidity. The kill fit the pattern, though. Ah, hell! Let the defense attorney pick at it if she catches it.

So, to date, he had eight murders, assuming Baruna died of cremation. He went over them again:

Date		Victim	Method
12/13,	Mon	Broman Tarper	Gunshot to brain
1/10,	Mon	?	
2/14,	Mon	Darryl Dunbar	Pushed out window
3/13,	Mon	Abdul Baruna	Cremated (?)
4/10,	Mon	Ramin Zander	Gunshot to ear
5/8,	Mon	Andy Harper	No body (cremated ?)
6/12,	Mon	?	
7/10,	Mon	"Tiny" Buggles	Poison – wood alcohol
8/14,	Mon	Willard "Willie" Lamarka	Poison – belladonna
8/28,	Mon	Leroy Luntz	Gunshot to ear
9/11,	Mon	Runyon Pilanski	Poison – curare Run over by SUV
9/24,	Sun	José Gonzalez	Poison – Belladonna

Summary
4 poisonings
3 gunshots to head
1 pushed out window
1 beaten to death
1 not found

Why couldn't the damned killer leave some fingerprints behind, or footprints, or a witness or two? Whatever happened to the good old days when the killer was still standing there with a smoking gun in his hand when you drove up? This just isn't fair.

Harry printed his chart, made a copy, and trooped back to Sergeant Brunkel's office.

Brunkel studied the document. "Good job, Shoe. The pattern stands out clearly. Ought to make Markova happy. Tell you what. Why not take a copy to her and see what she thinks? I'll come with you. If she's willing to run with it, we'll get out a warrant and pick up our Mister Smalter. Be interesting to hear what he has to say." Brunkel snorted and clapped his hands.

"What?"

"Perhaps then we can interview one of Mister Smalter's dummies. Care to take a whack at interviewing a block of wood?"

"It won't be the first time," Harry riposted as he walked out the door.

CHAPTER FORTY-FIVE

"I'd really like to go home," Jason pleaded.

"I know you would," Cally sympathized. "But the police are still investigating. They're trying hard to find enough evidence to arrest you again. You sure you want to take that chance?"

"I appreciate everything you've done for me, but I'd really like to go home. I have that presentation to make tomorrow — "

"What presentation?"

"I'm sure I must have told you. I've been invited to talk to the Phoenix Psychotherapy Council about how I use puppets with children. I've really been looking forward to it, you know. It's quite an honor for an ordinary guy like me to be invited to talk to such a large group of professionals. The biggest honor of my life."

Cally's mind began to race. "I see. And where will this talk be delivered?"

"The conference is this weekend, and I'm scheduled to talk tomorrow at ten. It'll be a general session in the ballroom of the Hyatt Regency. Miss Cally, I've really got to get Scootch and my notes so I can practice some more."

"Mmm. That's tricky. If I take you to your house for your puppet and the police see you walking in your front door — "

"They won't see me."

"Why won't they?"

"If you drive up to the garage behind the house, I can slip inside and be out of sight in just a few seconds."

"What good would it do to get into your garage? Is that where you keep your puppets?"

"No. They're in the basement. But I can get from the garage to the basement without being seen."

Cally's eyebrows went up. "Another secret passage?"

Jason smiled. "Uh-huh. Remember when I told you how the place got built by one of my uncles? And that every once in a while a body would be delivered late at night for cremation?"

"Yes. I remember. But you didn't say anything about a secret tunnel from the garage to the house."

"It didn't come up. Well, the car with the body would be driven into the garage. When the garage door was closed, the body was taken out and slid down a chute to the basement. There's a trapdoor in the floor — the chute is under it."

"I'll be darned."

"Somebody in the basement then put the body on the gurney and trundled it to the crematory."

"And how did it get from the bottom of the chute into the basement?"

Jason paused. "Uh . . . are you sure you want to know?"

"You're right. I *don't* want to know. I do, but I don't."

"The trapdoor hasn't been lifted for years now. I hope it's not all rusted in place."

Cally made up her mind. "Let's wait until it gets dark. Then we'll go. Okay?"

When Jason had gone back to the guest room, Cally picked up the phone and punched in a number.

"*Women for Jason*," a voice answered.

"There's something happening tomorrow I think your members will want to know about," Cally said.

"Who is calling?"

"Never mind. I have a suggestion that should interest you." Cally delivered her message and broke the connection.

"Impressive," Markova said after reviewing the documents handed her by Harry and Brunkel. "The pattern stands out loud and clear — you've got eight definite murders. All you need is something to tie your suspect to the murders."

Harry lifted a hand. "Wait a minute, what about Abdul Baruna? You already know we've got Smalter's fingerprints all over the oven and the gurney, and we can show he's the only one with access to the tunnel."

"That's good evidence, Detective, but it's still circumstantial. We've already talked about this. I can make a good case, but the defense will be able to create doubts."

Brunkel joined the discussion. "What about the fact that Baruna battered his family into the hospital where Smalter gets to talk to the battered kids?"

Markova scratched an ear. "That's useful. With witnesses from the hospital I can argue that Smalter selected his victims — some of his victims — from the information he got from the kids. Harry can testify about the basement, and the tunnel, and the crematory. Millston can testify about the fingerprints on the oven. Believe me, I can tell a convincing story. Unfortunately . . ."

Harry and Brunkel exchanged glances.

"Unfortunately," she repeated, "the defense gets a turn. And the defense would never allow me to mention the other murders."

"There is one witness," Harry said.

Markova looked up, surprised. "A witness? To the Baruna murder? Why in hell didn't you tell me?"

"No, not to the Baruna murder. To the attempted murder of Tara Tindall. She was there — she was the intended victim."

Markova stared at Harry like a school principal might stare at a wayward student. "I remember your telling me she wouldn't talk." She stood and turned to look out her window deep in thought. Turning back to her visitor, she said, "Okay. Here it is. I'll put that other nurse on the stand to testify that the Tindall woman told her Jason was the killer. Then I'll put the Tindall woman on the stand as a hostile witness and squeeze her guts dry. I'll get her to confirm she told that other nurse that Jason was the killer. *Then* I'll put on the Baruna case." She paused. "There's only one problem."

"What's that?" Brunkel wanted to know.

"I'm not sure how I'm going to introduce the *other* murders without being able to promise to link them to the killer. And if I can't do *that*, I can't show the jury the beautiful pattern you've established."

Harry's patience was wearing thin. "Well, do we have enough to arrest him, or not?"

"You have enough to arrest him, and I've got a good chance of a conviction on the Baruna case. I've also got a damned good chance of a conviction for attempted murder on the Tindall case. Bring me some evidence linking Smalter to *any* of the other murders, and I'll make it a slam-dunk."

It was late afternoon when Harry and Brunkel returned to Brunkel's office. "It may be too late to get an arrest warrant today, Harry, but let's try. There must still be a judge around somewhere. If not, get somebody to try the golf courses. Also get somebody to stake out the Smalter house."

Harry called Charlie Drummel and filled him in on the discussion with Markova. He then assigned him the task of obtaining a warrant for the arrest of Jason Smalter. He also assigned someone to sit on the Smalter house.

Wiping sweat from his brow, he called Tara at the shelter. She'd already gone home. He called her home number. No answer. *Damn!* Salivating for a cold beer, he put away the files on his desk and headed for his apartment.

After downing half a bottle of beer, he felt better fortified to tackle the Tara phone call. He tried her number again. This time there was an answer.

"Tara? Harry Shuman."

"Oh, it's so good to hear your voice," she said. "What's happening?"

"Tara, I'm glad to hear your voice, too. Look. But, before I tell you what's happening, I want to apologize for our last conversation. I said something I wish I hadn't, and it's been preying on me."

She remained quiet.

"It's just that, well, I was angry because you seemed too eager to put yourself in danger of arrest, and I was hoping not to have to see you in that kind of situation."

"Are you trying to tell me something?"

"I'm trying to tell you I'm damned fond of you and don't want to see you in the pokey, dammit. *That's* what I'm trying to tell you. Okay?"

"Yes," she said softly, "It's okay. Actually, it's more than okay, and I'm glad to know you care."

Harry wished he were there so he could wrap his arms around her.

"Harry, are you still there?"

Jolted from his fantasy, Harry responded, "Yes, I'm here. Just trying to decide how to tell you the next news," he lied.

"Maybe you could just come right out and say it."

"All right. We talked with the ADA this afternoon, and she's going to charge Jason with the murder of Baruna, and with the attempted murder of one Tara Tindall."

"Oh, my God! Are you serious?"

Harry took that as a rhetorical question. "The ADA has decided to call you as a hostile witness, and you'll have to tell what happened in the basement or go to jail for contempt."

"Harry, what am I going to *do*?" Her conflict returned in full force, slumping her into the chair behind her. Should she tell the truth and help convict Jason for murder, or lie and go to jail?

"I'd suggest just sitting tight. A lot can happen between now and the trial — that won't happen for at least three months — not until after the New Year. If we can find more evidence before then, your testimony may not be needed at all." There. He'd thrown her a straw to hang on to.

Sounding grateful, she said, "Thank you, Harry. That helps. A lot. I'm going to celebrate by going to the grocery store and buying myself a nice thick steak. Uh . . . dare I ask whether I should get enough for two?"

Harry quickly reviewed the situation. Concluding that nothing would be happening until tomorrow at the earliest, he said, "Sure, why not. But I've got to freshen up before I do any 'non-socializing,' so I couldn't make it before eight. That too late?" Harry hoped he didn't sound as eager as he felt.

"Perfect. Bring an appetite."

Cally hustled Jason into her Mercedes as nightfall approached; they reviewed their plan during the drive to Jason's house. "My car's in the garage," Jason said, "so you'll have to park in the driveway. You can drive up close to the garage door — I won't be opening it. I'll use the side door. It'll only take me about five minutes to get what I need. If you'll pop the trunk as soon as I get back, we can be on our way in no time at all."

"That'll work for me."

"You might want to leave your headlights turned off until we're out of the driveway and heading down the street."

The caper went smoothly. Jason had no difficulty opening the trapdoor in the garage floor — he had only to move the junk placed on top of it for camouflage. After sliding to the basement, he opened the secret door to the back of his hidden pharmacy. Once inside, he pulled open the door to the basement, collected his notes along with Scootch and Scrawk, and retraced his steps. Notches cut into the sides of the chute allowed an easy climb to the garage.

Turning the corner at the end of the street, they did not see the black unmarked police car sliding to a stop in full view of Jason's house.

CHAPTER FORTY-SIX

Harry was only ten minutes late, having stopped at a liquor emporium for something to lubricate their conversation. He didn't dare hope his offering — along with an apology — might be enough to rekindle the friendship. He had, after all, caused what he considered a fatal rift. He wished it weren't so. Having dressed in hunter green slacks and gray sleeveless shirt — as conservatively as the hot weather would allow — he collected the paper-bagged wine bottles and headed for the door.

"My God," Tara said, grinning broadly, "did you invite a busload of people to join us?"

"I didn't remember whether you preferred red or white with your steak, so I brought two of each." *Nothing like a little wishful thinking.*

Tara kissed Harry lightly on the cheek and pulled him into her apartment. Arms outstretched, she whirled with a dramatic flourish. "Look what I just bought."

Harry found that an easy request to fulfill. She wore a short lemon skirt that flared when she twirled, giving Harry more than a momentary peek at her long shapely legs. Her black sleeveless blouse looked to Harry as though made of fishnet — whatever it was, it allowed one to conclude without any detecting skill at all that she wore a dark green lacy bra beneath it.

"Very attractive," he managed to say, distracted by his dilemma. He didn't know whether to look at the legs, moving sensuously as she turned, or at her breasts, bouncing ever so invitingly as they flashed by. "A girl could make herself a target dressed as provocatively as that."

Tara's eyes twinkled. "You think?"

"Yeah. I think. I also think I'd better change the subject before I get arrested for drooling in public. If I remember correctly, you said something about a steak and things. I'm here to investigate the truth of that alleged allegation."

She liked the way he playfully mangled the language. "I spoke the truth, and I invite you to the scene of the crime to watch the deed being done. You can even be an accessory to the fact." She took him by the hand and pulled him toward the kitchen.

"To be accurate," Harry said semi-seriously, "the scene of the crime was wherever this terrific-looking piece of meat met its demise. We're merely intending to cre — . . . to create a suitable monument to the dear departed." He'd stopped himself just in time to keep from saying "cremate." But not soon enough to avoid changing the flirtatious banter to something more serious.

Tara, closing the refrigerator door after depositing the white wine bottles, turned to Harry and looked hard into his eyes.

Shit. I've blown it again.

"Harry," she said, moving slowly toward him, "ever since your call this afternoon I've been thinking about what you said. You know, about my being arrested and all." When he didn't respond, she continued. "I want to be sure I understand the situation." She took him by the hand and motioned him to sit across from her at the kitchen table. "I believe you said Jason is going to be arrested again. Right?"

"Yes. We should have the arrest warrant by tomorrow afternoon. He'll be arrested as soon as we can find him."

"And you said the ADA told you she has enough evidence to convict him of murder?"

"Yes."

"You also said she told you she'd charge him with the attempted murder of me, and call me as a hostile witness. Is that right?"

"Where are you going with this, Tara?"

She ignored the question. "Isn't that right?"

"Yes, it's right. You'll either have to tell the truth, or go to jail for contempt of court."

Tara studied her hands as she said, "I've thought long and hard about this, Harry — you know I have. In truth, I've thought about little else." The hint of a smile played across her face. "And I've sat on a certain park bench several times to contemplate the matter further. Just yesterday, while sitting there feeding a squirrel, I finally realized I was acting out of fear for my own safety, and for what might happen to Jason. We all like him, you know."

"Yes, I know. I started liking him as soon as I met him at the restaurant that night."

"You did?" Eyebrows raised.

"Yes, I did."

"Thank you, Harry. That helps. What I want to say is that I now see it's more important to catch a murderer than to keep a promise made in the heat of . . . of terror."

Harry held his breath, not wanting to risk interfering with what Tara was on the verge of telling him.

"I've decided to tell you what happened in the basement." *There. I said it!*

Harry emptied his lungs explosively, surprised at how long he'd gone without breathing. Taking her hands in his, he said softly, "I think you're doing the right thing, Tara."

She jerked them away, making it Harry's turn to be surprised. "But I ain't spillin' no beans until I git some food in me belly. Yours, too." That ended the serious mood. They prepared dinner and ate it without further reference to the promised confession.

During the excellent dinner, the banter was light, though punctuated with awkward moments of silence. Several times during the meal Tara stared hard at Harry, as if looking for any hint of lingering anger. Their "relationship" had, after all, almost imploded. Did she want to assure herself the storm was over? Fervently — she was terrified he might lose interest.

They reached for the salt at the same time and their eyes met when their fingers brushed. Both smiled, until Harry looked away.

Dammit! I can't stop being a detective. She's still not sure she wants to tell me what happened. She's still afraid she'll be charged with something, yet she wants to protect Jason.

Harry glanced at her for a moment and closed his eyes against the stunning picture she made, causing his thoughts to turn in a completely different direction.

God, I want to make love to her again. He wondered if that would ever happen.

"Penny for your thoughts." Tara smiled flirtatiously and lifted her wine glass.

"What?"

"You were a million miles away. I said, a penny for your thoughts."

"Oh. I was wondering whether you've got a beer I might borrow. All this wine is making me a little woozy."

"Yes, you can have a beer, but no, that isn't what you were thinking. Now give."

"Hey, lady, I'm the detective in this family — oops. There, you see what you've done? You've made me lose control of my tongue. See?" He stuck his tongue out and waggled it so she could see what it looked like with its control mechanism disengaged.

She didn't care about that at all. Harry's slip made her spirits soar, and her body tingled. *"I'm the detective in this family,"* he'd said. *Was that a Freudian slip, and if so, might he be thinking about a more permanent relationship?* Tara hoped that if she were right, he'd still feel the same way after she'd told him everything.

"I think," Harry said, "we'd better have our talk before I completely lose control and do something I could be arrested for." He placed his napkin on the table, picked up his dinner plate, and headed for the kitchen. "I noticed something that looked suspiciously like a pie last time you opened the fridge. Okay if we delay dessert until after you tell me your story?"

Tara was right behind him with her own plate. "I think that's a good idea. Let's talk in the living room. I'll clean up later."

Seating herself across the coffee table from Harry, Tara began her narrative. "It began when Narena joked one day that maybe Jason Smalter sent one of his puppets out to do the kills. She laughed when she said that, but it sent chills down my spine. Then I forgot about it until I read the article in the paper. It seemed to describe Jason to a 'T.' When I thought about Jason talking to battered kids, it dawned on me that he really could be the killer you were looking for. But he's so well-liked, and such a helpful person, I was reluctant to say anything until I was sure. So the next time Narena and I went to see Jason, I expressed interest in ventriloquism. That's when he invited me to see his workshop."

"So going to his workshop was his idea?"

"Technically, I suppose, but I'd wangled the invitation. Narena tried to stop me from going, but I just had to know whether he — well, I just wasn't going to say anything to anybody until I knew for sure. I couldn't risk destroying his reputation with an accusation that turned out to be false."

"So you went. Weren't you afraid?"

"Of course I was afraid. But I had to know for sure. I felt certain he wouldn't hurt me. I'm not the kind of person he makes 'go away'."

"Go on."

"So I went. He gave me a tour of the workshop and . . . oh, Harry, it's such a wonderful place. All those workshoppy smells, and all the body parts lying around — puppet body parts, I mean. It was absolutely magical — "

"And then?" Harry decided she'd go on all evening about the magic of ventriloquism without prompting to stay focused.

"Then I asked him some questions. I realized at once that I had done it clumsily, because pretty soon we looked into each other's eyes and each saw the truth. I knew, and saw that he knew that I knew. Right then and there, I thought my heart would stop. I didn't know what to do next." Reliving the experience in her mind, Tara hugged herself as if chilled by the thoughts. "We just pretended for a few moments it didn't happen. But it did. He said something like, 'The game's over.' Next thing I knew, when I was bending over the bench looking at the mechanism inside one of the puppet's heads, I felt a sharp sting in my behind."

"He jabbed you with a needle?"

"I guess I screamed — a little — when he stabbed me. It was such a surprise. It was only a little relaxant, he told me, so he could get me onto the gurney." She continued, describing the trip through the cobwebby tunnel, and the dimly lit room at the other end, empty except for the crematory. "I was in sheer terror, Harry — I'm a little claustrophobic, you know."

"No, I didn't know. What did you do along the way?"

"I had trouble talking for a while — my speech was slurring — but I kept pleading with him to let me go. I began saying anything that came to mind just to get him to stop . . . and to keep me awake. I asked him how he got to this country — things like that. Anything. He'd stop and explain — I could tell he really didn't want to do what he was doing."

"So why was he doing it?"

"I asked him that, too. He said he had important things to do, and I knew he wasn't talking about killing people. He has various performances lined up — you knew he performed at the governor's birthday celebration — and those were very important to him. Anyhow, he finally started pushing me into the oven." Tara shivered. "Then I was really terrified. He intended to burn me alive. He said he wouldn't hurt me — he'd give me something to make me sleep — but he didn't. At least not at that point. He had a hypodermic in his hand as he talked, but he didn't use it."

She was finally getting to the part of the story he was most interested in hearing.

"In desperation, I finally said something that made him stop — "

"What did you say?"

"I said a lot of things. I don't remember most of it. When I told him that killing me would be like killing his mother all over again — that really got to him. I said if he killed me I would never be able to have a family of my own — like his mother did — and watch my children grow up. But I think what made him stop is when I told him that if he killed *me*, he wouldn't be any better than his victims. He'd be no better than the bad guys he kills.

231

"When I said that, all of a sudden, he stopped. Tears began running down his cheeks and he stopped pushing me into the oven. He dropped to his knees, sobbing and moaning. He cried out, 'What have I done? What have I done?' wailing it over and over." She paused to catch her ragged breath as if reliving the tragedy of that remembered moment in all its fearful emotions.

When Tara began anew, her voice wasn't much more than a harsh whisper. "Jason stayed on his knees for a long time, sobbing and praying. Begging his dead mother's forgiveness, speaking as if seeing her and his little sister's bodies lying there mutilated on the floor. He moaned and prayed some more. After a while, he stopped . . . crying, pleading, moaning and shaking.

"He looked up at me and smiled. That was the last thing I ever expected to see . . . but, Harry, I don't think I ever saw a face so . . . so . . . peaceful and content. It was a true epiphany. He said, 'It's all right, Tara. Now it's all right. I don't have to do it anymore.'"

"And you really believe . . . after that . . . he won't kill again?"

"Harry, he doesn't think of it as killing. He 'sends people away.' That's what he calls it. He told me about the horrible memory of his mother and sister being shotgunned before his eyes when he was a little boy — blood spraying all over — his mother screaming, his sister bleeding to death." Tara reached out and grasped Harry's hands. "He said the torment was gone. What he said was, 'I don't hear Mother screaming anymore. The cancer chewing up my brain all these years has gone away.'

"At last he seemed to be at peace and I believed him. It made me cry, too, but I was crying for the joy he was experiencing and, of course, for my own relief. For a few minutes I actually forgot I was strapped to a gurney, halfway into that oven. I simply wanted to get up and hug and comfort him . . . and tell him, like I heard him tell so many children, 'It's going to be all right.' Harry, it was a moment I wouldn't have missed for anything."

"For anything?"

"Aw, you know what I mean. Like when soldiers say, 'War is hell,' but having survived it, they're glad they had the experience."

"Uh-huh." Harry took another sip of beer. "Well, give me the rest."

"He pulled me out of the oven and unstrapped me. When he helped me off the gurney, he closed the oven door and we both wheeled the gurney back through the tunnel to his workshop. All the while he was telling me how sorry he was.

"I kept promising not to tell anyone what happened. I even helped him close that heavy door to his workshop." Tara paused in her story.

232

Harry waited quietly, wanting more than anything else to take this woman into his arms and kiss her tears away forever. Finally realizing that having Tara in his arms would be worth far more than any five minutes of fame on the courthouse steps, he couldn't help smiling. It was as though he had just experienced the same sort of epiphany as Jason. Jason no longer needed to "send people away;" he no longer needed his moment of fame.

"Suddenly the reality of what almost happened hit me, and I had to run upstairs. I barely made it in time. I started shaking and threw up in the toilet. More than once, I think. That's why I didn't open the door as soon as you knocked and made all the commotion. It's also when I found out I'd wet my pants — I don't remember exactly when. I took them off, rinsed them in the sink, and slipped them into my purse."

Harry looked mischievously at Tara. "You mean you didn't have any panties on when I arrived?"

"None whatever."

"If I'd known that, I might have — "

Tara studied Harry's. "It's never too late, you know." Batting her eyelashes, she pulled her short skirt higher so more than half her thighs were exposed. "Would you like to try making love in the closet — with the light off?"

Harry stood, reaching out a hand as he did. Pulling Tara to her feet, he wrapped her in his arms. Just as he lowered his head to kiss her, she jerked back.

"Harry!" she exclaimed, eyes wide with surprise. "Did you hear what I just *said*?"

"Something about a closet?"

"Not simply *something* about a closet — *everything* about a closet. Listen to me, Harry. I just invited you to have sex in a *closet* — with the light off — that must mean my claustrophobia is gone!"

"I'm not sure I — "

"Harry, I get all sweaty in confined spaces. Palpitations. Heart pounding. The works. That basement experience with Jason must have done something to me. Something good. If it hadn't, I could never have said what I did about making love in a closet." Tara threw her arms around his neck and pulled him tight against her breasts. "Oh, Harry . . . let's! I feel so wonderful. Do you . . . would you . . . could we try — please? I've got to know."

Their kisses mounted rapidly from warm to hot to scalding, each becoming more extended. Arms enfolded, bodies burning, they sidled, virtually in lockstep, toward the bedroom closet with all thoughts of glory on the courthouse steps fading from Harry's mind.

Door closed, surrounded by darkness, each fumbling the others' clothes, he mumbled, "Let the experiment begin."

CHAPTER FORTY-SEVEN

When Jason's Sunday morning presentation to the Phoenix Psychotherapy Council was about to begin, the Hyatt ballroom was filled to standing-room-only. The air-conditioning equipment, working full blast, hardly cooled the large room to a tolerable temperature. Now, ten minutes after the session had been scheduled, committee members were still scrounging chairs from adjoining conference rooms.

"There's a door leading to a service hall behind the backdrop at the rear of the podium. Get the chairs that're stacked in the hall there," one called to the others. The crowd was so large the committee had to keep chairs streaming into the room from every direction.

Volunteers manning the registration table sat amazed at the number of visitor badges they were obliged to fill out.

"Where in the world are all these people coming from?" one volunteer asked another. "I don't think we have this many members in the entire Council."

"I don't know, but I do know we've never had this many paying visitors before. Ever."

When most of the standees were finally seated, the session monitor rose and spoke into the microphone mounted on the lectern. "Good morning. Our session this morning will be introduced by Doctor Laurie Cantrell, Director of the Phoenix Psychotherapy Council. Doctor Cantrell."

Doctor Cantrell stepped to the lectern and adjusted her notes. In her dark purple suit, one could imagine her as a perfect spokeswoman for one of those "Four out of five doctors recommend . . ." commercials. Tall, straight, and gray-haired, she looked every bit the professional she was. The gold medallion around her neck was perfectly highlighted by the high-necked lavender blouse.

"Thank you, everyone, and welcome. I can't tell you how delighted I am to introduce our speaker. I'm especially delighted with the unusually large turnout this morning. Out of curiosity, how many of you are guests?"

More than half the people in the room raised their hands, causing murmurs of surprise.

"Many of you know our speaker. For several years he's served as a volunteer, most often at the Marvella Snikskin-Pruitt Children's hospital. Those of you who work with him have told me repeatedly about his magical way of making the children forget about their aches and pains, and about the invaluable service provided by his lion puppet — Gweedo — in helping battered children talk about their traumatic experiences. This information has been priceless in our attempts to formulate the right treatment programs."

She smiled. "And . . . I don't want this to sound like a commercial, but if you haven't watched Jason Smalter at Bellissimo's restaurant trying to serve his customers while being nagged and harangued by that pesky parrot of his, you're missing a real treat."

The room broke into applause and laughter. Many present knew exactly what the speaker was talking about.

"We've asked Mister Smalter to share with us some of his secrets of communicating with battered children. While not a professional psychotherapist, he's as fine a virtuoso as I've ever had the privilege to observe. Mister Jason Smalter."

Again the room erupted in applause.

Jason, seated at a table on the podium, stood and approached the lectern. When the room finally quieted, he looked slowly around the room and began.

"Thank you for that warm welcome, but I must admit I'm a bit overwhelmed. I've never had such an appreciative audience in my entire life — and I haven't even done anything yet."

Loud laughter.

"Maybe I should sit down while I'm ahead."

More laughter.

"I was asked to tell you something about how I gain the confidence of the traumatized children. I'd be glad to try, of course, but I'm really not the one who should be talking to you. My friend Gweedo is the one who does all the work. So let me get him out here to help me out." The crowd murmured in anticipation as Jason reached under the lectern where Gweedo was waiting. When he'd arranged the puppet on his left arm, he raised Gweedo with a flourish and sat him on the front edge of the lectern.

Applause and laughter.

Jason hung a small microphone around Gweedo's neck, much to the amusement of the audience. "It helps create the illusion that the puppet is actually talking."

Gweedo looked at Jason, then turned to the audience. "Of *course* I'm doing the talking. You don't see *his* lips moving, do you?"

The audience enjoyed every minute of this interchange. It was true — Jason's lips weren't moving.

Gweedo roared. "Rroooarrr." Nothing happened. He looked around, he looked up, he looked down around the lectern, then turned to Jason and shrugged his shoulders. Then he roared again. This time the audience roared back.

Jason was off and running. He began by describing the lion puppet and the importance of creating a figure that wasn't threatening to the children. "If he's too large, the children might be threatened and be afraid to get too close to him. If he's too fierce, the same thing can happen. What's needed — and you need only look at the teddy bears clutched in a child's arms — is a cuddly-looking figure. Though you may not have thought about it specifically, the puppet needs to be soft and squishy."

Gweedo sat up straight and turned to Jason. "I *beg* your pardon. I resemble that remark."

Jason went on to describe the steps he took to gain the children's confidence, emphasizing the importance of making sure they understood that the puppets weren't real. Gweedo straightened and looked haughtily at Jason. "I didn't come here to be insulted, you know."

"Oh? Where do you usually go?"

"And that's *another* thing. That's *my* punch line and I'll thank you not to steal it."

By now, everyone seemed to be in love with Gweedo. Once the laughter died down, Jason continued. "Now it's time for you to hear from the horse's mouth, so to speak. After all, it's Gweedo here who does all the work."

"You better believe it," Gweedo responded. "But he gets all the cute nurses."

"Never mind. Without using names, tell the people about one of the cases you worked on recently."

"It's about time." Gweedo arranged himself on the edge of the lectern, fidgeting into position as he prepared to speak. After clearing his throat several times, he began.

"I remember the time I was called in on the case of a little girl who hadn't spoken a word after being checked into the hospital two days earlier. She just lay in her bed and stared at the ceiling. Well, I knew right from the start this wasn't going to be easy. No, siree. I had to think long and hard about how I was going to proceed. You can't just go up and lick somebody's face, you know. It can scare them. Besides, most of her face and head were wrapped in bandages."

The audience leaned forward, hanging on every word. The idea of being lectured by a puppet — a puppet talking about thinking things through — was totally entrancing.

Gweedo continued.

"I finally decided to use my most powerful tool — my unbeatable charm." Gweedo lifted a paw and preened. Most people present didn't even notice that the paw was being manipulated by Jason.

The audience laughed, but paid close attention to every word, aware they were in the presence of a rare treat.

"So I got about two feet from the little girl and said, 'Hi. My name is Gweedo.' I didn't ask her what her name was — it was too early for that, you see. I next wanted to compliment her on something. Usually I say something nice about their hair, but all her hair was under the bandages. She'd been very badly beaten. She had two black eyes, and some broken bones here and there. So I said, 'That's a pretty doll you have there. Does she have a name?' She nodded a little, so I asked her if she'd tell me the doll's name."

By now the audience had trouble remembering that Gweedo's words were actually coming from Jason.

"In a weak voice she told me the doll's name was Suzy — not her real name — and I asked the doll if she would tell me the little girl's name. Speaking through her doll, she told me her name."

Gweedo continued to explain how he gained the little girl's confidence, and how he slowly moved closer to her. Then he began to describe what the girl told him about how she got to the hospital.

"She told me that her father beat her a lot when she was bad. She told me she was hit when she left something on her plate, and when she got her clothes dirty while playing. Then she told me something that made me cry..."

Harry, still in his underwear the morning after a second late night with Tara, had just put his electric razor down when the phone rang. The warm memories of his two intimate evenings with Tara still occupied his thoughts as he picked it up.

"Harry, get your ass down here as quick as you can." Brunkel sounded excited.

"What's up?" Jarred by the abrupt wrenching from Nirvana to reality, Harry's mind resisted focusing on the intrusion.

"Drummel's located Jason Smalter."

"No shit? Where?"

"Right under our damn noses. He's giving a talk down at the Hyatt, even as we speak. I've got the arrest warrant in my hand — finally. Come get it while I get some backup organized."

"Be there in fifteen."

Gweedo continued his narrative. "She told me that her parents kept telling her what a bad little girl she was and that they didn't want her anymore. They told her they wished she'd just go away. I had to stop, then, because I was so choked up I couldn't talk.

"But you know what happened? When that poor little, broken up child saw how her story was affecting me, she put her bandaged arms around me and held me tight." Gweedo paused, choked up once again from the memory of the experience. "Then, in the sweetest voice, she said to me, 'Don't be sad. *I* would never treat *you* like that."

There wasn't a dry eye in the room. Tissue manufacturers were about to make a killing.

Just then one of the six double doors at the side of the ballroom squeaked open. Heads turned as Harry, Drummel, Skirms, and three other detectives, all in plain clothes, entered the room, trying to be invisible.

It didn't work.

Half the women in the room reached a hand into their purses.

Harry motioned his team to gather close. "There are more exits in this room that I thought." Pointing, he continued, "There are six double-doors along one side of the ballroom, two on the opposite wall, and two at the back of the room. There's another one behind the black curtain providing a backdrop to the podium. We might as well wait until he's finished. My CI said he's not likely to resist." He quietly assigned them to stations where they could observe and block as many exits as possible.

Gweedo described another session involving a little girl repeatedly raped by her father and his drunken friends. While Jason talked, the detectives couldn't help getting caught up in the narrative — they'd heard stories like this all their professional lives. And worse. They nodded in spite of themselves.

"This little girl didn't have a doll in her hands, so I gave her one — I always carry a couple in my suitcase — and then talked to her through the doll. It's easier for such children to talk to real people through a doll."

By now the audience was having serious difficulty distinguishing between the "real people" and the dolls.

When Gweedo finished his "case history" description, Jason concluded his presentation.

"As you know, we're not trained psychotherapists. But our job isn't therapy; it's to collect information to help you establish a treatment plan that will work. To reach that important goal, puppets are a very useful tool."

Gweedo nodded, and added the closing comments. "In a way, we're all psychotherapists, aren't we? We're constantly making our friends and associates feel better — or worse — about themselves just by the way we act toward them — by the things we say and do." Gweedo slowed his speech as he continued, "And every one of us has the power to help, by the oh-so-simple . . . act . . . of listening. Thank you."

Jason stepped to one side of the lectern, allowing him and Gweedo to bow in full view of the audience.

After a moment of silence during which the enchanted audience digested the words they'd just heard, the audience erupted as one. They applauded vigorously, and rose to their feet to express their gratitude for the remarkable performance they had just witnessed.

Jason bowed repeatedly, basking in the warmth of the appreciative audience.

Then something else remarkable happened. A strong voice from the audience rang out, "*Women for Jason* — NOW!"

At that signal, some two hundred women pulled their hands from their purses, each brandishing an autograph book. Waving their books in the air, they squealed in delight and shouted "Jason, Jason," as they surged toward the podium.

"Jeezus," Drummel mumbled, "it's a fuckin' stampede."

The two hundred plus *Women for Jason* packed themselves as closely around Jason as they could, surrounding him and brandishing their autograph books above their heads.

The therapists in the audience were mystified about what was happening. Those looking forward to asking Jason and Gweedo a question when the session had ended were disappointed. There was no way they could break through that solid wall of female flesh.

"C'mon," Harry shouted to Drummel. "Something's going on. Let's get in there and nab him before they crush him to death." The two detectives rushed forward, waving their badges.

"Police. Let us through." But that appeared only to make the wall of

bodies press more tightly together. "Police. Let us through," they repeated over and over.

Nobody took notice. Nobody stood aside to make way.

When the ladies did notice the detectives trying to push their way through, they locked arms and shoved back. Other women seemed to appear from nowhere to shower the detectives with a blizzard of long, brightly-colored scarves that covered their heads and tangled their arms.

Harry flailed his arms in a frantic attempt to push the scarves from his eyes and free his arms for action. That simply initiated another shower of the silken fabric. "Dammit, Charlie, I can't see. They're up to something. What's happening?"

Clutching at the scarves, the detectives tried even harder to wedge their bodies through the squirming, shouting, squealing, book-waving, scarf-throwing crowd.

It didn't work. The wall was solid.

Then, as if by an invisible signal, the wall of determined flesh began to dissolve. One by one, the women relaxed and peeled away, laughing and patting each other on the back.

By the time the two detectives were able to push their way to the podium, it was completely empty.

Jason Smalter was gone.

CHAPTER FORTY-EIGHT

Reactions to the disappearance of Jason Smalter came swiftly. "Special bulletins" and "breaking news" announcements interrupted radio and television programs, claiming that, once again, the serial killer had slipped away from the police. This time, however, no dramatic TV footage ran behind the narration, as no cameras had been present at the Smalter presentation to cover its astonishing conclusion. To cover the lapse, the police-booking photo of Jason Smalter again filled the screens, followed by old footage showing Harry Shuman breaking down the Smalter door, and emerging with the suspect in custody.

Radio talk shows, ever vigilant for grist with which to stir the blood of the public, quickly seized the moment. This time, the debate centered less on the morality of Jason's actions — the word "alleged" was seldom used now — than on the inability of the police to arrest a suspect making a speech in a public place less than four blocks from their headquarters.

"John, you're on the air. What do you think about Jason Smalter slipping away from the police?"

"Not much. There's a serial killer out there and I'm kinda worried about the safety of my family. Y'know?"

"I hear 'ya. But he only kills guys who beat up on women and children. Doesn't that make a difference?"

"Heck, no. The guy's a killer and that means he's crazy. Who knows who he'll decide to whack next."

"Thanks for the call, John. Linda, you're on the air."

"To tell the truth, I'm glad he disappeared. He used to wait on my husband and me at the restaurant and we think he's one of the nicest people we've ever met."

"Doesn't it bother you that he's a serial killer?"

"Not as long as he only kills the creeps who prey on women and children. By sacrificing a few lives he's saving many. Besides, the justice system is way too slow and lenient with those people. Sometimes women who are raped get treated worse by the police and courts than the rapists themselves. Just look at the number of cops and judges who don't even think rape is a

crime — "

"I hear you, Linda . . . Maria, you're on the air."

"Thank you for taking my call. I would like, please, the phone number to call for the *Women for Jason* people. I want to make a donation."

"We'll give you the number off the air, and thanks for the call. Priscilla, you're on the air."

"Okay, um, yes, you might as well give out the number *on* the air because that's what I'm calling about, too. Why keep it a secret? I'll bet there's lots of women who'd like to help."

"Thank you, Priscilla. I'll check with my masters to see if we can do that legally. I promise — if it's okay, we'll do it. Carlotta, you're on the air."

"I just want to say that I'm meeting here with my bridge club, and we think the callers who are afraid because Jason is out there are wrong. Actually, we feel a lot safer knowing he's getting rid of those creep predators."

"Shoe, what the hell happened?" Harry and Dutch Brunkel sat around the desk of Captain Portono, rehashing the events of the previous day.

"The damnedest thing, Sarge," Harry explained. "Totally unexpected. We had plenty of guys on hand to make the arrest. But just as the Smalter guy was taking a bow, half the audience jumped to their feet waving autograph books. They made such a tight ball around him we couldn't get through the mob of linked arms. By the time we did, Smalter was gone."

"You think it was a set-up?" This from Portono.

"Sure felt like it. Also felt like those women were somehow enjoying what they were doing. It's all in my report. It was that *Women for Jason* crowd."

"Maybe we should arrest them all for obstruction," Brunkel offered.

Portono snorted. "I think . . . not. We're already in enough hot water with the public. Besides, what would we arrest them for . . . standing too close together? Brandishing autograph books?"

"*Unlicenced* autograph books at that," Harry offered, joining the trend of the conversation.

Not to be outdone, Brunkel added, "Beating on the police with silk scarves? Hey, maybe we should lobby for a five-day waiting period on the sale of autograph books."

"That wouldn't do any good," Harry said, adopting a sonorous tone as he lifted a finger in the air. "Don't forget, autograph books don't obstruct justice — people do."

Portono put up his hands. "All right, all right. That's enough levity for a while. Now that we've vented a little spleen, it's time to get to work." Turning toward Brunkel, he asked, "Where's Lieutenant Stacy? She should be here."

"She's briefing every body she can lay hands on — so to speak. Said she'd get here as soon as she could."

"What's she done so far?"

"Full court press. I know she's got the Smalter house under 24/7 surveillance. Same for Cally Tunesco. Jason's smart enough not to show up at either of those places, but you never know. Bus station, airports, Border Patrol, Highway Patrol, APB . . . Stacy's going right down the list. But it takes time to set up."

Portono picked up his copy of Harry's report. "What about the Tindall woman? She covered?"

Harry hesitated. "No. She's the one who got him arrested the first time. Not likely he'll go anywhere near her."

Portono waggled a finger in Harry's direction. "I suggest it's assumptions like those that put the egg on your face at yesterday's fiasco."

"You made your point, Captain. I'll see she's covered, but we're already spread pretty thin, especially with this morning's copycat killing."

Portono's phone rang. He lifted the handset and listened, then handed it to Brunkel. It's for you."

"Brunkel." He listened, then said, "Send Drummel and Skirms to the scene. I'll be right down for the details." To Portono and Harry, he said, "There's been another murder."

"Smalter's work?" Harry asked.

"Don't think so. Too much evidence at the scene. Sounds like another copycat."

Tara finished preparing her lettuce and tomato salad. Adding another tablespoon of olive oil and a few drops of vinegar, she set the plate on her kitchen table and sat down to lunch. After a moment's hesitation, she stood again and grabbed the refrigerator door. Throwing caution to the winds, she reached for a bottle of cold white wine, and jabbed the refrigerator door closed with a pointed finger.

"I deserve it." The refrigerator simply hummed.

She was still reeling from the "Sunday uprising," as she called it, and that was three days ago. God, she was so grateful Harry had called her during his mad dash to the Hyatt. If it hadn't been for his thoughtfulness under stress, she'd have missed the entire event.

She had marveled at Jason's virtuosity in holding his audience's attention. Everyone had been completely spellbound by Gweedo's descriptions of his conversations with the battered kids. She was proud of his performance. Then, when that huge mob of women suddenly rushed to the podium to surround him, she was as stunned and confused as anyone else — it had come as a total surprise.

Looking back on it, she concluded it was as much a surprise to Jason as it had been to her. She had watched him closely as he ended his performance and took his bows with Gweedo. She saw no hint of anticipation, none of the tension one might expect of someone preparing to flee. Instead, she thought he looked panicky when the rush toward him began. *Besides,* she mused, *I don't think he even knew a warrant for his arrest had been issued less than an hour ago.*

Now, her feelings were again tugged in several directions. Yes, even though Jason had nearly cremated her — she could still feel the terror — she was both puzzled, and also disappointed, that he could do such a thing. She'd hated him for that.

Oh, yes, partly because of her own desperate words, he had experienced a violent emotional reaction to his actions — that churned her emotions in yet another direction. The sight of him on his knees, crying and praying, had softened her heart. She'd actually relaxed. She somehow knew then he would never hurt her. His emotion was so intense, it even made her forget her own terror — and claustrophobia — for a few moments.

Now that she'd had time to think, she worried about what would happen when Jason was caught and brought to trial. Would she have to testify against him? Of course, she would! Could she do it? Not by choice, but she'd be under oath — she'd *have* to testify. That would be a wrenching experience, but she would do it. It would be the right thing to do.

Nonetheless, the thought hung heavy in her heart.

Later that week, when the dust cleared and everyone realized Jason had disappeared, she began to feel serious sympathy for Harry. The poor man. It was the second time he'd been made to look the fool. He was no such thing, of course, but that's the way the media were painting it. He didn't deserve the ridicule. "At least," Tara said, remembering Harry's confession, "the dream of a brief spotlight on the courthouse steps no longer gnaws at him." She just wished she could put her arms around him and try to make him feel better.

Determined to transform her wish into reality, she reached for her phone.

CHAPTER FORTY-NINE

"I can't believe how delicately you're handling those tree ornaments," Tara teased. "For a detective, that is."

"You forget, dear lady, I'm a stamp collector. Delicacy is a requirement. Besides, 'tis the season to be gentle." Deftly catching the large red ornament she tossed in his direction, he added, "I just wish I knew how to be more delicate when it comes to handling *you*."

"Just what do you mean by that, Detective?"

"You *know* what I mean. I'm not very good when it comes to — what do women call it? — 'nourishing a relationship.'"

"That's a load of crap, Harry Shuman, and you know it. We've been seeing each other ever since Jason disappeared — what — three months ago? In all that time, have I ever creased your skull with a frying pan?"

"Not that I recall."

"Have I ever chased you with a meat cleaver?"

"No, but — "

"But nothing. Your only trouble is you think every woman only wants a man who'll listen to her talk endlessly about her *feelings*."

Harry spread his hands in defense. "Jeesus, lady, I wasn't trying to — "

"And another thing. You're doing just fine in the relationship department. Do you think I'd put up with some kind of a stamp-collecting, workaholic cop who's practically never around for a serious snuggle if I wasn't fond of you?"

Harry clamped his mouth shut.

"Let me amend that . . . if I wasn't *very* fond of you?"

Harry smiled. "See, that's the problem. I'm very fond of you, too, but I'm no good at doing all the romance stuff."

"What romance stuff are you talking about?"

"You know, sweeping you off your feet onto a white horse or something. Whispering sweet nothings — "

"Stop right there." Tara put a hand over his mouth. "Just stop right there." She pushed him toward a leather chair and shoved him into it. "All right, mister, I'm the interrogator here. You just answer the questions. Now then,

246

who went out and bought this fine Christmas tree?"

"I guess I did."

"And who bought all the ornaments?"

"I did that, too."

"And isn't it true it's the first tree — trimmings included — you've bought in many years?"

"Yes."

"*That's* romantic."

Tara pointed to the dining room table and continued. "Now then, who spread that nice new tablecloth and set the table with his finest cutlery?"

"Guilty."

"*Also* romantic." She stabbed a finger at his face. "And who procured the wine, along with a crystal decanter to pour it in?"

"Guilty again."

"And the large bouquet of flowers?"

"Okay, I confess. Guilty for another time."

"Of *course* you're guilty. You may be a little rough around the edges, but you are a romantic, my dear Shoe." She sat on his lap and wrapped one arm around his neck. She used the other to poke a finger into his chest. "Harry, you're just going to have to get over the idea that you're some sort of cave man in the romance department. It just isn't true." She kissed him hard on the lips and held him tight.

"Mmm, I like this part of the conversation . . . though I seem to be developing new holes in my chest," he mumbled through her lips.

"Besides, when I graduate from Police Academy — which starts right after New Year's Day, in case you've forgotten — I just may have to toss you flat on your back next time you say you're not romantic."

Harry beamed at her speech. "It'll be a proud day for me when you graduate."

Tara sensed this might be the moment, if only she handled it right. "Why?" she asked, the gentleness of her voice revealing the depth of her affection.

"What do you mean, why? Why will I be proud of you?"

"Yes," she said, nuzzling her nose against his cheek.

"Because I'm in *love* with you, dammit," he blurted. "*That's* why. And because I don't know how to tell you that in all the ways I want to. And because I like being near you way too much. And a whole bunch of other things."

Tara kissed his cheek and nibbled gently on his ear. "You're doing just fine, Harry . . . just fine, and what else . . . "

"And," he continued, ignoring her comment, "it's why I hid a little something in the tree for you — "

Tara leaped off his lap and rushed to the living blue spruce standing, half-decorated, in the corner tree.

" — hoping you might accept it, along with the implications of said item." Harry chuckled as she groped frenetically among the branches for what he assumed she was expecting.

When she found it, she held it up, squealing with delight. Harry slipped the engagement ring gently onto her finger, leading her to throw her arms around his neck and administer a lengthy, breath-taking, tongue-massaging kiss.

Over his shoulder she eyed the baguette diamond's bright glisten, turning it right and left to catch the light. "It fits perfectly. How did you know my size?"

"I'm a detective — remember?"

"Oh, yes. That's right, isn't it?" She feigned innocence. "Wanna make love in the closet again?"

Between more and more fervent kisses, he asked, "You're really proud of yourself, aren't you?"

"You *bet* I am. And I owe it all to Jason Smalter." She grasped the hand with which he had been caressing her breasts, and tugged him toward the closet.

The remainder of the tree-trimming had to wait while more serious expressions of love were exchanged.

Dinner waited, too.

CHAPTER FIFTY

Jason Smalter stood on a flagstone patio, high above a remote, hot, sandy beach. Shielding his eyes with a hand, he watched the single-masted sailboat glide lazily across the blue, tropical waters. As he watched, his mind kneaded the events of the past three months since his arrival in this special place, and experienced a deep yearning.

This has been a bewildering time. Activity-filled? Yes. Satisfying? Sometimes. It had been hard, getting used to unfamiliar surroundings and a foreign language, to unaccustomed luxuries . . . and, most difficult of all, to a covey of toadying servants constantly underfoot. Then there was the extensive variety of fascinating people who came and went, almost constantly.

No surprise, he found himself becoming more homesick every day for his workshop. *I miss my customers at Bellissimo's, I miss the children and staff at the hospitals, and I miss my performing and speaking engagements. I really love performing! And now, with Christmas approaching, I'm really getting homesick.*

He smiled at the memory of his recent "kidnapping," recalling how his latest adventure had started. It happened so quickly. He remembered stepping back from the lectern, and cringing at the sight and sound of the female stampede. After that he recalled only a whirlwind of action.

One minute he was speaking, the next a mass of shouting women surrounded him, brandishing a sea of autograph books and scarves. Someone said, "This way . . . this way," and hustled him out a back door behind the stage curtains. From there, it became a virtual dream sequence: they whooshed him into a long, white limo with heavily tinted windows. His suitcase — he hoped Scootch and Scrawk waited inside — already lay on the floor, Gweedo on top. A short drive and a long flight followed, taking several hours, and always in the company of four nice ladies. That made the time pass quickly. Then he arrived . . . here.

Now he was standing on the patio of an elegant six-room guest house in the center of a tropical paradise, gazing at two people flowing by in a sailboat. *I can't believe it. Yet those boaters out there are free. They can come and go as they please, do what they want, and be seen in public anytime . . . in safety.* He let out a long, wistful sigh. *I wish I were free again. I wish I were home in my workshop.*

"May I interrupt you, Jason?"

He turned as his exotic hostess glided into the room. The tall, Asian woman was in command of this villa on the sea. Her jet-black hair flowed down to her waist, held back from her face by a green jade clip. Her dark green dress, covered with brocaded gold dragons, reached almost to the floor. Around her neck she wore a hand-crafted gold chain. The large multi-colored opal swinging from the chain caught the light in hypnotic patterns as she moved. He wondered who she really was — where she came from — why she was here. He knew only that she seemed to have unlimited resources.

"Did I disturb you?"

Jason adjusted one of the upholstered chairs surrounding the glass-topped patio table. "Won't you sit down?"

"Thank you, I will — for a moment. I just wanted to ask whether you are comfortable and have everything you need."

"Oh, yes," he lied. "I've never stayed in such a lavish place. It still feels like a . . . a 'castle by the sea.'"

Her tinkling laughter made Jason smile — it reminded him of wind chimes on his porch . . . back home. "Are your houseman and maid to your liking? Have they done anything to displease you? You must tell me. If they have, I will have them replaced."

Jason frowned, unsure of the reason for the question. "They're just fine. Thank you. I'm not the least displeased. It's just that I'm used to doing things for myself. I — I never had the luxury of servants before, and I guess I just don't know how to make the best use of them. Every time I start to do something, one of them is there to do it for me."

"I am pleased to know this." Smiling, she added, "Perhaps I will ask them to let you do some things for *them*."

Taking her seriously, Jason said, "I'd welcome the opportunity."

"There is something else I would like to ask you. The holiday season fast approaches, and I have organized a little Christmas Eve dinner for a few special friends. You have already met most of them and I would like to invite you to join us."

"Will it be safe for me to be there?"

"Of course. It will be in the main dining room. Perhaps thirty people or so. They are all trusted friends and associates, all of whom know of your special talent with puppets. Will you come?"

Jason bowed slightly. "I'd be honored, and thank you for the invitation."

He had indeed met several of his hostess's friends, and marveled that each and every one had a special talent — musician, artist, mason, computer hacker, carnival knife-thrower, locksmith, bush pilot and more. All preferred to spend their time doing, rather than spectating.

"Splendid. Ah, dare I ask whether you would grace us with a performance with your little friends?"

Jason beamed. "I would be delighted. If you would tell me something about some of the guests maybe I can personalize the show a little."

"Ahh . . . perhaps I could provide a few tidbits, but please do not expect too much. Some of the guests may be a little, shall we say, sensitive about sharing much personal information. They will tell you what they want you to know about them. Of course, all of them will know about *you*, but only what you choose to tell them."

"I understand." My God, thought Jason, surely they can't *all* be fugitives. No, there must be other reasons for them to be secretive about their personal lives. Changing the subject, he asked, "Have you heard any news about my situation? I haven't seen anything in the newspaper for the past month or so."

"There is one bit of news. You know, of course, that after your departure there were three murders the press refers to as the 'Smalter copycat murders.'"

"Yes. I found that embarrassing — humiliating would be more like it."

"The police have now caught every one of them, all in a very short time. The detective who arrested you was the person mainly responsible for their capture. He has become a hero. There was even a ceremony in his honor on the courthouse steps."

"What about me?"

"Happily, there is no news about you. The public is jubilant about the capture of the three killers, and the police are once again seen in a favorable light. As for you, by now the public has forgotten about Jason Smalter — they have moved on."

"That's terrific news."

"The only unknown is the charge of the attempted murder of Miss Tindall. The District Attorney believes that case to be solid. If you like, however . . . I . . . I could perhaps arrange for her — "

"Oh, no. No! Please don't even *think* anything like that. She's a very fine woman, and I like her a lot."

His hostess smiled, bowing slightly. "Commendable. But I was thinking of something more in the line of a suitable inducement not to testify."

"I'm sorry, but I don't understand what you're telling me."

She placed a jeweled hand on Jason's. "Perhaps it is better if you know. When the Police Academy board learned your friend was to be called as a hostile witness, they considered that a smudge on her record and tried to remove her from the roster. My associates persuaded them to rescind that decision."

"So she enrolled after all?"

"Oh yes. She is now about to graduate and I believe the Academy staff will consider it in their best interests to take very good care of the lady."

Jason whistled, thinking the tentacles of this woman's influence seemed to have no end.

"In due course, it might be possible to make the entire Smalter case go away. Perhaps we should speak of it at a later time."

"Thank you. Ahh . . . there is one thing . . ."

"How may I serve?"

"If I might ask a favor. I would like to get a short message to Tara — not my location or anything like that — just a few words. She must be worried about having to testify against me if I go to trial, and I'd like to tell her that if that happens she has my blessing to do what she thinks is right. I'd like her to know that any promises she made to me are null and void."

"You are a very honorable person. If you will draft a note I will send to you, I will have it hand-delivered."

"Thank you for your kindness."

"It may take one or two weeks. Would that be all right?"

"Oh, yes. Of course."

"In due course, we will speak of your options. I have a few ideas that may interest you. Until then, it will behoove you to continue your martial arts and Mandarin lessons. I promise they will become useful. In the meantime, you are free to do as you please."

Free? Sure, I'm free. Free to do as I please in my guest house. Free to walk to the village and shop. Free so long as I wear my disguise. Free to swim in my pool, or in the clear water of the ocean. But the minute I move beyond those boundaries, I might be recognized.

Free? There may not be bars around this estate, but I'm anything but free. I can't go home again, ever. I can't work in my workshop, or perform for — or try to help — the damaged children. He ran his hand along the stone railing as his eyes scanned the horizon. *This is all very grand, but I want to go home.* He began humming, "I'm only a bird in a gilded cage . . ."

His picture of home now, however, was accompanied by the sound of clanking chains. Though he tried to picture himself in his workshop, ugly thoughts of jail intruded. The humiliation of standing barefooted on the concrete floor, of walking past that row of cells filled with sweating, vomiting derelicts on the way to the fingerprinting room, of being handcuffed and shackled before entering the elevator, of being put into a barren cell on the maximum security floor, of the door sliding shut with a clang. He shuddered at those images. He couldn't shake them from his mind. Maybe he didn't have to suffer the barren confinement of a concrete cell, and maybe he didn't have to shuffle through the days with what he thought of as the losers of society, but was he any better off here? True, he had enough to eat and a clean bed to sleep on. Nor was he confined to a tiny barren cell. But he was confined nonetheless. His mind was constantly filled with thoughts of home. Of the freedom he craved.

He wondered. *What would be my fate if I decide to return? I can't go back to that jail — I'd die.* Then he thought about the veiled promise, the possibilities hinted at by his benefactor. *Do they include my leaving this sun-drenched jail some day and going home? I wonder if it really would be possible. Some day?*

In the small hours, Tara awakened to lie on her side, one hand holding up her head as she examined Harry's chest with a minute closeness. A devilish expression on her face, she giggled. Moistening her fingers, she began tracing circles around Harry's nipples, off and on stopping to rub them, until they popped up like tiny asparagus sprouts. "Ever wonder what Jason's doing, and where he is, right now?"

Harry, already thoroughly disconcerted by her skillful manipulations, had to fight down a rising urge. "Oh, cowering in some hidey hole, I'd guess. Probably about the same as being in prison."

Tara muffled another giggle. "I don't see him like that at all . . . at least I hope not. I see him lying on a nice warm beach, somewhere, a lovely, exotic girl to each side, sipping on an icy margarita, enjoying his freedom." After a pause, she added, "I miss him, you know."

"I share your feeling — in a way, but right this minute . . . who cares?" Thoughts of Jason were being pushed farther and farther from his mind as her fingers moved southward. "Whenever he returns, we'll be waiting...but for the present... I have a gorgeous girl, right here in my arms, and...

Tara forgot all about Jason.

Printed in the United States
724700004B